I0822294

I Wish I May

Published by The Finding Press, LLC

Cover design by Adelyn Belsterling.

Editing by Ellen McGinty and proofreading by EditElle – Writing & Editing Services.

ISBN – Hardcover: 979-8-9906610-0-4
ISBN – Paperback: 979-8-9906610-1-1
ISBN – Ebook: 979-8-9906610-2-8

For Sam. Thank you for your unwavering belief in my dreams.

Contents

1. Chapter One 1
2. Chapter Two 9
3. Chapter Three 16
4. Chapter Four 22
5. Chapter Five 31
6. Chapter Six 40
7. Chapter Seven 47
8. Chapter Eight 54
9. Chapter Nine 59
10. Chapter Ten 67
11. Chapter Eleven 73
12. Chapter Twelve 81
13. Chapter Thirteen 91
14. Chapter Fourteen 100
15. Chapter Fifteen 108
16. Chapter Sixteen 113
17. Chapter Seventeen 120
18. Chapter Eighteen 127

19. Chapter Nineteen 135
20. Chapter Twenty 143
21. Chapter Twenty-One 151
22. Chapter Twenty-Two 160
23. Chapter Twenty-Three 167
24. Chapter Twenty-Four 173
25. Chapter Twenty-Five 178
26. Chapter Twenty-Six 183
27. Chapter Twenty-Seven 189
28. Chapter Twenty-Eight 194
29. Chapter Twenty-Nine 202
30. Chapter Thirty 210
31. Chapter Thirty-One 217
32. Chapter Thirty-Two 223
33. Chapter Thirty-Three 229
34. Chapter Thirty-Four 235
35. Chapter Thirty-Five 240
36. Chapter Thirty-Six 250
37. Chapter Thirty-Seven 257
38. Chapter Thirty-Eight 261
39. Chapter Thirty-Nine 266
40. Chapter Forty 270
41. Chapter Forty-One 276
42. Chapter Forty-Two 281

43. Chapter Forty-Three 287
44. Chapter Forty-Four 293
45. Chapter Fourty-Five 298
46. Epilogue 304
47. Bonus Scenes 307
Acknowledgements 318
About the author 320

Chapter One

Zelda picked at the corner of a pumpkin scone, a sick feeling growing in her stomach. The cathedral ceiling of the dining hall magnified the excited chatter of godmothers at the start of fall term, but Zelda couldn't muster enthusiasm for casting spells, brewing potions, or seeing *him* again.

A group of first-year godmothers bustled by their table.

Did I look that young when I first started out at Madame LeBleu's four years ago? Zelda could have sworn the first-years got younger every year.

Across a wooden table scarred by hundreds of years of school meals and magical mishaps, Imogen Yang took a deep swig of sweet, milky tea. She looked up at Zelda from behind black, curtain bangs. "What's wrong? Please tell me you're not still pining."

Zelda laughed dryly. "Pining? Of course I'm not pining. I'm totally over Dante." She popped a casual bite of scone in her mouth, but when she swallowed, her favorite treat stuck in her throat. "I'm just not ready to see him on a regular basis again."

Imogen picked every last crumb of her scone off her plate. "The tinkers don't start classes until next week. What's rotting your pumpkin *today*?"

Zelda shook her head. "Just nerves. I haven't felt like casting spells since the breakup."

Imogen sat a little taller. "Oh yeah. That's normal. I never feel like doing magic when I'm going through a breakup."

Zelda took another bite of her scone and it settled her jittery stomach.

"But you probably still practiced your spells more than me this summer." Imogen laughed.

"Well . . ." Zelda gave Imogen a sheepish grin.

Imogen's jaw fell open. "Zelda Ravensdale. How much did you practice?"

Zelda's grin turned into a grimace.

"You didn't practice at all?"

"No, I didn't," Zelda said, slumping back in her chair. "My heart felt too heavy to even pick up my wand. Still does."

Imogen groaned. "That's not like you at all, but you'll probably still sail to the top of the class."

"I really hope you're right."

If only magic were that easy. Zelda had talent, but she also had to work hard to get even close to beating Susan St. Germain to the top of the class. They'd been neck and neck for First Fairy since day one.

Zelda's insides knotted as students moved toward the hall to get to classes before the first bell. "Maybe it's not too late to be a tinker and transfer to the Erimount Academy of Magical Sciences."

Imogen scoffed. "Then you'd see Dante every day—besides, you almost had a mental breakdown trying to keep an A in Intro to Magical Mechanics."

Zelda let out a genuine laugh. A fairy godmother, like her mom and four older sisters, was all she'd ever wanted to be, and something as silly as a breakup wasn't going to get in the way of that.

They returned their dishes and joined the flow of students in blue berets toward the charms classroom. The latent scent of magic spells like crisp apple and peppermint fought against the acrid polish freshly coating the black-and-white marble floors of the crowded hall. It smelled just like Zelda's first day at Madame LeBleu's School for Godmothers.

The charms classroom was long, with desks at one end and a practice space at the other. Towering, arched windows filled the wood-paneled room with diamonds of morning sunlight. The class of fourth-years assembled, picking the desks they'd sit in for the term.

Would they need to perform any new charms on the first day? Zelda's wand was a weight in her hand when she pulled it out and set it on her desk.

Professor Blanche Hildebrandt glided into the classroom from her adjoining office. "Hello and good morning, my future godmothers," she said, her voice measured and musical, her hands clasped gently in front of her heart. "I hope you all had a restful summer."

She was a short, older woman with peach-kissed skin and round rosy cheeks, her white hair tucked into an immaculate French twist. Elegant, poised, and wise, Blanche Hildebrandt was everything the students of Madame LeBleu's strived to be.

The professor continued, her words serious but kind. "This year will be the truest test of your capability to be a fairy godmother, and I will warn you again, not every girl who goes through Madame LeBleu's will get their wings."

Professor Hildebrandt met Zelda's gaze and her stomach sank. *Why did she look right at me?* Was the glance a mere coincidence? Or had her professor cautioned her?

Wings were an essential part of a fairy's heritage. A personal emblem of everything it meant to be a godmother, and unique to each fairy. Fairies could still do magic without wings. A rare few even refused wings at graduation for their own protection. Wings helped focus a fairy's magic, but wings could complicate things and came with their own inherent risks.

Zelda's mom had warned her from a young age that after she got her wings she was to always protect them, and to use them only when absolutely necessary or when she was around someone she would trust with her life. Old legends said that if you could take a fairy's wings, you could take their magic. It was purely folklore, but that didn't stop some people from trying.

"You all have the talent; every one of you has the raw potential to become a fairy godmother, but Madame LeBleu is looking for polish, not just potential."

It was common knowledge, even outside the magical community, that Madame LeBleu's only accepted the very best and most promising fairies from around the world into its four-year, sixth form program.

Professor Hildebrandt turned to the chalkboard and the outline of the term's syllabus. "I hope you all practiced the basic and intermediate charms this summer. This first week will be a refresher, but next week we'll start on our first unit: ball gowns."

The mention of dressmaking spells sent a ripple of giggles and excited whispers among the fourth-years. Zelda wanted to join the excitement, but dread clawed up her throat. She'd never gone so long without practicing charms.

"At the end of this year, Madame LeBleu, the other instructors, and I will be choosing the First Fairy for your Wing Presentation Ceremony. This is the greatest honor to be bestowed upon a godmother and will give her first choice from the available territories she will grant wishes in until the end of her tenure."

The room quieted immediately at the mention of First Fairy. Zelda shifted to the edge of her seat. That was the price for admission into the school, a placement in an open territory for ten years, or longer if they desired. First Fairy got to pick hers, but the rest of the newly certified godmothers would have to apply for the other open territories.

"We'll make the choice based on many factors: your overall class performance, decorum and poise shown in and out of class, adherence to the standards of godmothers, service to the community, selflessness shown toward others, and whatever personal history that might impact your future as a fairy godmother.

"And I happen to know there will be one new territory in particular that might be an incentive for you all to put your best foot forward." Professor Hildebrandt paused for dramatic effect. "I have it on good faith from someone inside the International Council of Godmothers that the fairy godmother of Olisand is planning to retire this spring."

"Olisand is going to be open?" Henrietta Barnes said without raising a hand, earning her a glare from Professor Hildebrandt.

"Indeed. The post is arguably the most prestigious in the world, as Olisand has the highest concentration of wishes of all territories and the reputation as a kingdom of Happily Ever Afters."

The classroom buzzed with hurried conversation. In the halls of Madame LeBleu's, the godmother of Olisand was a legend. Like many granters, she kept her identity a secret to protect her privacy, but she was said to have the best record of Happily Ever Afters with the International Council of Godmothers.

"Oh dear. I fear we aren't going to be as productive as I would've liked today," Professor Hildebrandt said.

A flash of blond hair drew Zelda's attention to the row beside them as Susan St. Germain cut her friend a knowing smirk. Susan had a natural inclination for everything. So much so that a rumor even circulated that she was a descendant of the first fairy godmother. Imogen had a theory Susan started the rumor herself.

Susan's father owned St. Germain's Shoe Emporium, and if Erimount was known for anything besides Happily Ever Afters, it was shoes. George St. Germain had driven almost all the other cobblers out of town with shoes so well-made, many people suspected his process involved tinkering or fairy magic.

The St. Germain family was incredibly secretive about the whole operation, but locals knew the enigma was all part of the marketing and the shoes were made in a factory outside the city. Still, the shoes flew off the shelves for their quality rather than the mystery, and the profits made George St. Germain the most influential man in Olisand outside the royal family. This also made Susan an instant favorite among the students and professors. At least those she deigned to speak to.

The smug smile on Susan's pink-tinted lips confirmed that she thought First Fairy was as good as hers. Zelda glared at the back of Susan's head.

Don't count your pumpkins till they ripen.

If there was anything Zelda loved, it was the city of Erimount. She'd grown up within an hour's drive of the city, but in her four years at Madame LeBleu's she'd come to know and love the capital as much as the friends she'd made in it. It also helped that her parents were just a train ride away. For the other girls, Olisand was a premium territory.

For Zelda, it was home.

If she could have picked any place in the world to serve her mandatory ten years of service, she would have chosen Erimount. Olisand hadn't been open for more than twenty-five years. But now it was, and Zelda had to have it.

"Grab your wands and we'll do a quick review to start off the term," Professor Hildebrandt said as she headed through the desks to the practice area.

Nerves fluttered in Zelda's chest as she pulled out the long, sleek Blackwood wand she'd purchased for her first year at Madame LeBleu's. The wand specialist had selected it carefully for her, remarking that her magic was stronger than the usual fairy's and would likely be prone to surges. The Blackwood would mitigate these slight fluctuations, or so the wandmaker had insisted.

It had served Zelda well over the past three years. She gripped it in her left hand, relishing the familiarity of the hard, inflexible wood in her palm. It represented everything she wanted to be: strong and consistent.

Zelda rose from her seat and shuffled to the back of the room on wobbling legs.

"Attention, ladies," Professor Hildebrandt sang from the center of the practice area. "Attention." The hushed conversations stopped. "Let's get those wands in the air. I trust you all remember the charm to make snow?"

Zelda raised her arm shakily as she prepared to perform the spell. Casting spells came from the heart, and Zelda's was still healing.

"Goddlewollup et snoodle," they recited in unison. The air filled with a sudden chill and a gust of snowflakes erupted from wands. The flurries were accompanied by the fleeting scents of pine, cinnamon, and gingerbread cookies as girls recalled fond memories of winter to strengthen their spells.

Zelda's stomach tightened when nothing came from her wand. Palms sweating, she gripped her wand tighter and tried to coax snow from it, picturing icy blizzards and sledding down the hills of her parents' vineyard that winter when the snowdrifts reached almost to the eaves.

But again, nothing.

"Miss Ravensdale, is there a problem?" Professor Hildebrandt asked from the center of the circle. Her sharp gaze missed nothing.

A warmth surged in Zelda's cheeks. "N–no," she said with a shiver, but not from the cold. She could feel the gentle tingle of magic tracing the line of her arm.

"Are you having trouble with the spell?"

All heads turned toward her. The professor waved her wand and the rest of the glistening snow disappeared from the air. "There's nothing to be embarrassed about, Miss Ravensdale. Perform the spell again, and we'll see if we can't figure out the problem."

Zelda shifted her feet, placing them shoulder-width apart. She held her wand up and recited the spell, imagining peppermint on her tongue and the nip of snowflakes on her cheeks. Another shiver ran up her spine and down her arm, but nothing came from her wand. Her brows knit together. The magic was there; she could feel it trying to get out, but still nothing.

"It's all right, Miss Ravensdale. You can lower your wand. Perhaps another spell?" Professor Hildebrandt pointed her wand toward Zelda's feet. Sparks shot from the tip of it and swarmed around Zelda's leather flats. When the sparks disappeared, Zelda was left standing barefoot in front of her classmates.

"Can you make glass slippers?"

Zelda could've performed this spell in her sleep. "Fiddle ond faddle," she said and gave her wand two solid flicks. A few silver sparks leaped from the wand's end. Nothing more. For a brief moment she thought she could see the ripple of glass in the air around her feet, but the more she squinted at the outline, the more it slipped away.

"I don't know. I've performed this spell hundreds of times," Zelda said, struggling to keep herself composed.

"I've seen you perform magic much more advanced than this. You're probably having a bit of a mental block," Professor Hildebrandt reassured as she magicked Zelda's flats back onto her feet.

"Oh." Zelda swallowed hard. "A mental block?" It certainly felt more than mental.

"We see this every few years with one of our fourth-years. The pressure can be overwhelming at the start of the year, but once you get back into a school routine, it should work itself out—if you keep practicing."

For the rest of class, Zelda could only watch as the other girls performed a review of the spells and charms they'd learned the previous year. She was supposed to be excelling, shooting straight to the top.

As the ending bell rang, Professor Hildebrandt pulled her aside. "Just find a way to relax, Miss Ravensdale." She patted Zelda on the arm to reassure her. It didn't. "There's a lot of pressure on you girls, but I know how hard you've worked to get here. With your work ethic and talent, I'm confident you'll push through."

"Right." Zelda tried to sound unfazed. "Thank you, Professor." She ducked her head and rushed out of the classroom before her professor could see the tears welling in her eyes.

Eyes burning and cheeks hot with embarrassment, Zelda hurried through the empty cobblestone courtyard to catch up to Imogen and make it to potions on time. She swiped a knuckle under her eyes and swallowed the lump in her throat. She needed to shake off the doldrums or she really would fall to the bottom of the class.

This is just a minor detour, she assured herself. *I can bounce back, can't I?*

Her steps faltered when a boy in a hooded sweatshirt approached the wrought iron gates of the school's main entrance.

In some cultures, it was considered bad luck to approach a fairy godmother in search of a wish. In most others, it was just considered rude. In Erimount, when all else failed, the heartbroken, downtrodden, and weary-souled citizens wrote their wishes on folded sheets of paper and tied them to the wrought iron gates of the school.

The boy looked over his shoulder to make sure no one was watching and pulled a piece of folded paper from his pocket. His hood hid most of his features, but a golden lock of hair flopped over onto his forehead. He didn't notice Zelda as he tied the wish to the gate. When he turned to leave, he spotted her standing alone in the courtyard. Zelda met his clear blue eyes and was struck by their strange familiarity. He looked about her age, but she couldn't remember where she'd seen him before.

His lips parted into a brilliant smile. Zelda thought he might say hello, but the warning bell echoed off the white stone walls of Madame LeBleu's castle-like buildings. She took off toward the ivy-wrapped magical sciences building and the potions lab, desperate not to get a tardy mark on the first day of class. The boy's face lingered in her mind, but recognition still eluded her. When she glanced over her shoulder for one more look, he had already gone.

Chapter Two

The air of excitement and renewed competition carried through the day's classes as girls huddled together and shared predictions of the top competitors for First Fairy in whispers and carefully concealed notes. By some stroke of luck, Zelda hadn't needed to use a single spell after charms. Every other class had been filled with syllabi, lectures, and more final year expectations. When Zelda entered the dining hall for dinner, she caught a few sideways glances in her direction.

Imogen gave Zelda a playful nudge. "I think Susan St. Germain just sized you up. She must think you're one of the front runners."

"After charms class? I don't think so," Zelda said. Several heads turned as they passed tables on their way to the food line. "She's probably looking at you."

Imogen snorted and released a loud "Ha." More heads turned at the noise. "Susan isn't looking over her shoulder for me. My only goal is to not end up somewhere like Alaska. I'm hoping for someplace warm—white-sand beaches if, I'm lucky, or a Korean placement."

The thought of ending up anywhere but Olisand made Zelda's heart squeeze and the dining hall filled with hopeful fairies suddenly felt too small, suffocating.

"Do you want to go out for dinner?"

"I'm in," Imogen said without hesitation and tossed her empty tray onto the stack.

They signed out at the front gates of the school and hopped a trolley car to their favorite place in the city. The trolley slowed as it hit more traffic near the crooked streets of the city center. A hodgepodge of buildings ranging from ancient to modern passed by and a cool fall breeze cut through the open windows. The royal family's castle loomed from high on a hill above the city's jagged skyline, a familiar sight that brought a lump to Zelda's throat.

With or without magic, it was good to be back.

They hopped off in the River District, a quieter neighborhood dominated by stone houses with slate roofs, walled gardens, small shops, and cozy restaurants. A park ran along the bank of the Voeux River where they ordered galettes from a street vendor at the entrance. They found a bench close to the river where they could watch the punters pole by in their little, flat boats.

"Do you feel like there is way more pressure on us this year?" Imogen asked, picking at her ham and cheese galette.

"Oh yeah." She tried to laugh it off, but it came out too short and loud.

Imogen didn't seem to notice as she gazed across the river. "When I got my acceptance letter and said goodbye to my shot at the Royal Ballet, I remember thinking Madame LeBleu's would be all ball gowns and glass slippers."

"You're not thinking of going back to the Royal Ballet School are you?" Zelda's pulse fluttered. The thought of Madame LeBleu's without her roommate, Imogen, was almost too much to bear.

"No way. I mean—I've thought about it once or twice, but I'd never be able to catch up to the girls my age. I knew what I was doing when I turned down my admission to the upper school four years ago. You don't just come back to pre-professional ballet. When you're done, *you're done*, unless you want to teach."

"Well, I'm glad you're here. How was the band last night?" Zelda asked, changing the subject away from their worries.

Imogen shrugged. "Decent enough. It's too bad you didn't come out with us. Dante wasn't there, in case you wanted to know."

"Oh," was all Zelda managed to say. "Why should I care?" She rested her arm on her uneasy stomach. "I'll see him eventually, and when I do, it'll be him who's sorry he let me go. I won't even give him a passing glance." At least she hoped she wouldn't.

A loud whooping noise caught their attention as several boys on oddly shaped bicycles rode past at breakneck speed.

Imogen jumped from her seat. "The tinkers."

"Oy," Zelda called after them, waving her arms over her head.

Two of them kept going, but one stopped, turned, and began to pedal back up the sloping path through the park.

"It's Specs," Imogen said with a laugh. "Specs," she called with a wave.

They ran down the sidewalk to meet him halfway.

"Thaddeus," Zelda called, using his given name. He'd gotten the nickname Specs from them as he had a habit of leaving his magnifying spectacles atop his head.

The lanky, dark-skinned boy hopped off his bike. "Zelda." He wrapped her in a hug. "I missed you this summer. And Imogen." He Imogen before removing his goggles. His eyes were a shade of warm brown, rimmed with thick lashes.

Imogen stood on her tiptoes so they were eye to eye. "Are you taller? I think you got taller."

Specs straightened to his full height. "Two whole inches."

"Impressive." Imogen laughed.

Zelda laughed too. Finally, some of the day's weight lifted from her shoulders. "When do your classes start?"

If Erimount was known for anything besides shoes and wishes, it was known for its world-class tinkers—creators of intricate metal machines of limited magical capability. Thaddeus was a student of the Erimount Academy of Magical Sciences, EAMS, the most prestigious upper school for tinkers in the world. The EAMS campus sat right across the street from Madame LeBleu's, and as partner schools, they shared a library, dining hall, and athletic facilities.

"Next Monday, but how are my favorite GITs doing?" He swiped a hand across his sweaty brow and smudged bicycle grease across it in the process. GITs were what the tinkers called godmothers-in-training for short. "Didn't your classes start today?"

"Yep," Imogen said. "We decided to eat dinner out—take our minds off things."

"I'm glad." Specs smiled. "Well, glad I ran into you both. But what could you possibly have to take your mind off? It's only your first day."

"The pressure is on for First Fairy." Zelda groaned. "It's all our professors want to talk about. That and ICG certification exams."

"And?" Imogen prompted with a flick of her eyebrows toward Zelda.

"What?" Specs' eyes widened with concern.

"My magic is a little tiny bit stuck at the moment."

"How is that possible?" Specs grabbed Zelda's hand as if he thought he would feel the magic coursing toward her fingertips.

Zelda pulled her hand away. "I haven't been able to cast spells today, but I haven't practiced since the end of last term. I can feel the magic run up and down my arm when I say a spell, but nothing comes out of my wand."

Spec scrunched his brows together. "I've never heard of anything like this. Have you told a professor?"

Zelda swallowed. "Not intentionally. Charms class gave me away."

"If you don't figure out what's going on, would they expel you?" Specs asked. "Sorry," he added at the sight of Zelda's face. "You probably don't want to think about that."

She forced a meager smile to her face. "It's okay, Specs. I'll figure it out."

"Maybe it's a conductivity issue," he mused. His eyes unfocused, like when he was working on a complicated problem.

"Huh?" Imogen and Zelda asked at the same time.

"Have you tried a different wand?" Specs clarified. "Different wand materials have different conductivity. We tinkers use different metals to conduct aether, so I assume the same principle applies to wands."

Zelda instinctively grabbed her bag where her wand was tucked safely away. "A new wand? No, no, no."

"Yeah, Specs," Imogen said, a light censure to her voice. "Most fairies keep the same wand their entire life. That's like asking an Olympic sprinter to switch to a new pair of cleats right before a race."

Specs ran his hands through his hair. "Well then, I'll see what I can find, Zelda. That would really suck if you got expelled. Really."

Zelda's stomach flipped at the mention of expulsion again. "Sorry we took you from your friends. It doesn't look like they waited for you."

"It's fine." Specs' sympathetic frown turned into a proud smirk. "The bike I built was just walloping Alfred McKinney's. I'll probably get an earful when I catch up, but I'll get him in the next race." He mounted his bike and lowered his goggles.

"You're leaving us already?" Imogen pouted.

Specs shuffled his feet and ducked his head to hide a little grin. "Yeah, but the local tinkers are all heading to The Swan and Raven tonight to catch up with everyone who's back in town for school. Alfred told me to spread the word. D'you guys want to go?"

Zelda gave Imogen a nervous glance. "I'm not sure."

"Did Alfred say who exactly is going?" Imogen asked for Zelda's benefit.

Specs lifted a shoulder. "I didn't think to ask."

Zelda picked at the corner of her nail. She didn't know if she was ready to see Dante again after how things had ended and with so much left unsaid.

No.

They would run into each other eventually. Erimount wasn't that big of a city, and she wouldn't be the one sitting in her dormitory all year to avoid him.

"Let's go," she said, finding her voice.

"Really?" Imogen's brows rose, a tentative smile on her lips. "Are you sure?"

"Yes, you just have to help me find something to wear."

"Deal." Imogen reached out her hand, and they shook on it with a laugh.

"Cool," Specs said. "See you tonight."

"See ya," they echoed, and Specs took off down the path, whooping like a banshee.

After they finished their galettes, Zelda and Imogen headed back toward school. Instead of taking the trolley all the way to Madame LeBleu's, they got off near Founders Square with a specific destination in mind. Zelda filled her lungs with the pleasant evening breeze and the smell of Erimount as they turned the corner. Founders Square bustled with a familiar hum of city life. Street vendors roasted cinnamon nuts, couples rode past on bicycles, and people sipped coffees under striped umbrellas at tiny tables.

At the center of it all, a fountain filled the air with the musical sound of falling water. Atop the cascade, a sculpture of the first king of Erimount embraced his queen.

They headed for St. Germain's Shoe Emporium, on the opposite side of the square. At five-stories tall and an entire block wide, George St. Germain's behemoth of a store was the main attraction of the square. Imogen had tried on her school shoes from last year, but the soles had worn out in the toes. New shoes were in order, and no self-respecting resident of Erimount would be caught wearing anything but St. Germain's.

On the way, Zelda spotted a window display filled with colorful towers of macarons.

"You go without me," Zelda said.

"You're sure you don't want to go in?" Imogen prodded. "I can always find something in St. Germain's."

"I'm going to get a surprise for us."

"I love surprises," Imogen said before bouncing off toward the shoe store. "I promise I won't be long," she called over her shoulder.

Zelda passed Founders Fountain on her way to the patisserie. At the fountain's edge, a mother instructed a little girl wearing souvenir fairy wings to toss in a coin and make a wish. The fountain supposedly marked the spot of the first wish made by the founders of Olisand, a fact which most locals found suspect—a nice story fabricated to attract tourists to an otherwise average city square. Zelda liked to believe the story. She was a godmother in training for goodness' sake.

Her steps faltered, and whether it was a burst of sentimentality or just desperation, she got an inclination to make a wish of her own. She dug through her bag for a shiny, copper sovereign.

Zelda closed her eyes to listen to the ambient din of voices and the bubbling spouts of water at the base of the fountain. She wasn't sure if fairy godmothers even got their own wish. It was against the ICG standards of a fairy godmother to use magic for *excessive* personal gain. Still, she'd never been desperate enough to make a wish before. She hoped it wouldn't hurt to try as she squeezed the coin tightly in her palm.

"I wish," she whispered, holding her hand out over the water. All of the things she could wish for floated through her mind, but there was only one thing she truly wanted. "I wish to be First Fairy."

The coin fell into the water with a satisfying plop, and Zelda took a step forward to gaze into the shallow pool. Her coin was already lost among the many others covering the bottom, thousands of little wishes overlapping each other like copper dragon scales.

The godmother of Olisand must really have her hands full.

And suddenly her wish seemed quite insignificant in the grand scheme of things.

She purchased a box of assorted macarons, her reward for working up the courage to go out tonight, and returned to the fountain to wait for Imogen. It seemed this school year would take all her extra time and energy—if she didn't get expelled or forced out of the granter track. Even so, if these were her final days at Madame LeBleu's School for Godmothers, Zelda wanted to soak up every moment she could, and tonight would be the start.

Chapter Three

The Swan and Raven was a nearby, hole-in-the-wall pub favored by the students of Madame LeBleu's and EAMS when they reached Olisand's legal drinking age of eighteen. When Zelda and Imogen arrived, the crowd of students overflowed from the pub onto the sidewalks beneath the shingle depicting the fable for which the pub was named.

Zelda didn't know why the students had come to adopt this pub as their favorite—the city was full of nicer, newer pubs with all the same drinks. But walking into the Tudor, timber-framed building felt like coming home. Everywhere she looked, Zelda found a familiar face.

They snaked their way through the crowd and found Specs waiting at the bar. He and Imogen both ordered pints of fairy microbrew that gave one exceptional feelings of nostalgia, while Zelda ordered wine.

Up a steep and narrow staircase in the lounge on the second floor, they found some available tables and sticky leather couches to occupy. From their spot, they could see out a window overlooking the street and watch who came and went from the pub.

A steady stream of friends came by their table, stopping to discuss summer romances, faraway vacations, and expectations for the year ahead. It felt good to laugh and smile, and the happy conversations put all the pressures of the coming year out of Zelda's mind.

"I need a refill," Zelda said, shaking her empty glass. "Does anyone need anything while I'm up?"

Both Imogen and Specs declined and turned back to their discussion of Imogen's summer trip to Korea to see her extended family.

Zelda headed down the staircase to the bar. The light was dim, and she watched her feet carefully so as not to miss a step. As she turned down the first landing, she nearly crashed into someone as they rounded the corner.

"Sorry—" Zelda looked up from her feet and her stomach jumped.

The boy looking down at her had light-brown hair swept artfully to the side and a toothy smile. He was tall, bronzed from a summer spent sailing the Adriatic, and oozed a quiet charm Zelda had come to know well. He was still the most handsome boy she'd ever met—even if he had broken her heart.

"Zelda," he said in a smooth voice, stepping to the side so other patrons could pass them on the stairs. He sounded pleased to see her, which made Zelda's pulse swoop.

Does that mean he was sorry for ending things with her?

"Dante." His name rolled off her tongue—a forgotten familiarity.

"Hi." Dante lowered his voice, his lips pulling up on one side. It was a pained sort of smile, but Zelda could only stare at the single freckle on his cheek. She had kissed that freckle just three months earlier.

"Hi," Zelda said. Blood pounded in her ears as her mind reeled to remember all that she had to say. She'd rehearsed this meeting many times over, but all she could manage was, "Hi." She could've kicked herself.

"How've you been?" Dante rested an elbow to lean against the wall.

Zelda attempted a breezy shrug. "I've been fine," she said with a desperate hope the words rang true.

Another couple squeezed past them in the crowded stairwell and forced Zelda to move closer to Dante. Her breath hitched as the familiar scent of sandalwood and spiced citrus filled her nose.

"Want to go someplace to talk?" He jerked his head toward the bar area.

"Yeah." Zelda couldn't think in a small space with him so close.

Dante led her down the stairs, through the crowd, and outside to where people gathered in front of the stained glass windows of the pub. A few of Dante's friends gave them nods, though some wore curious looks that unnerved Zelda. Of course, he'd told his friends about their breakup. She'd told her friends. Why would he have done any different?

They stopped along the sidewalk out of earshot from the others. Zelda kept her eyes on the empty wineglass in her hand rather than the boy she'd once thought she loved.

"You look good," Dante said.

Zelda leaned her back against the stone wall of the adjoining building. The stones spread an inviting coolness through her canvas jacket. Dante propped himself up with a hand on the wall, the other shoved in the pocket of his cuffed chinos. The crooked smile on his lips made Zelda's pulse flutter traitorously. Dante looked cool. Casual. Zelda figured she probably looked like a flower folding in on itself during a frost.

"You too," she breathed.

With a sigh, Dante took a step closer to her. His closeness sent her head spinning with all the things she wanted to ask him.

He spoke before she could settle on where to begin. "I know things didn't end well with us last year. But I think what we had was really fantastic."

"Fantastic?" she asked incredulously.

It wasn't the word she would've used. She'd hardly call crying through her final exams fantastic. Things had been going well when they started dating during fall term, then Dante started to freeze her out in the spring with no clue or reason why. They'd been in love one month—at least Zelda had been—and then the next he'd suggested they spend some time apart, starting with the summer holiday.

"Fun," Dante said. His lips pulled back into a self-assured smile.

"Fun?" Zelda raised her voice. There was certainly nothing fun about getting her heart broken bit by bit over the length of spring term. There was nothing fun in replaying the events of that final week over and over again every sleepless night that summer. Fun. It was so ridiculous a notion, she could almost laugh. Almost.

"We definitely had chemistry, that's for sure. I'd hate to see that go to waste." He tucked a strand of Zelda's dark hair behind her ear with a gentle touch.

Zelda flinched as his fingers grazed her cheek. She could hardly believe what she was hearing. "Are you saying we should get back together?"

The smirk fell from Dante's face. "Well, no. I still meant what I said last year about not wanting a serious relationship. I'm still just looking for something casual. So, what do you say?" He lowered his head to bring his brown eyes to level with Zelda's.

"So just hook up?" Zelda growled.

She had never seen Dante like this. Full of bravado and cheek. He'd always had a subtle assuredness about himself, but the boy she'd known was intelligent and kind. More of a wallflower who preferred books and deep conversation. Not the swaggering jerk standing before her.

"You could put it that way," he purred, flicking his tongue over his bottom lip.

Something released in Zelda's chest, a feeling she'd been carrying with her all summer. She rolled her eyes.

"Goodbye, Dante." She pushed him away and headed toward the pub and the crowd of students, completely and utterly over him.

"Zelda, come on. Don't be such a prude." Heads turned to watch them now.

"No." Zelda rounded on him. The glass shook in her hand, but she felt taller than she'd ever felt before. "I will not *come on* because I've a little something called self-respect," she shouted, her shoulders back and head high. "And good taste."

The tinkers crowding the doorway of the pub snickered.

"Sweetheart, don't make a scene," Dante pleaded. Another emotion simmered beneath his honeyed words. Irritation? The conversation clearly hadn't gone as planned.

"I'm not your sweetheart. Not anymore." Zelda took a deep breath, her voice lowering to a cool, even tone. "I don't even know who you are, Dante Sadler. I can't believe I was ever sad over our breakup."

He sighed. "Zelda—"

"Bye." Zelda bit down on her lip, turned on her heel, then stalked back into the pub and up to the second floor.

She slammed her glass down on the table, causing Imogen and Specs to jump. The other tinkers hanging around the table scattered at the first signs of drama.

"What's wrong?" Imogen asked.

"We need to leave," Zelda shouted over the din of voices.

"Okay." Imogen nodded without further question.

They grabbed their coats and within the minute they were out the door.

"She's back for more," a boy yelled as they passed the group on the sidewalk. Dante looked wobbly on his feet with an arm around one of his rugby buddies. Imogen rounded on the crowd and told Dante to do something vulgar to himself, and Specs offered the crowd his best attempt at a withering glare before he and Imogen hurried Zelda down the otherwise empty street.

"Ugh, I'm sorry he was there. Are you okay, Zelda?" Specs asked, tucking Zelda under his arm.

"What happened? What did he say?" Imogen shook her head; she'd never been a fan of him.

Zelda clenched her jaw. "He wanted to hook up."

Specs made a disgusted sound.

"Yeah. I could have punched him. I should have. I can't believe I was sad about losing him. Now, I'm just mad." They turned the corner and found the main cobblestone street that led back toward Madame LeBleu's.

Imogen trembled with anger. "What a slimy worm. The next time I see him I'll—" She shook her fist in the air, and Zelda burst into giggles.

Specs laughed. "Did you really just shake your fist?"

"What? Was that funny?" Imogen said, her hand still raised in a closed fist.

"I didn't know anyone still did that," Zelda said as tears of laughter sprang to her eyes.

"I'm mad for you." Imogen's lips cracked into a smile.

Zelda put her other arm through Imogen's. "I know. I know. And I thank you for defending my honor."

They stopped at the corner, and Specs turned to Zelda. "What do you want to do?"

"Yeah, it's up to you," Imogen said. "We can get food, go back to school, or we can throw eggs at Dante's house. Your choice."

Specs laughed. "Or we can go to my house and gorge ourselves on day-olds from my parents' bakery?"

"That," Zelda said. "Let's do that."

"This will cheer you up too." Imogen dug through her purse and retrieved a glossy tabloid emblazoned with the face of Olisand's crown prince. The words "Leo Madness" were splashed across the page in neon block letters.

"A tabloid?" Zelda eyed the magazine with confusion.

"Prince Leopold is going to do his final year of sixth form at the Erimount Academy of Magical Sciences," Specs said. "We found out while you were with Dante. It was all the tinkers were talking about—the article explains everything."

Zelda hadn't caught Leo Madness even after three years in Erimount, but the thought of a real live prince studying across the street was a welcome distraction from her magic troubles. She took the magazine from Imogen and was struck by something. She'd seen the prince's face many times over the course of her life, but the image gave her a strange feeling of familiarity. Like she'd seen him recently.

The boy at the gate came to mind. Could that really have been the crown prince tying his wish to the gates? And what could a prince wish for that he didn't already have? She tucked the memory away, doubting she'd ever have the opportunity to ask him.

Chapter Four

Imogen met Zelda in the quad for their second day of classes, her highlighted brown hair in a slick pony with a pearl-embellished scrunchie, and a look of concern on her face.

"I'm fine," Zelda said cheerily before Imogen could even ask.

After her encounter with Dante, she had a new sense of clarity. She'd wondered all summer whether she would ever have a chance to change how things were with him, and now she had her answer. A part of her still ached for something to fill the space he'd left behind, but putting Dante firmly in her past would hopefully give her the focus she needed to fix her magic.

Imogen held up her hands defensively. "I didn't say anything."

"Really," Zelda insisted. "Last night was good for me. I've been dreading running into Dante since I arrived in Erimount, and now I'm cured."

"Good," Imogen said with a grunt, using the full weight of her body to pull open the heavy wooden door to the academic building. "So, you'll go on a blind date with me and Fletcher?"

"Fletcher Westbrook? The tinker?" Zelda asked as they ascended the stairs to the second floor. The well-groomed, preppy boy with dark hair and amber skin was in his final year at EAMS. If Zelda's memory was correct, he was on the rugby team with Dante.

"Yeah. We ran into each other over the summer; he lives in London too. I've been texting him." Imogen sighed. "*Fletcher*. I even like his name. You've seen him, right? Isn't he cute?"

Zelda laughed. "Yeah, he's definitely good-looking."

"Well, he's taking me out to dinner tonight." Imogen flicked her hair over her shoulder. "He says he can find a date for you."

"That's great, but I don't think I'm ready to be set up yet."

They turned into the potions lab. "Fine. But you'd better let me know the second you're ready. I have ideas."

Zelda's stomach lurched. "Oh no. Who?"

"I'll tell you when you're ready," Imogen teased with an impish arched brow.

The piteous looks of Zelda's peers made her cheeks burn as she and Imogen passed to take their spots at an empty lab table. Zelda threw down her book of potions and brews on the table and buried her eyes in the pages. Every fourth-year was probably glad not to be in her shoes after yesterday's disaster in charms class. Potions would be better. With Imogen as her lab partner, she wouldn't even need magic.

Professor Ballentine entered the classroom with the familiar click of heels on polished wood floors. "Welcome, students," she called out as she passed the rows of tables to reach the front of the room.

Professor Ballentine was young compared to the other professors and had only started teaching the previous year—right after the end of her tenure as a godmother. With four-inch pumps and a biting sense of humor, Professor Helga Ballentine had quickly become one of Zelda's favorites. Today she wore a camel turtleneck and white ankle pants with her cropped blond hair styled in a sleek finger wave.

"I hope you didn't forget everything over the summer holiday," she said, taking a seat on her desk at the front of the classroom. "Please prepare a simple sleeping draft according to the instructions on page ten of your textbooks. Mind the flames of your Bunsen burners. This potion requires lots of heat, and I don't want to have to restore any eyebrows today."

Zelda stifled a smile as she lit the small gas burner at her station. Most of the girls at Madame LeBleu's were intimidated by Professor Ballentine, probably because they didn't understand her dry sense of humor.

"All of the ingredients should be in your basic supply kits or the supply closet," Professor Ballentine said over the clatter of glass beakers and the clang of metal brewing instruments.

Zelda pulled out a set of scales from the drawer beneath their lab table and measured the ingredients for the brew.

"We need more night-harvested lavender. I'm out," Imogen said as she riffled through the glass vials that filled her leather potions kit.

Zelda went to the supply closet and found a half-empty vial of lavender. After she double checked the label to make sure it had been cut by the light of the moon, she turned to see Susan St. Germain blocking the door, a meek grin on her lips.

"Hi, Zelda," she said, almost hesitantly.

"Hey, Susan." Zelda's brows knit in suspicion. The times Susan had condescended to talk to her were few and far between. Zelda took a step forward, but Susan didn't move from where she was rooted in front of the door.

"I just wanted to stop by to offer my condolences about what happened in charms class. That must have been so terrifying," Susan said with what looked like genuine concern on her dainty features.

"It really wasn't," Zelda said, straightening herself.

"I'm sorry . . . well . . . I confess that wasn't my intention for this little tête-à-tête. I know we've never been close, but I have the utmost respect for you as a fellow fairy, Zelda." She moved her braid from one shoulder to the other as she spoke.

"Okay," Zelda said slowly, not entirely sure what Susan was getting at.

"I know you and Dante Sadler were separated for the summer; our families linked up in Montenegro for a few weeks. He asked me out, but I heard about the spat in front of The Swan and Raven. If I were to go out with him, I just wanted to make sure there wasn't anything still between the two of you. I always thought you two made a cute couple, and I'd hate to be the one to get in the middle."

Zelda's jaw clenched. She hadn't been prepared for this. She hadn't even known the St. Germains were close with Dante's family. It took a slow breath to steady her nerves, but she managed to give an even, albeit short, response. "Yeah, we're over. He's all yours."

Susan's face lit up with a smile. "Oh good," She clasped her hands together. "I would hate for there to be any unpleasantness between us." She grabbed a vial of powdered moonstone and returned to her lab table.

Zelda hurried back to Imogen who gave her a confused look.

"Were you talking to Susan in there?"

"Yeah," Zelda said.

Imogen leaned in, her voice lowered to a whisper. "What did she want?"

"She wants to date Dante. She was checking to make sure I didn't still have a thing for him."

Imogen emitted an actual growl. "Typical. She's just trying to get in your head."

Zelda's lip curled in disgust. "Ugh. She can have him. It's going to take more than that to get in my head," she said, portioning the lavender onto the scale. "I hope they're happy together. I honestly don't care."

Until last night, she'd entertained the idea of a rekindled romance with Dante, that whatever had broken between them could be fixed. But that idea was long gone. As much as she tried not to care, it would take some getting used to. Dante would see other people and so would she. Maybe. Eventually.

At the end of the class, Ballentine visited each table to examine their work. She lifted Zelda and Imogen's flask for examination first. "Good work, Miss Ravensdale, Miss Yang." She swirled the liquid inside and waved a hand through the steam to waft it toward her nose. "Potent yet palatable, I expect."

"I added a little crushed frankincense," Zelda said.

Professor Ballentine's angular brows rose with surprise as she offered Zelda a rare smile. "Ingenious." She wrote something down and moved on to inspect the next potion.

Zelda relished the small victory. Everyone produced satisfactory sleeping drafts, but none quite to the level of Zelda and Imogen's.

"Excellent job today," Professor Ballentine said to the room, her voice approving but still severe. "I expect you all to carry this momentum through the rest of the year. I don't need to remind you how important potion brewing will be while granting wishes."

The bell rang, and the girls began to pack up their supplies and ingredients.

"I want a five-hundred-word essay on the methodology and side-effects of sleeping drafts by next class," Ballentine called after the girls as they filed out into the hall. "The assignment is in the syllabus."

Despite Susan's attempt to throw her off her game and charms class lingering in the back of her mind, Zelda walked lighter on her feet. Even without magic, she had helped produce the best potion of the day. If this wasn't the start of the end of her mental block, it sure felt like it.

For the last block of the day, the fourth-years had a new activity on their schedules. Zelda arrived at the room on the second floor and found it occupied by rows of wooden study carrels, each with its own powder-blue telephone. Zelda took a seat near the window and eyed the peculiar phone. In addition to the numbers zero through nine, it featured three buttons: red, yellow, and blue. She checked the back of her phone and didn't find any cords connected to it.

Old phones like this must be plugged into a wall, right?

Girls chatted excitedly as they waited for someone to arrive to explain what they were doing. Imogen picked up the receiver impatiently and held it to her ear. "No dial tone."

"Imogen? What are you doing? Hang that up." Zelda grabbed the handset from Imogen's grasp and replaced it on the base. "Does your phone have cords? I think I have gotten a broken one."

"No," Imogen said. She snatched the receiver to her ear again and stabbed the hook with her index finger. "I think they're all broken."

Zelda nudged her as Professor Weymouth, their history professor, entered the room. He was tall with a pale complexion and light-brown hair that was always a little wild.

The only male instructor at Madame LeBleu's, he was also a common favorite among the students. According to Zelda's older sisters, the last history professor had been a terrible bore, an old lady with bad breath and a monotone voice. Professor Weymouth, on the other hand, had a way of making an otherwise dull subject interesting. Magic was his passion, even if he didn't have the gift—fairies only passed on their magic to their daughters. His fascination with the magic arts showed in his teaching. It also didn't hurt that he was in his early thirties and easy on the eyes.

He deposited a heavily scuffed leather case and a tweed jacket onto the desk at the front of the room. "Good afternoon, ladies." He hooked his thumbs into the pockets of his trousers. He wore a vest over his white shirt. With the sleeves cuffed at the wrists, he looked far more disheveled than usual—like he'd already left for the day when he realized he had another class.

"Good afternoon," the girls replied in harmonious unison.

"I must apologize. There was a mix-up in the scheduling, and I just got word they needed a professor to advise your class on your field experience. Professor Ballentine would've been your advisor, but she had a scheduling conflict," he explained. "But that is neither here nor there." He popped open the briefcase and set a stack of cards on the desk.

"The phones you see before you are direct lines to the ICG Regional Field Office Wish Processing Center," he began. "The godmother of the Olisand region has always generously allowed Madame LeBleu's students to grant wishes in her territory to gain the invaluable experience of granting real wishes outside the classroom. She and the fairies at the processing center have specially selected these wish cases for you. I will be monitoring the wishes you grant and how you grant them, and so will the local office of Ever After Assurance."

He held up a pale-blue card from the stack on the desk. "Each card has a brief description of a wish, which I will distribute. On this same card, you will mark your name and actions taken should you decide to grant the wish."

He slid half of the chalkboard aside to reveal a list of the official standards of a fairy godmother. "As you've learned in ethics, you would do well to keep these standards in mind. A godmother must be selfless and put her godchildren before herself," he recited. "She must be conscious of the greater good and only grant wishes that will not harm it. A godmother must be kind and respectful, treating each wish as if it were her own. A godmother must have her wand ready at all times, and finally, a godmother must not use her magic for excessive personal gain. Your performance in the field, and your adherence to these standards will be a major factor in our consideration for First Fairy."

"But how will we grant wishes by phone?" Felicity Dunn asked.

"Good question, Ms. Dunn. These phones have been magicked specifically for this task. I'm sure you've all noticed the buttons. There's an anonymous case number assigned to each card; dial the case number, and you will be connected to the phone nearest to your godchild. The red button will transport you to their location when you're ready. When you finish, click your heels twice to return to this classroom."

"There's no place like home," Maud Woods said, inciting a chorus of giggles.

Even the professor cracked a smile. "Yes, Ms. Woods. Now, the yellow button will hold the call if you need to ask me a question. Blue sends the caller to the fairy godmother of Olisand's voicemail if you aren't sure whether to grant the wish or if you aren't sure your skills will allow you to."

Zelda's breath caught in her throat as Professor Weymouth spoke. They were granting real wishes on their second day, and she hadn't even figured out how to use her magic again. Nervousness turned in her gut, but excitement thrummed beneath it. She'd waited to grant wishes for years. Now, that moment had arrived.

Weymouth erased the standards and began to write out the rules for wishes. Granting wishes for people often delved into morally gray areas, but godmothers were trained to be prepared with a clear and wise mind should someone wish for something that was challenged by their conscience. That was one of the good things about being a godmother; there was no obligation to grant any wish, and each wish was up to the interpretation of each fairy and how she granted it.

Professor Weymouth stepped aside to reveal the list on the board.

1. Everyone is allowed one wish. A person may choose not to use this right, but wishes are not transferable and may not be sold, bought, or traded.

2. No wishing for more wishes.

3. No wishing for magical powers.

4. No wish will be granted which harms the greater good or the physical, mental, or emotional well-being of another.

5. No fairy shall use banned magic, nor grant wishes that conflict with the laws of the International Council of Godmothers (ICG) or their territory of residence.

6. These rules are binding to all wishers and may not be altered by wishing. Rules are subject to change only by the ICG. Awarding wishes is at the sole discretion of the godmother to whom the wish was wished.

7. All wishes and subsequent Happily Ever Afters are subject to the known and unknown limitations of magic.

"I must emphasize, each wisher must sign a contract agreeing to these rules before their wish is granted. This is both for their protection and yours. Once signed, the contract will be stored in the Library of Wishes, which is maintained by the ICG. In addition to the contract, the actual wish and the spells cast, or potions used, will go into that individual's file," Professor Weymouth said.

The mood of the room shifted as a few girls rustled in their seats. It made sense that godmothers had to be regulated, but Zelda wondered how strict they'd be if wishes were to be granted based on the discretion of each godmother. She imagined a bunch of fairies in a file room, looking through her own file with disapproval on their rosy-cheeked faces.

"Now, get your wands out, and I'll assign you your first wishes. Are you ready to make some Happily Ever Afters?"

Nervous laughter rippled through the room in response.

The professor cracked his knuckles and picked up the stack of cards. He shuffled them and examined the top one with a dark, furrowed brow. "All right, Miss Pickett, you're first."

Iris straightened in her seat and eagerly snatched the card from his hand. The room stilled as she dialed the case number from her assigned card. After a brief exchange, Iris pushed the red button and disappeared from her seat, sending a small current of air through the room.

Excited chatter erupted.

"Quiet please," Professor Weymouth instructed.

He handed out cards slowly at first, passing them to girls in no apparent order. Zelda waited patiently for her turn, but soon the room was almost empty, and she began to eye the clock on the wall as it neared the end of the block.

Has Professor Hildebrandt warned the other teachers about my magic failing?

Girls soon reappeared in their seat with wide grins. They each filled out their card and returned it to the professor, who then dismissed them from the room. Zelda sat rigid in her seat. Imogen had been one of the first few girls to get a card. When she returned, she gave Zelda an encouraging smile and grabbed her bag to leave.

Perhaps Professor Weymouth would dismiss her once all the others had gone to save her from further embarrassment. That seemed like something he would do, but Professor Weymouth didn't glance her way until he reached the very last card.

"Are you ready, Miss Ravensdale?"

Zelda jumped at the sound of her name. "You mean I get a chance?"

Professor Weymouth nodded.

"I'm ready," she said, her hand tightening around her wand.

He handed her a card, and she read it hungrily. The card was sparse, the description of the wish left blank. The only information on the card was the case number.

"Professor, the card doesn't have a wish description."

"I saw that," Professor Weymouth said with a curious grin.

"What does that mean?"

He rubbed the back of his neck. "I'm not sure, but the fairy godmother of Olisand wouldn't have passed it to a student without reason. I guess you'll have to dial the number and see."

Zelda took a deep breath and picked up the receiver. She dialed the four numbers listed on the card, and the speaker against her ear clicked to life.

The phone rang twice before someone picked up.

"Hello?" The voice was deep. Hesitant.

"Oh—uh, sorry. My name is Zelda Ravensdale, and I'm, um, calling on behalf of the fairy godmother of Olisand. How can I help you?"

"Well, I have a wish—" He laughed a little, the tightness in his voice slipping.

"Right." Zelda laughed too.

"It's kind of a big wish and a bit sensitive. I'm hesitant to ask it over the phone."

"I can come to you," Zelda said, her voice rising at the end as if to ask for permission.

The voice paused, and she thought for a moment he might have hung up on her.

"Okay," he said.

Zelda held her finger over the red button but looked up to see Professor Weymouth watching her over the top of her study carrel. He gave her a nod as if to say, "go ahead." She pressed the button and all the air was sucked from her lungs. The room went black, but not before Zelda caught a glimpse of a concerned frown on Professor Weymouth's lips.

Chapter Five

Zelda drew in a desperate breath, and a moment later, all she saw was an ornate rug tilting beneath her feet. A steady hand grabbed her arm, and her head stopped spinning. Her legs wobbled, but when her vision cleared, Zelda found herself standing in the most lavish bedroom she'd ever seen. Ornate tapestries hung on stone walls lined with showy, antique furniture, darkened with age.

"Are you all right?" asked a voice at her side.

"Yeah," Zelda rasped, but her voice dropped off when she saw the handsome boy who stood next to her. "You're—"

"Prince Leopold, at your service," said the boy with a face she would recognize anywhere. "You look a little sick. Do you need to sit? If you're going to get sick, I ask you don't do so on the rug. It's older than . . . well it's really old."

"No, I'm fine," Zelda said, trying to reconcile the person she saw on tabloid covers with the face in front of her. He was handsome in photos, but photos didn't capture a certain charm to his features. Whether it was the clear blue of his eyes, or the slight upturn of his nose, or the fact his smile reached a little too wide, there was some quality of his that she couldn't quite put into words.

Composing herself, she adjusted her navy sweater and tucked her hair behind her ears. "Travel by phone just takes a second to get used to. This is my first experience in the field." She silently cursed herself for babbling, then shook her head to clear it. "You have a wish?" She gave the prince a smile, hoping it showed a bit more confidence than she actually had.

"Yes." His blue eyes danced in the warm light of what Zelda now assumed was his bedroom.

"And what is this wish, Your Highness?" She tried her best to ignore the fact that she was in the presence of royalty—royalty with symmetrical features. Her stomach felt unnervingly jumbled and giddy like she'd eaten too many macarons.

How am I supposed to grant his wish without any magic?

"You can call me Leo."

"Zelda." She extended her hand to him, which he shook graciously.

"Zelda," he repeated. "You don't hear that every day." He took a seat in a plush leather armchair and gestured for Zelda to take the one opposite.

He looked relaxed. His golden-brown hair was playfully disheveled, the ends of it curling around his ears and every which way. The rolled sleeves of his white collared shirt added to the prince-at-leisure look.

"You don't hear Leopold every day either," Zelda said.

He smiled, and Zelda couldn't help but smile too.

"So, your wish?" she prompted, remembering why she was here in the first place.

He leaned forward to rest his elbows on his knees. "As I said, this is sensitive." His voice was low, and Zelda had to lean in to hear him clearly. "You can't tell a soul."

"Well," Zelda paused, "any wishes I grant are reviewed by my professors. They go in my file while I'm still in training."

"Oh," Leo said. His eyes flicked to the Madame LeBleu's crest sewn onto Zelda's sweater.

"And what if this is a matter of utmost secrecy? For the sake of the monarchy?"

Zelda's stomach clenched. "I'm sure my professors will understand the need for secrecy if I intentionally leave my reports vague."

"All right then." Leo's shoulders sagged. He breathed a long sigh and locked eyes with Zelda. "I wish I wasn't a prince."

His words took the wind out of Zelda's lungs. "W-wow, that is . . ." She fumbled for words as she tried to wrap her mind around the implications of his wish. "That's a *really* big wish."

Why is the godmother of Olisand passing the wish of a prince to a student?

Leo gave her a small smile, but it didn't reach his eyes. Only then did Zelda realize what made him so different from the face on the cover of Imogen's gossip magazines; he had a sadness about him that he hid in front of cameras.

"Yeah." The prince hung his head. "I'm sorry. I shouldn't have put this on you."

"Don't apologize. It's why I'm here." Zelda flicked her wand without even thinking, and magic rushed to her hand. "*Provisious Contractiment*," she said before the feeling ceased. For the first time in months, the ripple of magic begrudgingly traveled from her hand to her wand to make the wish contract appear in her lap. Her heart leaped. She hadn't lost her magic entirely, but why had it returned now?

"Are you okay?" Leo asked.

She must have looked strange, holding the paper in stunned silence. "Here are the rules of wishes." She handed him the contract. "You have to sign on the bottom stating that you understand the rules before we proceed."

"Does this mean you will grant my wish?" he asked hopefully.

"Well," Zelda started, but had to laugh a little at her own luck. She couldn't have gotten a more complicated wish for her first field experience. "This is no simple wish. Are you certain you don't want anything else?"

His eyes scanned the contract, and Zelda noted the heavy lashes which framed his eyes. She tried not to dwell on such things, even though they made her chest tighten in a strange and pleasing way. Especially when she had just cast her first small spell in months.

"You know where we are, right?" Leo asked with a chuckle. He stood, crossed to an ornate wooden desk, and scribbled a signature across the bottom of the page. "We're literally sitting in a castle right now. I could have almost anything I want if I just pull that bell by the door." He returned to his seat and gave the contract back to Zelda, his smile wide and disarming.

Zelda laughed, and it chased away the last of her nerves. *Curious.* She hadn't thought much about meeting the crown prince, but she'd expected that any encounter with royalty would have been more than uncomfortable. Instead, he'd put her at ease within minutes. She wondered if he was that way with everyone. A true Prince Charming.

Leo sat a little taller for having pulled a genuine laugh from her. "Please don't think me ungrateful. I know millions of people would happily trade places with me, but I want for nothing in this world except control over my own fate."

Zelda shuffled in her seat. "I only caution you because what you're asking for is much more complicated than it seems. Complicated political ramifications aside, it would take a spell of its very own. A big one. A made from scratch, one-of-a-kind type of spell, and I need to know that granting your wish won't harm the greater good," Zelda said quietly, trying her best to give Leo a reassuring smile. "Why not just abdicate?"

Leo nodded, and the smile faded from his face. "I don't want to hurt my family. An abdication would be a scandal on a global scale. The aftereffects could hurt the monarchy for ages. I'd hate myself if I left an embarrassing mark on my father's reign."

His hand suddenly reached out for hers, and he wrapped her fingers up in his. The sudden contact made Zelda's breath stop. "And this country will be much better off if I'm not king, believe me."

Zelda tried to ignore the warmth of his hand spreading into hers, but her lips parted in a short gasp at the intimacy of the gesture.

Leo seemed to sense his blunder and released her hand. "Sorry," he said as a blush colored his cheeks. He shoved the offending hand into his hair.

Zelda found her voice haltingly. "W-what makes you say that?"

Leo's brows cinched together in confusion. "Because I grabbed your hand?"

"No. Why do you think the kingdom would be better off without you as its next king?"

"No one wants me, of all people, running this country." Leo's face was full of earnest sincerity as he spoke. They'd only just met, and he was pouring his soul out for her. This was all part of being a fairy godmother, wasn't it?

"But your father—he can teach you, can't he?"

"Oh, he has, but he thinks I'm too soft. He's told me I don't have what it takes to be the ruler of a country."

Zelda remained silent as she watched Leo's eyes cut to the family crest hanging proudly over the carved stone fireplace at the far end of the room. With the hurt written so clearly on his face, it took every ounce of self-control Zelda possessed not to grant his wish right then and there. Or grab his hand.

Zelda shook her head. "Sorry," she said. "I need time to process this."

"Oh, no. I apologize for springing this on you," Leo said. "I realize what implications this could have."

Zelda's chest tightened. "I can pass the wish on to the fairy godmother of Olisand if you'd be more comfortable with that?" Her eyes swept the lavish chamber with its high stone walls and cascading draperies.

I'm in way over my head.

This was a job for a professional fairy.

"I don't think that's necessary," Leo reassured. "I know Madame LeBleu's only takes in the best and the most promising fairies."

"But perhaps Olisand's godmother would be better suited to give you your Happily Ever After."

"No, no, no," Leo said with a bit too much force. "The fairy godmother of Olisand and my father know each other. If he found out about my wish, he would make my life miserable, and it would break my mother's heart. I-I'd like to keep this between us. Can I trust you to do that, Zelda?"

"I think so," she said, though she didn't understand why he wouldn't want a professional fairy to grant his wish. "Although I am having a bit of a dry spell when it comes to magic."

Leo tilted his head with a confused look that was hard not to find adorable.

"I have what my professor calls a block, but even if I could grant your wish, I'm not entirely sure I should. There's a potion for helping people who need to disappear. Magic can't change the past, but it can change what you know of it. I would need time to prepare the potion, but it would alter your personal history. Once you drink it, you won't remember being a prince and neither will anyone who has ever known that about you. It's not a pleasant solution; you'd be an orphan. Along with everything else there is to consider, I want to make sure you won't regret this decision—that this is really your Happily Ever After." Zelda studied the prince's face for any sign of dismay, but he only nodded serenely. "You'd be very lonely."

"I already am."

Zelda was about to reply, but a pressure built in her ears like they were filled with cotton. Darkness bled into the edges of her vision and slowly enveloped the room. She gasped as Leo's alarmed expression disappeared from view.

A brief moment later, she was sitting in her desk chair back at Madame LeBleu's. Coming back was just as strange, but her eyes adjusted faster this time.

Professor Weymouth stood over her desk, his finger on the red button of her phone. "Miss Ravensdale, I apologize for pulling you back, but you have to come with me." His voice was low and hurried. He turned quickly on his heel and headed for the door.

Zelda scrambled to collect her things and followed the tall man's lengthy strides out of the room. "Where are we going? Professor?" Her grip tightened on her wand in alarm. "Did I do something wrong?"

Professor Weymouth didn't pause to reply. He merely turned the corner and all but ran down the wide marble staircase. He held the door for Zelda that led to the courtyard between the academic and administrative offices. Silently, he directed Zelda to a low brick cottage with a slate roof and short chimney puffing tendrils of smoke into the afternoon sky.

Madame LeBleu's personal residence.

The professor pushed open the arched wooden door and ushered Zelda inside. The entryway was a bit cramped and Professor Weymouth stooped his head to clear the first archway into the main hall. He didn't duck low enough—the average fairy was lucky if she reached five feet and five inches—and the top of his head hit the frame with a thunk.

He swore, then seemed to remember he was with a student.

"Grayson?" a voice sounded from a room adjoining the hall. Heels clunked against an old wood floor, and Zelda's heart pounded. Girls never went into the headmistress's cottage unless they were in serious trouble.

"Evening, Headmistress." Professor Weymouth followed the voice, rubbing the top of his head. He turned into a brightly lit room, and Zelda trailed behind.

They entered a large study with walls of shelved books. It was neat and orderly, with a broad desk facing away from a large glass window. A fire roaring in the fireplace helped ease Zelda's nerves as she stepped out of Professor Weymouth's shadow.

"I see you have company," the headmistress said from the center of the room, a French accent softened the edges of her voice. She wore her black, gray-streaked hair in large curls, which brushed the tops of her shoulders. Her cream-colored, satin dress was cinched at the waist with a belt. The skirts bounced around her knees as she crossed the room and took a seat behind her desk. "Welcome, Miss Ravensdale."

"Headmistress."

Madame LeBleu gestured for them to take the seats in front of the desk.

"What brings you in, Professor Weymouth?" Her eyes crinkled with a smile.

"Miss Ravensdale had an interesting conversation with Prince Leopold this afternoon."

Madame LeBleu's eyebrows shot up. "Prince Leopold? How did it go?"

Zelda opened her mouth to reply, but Madame LeBleu had addressed her colleague.

"She handled herself admirably. I think I chose well. Any other girl might have been too starstruck to help the poor boy." Professor Weymouth smiled as he spoke.

How does he know any of this? Zelda sat in her seat dumbfounded as her head filled with questions. *Had Professor Weymouth known the prince was associated with the card he gave me?*

"What's going on?" she asked before they could continue.

"Oh, I'm sorry, dear." Madame LeBleu addressed Zelda. "This is a very delicate situation and, truthfully, we need your help."

"My help? What for? How did you know I went to see the prince? The wish case numbers are supposed to be anonymous." Zelda's eyes flicked between Professor Weymouth and the headmistress. She'd given Leo her word that she would keep his wish as private as possible.

"Tell me. He wished away his crown, correct?" Professor Weymouth asked.

Zelda's lips parted in confusion, but she didn't answer.

"Clairvoyance," he said, touching a finger to his temple. "My mother was a fairy so magic is somewhat part of my DNA."

Zelda's confusion turned to shock. Professor Weymouth had some magic after all—and a rare magic at that. Only the best fairy godmothers developed the ability to look into the murky future, and while fairies passed their magical abilities onto their daughters, it was unheard of for them to pass it on to a son. Unheard of, but apparently not impossible.

"Your discretion would be much appreciated," Weymouth said. "I don't want that broadcasted to the whole school. The ICG isn't sure what to make of me yet."

Madame LeBleu rose from her seat and picked up a long quartz wand that sat on the mantel. "You look like you could use some tea," she said. "I'm sure this is a lot to take in, but any information we share with you must not leave this room." With a flick of her wand, a cart rolled up to the desk and a teapot floated through the air as if a pair of invisible hands prepared them tea.

"Of course," Zelda said. "Did you see something about his Happily Ever After?"

Professor Weymouth shifted to cross one leg over the other. "Not necessarily, but when he decided he no longer wanted to be king it set a very different political future in motion. One I don't think we'd like to see."

Zelda inched closer to the edge of her seat. "What happens?"

Weymouth glanced at Madame LeBleu. "I probably shouldn't say. The future is," he searched for the right word, "fluid. Tangled."

"If all goes well, Professor Weymouth's premonition will be of no concern to anyone."

Zelda didn't like that answer much. "So, I shouldn't grant his wish."

"I'd advise against it," Madame LeBleu said.

"Nothing is set in stone. For now, we'd like you to convince Prince Leo to keep his throne," Weymouth said.

Is that possible? If the prince really didn't want to rule Olisand, could there be other ways for him to avoid it?

Teacups on saucers rose off the tray and traveled to hover patiently in front of each person. Zelda plucked her saucer out of the air and held it in her lap.

"We know this is a lot to ask of you, Miss Ravensdale," Madame LeBleu said.

Professor Weymouth placed a heavy hand on her shoulder. "The future is always shifting. I have no doubt you'll be able to help the prince."

"You can say no," Madame LeBleu said. "But you have always been at the top of your class and one of our contenders for First Fairy. In all my career as headmistress, you are one of the few students I'd trust with such a task. The prince is starting at the Erimount Academy of Magical Sciences on Monday, and he could use an ally in the halls. One who steers him out of harm."

Harm? Zelda wasn't sure she liked this—turning against her godchild's wish. She didn't have clairvoyance, but if Professor Weymouth said Leo's wish would hurt him or the greater good, then she had to follow his lead. That was what he was supposed to do: guide them through their field experience.

Zelda nodded and meet the headmistress's gaze. "I can do it."

"You chose very well, Professor Weymouth," Madame LeBleu said.

"I have the highest confidence in her ability to help the crown prince toward his Happily Ever After," Weymouth said.

Zelda wished she shared their confidence, but she was going to try.

Chapter Six

Zelda walked into the dining hall standing a little taller. She'd been chosen for a special mission, and it was up to her to make sure Leo didn't give up his right to rule. With her objective in mind, she began to wonder how to convince him to keep the crown. They'd only just met when she'd left without giving him any hope for a Happily Ever After. That fact didn't seem to bother Professor Weymouth.

Zelda joined a large group of fourth-years at their table for dinner.

"Where have you been?" Ava Spencer asked, her blond ringlets bouncing.

"Naomi said you were the last to be sent into the field," Iris Pickett said, leaning around Ava.

"I was out on my assignment. When I got back, I had to fill out a request to give to Madame LeBleu since I can't use my magic." That answer seemed to account well enough for her absence.

Between bites of coq au vin, they traded stories of their first field experiences. When asked about her own experience, Zelda lied and said the woman had wished to be famous. It was a common enough wish.

After dinner, Zelda hunkered down in her dorm room to start on their first batch of assignments. Imogen returned from her date with Fletcher, bubbly and beaming. She, too, began her homework but kept her attention on her phone, which buzzed on the minute with texts from Fletcher. A silly grin spread across Imogen's lips as she read each message. Zelda looked at her own phone. She'd missed a call from her mom, and her oldest sister had sent a group text to the whole family with a picture of her one-year-old with cake frosting smeared across her face.

Cute, she replied, making sure to add the baby, cake, and heart eyes emoji.

Zelda turned back to her homework, but her gaze snagged on a glossy tabloid on Imogen's desk with Prince Leo's face splashed across the cover. She wasn't sure why, but she felt guilty for having it in their dorm—and for the fact that she wanted to read what was inside.

It'd been strange to see the prince in real life. Surreal enough that now, only hours after their meeting, it seemed like it hadn't happened. But it had—he'd even grabbed her hand. *Am I still a little starstruck right now?*

By the time Imogen went to brush her teeth, Zelda had finished the day's reading assignments. Curiosity won out over her guilt as the magazine called to her from Imogen's desk. She could read the neon-colored headline from where she sat on her bed: Leo Madness.

It's just for research, she justified as she slid off the bed and padded over to Imogen's desk. The cover glowed under the lamp. It struck Zelda once more just how different the prince had looked in real life. As if they had a will of their own, her fingers drifted out and flipped open the magazine.

It opened to a two-page spread dedicated to photos of Prince Leo in uniform. The sidebar discussed whether he had the buttocks to pull off white pants. Zelda's cheeks heated. From the photos, it didn't look like there was much to be discussed on the matter.

"You know, I've never seen you pick up one of those," Imogen said.

Zelda nearly jumped out of her skin. "Sorry. I didn't hear you come in."

Imogen laughed. "You can have that. I already finished it."

"It's okay." There was something so degrading about the way every photo had been taken from an angle so the perfect curve of the prince's posterior could be analyzed by anyone with three sovereigns in their wallet. "I was just curious if there were any interesting articles." She would have to get to know Leo better if she was going to help him, but this was definitely not the way.

"Loads." Imogen picked up the magazine and shoved it into Zelda's hands. "I'm glad to see even you're excited about the prince coming to EAMS this year."

"What? Why?"

"There's more to life than schoolwork and beating out Susan St. Germain for First Fairy." She cocked her head to the side. "And I need someone to fangirl with."

After another miserable performance in charms class, Zelda signed out at the front gates and headed to the Erimount wandmaker's shop. In desperation, she hoped Specs was on to something and a new wand would help coax the magic out of her. She was willing to try anything rather than fall behind.

Wand-making was a valuable skill for fairies, but a difficult one. Madame LeBleu's only accepted five fairies per year into the wand-making track, and the wandmaker of Erimount was widely proclaimed as one of the best. The shop sat out of the way of the bustling city center. Even in a quiet corner of the city, it attracted a fair amount of attention. Joggers, tourists, and couples out for afternoon walks all slowed as they passed the mint-green storefront.

For the average passerby, it might look like a patisserie with its striped awning and gold-painted scrollwork trimmings. But on closer examination, the smudgeless front windows weren't filled with ornately decorated cakes, but a display of glittering wands of every make and size.

A bell rang when Zelda pushed the door open by its ornate brass handle.

"Be there in a minute," a voice called from somewhere in the shop.

Zelda stepped up to the register and waited. The black-and-white tile floor gleamed under her shoes like it had just been washed. Large glass cases flanked the register, each with a meticulous array of wands in brass holders. A dark wood wand inlaid with blood-red gems caught Zelda's eye.

A beautiful older woman emerged from behind a green velvet curtain. Her face was heavily lined, and her gray hair was pulled back into a loose French braid. Zelda vaguely remembered the woman from when she'd bought her first wand.

"What can I do for you?" the wandmaker asked, pulling on a pair of dark-framed glasses from the pocket of her mint-colored apron.

"I'm having some trouble casting spells with my wand." Zelda produced the Blackwood wand from her bag.

The wandmaker took the wand and turned it over in her hand. She gave it a little flourish and a pink bubble floated from the tip. It drifted low and landed serenely on the marble countertop. She muttered something to herself and pushed the glasses up her nose to examine Zelda. "The problem isn't the wand."

Zelda's stomach sank. "Oh," she said. "My professors seem to think the pressure of school is *blocking* my magic. I can feel the magic travel through my arm, but it just stops at my hand."

"A true magic block is very rare. Tell me, have you produced a spell of any kind recently?"

"I managed to conjure a wish contract, but that's all."

The woman snorted a sharp laugh. "Well, I'm sure you'll be glad to know that a block isn't the problem either. Magic matures with the fairy. It changes and shifts and, in rare cases, sometimes a different wand is in order. Your magic has some volatility. It must, or else I would never have sold you a Blackwood wand."

"Volatility? What kind of wand should I use then?" Most fairies chose to use wood. It had a great way of grounding magic, making it easier to use, easier to control.

"We'll test them all, but I think we can rule out wood," she said, gliding over to one of the display cases. She pulled out a black onyx wand and held it out to Zelda with two hands. "Give this one a try. It should offer you a little less resistance."

Zelda took the cold, stone wand in her hand and waved it slowly. Goosebumps rippled over her skin as the magic traveled down her arm, but try as she might, it stopped in her hand. The wand grew suddenly hot, then shot from her hand. It shattered a glass jar filled with training wands on the shelf behind the register.

"I'm so sorry."

"No worries, dear. But I think I've solved the problem." The wandmaker picked the wand out of the debris and pointed it at the shattered glass which reassembled itself and its contents on the shelf. She retreated behind the emerald curtain and came back with a long wooden box, which she placed on the counter.

Zelda watched the box curiously. The woman lifted the lid to reveal a wand of cut crystal set on a regal velvet pillow. It had a slender glass handle and at the tip, a multifaceted star which refracted the light of the glittering chandelier above the counter.

"The wand is the conductor of your magic. The stronger the magic, the less resistance your conductor must have for magic to pass through it. It seems the strength of your magic outgrew your old wand."

"I see," Zelda said. "It's beautiful."

"Indeed, but it's also dangerous. There is almost no resistance in this wand. Without proper training and supervision, you can lose control of your magic," she cautioned.

Zelda reached for the wand but paused, hand hovering over the case. "May I?"

The woman nodded, a tender smile creasing her cheeks. Zelda lifted the wand carefully.

"It's not delicate," the wand maker said. "It's made of pure diamond."

Zelda's jaw fell open. It looked flawless; she could only wonder how much such a treasure would cost. "I don't think I can afford this."

"Nonsense. Give it a whirl."

Zelda waved the wand over her head and a flurry of golden sparks shot from the wand. They hovered in the air like little stars until they faded out one by one. Relief crashed over Zelda in a wave. She hadn't even felt the magic travel to the wand. Perhaps First Fairy wasn't as far off as she hoped.

"Marvelous," the woman sighed. "The diamond is not a natural diamond. It is manufactured with tinker technology—fifty sovereigns will do nicely."

Zelda placed the wand back in its box and took out her wallet. Fifty sovereigns was a lot for a student, but she paid the woman and returned the much lighter wallet to her bag.

"Now don't go waving that thing around in public. It's a bit flashier than your old wand," the woman said, placing the bills neatly into the register.

Zelda tucked the box into the deepest pocket of her bag. "I won't."

"And don't try any advanced spells until you get the hang of it."

Zelda nodded. "Thank you so much for your help."

The wandmaker smiled. "It's my pleasure."

Out in the cobblestone street, Zelda gripped her bag tighter, conscious of every movement around her. She headed back for the school, trying to look like she wasn't carrying a treasure in a worn leather sack.

Imogen was out when Zelda reached the safety of the dorm. She opened the box with great care, slipped out the beautiful and dangerous instrument from its holdings, and gripped it. A shiver of magic shot down her spine, itching to be released now that it had a proper conductor. With the wandmaker's warning in mind, Zelda worried she might cast a spell that would shatter the window between their beds, so she quickly placed the wand back in the box.

Imogen gasped in shock when Zelda took out her new wand at the start of charms class the following day.

"What is that?" Imogen asked as the faceted star caught the light from the window.

"A crystal wand," Zelda said with a grin. It was probably best to leave out the diamond part.

"No. Way." Imogen ogled the wand with a hungry gaze.

"Specs was right. Apparently, my magic got stronger over the summer, and I needed a wand with less resistance," Zelda said, giddy with relief to have figured out the source of her magic troubles.

"Let's see it then." Imogen nudged her in the ribs.

Zelda could barely contain her excitement. She entered the practice area, eager to prove herself to the others after three humiliating days without magic. The room fell silent as the fourth-year GITs observed Zelda and the wand in her hand. She extended her arm, lifting the wand to shoulder level. She moved her wrist in a circular motion and recited the snow charm.

Barely perceptible, the magic shivered through her. A swirl of dark clouds ripped from her wand and a biting cold wind cut through the thin layers of her uniform. Girls screamed as the clouds pelted them with icy rain rather than the gentle flurries she had intended to create. Zelda grabbed her wand with both hands to keep her arm steady, but cold dread drenched her like frozen sleet as the charm grew beyond her control. Students crawled under desks to avoid the pellets of hail pummeling the classroom floor.

"Stop," a high, clear voice called out above the panic.

Professor Hildebrandt rushed to the center of the room. With a dance-like flourish of her wand, the clouds disappeared along with the hail and wind and freezing rain.

"Miss Ravensdale?" The professor regarded Zelda at the center of it all, diamond wand in hand and hair in dark, wet clumps from the sleet. Her eyes fell to the wand. "That is a dangerous wand, Miss Ravensdale. You should know better than to use a new wand without supervision."

"I'm sorry, Professor. I didn't know that would happen," Zelda sputtered. Despite her shivers and her cold, sodden uniform, her cheeks burned with shame.

"You have a head on your shoulders. Use it," Professor Hildebrandt scolded. "That's one demerit."

Zelda wanted to object, but she didn't want a second demerit. *How was I supposed to know I had a hailstorm bottled up inside me?*

For the rest of the lesson, Zelda cursed herself and her foolishness as she practiced basic spells along with the other girls, but she couldn't focus on her guilt for long. Using the new wand required twice as much concentration to keep her magic from surging out of control. She kept it in check for the duration of the class, but even Imogen gave her a wide berth when she was casting charms. As Zelda packed up her wand, she couldn't stop the bitterness rising in her heart. For a few fleeting hours it had seemed a new wand had solved all her problems. But had it really? She finally had access to her magic, but at what cost?

Chapter Seven

Anxiety and excitement warred for dominance in Zelda's mind as their next field experience approached. When she walked into the room, Professor Weymouth lit up with a conspiratorial smirk. Zelda's stomach pitched with the reality that she would see the prince again—and she'd have to convince him not to throw away his crown.

"Take your seats. Take your seats," Professor Weymouth said. He took out a stack of cards and began assigning calls to the eager group of soon-to-be godmothers.

As Zelda waited for instructions on how to reach Leo again, she tried to remind herself to trust Weymouth's clairvoyance. She only knew a little about the incredibly rare gift. It was most useful in granting wishes, but it couldn't be taught. Madame LeBleu's only monitored their students for the gift. As far as Zelda knew, no one in their year had it. It'd never occurred to her that their only male professor would. He'd never hinted at having his own powers in his lectures, but Zelda understood his need for discretion. Being able to see into the future seemed more like a curse than a blessing.

As before, the last fairy disappeared from her seat and returned before Professor Weymouth passed Zelda a card.

She dialed the case number quickly and Leo picked up on the second ring. "Hello?"

"Fairy godmother at your service." A smile creeped across her cheeks without meaning to.

The prince laughed. "I was hoping—wondering when I would hear from you again."

"I'll be right there."

"Wonderful."

Zelda pressed the red button, and the classroom faded to black. When her vision came to, she saw the same antique rug as before, but now a pair of cognac loafers mirrored her saddle shoes. She wobbled a bit but quickly steadied herself.

"Are you all right?" Leo held out an arm, ready to catch her if necessary, but his hand hovered politely inches from her waist.

"Traveling was much better that time," Zelda said. She took a few steps to make sure her legs worked. They were in the prince's bedroom again. The room was draftier than she remembered despite a roaring fire in a massive stone fireplace. A cup of unfinished tea with the bag languishing inside sat on the table between the two seats they'd occupied on her last visit. Only at the sight of the unmade bed did she remember her manners.

Her cheeks burned. "I'm sorry, Your Highness. I should have asked your permission before intruding on you," Zelda said. She would have to look up etiquette for godmothers serving royalty when she got back to Madame LeBleu's.

"Nonsense," Leo said, brushing off her apology. "I was waiting for your call." He took a seat in an armchair and picked up his cup. "Would you like me to order you tea?"

Zelda took the seat opposite of Leo. "I'm more of a coffee drinker."

He smiled. "I can have the best pour over you've ever tasted here in about ten minutes. The espresso is pretty good too."

"I'm fine." She didn't need any caffeine when her heart was already pounding its way out of her chest.

The scent of lemon and ginger lingered in the air. Leo looked eager as he took a sip, but he said nothing. The collar of his white shirt was undone in a way to suggest he'd taken off a tie in a rush. It was a good look on him.

"You left before you gave me an answer," he began with a sheepish grin.

"Yes, about that." Zelda laughed dryly, the smile falling from her face.

Leo sank in his chair. "Oh no. I don't like the sound of that."

Zelda didn't want to deny her first godchild's wish, but she wasn't ready to go against Madame LeBleu's advice. "I don't think it's in your best interest, or the best interest of the country, if you give up your crown." She left out the part about her professors knowing his wish after he'd specifically requested her confidentiality.

Leo covered his mouth with a hand and turned his head toward the window. It was typical for royalty to hide emotion, but the taut muscles that lined his forearm gave him away.

"And I think you would eventually regret the wish," Zelda said.

The prince turned sharply to look at her. "How would you know?"

The direct nature of his words caught Zelda off guard, but she steadied herself. "Because I know a little bit about wishing. And regrets. I am your Happily Ever After Specialist, after all." It all came out more hurried than she intended, but she hadn't been prepared for such a sharp reaction.

"I think I know more about my happiness than you." He rose abruptly from his seat. His leg jostled the table as he passed to lean against the fireplace.

Zelda had expected he wouldn't be thrilled, but the display of emotion left from the young royal was surprising enough to leave her speechless.

"Maybe this was a bad idea," he said. "I shouldn't have expected anyone to understand. If you aren't going to grant my wish, you can go."

Panic coursed like ice through Zelda's veins. She had a mission from her headmistress to complete and leaving was not an option if she didn't want to risk him taking matters into his own hands.

Zelda gathered her nerve and pulled out her wand. "Listen. I never said I wouldn't grant your wish. Your wish is still on the table, but it—it has to be part of a package deal."

Leo turned back to Zelda with a wary look. He took a hesitant step toward her, eyes narrowing at the glittering wand in her hand. "What kind of deal?"

Zelda paused. She hadn't quite thought this through yet. There had to be a way to keep the prince's interest while she made sure he wouldn't give up the crown on his own. "I'll grant your wish, but before I do, I will give my best attempt to convince you otherwise. If by . . ." *How long was enough time?* "The spring—if by the Wishmaker Festival, you still wish to relinquish your right to the throne, then I will free you of your obligation to the crown of Olisand."

Leo cut her a sideways glance. "Really?" The sadness on his face was replaced by intrigue.

"If you give me till the festival, then yes."

He rubbed a hand over his jaw. "I think that will work."

Zelda squared her shoulders. "I can't let you make such a decision on a whim."

His brows rose. "Fair enough. So, when does the convincing begin?"

Zelda swallowed the last of her nerves and thrust her chin a little higher. "Now."

Leo took a step toward her, the smile on his lips a challenge. "Okay then. Why should I be the King of Olisand?"

In the glow of afternoon light, Zelda had to admit something about his appearance made her chest ache in a good sort of way, but she wasn't one to let a pair of clear blue eyes throw her out of sorts. "Because it is the greatest country in the world," she said. "The land of Happily Ever Afters. That is the *actual slogan*."

"But not the Happily Ever After I want."

Zelda closed the distance between them. "I get it, Your Highness. You don't want to be king. But why give up such an honor? There are probably hundreds of people who'd line up to take your position."

"Then let them have it," Leo grumbled. "I'm certainly not inclined to be king."

"Why not?"

Leo folded his arms, looking fully like he didn't intend to answer. He really was the obstinate sort.

"Fine then. What sort of Happily Ever After do you want?" Zelda asked with an annoyed huff.

"I-I don't know," Leo said. "All I know is I don't want to be irrelevant." His shoulders slumped in resignation.

Zelda straightened, surprised and a little annoyed by his answer. "How can you call being king irrelevant?"

Leo released a slow breath. "You wouldn't understand."

"Then help me understand." Zelda moved away from the fire and seated herself on a velvet bench near the towering arched window.

"Olisand is a constitutional monarchy," Leo said with his back to Zelda as he retrieved his tea.

"I'm aware."

Leo joined her at the window and sat a respectful distance away on the same bench. "The monarch is just a figurehead, a fancy puppet in a crown." He dragged a hand through his golden-brown hair, messing the perfect coiffure.

"Are you sure that's all it is?"

"Yes," he said obstinately, then sighed. "Sorry. It's been a long week. I resorted to screaming into a pillow," he said drolly.

"And did it help?" Zelda asked, glad to see a change in his emotion.

"Not really." Leo's mouth lifted into a half-smile as he twisted the string of the tea bag around his finger.

Zelda laughed. He was quite agreeable when he wasn't being so difficult. "I accidentally made a blizzard in class this week," she offered in a display of empathy.

"Impressive." Leo nodded his head in approval. "My bitter ex-girlfriend told the press what kind of kisser I am—among other things."

"Ouch." Zelda silently vowed to burn that tabloid once she got back to the dormitory.

Companiable silence fell between them as Zelda realized they maybe had more in common than she thought.

"Do you have a phone?" Leo asked abruptly.

"Not on me. Just a wand."

Leo set his cup aside and retrieved a phone from a table beside the four-poster bed. "Put your number in."

He handed the phone to her and their fingers brushed. Zelda tried to ignore the tingling sensation that lingered in her hands at his touch. She typed in her name and phone number.

Leo took back the phone and stashed it in his pocket. "Just in case."

Zelda stood. Adjusting her skirt, she turned to the prince. "We need to talk more about this 'irrelevant' thing."

"It's complicated. Do you have a couple more hours?"

"We should get more time soon. We'll be eating in the same dining hall as of next week."

"Right." Leo shuffled his feet. "I was hoping to have at least one *normal* year of schooling. Instead, I'll be starting my fourth year with six bodyguards at an entire school full of people who think they know me because they've seen my face on TV since before I could walk."

"It could be worse," Zelda said.

Leo shot her a pointed look.

"You could be starting your fourth year with no name and no friends at all. You'll have me."

"Right." Leo's smile was genuine. "But how will we explain how we know each other?"

"I suppose you have a point."

"I guess I could introduce myself when I see you on Monday."

Zelda smiled. "Simple enough."

"No need to complicate it." Leo's smile deepened the dimples on his cheeks.

"But remember, you're my godchild. I'm your ally, so if you need anything before Monday, let me know."

"I will," said the prince. "I have your number."

Zelda wasn't sure if she should curtsey or shake his hand. When he smiled expectantly at her, she panicked and clicked her heels together. The room went black and just as quick as the castle had fallen away, the classroom emerged from the crushing darkness.

"How did it go, Miss Ravensdale?" Professor Weymouth asked with a knowing grin.

How much could he actually see with his clairvoyance? She'd just cut a deal with the prince that she hadn't quite been authorized to make.

"Good," she said, but perhaps he already knew the answer. She checked to make sure the classroom was empty. "So how does the clairvoyance work?" It might have been a personal question, but she had to know how closely her professor and Madame LeBleu were watching her.

Thankfully, he laughed at her directness. "Clairvoyance is a fickle thing. I can direct it toward certain people, but it's easiest to see big picture things."

Zelda nodded.

"I'm keeping my eye on the big picture, Miss Ravensdale. Not you."

"Okay." Some of the weight lifted off her shoulders.

"Madame LeBleu and I know this is a lot to ask. You can stop at any time."

She straightened. "I can do it."

"Good." Professor Weymouth smiled, his expression comforting in every way. "You're free to go."

That night Zelda lay awake, restless, her thoughts scattered between classes, her mission, and alarmingly enough, whether Susan St. Germain really had any interest in Dante Sadler. Imogen slumbered soundly in the bed opposite hers. She'd been asleep for an hour at least, snoring happily into her pillow. After a spate of feelings marked by self-doubt, Zelda briefly considered redoing a history position paper, but her phone on her bedside table buzzed. The screen showed a text from an unknown number.

She snatched the phone and turned toward the whitewashed wall so the light wouldn't bother Imogen.

Hey, it's me.

Her pulse jumped. She wasn't sure why she was both excited and nervous at the message. It could only be from one person: a certain obstinate prince who had only confessed his deepest wish to her.

Hello.

His reply came seconds later. **You know this is Leo, right?**

She laughed quietly and added his contact as P. Charming to her phone. Imogen stirred in her bed, and Zelda checked over her shoulder to make sure she was asleep before she typed her response.

I figured as much. Do you need something?

I'm just saying hey. And I want to make sure you have my number.

Hey, she replied.

Made any blizzards since I last saw you?

Not lately.

Glad to hear it.

Leo's dimpled smile formed like a perfect picture in Zelda's mind. The following morning, she woke with her phone in her hand, and a smile plastered on her face.

Chapter Eight

When Monday came, a new energy crackled in the air on campus. Across the street, boys and girls in crimson blazers streamed through the archway to the Erimount Academy of Magical Sciences. Built by the Scarlet family when the school was founded at the end of the nineteenth century, the network of Victorian Gothic stone buildings blended into the classical elegance of Madame LeBleu's, joining the students of the old magic and the new.

"I wonder what it would be like to go to EAMS," Zelda mused.

She and Imogen gazed down at the new and returning students from the dining hall windows, hoping to catch a glimpse of the prince's arrival.

"Interested in sitting next to Prince Leo in class?" Imogen bumped Zelda in the ribs with her elbow.

"No," Zelda said, squirming out of the way of a second jab. "I just wonder what it would be like—to make all those contraptions."

Imogen shrugged. "It must take creativity to think up all those crazy things. Did you hear what Specs is working on this year?"

Zelda shook her head.

Imogen didn't take her eyes off the scene across the street. "He's making a pocket hourglass that only moves when you're wasting time."

"That sounds interesting—"

"That's him," Imogen said as four black sedans pulled up to the front of EAMS. "That's gotta be the prince."

Zelda was jostled as a bunch of first-years pushed their way to the front of the growing crowd at the window.

A head of tawny hair appeared from one of the middle cars. Zelda recognized the hard set of his shoulders. Prince Leo. He was immediately surrounded by security guards in dark suits and ushered through the crowd and into the school. It was maybe thirty seconds and then he was gone.

"Woah," Imogen said. "It was really him."

"I know," Zelda said.

During classes, all anyone could talk about was the prince. Some girls claimed to have seen him in the library already, but most shared rumors that were smuggled in through texts from the girls and boys at EAMS.

"He's much shorter in real life."

"He's kind of quiet."

"I thought he'd be more handsome."

"Are you kidding? He's gorgeous."

"Do you think he's made friends with anyone yet?"

The professors seemed frustrated with the chaos. Demerits were handed out left and right for improper use of cellphones in class. Few lessons stayed on track and pop quizzes were threatened by all. Even Zelda felt a bit giddy with the excitement, though she was sure she'd taken immaculate notes despite the distraction.

By the time lunch block rolled around, Zelda still hadn't heard from Leo. She had no idea if they even had lunch scheduled at the same time. It seemed that the other girls had the same thought. Since no one had seen him yet, their chances of sitting together for lunch were getting better with every passing hour.

Zelda had never seen girls head for the dining hall so fast. No one ran, of course. No one wanted to seem too eager, but usually they lingered in the bathrooms and at their lockers until they were chased toward the cafeteria by the hall monitors.

The lunch lines were jammed before the starting bell rang, but Zelda and Imogen were seated before most of the tinkers had arrived. Zelda picked at her croque madame, the little bites sitting thick in her throat.

Now that the day was here, she had no idea how this scene would play out. How would she and Leo pull off their *flawless* plan to fake their introduction? Zelda was certain that Imogen would catch on. Before she could run through every conceivable scenario, a large pack of excited tinkers entered through the west doors to the dining hall, the ones that led to the EAMS side of campus.

Leo led the pack of students with Alfred McKinney, Specs' friend with the cloud of red curls, by his side. Alfred talked animatedly about something Zelda couldn't hear. Behind them, Leo's security kept the tide of students from reaching the prince.

Zelda didn't realize she was staring until a sharp pain shot up her arm. "Ow. Imogen, you're clawing me."

"It's him," Imogen said, loosening her grip on Zelda's wrist. "It's Prince Leo."

"I see him."

Leo's gaze darted across the dining hall in search of something. Perhaps he was just taking it all in, but he seemed to have forgotten he was talking to McKinney. When his eyes landed on Zelda, he stopped. A smile twitched at the corner of his lips. Zelda's stomach did a little flip when she realized he'd been looking for her.

"Zelda," Imogen whispered. "He's looking right at us. Do you think he's going to come over here?"

Zelda's heart raced. She wasn't sure how it would appear if Leo singled her out the moment they were in the same room together, but anything was better than having to pretend they didn't know each other. Just as it seemed the prince was about to cross to their lunch table, Madame LeBleu swept into the dining hall, bringing a hush with her. Very rarely did the head of the school show up to a lunch block.

"Your Highness," the headmistress said with a graceful bow of her head to the prince. "I am Madame LeBleu, Headmistress of Madame LeBleu's School for Godmothers, and I would like to welcome you to the shared space of our two campuses."

Leo shook Madame LeBleu's hand with a stiff regal bearing. "I'm delighted to meet you again, Madame LeBleu. I believe we met at my father's fiftieth birthday party."

A grin spread across Madame LeBleu's face, the pleasure of being remembered written in her delicate features. "Your memory serves you right. I also want to introduce you to a student of Madame LeBleu's who I've chosen as our ambassador to provide you with a tour of our school."

Zelda's chest clenched against a breath before Madame LeBleu even called her name.

"Zelda Ravensdale," the headmistress said. She gestured to Zelda and every eye in the dining hall turned from the prince to her.

This phony "ambassador" business had Professor Weymouth written all over it, but it was a much smoother introduction than their flimsy plan.

Leo crossed the room and extended a hand to her. "It's a pleasure to meet you, Miss Ravensdale."

Zelda stood, nearly toppling her chair as she shook his hand. "It's all mine, Your Majesty."

Leo broke his princely composure to give her a real smile. Before Zelda could say more, Madame LeBleu inserted herself at Leo's side. "Miss Ravensdale, you are excused from classes for the afternoon so you may give Prince Leopold a tour of our campus. Perhaps show him the flow of the dining hall first so he may eat?"

Zelda nodded. "O-of course." She glanced back at Imogen who gaped open-mouthed at the prince. "I'll show him around."

Madame LeBleu was about to leave when someone cleared their throat. She turned to see Alfred McKinney standing behind her. "Pardon me, Headmistress, but it would be social suicide for a tinker to hang around the GITs on his first day. You know, the rivalry and all."

Madame LeBleu gave Alfred a withering look that made the tinker blush so hard his freckles disappeared. "I won't pretend to understand dining hall politics," she said, "but friendly rivalry or not, I hope that all students will treat the cooperation between our schools with the utmost respect."

Madame LeBleu, like most fairies, wasn't imposing in stature, but she could certainly put students in their place. It seemed Alfred had shrunk a full foot since she'd started speaking.

"Yes, Madame," he squeaked and scurried back into the crowd of tinkers.

After eyeing the rest of the dining hall to make sure everything was in order, Madame LeBleu swept from the room in as grand a fashion as she had arrived. A din of voices returned, and though many students still watched the prince, Zelda almost let out a sigh of relief.

Imogen reached around her shoulder to shake Leo's hand. "I'm Yang Eun-A, or Imogen Yang if you prefer, Your Highness," she said. Zelda had never heard her introduce herself with her Korean name before.

"What do you prefer?" the prince asked with a polite smile.

"Imogen."

Leo smiled. "Excellent. I think Leo will do just fine for me."

Imogen giggled. "Cool."

"Should I show you how to get lunch?" Zelda gestured to the line that queued up to a buffet of lunch options. "It's not too complicated."

The prince didn't seem nervous, but his hands fluttered at his sides. "I wouldn't mind the company."

They joined the lunch line, and Zelda was sidelined as everyone with enough courage took turns introducing themselves to the prince now that he was pinned down by the queue. Once they got Leo a tray of food and found their seats at the table with Imogen, the situation failed to improve. A stream of eager students took turns in the open seat at their table, each taking care to invite Leo to their club or ask what sports team he was joining. Leo held up well at the start, but even Zelda was feeling overwhelmed by the time he glanced at her and silently mouthed the word "help."

"Should we start our tour now?" she suggested.

Zelda could almost see the weight lift from his shoulders. "That sounds like a wonderful idea."

They bid Imogen goodbye, deposited the remains of their lunch in the compost bins that would be sent to the gardens for growing pumpkins, and all but ran from the dining hall. Zelda only paused to sneak a glance at Susan St. Germain. She was pleased to find her staring at them, most likely bitter at having been passed over for a special position. No one knew it was a sham, and Zelda was going to do everything she could to keep it that way.

Chapter Nine

The halls of Madame LeBleu's were empty during classes, though Leo's security team filled them up a fair bit. When Zelda's impromptu tour reached the library, the prince's composure dropped, and he let out a long sigh.

"Everything all right?" Zelda asked.

"More than all right," Leo said. "This place is amazing. I mean, I feel more than overwhelmed trying to remember the names of everyone I've met, but look at this place."

With a sweep of his arm, he gestured to the massive library. It was three stories tall, and each level looked out over the long rows of study tables on the first floor. The large glass domes on the ceiling provided bright natural light to the entire library.

"I love the library," Zelda agreed.

"You should see the tinkering labs at EAMS, but you've probably already seen those." Leo laughed. "Sorry, I'm rambling."

"I don't mind. It's nice to see you enjoying yourself here."

"I know what you're thinking," he said.

"Do you?" Zelda couldn't help but smile as she watched Leo tilt his head back to take in all three floors of books and the shelves stretching to the rafters.

At the prince's silent signal, his security held back so Leo and Zelda could move out of earshot. "You're thinking my worries were unfounded, that I'll do fine here even though I'm a prince."

Zelda shifted between her feet. Perhaps she had thought that briefly. Really, she'd been admiring the gentle angles and curves of Leo's profile as he'd taken in the library. "What do *you* think?"

Leo shrugged. "The things I can learn here . . . they make me want to forget all about being a prince. But I can't, can I? Everyone I meet makes me wonder if they're really interested in getting to know me, or if they just want to befriend me because I'm royalty."

"Oh, Leo," she said. "Welcome to boarding school. You'll never figure out people's true intentions until you figure out who you can and cannot trust. The same goes for being a godmother."

"You're right."

"At least you know you can trust me, and I know exactly who to stick with here."

"I know, I know," Leo said, and he reached up to rub the back of his neck. It was a casual gesture, unbecoming of royalty, and Zelda liked it. "I've been dying to find you all day. That was lucky with the ambassador business. I was just going to walk up and say hello."

"Yeah, I suggested it to the headmistress this morning." A lie. "I'm just glad she went for it." Zelda hated lying to Leo after just telling him that he could trust her. The guilt hit her like a gut punch, but she couldn't let him know that her headmistress and professor knew about his wish when Leo had requested her secrecy. Not only would such a revelation betray his trust, but above all, she feared he would spook and take matters into his own hands.

"What are your plans for the rest of the day?" she asked, changing the subject.

"Not much. I'd planned to unpack my things in the dormitory, but that can always wait. Do you have something in mind?"

"Well, I'm excused from classes. We could really use some time to talk about, you know, you, among other things. I could teach you how to sign in and out of campus?"

Leo's face lit up at the idea.

"You can leave school grounds, can't you?" Zelda asked as the security team caught her eye.

As if on cue, one of them peeled himself from their group and approached. "Can I help you with something, Your Highness?" he asked, his deep voice brushed by the distinction of a Castilian accent.

"Yes, Felix," Leo said. "We were hoping to take a brief trip away from campus."

Zelda guessed this was his head of security. His dark brows pushed together. "Where away from campus?"

Leo looked from Felix to Zelda as if telling her to answer.

"There's a little coffee shop in the Castle District. They have the best peach pie in Erimount," she said.

"And we'd like to go alone," Leo said.

Zelda's pulse stumbled. That hadn't exactly been part of her plan.

Felix looked even less pleased. "There are a lot of risks for something like that. We haven't made any plans, done a security sweep—"

"Zelda can whip up a blizzard," Leo said. "She's my security should anything go wrong."

"And I can make him a disguise," Zelda said.

Felix looked between them. "One guard."

"Fine," Leo said. "But he needs to tail us. I don't want one of your brutes over my shoulder the whole time; it would be more than conspicuous."

"Deal." Felix and Leo shook on it. "But it'll be me tailing you, and we need to be back here in a timely fashion. Straight to the coffee shop and back. Your father will want a call to know how things went here."

"Fair enough." Leo placed a gentle hand on Zelda's elbow.

"We should probably head out the back entrance," she said. "Best to avoid the media circus waiting outside the front gates."

After signing out with the attendant at the back gate, Zelda and Leo slipped into the alley between Madame LeBleu's and a clock repair shop. Felix hung back and propped himself against the stone wall around Madam LeBleu's. Before they moved from hiding, Zelda needed to fashion Leo a disguise. Today, he looked more like a prince on a magazine cover with his narrow cut, navy suit and a crisp white shirt. His hair was finished and styled, falling perfectly around his ears and hitting right above his collar.

"Is this the part where I get a pair of glass slippers?" Leo asked as he watched her assess his outfit.

Zelda chuckled behind pursed lips. She snuck a glance at Felix, who stood a respectable distance away. "I could do a nice pair of glass loafers, but we're going for subtle here, and you already stick out like a sore thumb."

Leo feigned offense. "This is my worst suit."

"You can keep the shirt and blazer, but we should do something about the trousers." Zelda withdrew her wand from her bag. "Jeans perhaps."

She turned her wand on the prince and took a steadying breath as she prepared herself for casting. With a wave of the wand and a steady roll of her hand, magic zipped through her fingers. A flurry of sparks swarmed from the star at the end of her wand. The enchantment had barely formed on the tip of her tongue when the golden flurry settled around Leo. She blinked and Leo no longer wore tailored trousers but a pair of jeans.

It felt good to cast again, but the magic had barely been under her control. Zelda made a mental note to be more conscious of her thoughts. An altering enchantment was nothing, but her magic had rushed out of her without restraint. She would need to be on her guard when casting more advanced spells. How many demerits would she get if she accidentally gave the entire city a case of the hiccups with a giggle charm gone wrong?

"Wow." Leo bent to examine his new look. "You got the size perfect."

"I just altered the appearance of the suit pants, but we need a little something more."

"A hat?"

Zelda laughed. "We need a little more than a hat."

"What do you suggest?" Leo took a step closer to Zelda.

They were standing quite close, and she had to tilt her head back to meet his eyes. *Eyes!* She centered herself, holding the muscles of her arm taut to make sure her magic was in control. With a twirl of her wand, Leo's irises darkened from blue to warm brown. Another flick of her wrist and his hair shifted to a deep brown.

"What just happened?" Leo asked. "Why do I smell chocolate?"

"That's a side effect of the spell." Zelda stuck a hand deep into her bag and pulled out a macaron-shaped compact. She passed it to Leo. "And my inspiration."

He drew his nose inches from the mirror to look at his new eyes. "I don't look like me."

With great focus on what she wanted to fashion, Zelda tapped her wand to her palm and a pair of dark-framed glasses appeared in her hand.

"Here." She handed the glasses to him, and as his hand brushed hers, it felt like a bit of her magic jumped from her fingers to his. The sensation was strange, but she pushed it quickly from her mind. "It's the eyes that matter most. Now people will assume you bear a passing resemblance to the prince."

Leo peered into the compact once more. "Ingenious."

He started down the alley, but Zelda stopped him. "Wait. Just one more thing."

Before she could stop herself, she reached up and ruffled the crown prince's hair. Time slowed like watching a car crash, and Zelda panicked.

What am I doing?

It was poor manners to just stick your hands in a near stranger's hair.

Zelda withdrew her hand, and her face flushed with warmth. "There," she said. "Are you ready to test your disguise?"

Leo's cheeks turned pink. He was clearly embarrassed by the hair mussing. "Let's do this," he said with a little smile.

As they headed into the city, Zelda wished there was a spell to turn back time, so she could erase ever putting her hands through Leo's heavenly soft hair. Unfortunately, there wasn't.

A case of freshly baked pies greeted them at the door of Blackbird Café, and they took an empty table for two at the window.

"Interesting place," Leo said as he scanned the disinterested patrons.

"Cafés are the best places to talk," Zelda said. "And when you can't think of anything to say, you people watch." She nodded to the window.

"You think we won't have anything to talk about between a prince and a fairy godmother?" Leo laughed. His brown eyes twinkled with warmth in the shop's golden light.

A waitress appeared at their table and pulled a notepad from her apron pocket. A pink hijab framed her heart-shaped face and welcoming smile.

Zelda ordered two coffees and peach pie for both of them. The waitress narrowed her eyes at Leo for a moment like she'd seen through his disguise, but she only gave him a coy smile before leaving to fill their order.

"The best peach pie in Erimount," Leo mused. "I take it you come here often?" He leaned forward to rest his elbows on the table.

"It's a little far from school." They'd taken a trolley all the way across the city to get to the café. "But it's the best place to study in town. It's small and quiet and not cutesy enough to attract tourists."

"I like it so far."

"Good. We should probably talk about what you told me. Tell me, how does a future king feel irrelevant?"

Leo brushed a hand through his hair. "It's complicated."

"Try me. I've lived in Olisand my entire life."

"Being a monarch in a constitutional monarchy is a strange role. As king, I'll be the Head of State, a symbol, our national identity embodied. That's it. I get to hand out awards and ride in parades, but I can't have political influence. The power of the crown lies in the notion that it's above politics."

Leo paused abruptly as the waitress returned to place steaming mugs of coffee and plates of peach pie with vanilla ice cream between them.

"I want to be useful, not just a figurehead," Leo said once she'd gone.

"I see, sort of." Zelda was sure the king had more power than a glorified mascot, but Leo probably knew this better than she did.

She took a bite of pie and gave Leo a nod to try his. He gave the pie a suspicious glance but tried it all the same. His eyes widened.

"Good, right?" Zelda said with a smirk.

"Okay, it's delicious. I should've never doubted you." He shoveled in another mouthful.

Zelda sipped her coffee and Leo speared every last crumb on his plate before she brought up his wish again. "What would make you feel useful?"

Leo leaned back in his chair and fiddled with his new glasses. He gave her a shrug which she returned with a playful glare. "Fine. I'm not sure, but I like to make things. Tinkering has always been my favorite subject. Making things that can be used to help others feels like something I was meant to do."

Zelda took a bite of her own slice before answering. "That's great. I can use that for your HEA, but as king you *could* make things in your free time, right?"

"But it's not just being useful." Leo took a sip of his coffee. "A part of me wants a private life."

"And you can't do that as Head of State?"

"Not easily."

Zelda mimicked Leo's shrug, but she didn't pull it off so nonchalantly. "If I had to give my best guess, I'd say dating supermodels, starlets, and socialites probably plays a part in the media circus."

Leo placed his elbows on the table, filling what little space remained between them. "So, you've read the tabloids?"

"No," Zelda insisted. Leo flicked his eyebrows up at her. "Really. You eventually hear things living in Olisand."

"But you see my point?"

"Yeah."

"And what am I supposed to do? Those are the only types of people I meet. Plus, is it really dating if your schedules only allow you to have a date every two months?" Leo's eyes fell to her pie, and she quickly pulled it further away from him.

"You're insane if you think I'm sharing." She put the biggest forkful she could manage into her mouth.

Leo laughed as he watched her try to chew and swallow the massive bite. Zelda washed the sugary pie down with a swig of bitter coffee. They remained quiet for a few minutes as they watched people move past the café window.

"It gets lonely," Leo said softly, then downed the rest of his coffee. He kept his eyes on the empty porcelain mug.

Zelda couldn't think of anything to say that wouldn't sound silly or dismissive. Instead, she acknowledged his confession by sliding her plate to the center of the table so they could split the remainder of her pie.

They stayed and talked at the little table by the window long after their cups were empty, their knees occasionally bumping. Not many people were in the coffee shop. Felix had posted up in one corner, but a woman sitting against the far wall seemed to have taken an interest in them and kept glancing their way.

Nervous they'd been spotted, they each paid for their coffee and pie and headed back to campus. Leo had offered to pay for Zelda's, but she'd insisted on paying her own way. When she did so, he didn't push either, which felt like being respected.

In the alley behind Madame LeBleu's, Zelda changed Leo's features back to normal.

"That was nice," Leo said.

"Peach pie makes everything better."

"Maybe next time we'll talk more about you?"

Zelda smiled as her stomach flipped. "Maybe."

Chapter Ten

When Zelda entered the charms classroom, she found twenty-four canvas dress forms all in a row. She took a place in front of one in the middle. Their review of the previous year's spells had gone on for an agonizing extra week, and Zelda was more than eager to begin the real work. Her performance so far had been inconsistent at best, but there was still time to make up lost ground.

As girls took the mannequins around her, Zelda's phone vibrated from the depths of her school bag. The little buzz sent a shiver of excitement down her spine. She fished it out and found two notifications from P. Charming on the lock screen.

You have lunch next block, right? I really need to see you.

I sat at the worst table yesterday.

Zelda didn't have a chance to stop the smile that slipped over her mouth. What was she thinking? Yes, Leo was handsome and charming and easy to talk to. But if she was going to be First Fairy, she had to stay focused on his Happily Ever After, not how his texts made her heart do flips inside her chest.

She stuck her phone back in her purse before Professor Hildebrandt could catch her and give her another demerit. *They could only be friends.* Friends would leave her enough room to be the mature and emotionally collected fairy godmother he needed her to be.

Professor Hildebrandt arrived, and they spent the beginning of class watching as she produced yards upon yards of glimmering silk and draped it artfully over a dress form. Her wand then poured out strands of gossamer-thin thread that wove each panel of the dress together. She made it look easy, but there were a lot of elements to work together. The thread, the fabric, the boning, the ribbons, the crinolines. Zelda made note of each as the professor worked.

The professor wheeled her form to the center of the room for them to use as an example. "Today, I only ask that you practice creating fabrics and draping them. We'll add new elements each day until you're able to create an entire dress. Mastery of clothing making will come in handy when you're out in the field."

Zelda examined her mannequin and tried to envision a gown on it, but too many ideas came to mind. Beside her, Imogen created ruffles of stiff, hot pink satin on hers. Zelda turned back to her empty canvas and settled on a midnight blue sky flecked with winking stars as she lifted her wand. A lush blue velvet with the faintest sparkle unfurled from the air and wrapped around the dress form like a dark embrace.

Imogen eyed Zelda's handiwork. "That fabric is very you."

"Thanks. Yours is too."

The classroom tittered with excitement as they all sized up each other's choice of fabric.

"I love the ruffles, Miss Yang," Professor Hildebrandt said when she passed Imogen's form. She wore pink herself today. "Miss Spencer has created a lovely pattern as well." The professor waved her wand, and the fabric disappeared from each dress form. "Begin again, girls. This time, try something new."

Felicity Dunn occupied the dress form on the other side of Zelda, but she seemed more interested in gossiping with Maud Woods than draping fabric. Zelda tried to focus on draping layers of sheer, blush silk on her form, but she couldn't stop herself from turning an ear to their conversation.

"I can't believe she's already together with Sadler. That didn't take long," Felicity said.

"What?" Zelda interjected. She lowered her voice. "I mean, who are you guys talking about?" She inched closer to Felicity.

Maud leaned around Felicity and gave Zelda a pitying frown. "Susan St. Germain. She wouldn't shut up about it at breakfast this morning."

Felicity rolled her eyes. "I'm glad you missed it, Zelda. She was talking loud enough for all the room to hear."

"I'm sorry," Maud said as Zelda turned back to her dress form.

A tender feeling quivered in her chest. This was all her fault. She'd told Susan outright that she was free to date Dante, but she hadn't expected anything to happen so soon.

The Dante she'd known was quiet, thoughtful. He took things slow. She hadn't dated the swaggering boy she'd run into at the Swan and Raven. That was a different Dante, flitting from girl to girl, proposing a casual hookup with her and dating someone else two weeks later.

Or was he? Have I ever known the real Dante?

With her mind on the idea of Susan and Dante, Zelda didn't notice the mountain of angry black tulle she was creating on her mannequin.

"Ms. Ravensdale," Professor Hildebrandt shouted from behind, causing Zelda to jump.

This only caused more of the spongy black fabric to fly from Zelda's wand. Panic rushed through her veins as she tried to break the spell. With gritted teeth, she willed it to stop, but her wand was relentless. Tulle spewed out with no end in sight, and the mass of fabric grew to engulf the two dress forms beside hers.

Professor Hildebrandt stepped in front of Zelda and with a wave of her wand the spell stopped. With another flick of her wrist, she cleared away the giant tulle beast that filled the practice area.

The room quieted as Professor Hildebrandt rounded on Zelda. "Ms. Ravensdale, I highly suggest you get your magic under control. This kind of performance is unacceptable from a fourth-year." Her mouth formed a thin line.

Zelda resisted the urge to turn and run from the room, determined not to let Susan, or anyone, see her lose her composure any more than they already had.

Professor Hildebrandt stepped closer. "I expect more from you, Ms. Ravensdale." She lowered her voice so only Zelda could hear her. "Please see me after class."

Zelda kept her eyes on her shoes, unable to look at the faces of her classmates.

After class ended, Zelda waited by Professor Hildebrandt's desk as the others filed into the hall. Susan, of course, sent her a pitying sort of frown as she passed. Zelda pretended not to notice.

Professor Hildebrandt finished clearing fabric scraps from the practice area before she turned her attention to Zelda. "Don't worry. I won't scold you again." Her round, rosy cheeks creased as she offered a tiny smile. "I'm only firm because I know your potential."

Zelda tried to swallow the lump that formed in her throat. "I don't know what's happening with my magic."

Professor Hildebrandt smoothed out the wrinkles in her sweater. "You've done well in your practice. You have the right forms. The right pronunciations. But that's only half the battle. Spells guide magic, but it's ultimately your heart's intention that has the final say. I've seen emotions interfere with spells in far worse ways than this. With that new wand, you will need to guard your emotions well when you're casting."

Though she didn't want to, Zelda thought of Dante. He was firmly out of her life, but she could still feel his influence. Emotion burned in her chest. She wanted to call it anger, but hot tears sprang to her eyes.

Her phone buzzed, pulling Zelda from her thoughts. She glanced at the clock.

"I'm sorry to hold you up," Hildebrandt said. "You may go. I don't want to make you late for your next class."

Zelda arrived to potions just after the late bell, but Professor Ballentine didn't seem to notice. She took her seat beside Imogen and pulled out her phone. She held it in her lap so the professor wouldn't see.

I don't have lunch till fifth block today.

She took out her copy of *Lady Wilton's Compendium of Punishingly Advanced Brews* and flipped to the page number marked on the board.

"The Draft of Endless Fog." Professor Ballentine sat on her desk. With one leg crossed over the other, she bounced her red-bottomed, patent-leather pump up and down. "This is a great brew to keep on hand. Once completed, it will produce a dense fog that can be used as cover should you get yourself into a precarious situation."

Zelda unzipped her lab kit and pulled out the ingredients from the supply list in her book. Imogen lit a Bunsen burner and found the correct size of Erlenmeyer flask for the brew.

Professor Ballentine hopped off her desk and moved through the room. "Work quickly. You'll need every minute of the lab period to finish this potion since there's a long simmering time at the end."

Imogen leaned over Zelda's side of the table. "Professor Ballentine was a granter, wasn't she?"

"Yes. Why?"

"Did she say where she did her tenure?"

"Venezuela, I think."

"She seems to know a lot about all the sorts of trouble a fairy can get into while on the job," Imogen mused.

Zelda tried not to imagine the sort of precarious situations she would encounter during her own tenure.

"Venezuela might be an interesting territory," Imogen said with a flick of her hair. "I'd never considered South America before."

Professor Ballentine passed by to examine their progress and they turned their full attention back to their brews. Soon the calm of measuring and stirring banished all lingering thoughts of Dante and Susan. After their brew cooled to the proper temperature, Zelda added the final drop of summer rain and gave it a swirl. Thick, gray smoke began to pour from her flask. Around the room, other lab stations spewed a similar fog. Some were thinner than others and some had funny colors. Georgia Rollins' brew produced a green fog with putrid egg smell that earned her a reprimand from Professor Ballentine for overheating her solution.

"Fill a vial and leave it on my desk to be graded," Ballentine said. "If you've had some success today and you'd like to keep one for yourself, feel free. This draft has a particularly long shelf life and should keep for at least a year."

Zelda took out three vials and ladled a small supply of the milky white liquid into each. She wasn't sure if it would come in handy, but a fairy godmother should be prepared for every possible scenario when granting wishes. She stoppered the vials and slipped one into her bag. One she gave to Imogen, and the other she labeled with their names and delivered to Professor Ballentine's desk.

After returning to their lab table, Zelda hazarded a glance at her phone and found another text from Leo.

Will you be in the library after dinner then? I really need to talk to you.

Again, Zelda couldn't stop her grin. Something about his eagerness made her heart stutter in her chest.

She couldn't reply fast enough. **Yes, I'll be there.**

Chapter Eleven

Zelda, Imogen, and Specs sat at a study table on an upper level of the library. Stashed between towering shelves, Zelda tapped furiously at her laptop while Specs disassembled the guts of a brass pocket watch. Imogen's head lolled in her hand. She yawned lazily as she flipped through a book of complexion clearing charms. The setting sun cast long beams of diamond-patterned light through the library windows.

"Are you even reading anymore?" Zelda asked.

"Huh?" Imogen sniffed and lifted her head. "No. I ate too much bread pudding at dinner. All I can think about is crawling into bed."

Specs snorted but didn't look up from the inventory of gears spread out in front of him. Zelda finished the last sentences of her essay on the role of fairies in World War II and the Paris Peace Conference when Prince Leo approached their table.

He motioned to the empty chair beside Zelda. "May I take this seat?"

"Sure." Zelda had hoped he'd show up. He still had important royal duties to fill in addition to his schoolwork, but the urgency of his last message worried her.

Imogen sat upright and pointed. "Prince!"

He chuckled. "Leo is fine."

Imogen flushed as she let out a squeak. "Sorry. I just got really excited."

Specs finally looked up from his tinkering. His eyes widened as Leo pulled a stack of notebooks from his backpack.

"Have you met Specs—I mean Thaddeus?" Zelda asked.

"Specs is fine with me." He extended his hand across the table. "We haven't had the chance to meet yet."

Leo reached for Specs' hand. "No, we haven't, but I'm pretty sure we have Advanced Magical Mechanics together."

"Yeah," Specs said. His mouth turned up into a grin. Never one for chitchat, his attention returned to his work.

Zelda looked from Leo to Imogen. Leo watched her with an expectant sort of smile like he wanted to tell her something. Imogen stared at them, her eyes wide and mouth parted in unveiled shock. Zelda met Imogen's gaze and raised her brows.

Be cool, Imogen.

Imogen seemed to understand and busied herself a little too intently with the task of deciding which of her fifteen differently colored gel pens to use for notes.

Leo didn't seem to notice. He fiddled with his notebooks until he finally asked, "Can you show me where the library catalogue is?"

"Sure." Zelda's mind raced. *What will he tell me once we're alone?*

Zelda escorted Leo to a desktop computer where he could search for book titles.

Leo typed in a title. "It's in section 300."

"Third floor then." Zelda's insides knotted as they headed silently for the stairs. Was he about to call the whole wish off? Take matters into his own hands?

As soon as they were alone and out of sight, Leo's demeanor shifted. The calm, composed, regal mask slipped away, and a normal eighteen-year-old boy moved beside her. "How are you?" he asked earnestly. "I feel like we only ever see each other in passing."

Some of Zelda's nerves slipped away but not completely. He still had that air of sadness, of loneliness, that he hid from everyone else.

"I'm fine. And you?" Her miserable performance in charms class came to mind, but it was the last thing she wanted to talk about.

"I'm okay." He tugged nervously at the sleeves of his crimson blazer.

They turned down an aisle and wound their way through the shelves. Leather-bound books with shimmering gold lettering on their spines sat between books covered in plastic to protect their paper jackets. Somewhere among the towering wooden shelves lurked a book with a lemon-scented, anti-staining charm left by a fairy with a proclivity for spills.

"Just okay? Isn't boarding school everything you thought it would be?" Zelda asked.

Leo chuckled behind closed lips. "The tinkering labs are as fantastic as I thought they'd be."

"So, what's bothering you?"

"It's my dad."

"Yeah?" It was weird to hear the king of Olisand called "Dad."

"I made the rowing team, though," he said as if it were a consolation. "But my dad just seems interested in reminding me that he thinks I'm wasting my time here when I could be finishing my schooling faster with a private tutor."

And I thought Dante's parents were intimidating. Something twisted in Zelda's insides. Not pity. Sympathy, maybe. Hopefully not remorse for refusing to grant his wish. It was the first time she'd questioned the will of her headmistress. What if giving up his title as prince really was Leo's Happily Ever After in spite of the political consequences? Would she be able to go against Madame LeBleu if Leo still wished his crown away? And if he did, would she lose her shot at First Fairy?

"Leo," Zelda said, his name like a sigh. "You're not wasting your time here."

"I know." Leo ran a hand through his hair. "I just need to make my dad see that."

"Have you settled on a capstone project?" Zelda pulled to a stop in front of a window overlooking the grounds of the EAMS side of campus.

"Not yet. My dad wants me to focus on befriending students from influential families."

Zelda straightened. "Like who?" Her mind instantly went to Susan St. Germain. The thought of Leo cozying up to Susan made her stomach queasy.

"Thora Green, Bertrand Dupuis, Dante Sadler—"

Zelda's heart skipped a beat and the dread must have showed on her face.

"Do you know him?"

Zelda wrapped a hand around her waist. "I dated him last year."

Leo almost froze. He watched Zelda with confusion, as if he couldn't be sure she wasn't kidding. "You and Sadler?"

Zelda winced. "Yeah."

"But he's . . ." Leo fumbled for the right word. "Not nice."

"You can say it. He's awful."

Leo sighed. "How did *that* happen?"

"He wasn't horrible until the end. It seems to have gotten worse over the summer. As far as I can tell, the Dante I knew and the Dante you met are completely different people."

Leo grimaced. "I'll keep my distance then."

"But if it's part of your duty, I don't want to get you in trouble."

"He's just the nephew of a Lord—he's not as important as he seems to think."

Zelda smiled. She liked to think of Dante being put in his place. Leo's dimpled smile mirrored hers. Her phone rang with a jarring *beep* in the quiet library.

Reminder: ***pick up more First Snow of Winter for potions.***

Her face fell. "I have to go."

"What? Already?"

Something stirred in Zelda's chest to see Leo so disappointed in her leaving. "I have to get some potions ingredients before my next class. I'd go tomorrow, but we're doing our fieldwork all afternoon, and Imogen and I have our first fencing team practice after dinner."

Leo checked an expensive-looking watch. "It's eight. Curfew is at nine thirty."

"There's a shop with potion ingredients not far from campus."

"Hang on."

Leo dashed down the aisle to retrieve his book, then returned to her side. "Can I come with you? I've never been to a potion shop before."

She wanted to say yes, but she had to be more sensible than that. "Can you leave campus with me, or do we need another security escort?"

A deep voice came from behind them that made Zelda jump. "Yes, the prince needs a member of his security team present for all public outings."

Leo spun around at the sound. "Come on, Felix. Let me go—just this once."

Zelda's pulse thundered in her ears. "Where did you come from?" She turned to Leo. "Was he following us that whole time?"

“Please, Felix,” Leo begged, ignoring Zelda’s question. “I’m already rooming with you, and I’d like an hour and a half of privacy. I’ll wear a disguise. I’ll carry pepper spray if it makes you feel better.”

Felix folded his arms across his broad chest in disapproval. Zelda didn’t like the way his dark-brown eyes sized her up either.

“Felix,” Leo pleaded. “We’ll be back before curfew.”

“You know, it’s really not that interesting,” Zelda said as Felix turned the full weight of his cold, appraising gaze on her. “I should just go alone.”

Felix’s eyes darted between Leo and Zelda, his face unreadable. He let out a sharp breath through his nose. “Fine. But the prince will not remove his disguise under any circumstance. And, under penalty of death, you will not be late.”

Zelda’s brows pushed together. Felix wasn’t a particularly large man, but his black suit jacket was doing a poor job of hiding the bulge of well-honed muscles.

Leo’s head fell back, and he let out a sigh of relief. “Thank you. You won’t regret this.”

Felix didn’t look pleased.

Zelda swallowed hard. “He’s kidding about the penalty of death, right?”

Neither Leo nor Felix answered her before Leo grabbed her hand and pulled her along after him.

Zelda and Leo slipped through the door to the potions shop at 8:50 p.m. The hours posted in the window said it was open till nine. The store clerk was in the process of dusting shelves full of amber glass bottles. She looked less-than-pleased to have patrons come in right before closing. Zelda gave her a friendly nod and headed to the elemental section in search of snow.

She stole a glance at Leo, who meandered through the tiny shop just behind her. He looked like a kid in a candy store as he perused the thousands of neatly labeled ingredients.

He caught her watching and his mouth turned up on one side. “What?”

A violent warmth reached Zelda’s cheeks. “Nothing”

Leo read off the ingredients. "Snowball, snow drift, yellow snow." He laughed. "Are all these used in potions?"

Zelda smiled. "Of course." She found a vial of first snow and grabbed it from the shelf. The glass was cold to the touch.

"That's not going to melt is it?" Leo asked.

"No. It's charmed, but the spell will break when the seal is broken."

Zelda paid for the vial, and they headed back toward campus. The night was cool for September, and Zelda pulled her coat tight against the chill. To her surprise, Leo walked close to her. His shoulder bumped hers on occasion as they walked. Zelda shivered, her skin too attuned to the prince's movements at her side, but she didn't know how to make it stop. *And do I really want his arm to stop brushing mine?*

"So," Zelda said after they'd walked a block in silence. "Now that Felix isn't over your shoulder, can we talk about godchild stuff?"

Leo seemed to flinch. "If we must."

"I've been thinking," Zelda said.

"About me?" A grin brightened his voice.

"Yes, I suppose so." This earned her another shoulder bump from Leo, but she was pretty sure this one was intentional. She calmed the smile that threatened to burst from her lips. "I think I disagree with your stance on the king's role. I think your father has considerable influence over current affairs in Olisand."

"It looks that way, but it's much worse than that. If we don't act on an issue, we get called useless. If we do, we get called tyrants."

Zelda shrugged. "That's part of the challenge of being a monarch, isn't it? It's a balancing act."

"You sound like my mom."

Queen Antonia. It was almost as strange as hearing the king referred to as "Dad." Zelda shook off the weirdness. "So, you'd rather make things? Doesn't a king do that?"

Leo scrubbed the back of his magically darkened hair. "Politics moves too slow. It involves compromise and acquiescence to people's underlying agendas."

"Maybe if the people knew where your heart is, they'd let you rule in your own way."

Leo scoffed. "I don't think my dad and all his advisors would agree with you."

"I wish I could take this burden from you." Guilt and the desire to help mingled to form an ache deep in her gut. "If I didn't think the consequences would be too great."

"Thanks," Leo said. "I know you don't take your job lightly. Neither did I make my wish casually."

They turned the corner to pass through Founders Square. Shoppers and tourists had moved to bars and restaurants in the River District. The shop windows were dimmed for the night, even the brilliant display in the windows of St. Germain's. Leo slowed as they passed the emporium.

"I don't think we have time to linger. It's almost curfew," Zelda said.

"No," Leo said, distracted. "I-I thought I saw something."

"What?"

He stopped in front of the towering window and its shadowy display of men's dress shoes. "Movement."

"I'm pretty sure the emporium is closed."

"No, there," Leo whispered. He grabbed Zelda by the waist and guided her, so she could see better.

Something moved on the display. At first, she thought it might have been a mouse as a hairy head darted behind a pair of leather loafers, but a movement to the left caught her eye.

Zelda blinked, losing trust in her eyes. But there she was, carrying a rag and rolling a tin of shoe polish: the tiniest person Zelda had ever seen. The girl was small enough that she could have fit in Zelda's hand.

"Do you see what I'm seeing?" Zelda whispered.

"I see." Leo's breath brushed her ear as he leaned closer to get a better look at the creature.

The tiny figure polishing shoes on the display wore a smudged white smock and navy dress that looked like it belonged on a doll. Pointed ears stuck out from the girl's hair.

"I haven't lost my mind, have I?" Leo asked.

He must have spoken too loudly. The girl spun around when he spoke.

"It's an elf," Zelda squeaked as she finally put a word to what she was seeing. She realized the girl was actually much older than she'd first thought.

The woman must have heard them through the glass. She gave a tiny screech and scurried out of sight, leaving her rag and polish behind.

Zelda and Leo stood silent in front of the window for several long beats.

Leo rubbed his eyes and nearly knocked his fake glasses off his nose. "That was real, right?"

Zelda's mouth flopped open and closed as she tried to understand what they'd seen. "It can't be. Can it?" Elves were things of fairy stories—mischievous creatures grandmothers warned young fairies about when they left their training wands unattended. But that didn't mean they were real, did it? Zelda's hand flew to her purse in panic to make sure her wand was still there.

Leo shook his head. "You're a fairy. Shouldn't you know?"

"I have no clue," Zelda said.

Leo glanced down at his watch. "We'll have to talk about this tomorrow. We have to go. It's almost curfew."

They ran back to the school gates barely a minute before curfew. Zelda undid Leo's disguise before they checked in and returned to their rooms. That night, Zelda dreamed a team of miniature people climbed through her window and polished her shoes.

Chapter Twelve

Zelda couldn't get the thought of elves scurrying through the spaces in the walls out of her head. What would the discovery of elves in their midst mean for the world? And who already knew about it? It was the sort of groundbreaking discovery she didn't have time for. She was supposed to be focusing on school and First Fairy.

Leo was enough of a distraction. A tired, desperate part of her didn't want to have to wonder what elves were doing polishing shoes in St. Germain's. It was becoming too much—more than enough to distract even the most diligent student.

She hadn't discussed telling a professor with Leo, but Professor Weymouth might have answers and she could at least put the elf out of her mind. After history class, Zelda hung behind to see what he thought.

"Can I help you with something, Miss Ravensdale?" Professor Weymouth asked as he erased the boards.

"Yes." Zelda approached his desk hesitantly. "I have a question about other magical beings." If anyone knew something about the history of magical creatures, it would be Professor Weymouth.

The professor turned and gave her a curious look. "About *what*?"

"Other magical creatures. Aren't they just a myth?" She hoped she didn't sound completely insane. She didn't have any proof of what they'd seen.

"Well . . ." He smiled and took a seat at his desk. "I wouldn't say they are *just* a myth. There is great debate among magical scholars whether the creatures in fairy tales actually existed. Strange magical occurrences throughout history have convinced some historians that there may be magical creatures that have been moving through our world unseen since the Dark Ages. Why do you ask?"

"I think I saw an elf." She thought it would be best to leave Leo out of it for now. "She was in the window of St. Germain's Shoe Emporium."

His eyes unfocused for a brief moment.

Is he looking into my future?

When he returned his gaze to Zelda, a deep crease formed between his brows. He rose from his chair and rubbed a hand over his angular jaw. "Interesting. Are you sure that's what you saw?"

"Yes. Tiny. Pointy ears. Polishing shoes," she confirmed. "I thought for a second I was losing my mind, but she spotted us—*me* and darted away."

"Very interesting," he murmured, lost in thought again. He pressed his eyes shut for a moment before continuing. "I must talk with Madame LeBleu about this, but take heart. You're certainly not losing your mind." Professor Weymouth shoved papers and books into his worn briefcase.

Zelda's heart sputtered. "What are you going to tell Madame LeBleu?"

"I can't be sure, but I'll let you know what Madame LeBleu says."

"Okay," Zelda said, but the professor was already rushing out of the room.

When Zelda and Imogen returned to their dormitory after fencing practice, a thick, powder-blue envelope sat on Zelda's desk. It had a gold wax seal on it which she worked open with her finger. She pulled out a card of the same color as the envelope embossed with a gold, ornate "ALB."

"What's that?" Imogen asked.

Zelda skimmed the letter's contents. "It's from Madame LeBleu."

"The headmistress? Are you in trouble?"

Zelda shook her head. "She's invited me to tea."

"Tea?" Imogen gave Zelda a suspicious look.

"Don't give me that look. I know as much as you do. It only has a date and time."

Zelda wished she could tell Imogen about Leo's wish. It would have been nice to bounce her thoughts off someone other than her professor and headmistress. She wanted to know what Imogen would say about her deal with Leo. Imogen probably wouldn't have been afraid to go against the wishes of Madame LeBleu for the happiness of a godchild.

Could I be that brave?

The following Wednesday at promptly three o'clock, Zelda knocked on the door of Madame LeBleu's cottage. To her surprise, Professor Ballentine opened the door.

"Who is it, Helga?" Madame LeBleu called from within.

"Miss Ravensdale," Professor Ballentine called over her shoulder. She eyed Zelda suspiciously and ushered her into the cottage. "Come in, come in. Professor Weymouth will be joining us shortly."

Ballentine led Zelda into the study where Madame LeBleu was sitting at her desk. Zelda took a seat in one of the plush armchairs and gave the headmistress a weak smile. She wasn't sure why Professor Ballentine was there, but judging by her pacing, Ballentine wasn't too happy about it.

Was she in trouble? Did they know about her deal with Leo? It probably wasn't the most prudent thing she'd ever done, but they'd entrusted his wish to her for a reason.

As they waited for Professor Weymouth, Madame LeBleu inquired about Zelda's mother and sisters and recalled them all being bestowed with the honor of First Fairy. They didn't have to wait long before Weymouth entered, hitting his head on the low beam and growling out a curse. He entered the office like a gale force wind, a stack of papers under each arm and his hair and bow tie askew. He dropped the papers on Madame LeBleu's desk with a thud.

Ballentine snatched one of the pages from the top of a pile. "What's all this?"

"Research." Weymouth grabbed the sheet and stuck it back with the others. "Don't get them out of order."

"Settle, Grayson," Ballentine cooed. She sank into her chair with a half-smile curling on her lips.

Madame LeBleu motioned for Professor Weymouth to sit, and he begrudgingly complied.

"Tea first, then business." Madame LeBleu waved her wand and her kettle poured them each a steaming cup. "Are things going well with the prince, Zelda?"

Zelda's cup rattled in her hand as she stilled. She glanced instinctively at Professor Ballentine.

"It's okay," Madame LeBleu said. "You can trust everyone in this room."

Zelda nodded, but she wasn't sure what to call her progress with the prince. He was still a prince and that was what mattered. "As far as I can tell, he still doesn't want to be king, but he's considering it."

"Wait," Ballentine interjected. "What are you two playing at? Grayson won't look me in the eye. Is the prince Zelda's godchild? Are you interfering with a wish?"

"We have good cause—" Weymouth chimed in. "The prince tied an anonymous wish to the gates in September, and the future of Erimount changed for the worse. I sent Zelda in to manage the situation, and so far, she has done a splendid job. We all know the king's health has been suspect of late. If that boy gives up his throne and the crown falls to Astara, she can't rule until she turns eighteen. Prince Leopold's cousin, the Duke of Brockford, will be made regent and he's already been a hassle to the ICG." He looked only at Ballentine as he spoke.

She glared back in return, but she nodded once he had finished. "So, it's a greater good sort of situation with this wish?"

Weymouth nodded. "All I saw were pieces. I knew Brockford was involved with the St. Germain family, but I didn't know why. When Zelda came to me after class to tell me she saw an elf in St. Germain's Shoe Emporium, my inner eye told me there was danger in the prince's future. It's hazy, but I think Brockford is going to make a play for the crown—"

Danger? Zelda's mouth went dry.

"That's quite a leap, Grayson. Especially when your inner eye is spotty at best," Ballentine said. She turned to Madame LeBleu. "Aurelie, I can't believe you're letting a student get wrapped up in this mess. This sounds like a whole conspiracy, not a cut-and-dry wish a fourth-year should be handling."

Zelda straightened. "I knew what I was getting into."

Ballentine's face softened. "I know, but these are the kinds of wishes that should be handled by a seasoned professional."

Zelda's heart sank as she realized one of her favorite professors really saw her as just a kid. A lump formed in her throat, but she wouldn't let herself cry. It was clear Professor Ballentine didn't have much faith in her, but at least it was two against one. She swallowed to make sure her voice wouldn't shake. "I'll do whatever needs to be done to help the kingdom and to save the prince, if need be."

Ballentine pressed her lips into a frown. "I guess I'm outnumbered on bringing the student in on this conspiracy."

Weymouth's shoulders slumped. "Please, Helga. You know the studies. A wish is most likely to end in a HEA if the godchild is still young and full of hope and optimism. Godchildren trust their peers most readily and I think we picked the perfect peer for Prince Leopold. He trusts her, which means he won't take matters into his own hands. We need you on board. We need your help."

"Fine," she spat, before she turned to Zelda. "Miss Ravensdale, you're going to have to learn what you're capable of handling as a godmother sooner or later, so I'm not going to put a stop to this. But, if you ever feel over your head handling this wish, please let one of us know. You're one of our top students, but you don't have to do this alone."

The lump returned to Zelda's throat. She knew Ballentine meant well, but all she heard was failure, failure, failure.

Madame LeBleu seemed to sense her distress. "You're handling things just fine. Keep doing what you're doing. Keep Leo away from the elves and the St. Germain family. We'll mount an investigation into their doings. You just make sure Leo doesn't give up his crown."

Zelda nodded, but it was easier said than done.

The elf in the window haunted Zelda the rest of the week. Zelda and Leo were both too busy with classes and the start of extracurriculars to find a time to talk about what they'd seen, but that might have been a blessing in disguise. She needed him to focus on all the reasons to keep his crown, not chase fairy tales.

Saturday was unseasonably warm, so Zelda, Imogen, and a number of GITs spent the day at a large lake which bordered the city of Erimount. Zelda and Imogen sunned themselves on colorful towels while Ava Spencer sat cross-legged beneath a lace parasol to keep her pale complexion from turning a shade of crimson. The water was barely warm, so most girls stuck to the sandy shoreline. Zelda had brought her homework, which earned her a few groans from Imogen who'd brought only magazines and gummy worms.

After a quarter of an hour, the EAMS students started showing up. Girls joined their friends along the shore, while the boys appeared in gaggles to cause a ruckus. Some insisted on showing off by tossing each other into the tepid lake.

Leo arrived with a rowdy bunch of popular tinkers. He gave off almost as much warmth as the sun with his brilliant golden hair and a laugh that made you feel like the funniest person in the room. Felix trailed twenty paces behind Leo like a dark cloud in a tailored black suit.

Leo peeled off from the group with a friendly wave and headed straight for her. Zelda's heart clenched strangely when their eyes met, and her hands tingled like magic coursed through them.

"Can I join you?" he asked.

"Of course you can." Imogen patted an empty space at the foot of Zelda's towel and shot her a mischievous grin.

Zelda's cheeks heated. *What are you doing, Imogen?*

Leo seemed to think nothing of it and took the empty spot. Specs arrived soon after and dropped on the towel at Imogen's feet. "So, I've been reading about wands," he said in lieu of a greeting as he stole a handful of gummy worms from the bag in Imogen's purse.

"Hey." Imogen slapped him away playfully with her magazine. "Get your own."

Zelda snuck a glance at Leo as he sat by her side. He gave her little smile that dimpled one of his cheeks. It was strange to see Leo in something besides a suit or a school uniform. He wore a crew-neck rowing T-shirt and athletic shorts.

"Why are you reading about wands?" Imogen asked.

"Zelda's magic troubles made me wonder," Specs said.

"What did you find?" Zelda asked. "My new wand works, well, aside from my blizzard it works fine."

Specs smiled. "Can I see it?"

Zelda retrieved the wand from her bag. The faceted star glittered in the sun and cast little rainbows across the towel when she passed it to Specs.

"Whoa." Specs tilted his head to examine it. "That would explain the blizzard. Diamond is much more conductive than wood."

"Diamond? Not glass?" Imogen propped herself on her elbows to get a better look at the treasure in Specs' hands.

Zelda shoved him in the shoulder. "You blabbermouth. I was trying not to broadcast that."

Ava looked concerned. "Zelda, diamond wands can be very dangerous. I've read some articles that claim diamond amplifies a fairy's magic."

"I didn't have much of a choice," Zelda said, lowering her voice. "No other wand material works for me."

Ava nodded, but she kept her eyes on the wand—like it might jump out of Zelda's hand and bite her.

"Why's your magic different?" Leo asked. He didn't look scared, only curious in the way Specs was curious about the science of magic.

"I've been asking myself the same thing," Zelda said.

Without warning, Imogen jumped up from her towel. "Fletcher," she called, waving.

A tall, brown-skinned boy strolled shirtless along the lakeside. His figure turned heads and inspired preening and giggles as he passed. He gave Imogen a casual wave. When she bounded up to him, he threw an arm around her shoulders, and they started off down the shoreline.

"Who's that?" Leo asked.

"Fletcher Westbrook." Specs didn't seem enthused. "He's in the year behind us at EAMS."

"Have you talked with him? Is he nice?" Zelda asked. She trusted Imogen to make her own choices, but she was easily swayed by rippling abdominal muscles.

"We don't talk much, but of course he's nice. Normally guys who look like him don't have brains, but he's got it all. Looks, brains, a spot on the rugby team, and, on top of that, he's nice to everyone," Specs said. The sparkle had left his eye as he watched the pair move farther down the beach.

Was Specs jealous of Fletcher? Zelda hated to admit that "tall, undiscovered model" was Imogen's type. Specs was handsome in a more whimsical way. He had an elegant bone structure that gave him a delicate sort of appearance. With the exception of his strong chin, he looked far more breakable than the muscled rugby player at Imogen's side.

A breeze carried the smell of burned sugar and almond out to the lake. The wonderful scent in the air distracted Zelda from the wounded look on Specs' face.

Leo sighed. "Something smells amazing." He smiled at Zelda pointedly.

Zelda scanned the lakeside. "I think a vendor is selling pizzelles over there." She pointed to a yellow umbrellaed cart.

Leo stood and offered Zelda a hand up. "Shall we get some?"

"Do you guys want any?" Zelda asked.

Ava shook her head.

Specs' face brightened. "Strawberry, please."

Zelda took Leo's hand, and he pulled her to her feet. She grabbed her wallet, and they joined the long line of young locals, eager for crisp sugar pastries. The treats were more of a doily than anything of substance, but that was half the fun.

The line moved slowly, and Zelda's stomach knotted as she realized how many people watched her and the prince. And just how close Leo stood beside her. Felix hovered out of earshot but conspicuously close. Self-conscious of what people would say, she took a step farther away.

Leo didn't seem to notice. Perhaps he was used to everyone staring. "I've been meaning to talk to you."

"Yeah," Zelda said. Their last meeting had certainly been eventful. "Me too."

"I can't stop thinking about what we saw on Wednesday night. That wasn't normal, was it?"

Zelda rubbed her arms as if to chase away a chill. "No. No, it wasn't."

"I'm trying to wrap my mind around it. I tried searching for elves online, but all I got was a bunch of conflicting folklore and fantasy movie stuff."

"The internet is very unreliable about magic history," Zelda said with a laugh. "You can really only trust books and journals vetted for approval by the International Council of Godmothers."

"But aren't you curious?" Leo moved closer.

"Of course I'm curious. Would your father know about this?" Zelda's cheeks heated when she realized how close his face was to hers. She resisted the urge to take a step back, but she didn't want to risk being overheard.

"I doubt it, unless it's some great state secret I'll only find out about once I'm king."

"Could you ask him?"

Leo backed away and picked at a cuticle anxiously. "Sure, but he'd probably accuse me of reading tabloid headlines instead of my schoolwork."

Professor Weymouth's warning came to mind; Zelda had to get Leo's mind off the elves. "Fairy godmothers have been working in the public eye since the Dark Ages, but that doesn't necessarily mean that other magical creatures were forced out of hiding too. There's, of course, the nonsense the tabloids publish, but in all our history lessons, we've never covered anything of the sort. I asked my history professor what he thought—"

Leo's eyes lit up. "And he believed you?"

"Sort of, but he says we should leave it alone. It could be dangerous for a student to be poking around the St. Germains so he's going to look into it," Zelda said, hoping Leo would let it go for his own sake.

The excitement fell from Leo's face. "Did you tell them about me?"

"No. I didn't want to draw their suspicion."

Leo's shoulders dropped in relief. The line moved up, and Leo took a step forward to turn and face Zelda. His brow was furrowed, eyes bright. "Do you think St. Germain knows there are elves running around his store? He *has* to know."

"I don't know. Maybe, but I think we should just drop it—let my professor investigate."

Leo smiled. "Are you chickening out on me, Ravensdale?"

His teasing grin made her chest glow with warmth. "No. I just . . . we have enough on our plates. As your godmother, I think you should focus on your Happily Ever After."

"Perhaps you're right," Leo said, but he didn't seem convinced.

With treats in hand, Zelda led the way back to their spot on the beach. Imogen and Fletcher had returned; she was draped across his lap while he played lazily with her hair, and she chatted with Ava. Specs looked like he wanted to be anywhere but there.

Zelda handed Specs his strawberry pizzelle and settled herself on her towel.

"Thanks," he mumbled.

A musical laugh floated over the sounds of the lake lapping at the shore. The familiar low voice accompanying the laugh made the elderflower cream-filled pizzelle stick in Zelda's throat. Susan strolled past with her arm through Dante's, hanging convincingly on his every word.

Zelda lost track of her group's conversation, but Leo's unmistakably warm voice floated toward them. Susan's head snapped to look their way. Dante looked too. Zelda met their gaze. There was no hiding the fact that she'd been watching them.

In a gesture she hoped looked cool, calm and utterly unfazed, Zelda slipped on her sunglasses and gave them a little smile and a wave. There was also no missing the crown prince at her side. He may have been more than what she'd planned to take on during her final year, but the look on Susan and Dante's faces was more than worth it for tackling the fate of Olisand's future king. She didn't care what they thought of her. She didn't look sad, and for the first time in a while, she didn't feel sad either.

A hand on her elbow brought her back.

Leo's fingers were gentle as he held her arm. "Are you okay?" His eyes flicked to Dante and Susan's backs as they continued down the beach.

"Yeah." Zelda swallowed the thick feeling that fluttered in her throat. A tender, sincere concern painted Leo's face.

"Didn't take him long," Imogen growled under her breath.

"Down girl," Zelda said. "He can date whoever he wants."

Zelda glanced at Leo and was surprised by the relief on his face. The strange warmth filled her chest again. "I'm over him."

She meant every word of it.

Chapter Thirteen

Leo's text came through as Zelda was getting ready for bed. **I'm craving the best peach pie in Erimount.**

Zelda smiled to herself. **We can't leave school grounds. It's already past curfew.**

I need to talk to you. Meet me at the bike racks behind the dining hall.

The night was cold and clear. Zelda pulled her coat tight around herself. Students passed her on their way back to the dormitories, but few gave her a second glance. Just when Zelda thought to check the time on her phone, a familiar figure turned a corner around the athletic building and moved in her direction.

Something fluttered in Zelda's chest as she recognized Leo's stride.

When he spotted her, he hurried to close the distance between them. "Hey. I was hoping to beat you here. Have you waited long?"

Zelda smiled. "Not long. This is an odd place to talk, don't you think?" A shiver ran the length of her spine.

"We're not talking here," Leo said with a sly little smile.

Zelda tilted her head. "Where then? I see you managed to ditch Felix."

Leo pulled out a key. "I called in more than one favor tonight."

Zelda had never been in the school kitchens before. She'd expected something more cafeteria-like, not flagstone floors, and shiny copper cookware hung from the ceiling in carefully arranged rows.

"Are we allowed to be in here?" Zelda whispered.

"I was given permission," Leo said as he walked to the fridge. "I stress bake."

Zelda laughed. "That must be a perk of royalty—getting your every whim accommodated."

Leo shot her a playful glare from around the door to the walk-in fridge. "Not true. These are my personal groceries, and I'll have you know that I spent lots of time talking with the cooks. And, with Madame LeBleu's and Lord Scarlet's permission, I personally purchased the new range they needed." He jerked his head toward a shiny, new-looking stove.

Zelda eyed the copper-plated cooking range. Guilt needled at her insides for her snap judgment. "Right," she said. "I'm sorry. I should have expected as much from you."

Leo removed various ingredients and placed them on the table in the center of the room.

"We're really baking peach pie?" Zelda asked.

Leo fixed her with a dimpled grin and pulled out a set of notecards. "We're really baking peach pie."

"I'm impressed you know how to bake."

"What? The spoiled prince doesn't know how to crack a few eggs?" Leo grabbed a bowl and pulled up an egg carton. He cracked one single-handed on the edge of the table. The whites and golden yolk slid languidly from the shell and into the bowl. He tossed the shells into the trash bin and repeated the action.

"That's not what I meant," Zelda said. "My dad does most of the baking at my house. I've never had any luck with it. It's too complicated."

"Seriously? You brew complicated potions all the time."

"That's different."

Leo stopped beating the eggs and fixed her with a curious look. "It's just following directions, you scaredy-cat." He grabbed her by the arm and pulled her to stand in front of the bowl. "You get to take over now."

"I'm going to ruin it. There's no way I can make anything to compare to the best peach pie in Erimount." Zelda tried to take a step back, but Leo caught her by the waist and held her in place. Her breath hitched as Leo's steady, sure hands captured her hips.

"No, no. You're not getting away that easy." He slowly released her, but his hand lingered on her back long enough for her to notice. "I'll walk you through it, step by step."

Baking wasn't as hard as Zelda had expected. It required the same methodical attention to detail that a potion required, and it was indeed just as relaxing. Leo put Zelda in charge of the filling while he prepared the dough. Soon, they had a pie that bore a passing resemblance to what they'd eaten on Leo's first day.

"The prince even knows how to make a lattice crust." Zelda shook her head as Leo crimped the edges.

"The castle chefs and cooks taught me a lot. I liked to hide out in the kitchens when I was little—I was a chubby kid."

"I bet you looked adorable with those dimples," Zelda said with a giggle.

Leo cocked one of his brows at her. "You like my dimples?"

Zelda's cheeks flushed. They were dangerously close to flirting. *Why does he have to be so charming?* "I like smiles that have parentheses." As the words left her mouth, they felt like a confession. *Am I flirting back?*

Leo ducked his head to smile at his feet. He crossed to a cabinet and pulled out a small bowl. He wore the remnants of the smile on his lips as he cracked an egg and beat it.

Zelda watched in silence as he brushed egg over the crust. She could feel the ghost of his touch on her waist. A warmth sat high in her chest as she watched Leo, overwhelmed with a feeling dangerously close to affection. *Is it friendship or something else?*

They slid the pie into the oven and began cleaning the kitchen.

Leo washed the dishes and Zelda dried.

"So, what did you want to talk about?" Zelda asked.

"I wanted to talk to you about the elves again."

"Leo." She sighed. "I really don't think we should be getting involved. It's none of our business."

"Just hear me out. I can't stop thinking about it. My gut is telling me something is off. We don't know why St. Germain has kept something as special as formerly thought to have been mythological elves to himself."

He had a point.

"Knowing Susan, that seems like a discovery a St. Germain would shout from the rooftops," Zelda said. "If he uncovered the existence of elves outside of the old fairy stories, his name would be written in history. You don't think there's a chance St. Germain doesn't know the elves are there?"

"Maybe, but would you go around polishing shoes for someone out of the goodness of your heart?"

"Good point." She chewed her lip as she considered the implications of getting involved. She wanted to follow Madame LeBleu's orders, but she couldn't tell Leo why she was saying no. Leo's argument was convincing. How could she keep him from heading into danger without telling him what Madame LeBleu and her professors knew about his wish?

"I have access to resources your professors don't and I might be of some use to their investigation. Please." Leo placed his hand on hers. "I want to be useful. Let me just make sure everything is above-board."

The newly familiar magic-like tingle surged from her hand and up her arm.

"What does your fairy godmother's intuition say?" he asked.

Zelda's face flushed with heat under Leo's gentle, pleading gaze. "I don't like secrets. I don't trust secrecy even if it's done with the best intentions. There's no accountability in it so I guess that means I'm in—but we *must* be careful."

"I could probably score a tour of their facilities to get a better look around. It's good PR for a prince to be seen out and about. My father would approve."

"No. That's too risky. We need to keep our investigation under wraps. I think the library should be our next step," Zelda said. There was nothing *too* dangerous about the library.

"Of course. We should probably find out all we can before we continue. If we know what to look for, I can send in an inspector from the labor office."

"Can you send one anonymously?"

Leo's eyes narrowed with playful suspicion. "I'm sure there's a way. Why? Are you nervous?"

Zelda folded her arms. "I'm just not used to ignoring the advice of a professor. I don't break the rules."

"Never?"

"Not if I can help it."

Leo turned toward her. "Trust me. You're in good hands. My life is filled with more rules than you can imagine and I've been bending them since I could talk."

Zelda laughed mirthlessly. "I'm sure you have, but a toe out of line this year could cost me First Fairy."

Leo's side smile dimpled a cheek. "Then we'll be extra careful."

They finished the dishes and took a seat at a small table in the corner of the kitchen, the sweet smell of peaches swelling in the air.

"This reminds me of my parents' kitchen," Zelda said as she settled into her chair, trying to shift the topic away from elves and her general flaunting of Madame LeBleu's guidance. "They love old places."

Leo's brows rose. "Your parents have a professional kitchen?"

"Sort of." She smiled at the memory of the thick plaster walls, of lavender drying in the arched windows. "They own a vineyard and winery in the south of Olisand. The vineyard has a restaurant on the property. It's all part of the wine tourism industry."

Leo leaned an elbow on the table. It was a rather small table, and the posture brought his dimpled smile closer to Zelda. "And was your mother a fairy like yourself?"

"She was the regional godmother of Southern France once she graduated from Madame LeBleu's. That's where she met my dad. She did two tenures in France before they moved to Olisand and bought a vineyard." Zelda's chest fluttered under Leo's gaze. They were supposed to be discussing his Happily Ever After, not her.

"Any siblings?"

"Five of us. All girls."

Leo laughed. "Ouch. And I thought one sister was enough."

Zelda giggled, but then she paused. Could she ask him about his family? It would be polite to ask, but his family was the subject of national headlines on a weekly basis.

He seemed to sense her hesitation. "Go on. You can ask me anything."

Zelda released a slow breath. "How about your family?"

"You've probably heard about them: King Theodore and Queen Antonia of Olisand. They make the papers a lot more than my sister Astara." A slanted little grin formed on Leo's lips.

"She's much younger than you, isn't she?"

"She's ten. We're eight years apart, but she's been watching way too much TV, so she thinks she's a teenager."

"She sounds awesome."

"She is, but you probably know all about my family already. Everyone does." Then his eyes seemed to light up. "I want to know more about Zelda Ravensdale."

Zelda's mouth went dry. *Me?*

The oven timer chimed at the perfect moment to change the subject. Leo crossed to the oven and pulled the golden pie from within. Zelda joined him at the long wooden table at the center of the kitchen. Steam rose off the crust while the overwhelming aroma of peaches made her mouth water.

Leo cut two large slices and slid Zelda her plate. "Don't go easy on me. You won't hurt my feelings if you like Blackbird's pie better."

Zelda dug her spoon through the crust and into the peachy flesh beneath. Leo watched her take a bite, his eyes alight with something Zelda couldn't quite place. Her mouth was too full of crispy crust and soft, tangy peaches to tell him not to watch her eat. She smiled with her mouth closed, savoring the flavors.

Leo wrung his hands on his apron. "Is it terrible?"

Zelda shook her head and swallowed. "*This* is the best peach pie in Erimount." She broke into a laugh at the sight of Leo's relief.

He stuck a spoon in his own piece and took a bite. His eyes widened in delight. "I'm amazing," he said around a mouthful of pie.

Zelda laughed harder and let her shoulder bump into Leo's. She wasn't sure what she'd meant by the gesture, but Leo leaned in, and his arm remained pressed against hers. Zelda's pulse sputtered. Leo turned his head toward her, his lips only inches away. His eyes fluttered closed, and in a moment of panic, Zelda took a giant step back.

"Did you just lean in?" she asked, bewildered, shocked, and the slightest bit breathless. Her heart hammered in her ears. Had she wanted this? She glanced at Leo's lips, pulled up into a charming half-smile. Her stomach gave a flutter that gave way to an ache that seemed to say *yes, please.*

Leo watched her, his cheeks twinged pink. "So, what if I did lean in?"

Zelda took another step back. This time she put a chair between them. "You can't just go and plant a kiss on your fairy godmother."

Leo took a step toward her. "Says who? It wasn't in the rules. Or the contract." He moved the chair aside.

"Says me." She sidled around the table in the center of the kitchen. "I can't have you trying to flirt, kiss, or *whatever* a wish out of me."

"I wasn't going to kiss you," he said.

Zelda's brow furrowed as heat rose to her face. Embarrassment threatened to burn her from the inside out. If she had misread the situation so drastically . . .

Leo smiled. "You had a little sugar on your lip. I was going to wipe it away—"

"With what? Your mouth?" She almost laughed.

"Precisely." His dimples deepened.

"Leo." The name was heavy with reproach, and he stilled. Zelda's heart pounded in her chest as if it tried to push her closer to him with each wrenching thud. "You can't kiss me."

"I promise I'm not trying to kiss you to get a wish." He rounded the corner which left nothing but empty, empty space between them. "I just . . . you look . . ."

"I look like what?" Zelda asked, desperate to hear the end of that statement.

Leo's eyes looked a darker shade of blue as he watched her through lowered lashes. "Beautiful. Kissable." He took a step toward her with each word.

Zelda swallowed hard. "There will be none of that talk either."

Leo heaved a sigh and ran a hand through the waves of his hair. "May I ask why? You don't have to answer if you don't want to. I just thought for sure you felt something too."

I do. I do too. Zelda wanted to confess, but she knew better.

"There are serious ethical implications for me to develop romantic feelings for my godchild. There aren't any official rules against it, but they're mine. Your wish is huge, and the consequences could be too. If by spring you haven't changed your mind, and I agree that to give up your crown would be the best decision for your Happily Ever After, I wouldn't want anyone to question whether our relationship affected how I granted your wish."

Leo nodded. "I see." He laughed. "I was worried it was because you really weren't over Dante or something."

Zelda laughed too. "It's definitely not that." There were no good feelings left there, but she'd just started to regain a feeling of normalcy after Dante. She wasn't sure she was ready to open herself up again. There was also all of her fourth-year coursework and First Fairy and a thousand other "ands." An adorable, kissable prince was at the bottom of her list of priorities.

"I can wait," Leo said. He placed his hand on Zelda's which rested on the table. The heat of Leo's hand on hers shot through her arm. "I'm asking now. No matter how this Happily Ever After shakes out, prince or pauper, I'd like to take you to the Wishmaker Festival Ball with me."

With his hand on hers, Zelda could barely think. "Fairy godmothers don't get to attend balls. We're always working."

"It's months away." Leo cocked his head to the side. "You can't request off?"

"There are too many wishes made that night for one fairy to handle." Zelda withdrew her hand before Leo could stop her. Technically, fourth-year GITs were allowed to request off if they had a date, but Zelda wasn't sure she could trust her heart to agree to a date with Leo—no matter how far away it was. "I don't know. I have to go."

She ducked past Leo, trying to ignore the look of disappointment on his face. His hands were stuffed in his pockets, his shoulders slumped. He had dropped most of his regal bearing, but his eyes still had enough sparkle to make her regret running out. She gave him a smile. "I'll see you at lunch tomorrow?"

"Yeah," he said, his lips lifting at the corners. "I'll be there."

When Zelda returned to her room breathless, she found Imogen sitting on her bed, a pile of books around her. Her eyes went to the clock on her nightstand when Zelda closed the door.

"Where have you been? I was just about to call," Imogen said. "I came back to the room, and you were gone."

"Sorry, I had to do something."

Imogen's eyes narrowed. "Can you be more specific?"

"I needed a library book for our History essay."

Imogen's shoulders slackened, but a worry line creased her forehead. "Oh, okay. Where is it?"

"What?"

"The library book."

Zelda's mouth fell open as she scrambled for an answer. "It was a reference book. I couldn't check it out."

"I see," Imogen said, but she didn't seem convinced.

Fumbling to change the subject, Zelda spotted an unusually large spread of books and cosmetics across Imogen's bed. "And what are you up to?"

"I've got an idea," Imogen said, and her face lit up. "I want to see if I can spell my foundation with a complexion clearing charm. Wouldn't that be amazing?"

Zelda laughed, the sound tight and strangled. "That would be amazing. If you get it to work, will you charm mine too?"

Imogen smiled half-heartedly as if she hadn't yet forgotten about Zelda's disappearance. "Absolutely."

Chapter Fourteen

Eager to be out of the cold, Zelda and Imogen hurried through the dimly lit courtyard of the main EAMS academic building for the Halloween mixer. The gravel path was lined with intricately carved pumpkins, and the rhythmic din of music carried outside the school walls. They entered through the main doors and Zelda found herself in what had once been the foyer.

In keeping with the annual tradition of years past, the tinkers had transformed each of the halls and labs into a spooky and spectacular scene. This year, they'd made the school into a prehistoric jungle complete with mist, giant foliage, and a mechanical brass dinosaur that roared at the entrance.

Imogen squealed in delight and jumped behind Zelda to use her as a shield when a large raptor ducked its head from the cover of the trees to greet them.

"They've outdone themselves this year," Zelda said.

They rushed from the foyer, fearful of finding other monsters in the brush, and followed the flow of students to the main auditorium. Vines hung between dimmed chandeliers, wooden benches had been removed, and the walls were made to look like a dense jungle.

A band of tinkers played music on homemade instruments from a red-curtained stage. Imogen grabbed Zelda by the arm and dragged her into the crush of dancers. Zelda wasn't a fan of dancing, but she knew it was Imogen's favorite, so she swayed along to the song. Her heart gave a funny twinge as she eagerly scanned the crowd for Leo.

Imogen caught her eye and gave a knowing smirk. "Who are you looking for?" she yelled over the music.

"No one." Zelda's pulse raced as a heavy tap landed on her shoulder. Was she really so eager to see Leo?

She turned and found Specs behind her, a grin on his face and glasses perched on his head. He pulled her into a welcome hug that made her feel guilty for hoping he'd been Leo. "This place looks amazing."

"Thanks." Specs glanced at Imogen for her approval as well, but she seemed to be looking for someone in the crowd too. "I'm one of the official 'dinosaur wranglers' for the first half of the night. The giant alligator in the lab keeps getting jammed. You'll have to check it out; we turned the lab into a swamp."

Zelda laughed. "Yes, we will."

Specs turned to Imogen. "You look great."

"Thanks," Imogen said, her head on a swivel. "Have you seen Fletcher?"

Specs' shoulders fell. He glanced at his watch as if to hide his disappointment. "He's working the snack and drink table for the next hour."

Imogen bounded off in search of Fletcher, and Zelda felt a pang of sadness to see Specs look so down. She loved them both, but sometimes they could be oblivious. Specs didn't exactly fit Imogen's type. He didn't look like a guy who could be in a music video, but a number of students had developed crushes on him over the last four years. Zelda suspected the only reason he hadn't turned Imogen's head was because he was too terrified of changing their friendship.

She wound her arm through Specs' and pulled him away from the crowd of dancers. "Come on. I want to see the swamp."

Specs led her out of the auditorium and down a long corridor where a group of tinkers and GITs waited in a short line outside a pair of ornately carved doors that led to the magical mechanics lab.

"It's a ride," Specs explained. "Like at a carnival, but with dinosaurs and stuff. It exits on the other side."

They took their spot at the end of the line and waited as students entered in small groups. The line inched forward as Specs detailed a list of everything he'd helped build for the event.

"It takes the help of the entire school to put this thing together," he said.

Zelda cleared her throat. "Did Leo help out?" She'd wanted to ask about him since she arrived, but she didn't want to seem too eager.

Specs nodded. "He helped lots. It's a shame he couldn't be here tonight."

Zelda wanted to ask why he wasn't at the mixer, but a deep voice behind her made her freeze.

"Hey."

Zelda froze at the sound of Dante's voice. Being stuck in a line with him was the last place she wanted to be. She schooled her lips into a smile and turned to see Dante standing behind her. He wore his usual uniform: blue, collared shirt, crew-neck sweater, and cuffed jeans.

Play it cool, she told herself.

"Hey." Zelda hoped her greeting sounded as aloof as his, but since he was only her first ex, she was woefully underprepared for this sort of interaction.

She made to turn around, but Dante grabbed her arm.

"What do you want?" Angry heat rose in Zelda's face. Around Dante, the concept of aloof seemed to fly out the window.

"Um, Zelda?" Specs placed a protective hand on her shoulder. "Do we have a problem?" His voice hardened as if to warn Dante away.

"I'm fine," Zelda said, hoping Dante wouldn't see how much he bothered her.

"We're going in next," Specs said. He jutted a thumb over his shoulder.

"I need to talk to Zelda, Asher." Dante spat out Specs' surname like it left a bad taste in his mouth.

"No, you don't." Zelda glared at Dante and stepped back to put space between them.

Dante's face softened. "I really need to talk to you. It's important."

Really? What is so important that he needs to talk to me right at this moment?

Curiosity won out and Zelda gave Specs a look that said it was okay for him to join the group ahead of them. He nodded and threw a nervous glance at Zelda before he headed into the swamp. Zelda turned back to face Dante. "What do you want?"

Dante gave her a look of feigned injury. "I can't just come over to catch up? From what I hear, you're having a busy year. Being a fourth-year GIT and all." His voice had gotten all slippery like he meant more than he said.

"You heard this from Susan, I assume?" Zelda casually adjusted the stack of bracelets on her wrist while her heart hammered. What did he mean by "and all"? What had Susan told him? It was easy to assume Susan would've told him about her magic issues. It was impossible he knew about the elves and her troublesome royal godchild.

"Yeah, Susan tells me things. We've been seeing a lot of each other, you know."

Zelda forced an overly pleased smile. "Of course. I gave Susan my permission when she was nice enough to ask for it at the start of the semester."

The smug smile fell from Dante's face. He knew Zelda disliked Susan. If this had been a ploy to make her jealous, it had been a serious miscalculation on his part.

"Oh. Cool," he said with an offhanded shrug. A silence stretched on between them, but he didn't make a move to leave.

What more can he have to say? Did he really just want to catch up or was there actually something important he wanted to tell me?

"Hey, it's your turn," one of the tinkers said, drawing Zelda's attention away from her thoughts.

"After you," Dante said with a slice of a grin. He ushered her into the darkened room with a sweep of his hand, and Zelda's confidence slipped away. All the lights were out save for tiny twinkle lights, which hung from the ceiling to form a semblance of stars in a black sky. Heavy mist filled the entire room, hiding anything more than three feet away from view. A roar filled the foggy air followed by screams.

A mechanical sound came from near them, and Zelda jumped. Out of instinct, she grabbed Dante's arm. He laughed, and she instantly released his sleeve.

"Don't worry. That's just the boat. They're on a track that takes you through the swamp."

"I know," Zelda said as a boat with a flickering lantern hanging over the bow came into view and she cursed her curiosity. She knew how jumpy she got when she was scared. Why hadn't she expected the swamp to be scary? It was Halloween. Of course, the tinkers had made it scary.

Zelda wanted to run and leave Dante behind, but she reminded herself how serious he looked when he'd asked to talk. Her curiosity got the best of her, and she climbed into the boat.

Dante sat beside her. "Please keep your hands and feet inside the ride at all time," he said, mimicking a carnival ride operator.

He grinned at his own silly voice, and Zelda caught herself at the edge of a laugh. Her stomach dropped. The Dante she'd dated was sitting beside her making silly voices. She shook her head as the boat jerked into motion. Had he just dropped this new act of his? He caught her staring, and the rakish smirk reappeared.

The boat pushed aside a row of reeds as it plunged further into the mist.

"What do we need to talk about?" Zelda asked. She flinched as a blade of tall reeds brushed her arm.

Dante sighed, his smirk retreating.

"What?" she snapped. She didn't like how he was looking at her: like how he used to look at her. The swaggering jerk-face had made their breakup easier to understand, easier to move past; he'd changed. *But was that all an act?*

"What are you doing outside of class, Zelda?" he asked.

"You want to hear about my homework assignments?" She narrowed her eyes at him. *That's a pointed question if I've ever heard one.* It put her on her toes.

"No." Dante pushed his fingers through his hair. "I mean, have you made any new friends?"

Leo's face flashed in Zelda's mind. What did he know about Leo? "Why do you care who I spend my time with? In case you don't remember, we aren't together anymore."

A brass bird with long legs appeared from the fog. It tipped forward and dipped its curved beak into the nonexistent water, but Zelda wasn't paying attention. Dante leaned in closer. Even in the dark, Zelda could see the concern written on his face. "It doesn't matter why I care. If my suspicions are right, you're getting quite close to Prince Leopold." His brown eyes poured into her, and Zelda's pulse stuttered.

"Close isn't exactly how I'd describe my relationship with Leo."

"You call him Leo?"

Zelda crossed her arms. "He's a friend."

Dante mimicked her posture, a smile on his lips and a challenge in his eyes. "Whatever you want to call it, I don't care. I'm not here to play the role of jealous ex-lover."

"Then why are you here?" Frustration rose in her chest.

Dante shifted uncomfortably in his seat. He was never uncomfortable. "I wouldn't be able to take it if you were hurt."

"Hurt?" Zelda's voice rose. "Why on earth would I get hurt?"

Dante shook his head. "I don't know."

"It kinda sounds like you do," Zelda retorted.

"The prince is trouble," he blurted. "You shouldn't be getting involved with him. In fact, I think you should get as far away from him as possible."

Zelda searched his face to find the evidence of a lie, mockery, or condescension, but he seemed serious, even concerned. "You're serious? I should stay away from Leo?"

Dante clenched and unclenched his fists. A familiar smirk slipped over his lips. "He's going to use you. That's what people in power do. It's the same for the royal family. They only care about politics and who they can bleed dry before they move on to the next willing victim. You're naive if you think he cares about you."

"You're unbelievable." Zelda jumped as a brass dinosaur appeared. Its tail swished over their heads, and Zelda ducked out of instinct. She was too angry to appreciate the mechanical gears that made the creatures move as if alive. What was wrong with Dante? She couldn't make up her mind whether he was concerned for her, or he just wanted to injure her.

Out of nowhere, the massive jaws of an alligator appeared. It roared and snapped its brass teeth. Zelda jumped, nearly falling from the boat. She collected her breath as the boat pulled up to the exit. It stopped on the tracks, and Zelda clambered out and rushed for the door. She burst into the lighted hall.

Dante's gentle touch on her arm made her stop. She spun on her heel and fixed him with what she hoped was an intimidating glare. "What? What else do you have to say? Because I'm not sure whether you're trying to protect me or insult me. Which is it?"

Dante moved in close. There were other students within earshot now. He slid an arm around Zelda's waist. His hand on the small of her back, he leaned in close to whisper in her ear. "A little of both."

An angry tremble coursed through her limbs, but Dante didn't wait for her reply. He released her and started off toward a group of tinkers down the hall. "You're smart," he threw over his shoulder. "You'll figure it out yourself soon enough. When you do, I won't even say I told you so."

Her face heated, and every nerve ending in her body buzzed with indignation. The need to get away overcame her and she took off in search of the first friendly face she could find. Imogen was easy enough to spot wrapped around Fletcher in an window well. They were still in a lip-lock when Zelda tapped on her shoulder.

"Kinda in the middle of something," Imogen groaned before turning to see Zelda. She must have looked terrible because the moment Imogen's eyes met Zelda's, her face fell. Imogen peeled herself away from Fletcher's muscled arms. "Are you okay?"

"I—" Zelda cut a glance at Fletcher. He was on the rugby team with Dante.

Imogen put a reassuring hand on Zelda's back and led her out of earshot.

"I just had a rather unpleasant encounter with Dante," Zelda said. She wrapped her arms around her waist to stifle the sickening feeling that gathered deep in her gut.

"Dante? I'm so sorry. What happened?"

Zelda tried to find the words to describe their confusing encounter. "I don't even know. He was being weird."

"He didn't hurt you, did he?" Imogen pushed up her sleeves as is she was readying for a fight.

"No. No. He was just Dante, I guess."

"Oh," was Imogen's only reply.

Zelda hated this. She didn't like that Dante could make her feel so unsure of herself, of her judgment. She didn't like that Leo wasn't there to defend himself either. "I think I'm going to go back to our room."

Imogen's face fell. "Are you sure? Do you want me to come with you?"

Zelda shook her head. "It's okay. Have fun."

"Okay then."

But Zelda didn't head back to the dorm. She should've headed straight for the front doors, but instead her feet carried her away from the sounds of the Halloween mixer and deeper into the halls of EAMS.

Zelda pulled out her phone once she was far from prying eyes.

Where are you tonight? she texted Leo.

The hallway was mostly dark. She leaned against the cold stone wall as she waited for his reply. Everything was uneven again. Dante had a way of tipping her world off its axis, and Zelda didn't know how to right it again, to put things back where they belonged. Was she going to cry? The lump in her throat sure made it feel like she could.

Her phone chimed, and relief washed over her as Leo's text broke her downward spiral.

I'm in my dormitory. Felix wasn't comfortable with me going to such a large function yet. Why? Are you missing me?

Zelda couldn't stop the smile that burst onto her lips. She could almost hear the laughter in Leo's words, see the teasing smile on his face.

Can I come see you? Her fingers shook as she typed the words.

Leo's reply came faster this time.

I'd love that.

Chapter Fifteen

Zelda tiptoed through the halls of the Erimount Academy of Magical Sciences as she headed toward the boys' dormitory. The last time she'd ventured this far into EAMS it had been to visit Dante or Specs' room.

She was cutting across the small, manicured lawn of the cloisters when she heard the echoing click of heels from the open arcade. Her heart sputtered at the noise, and she glanced around for a place to hide. She was far from where GITs were supposed to be, so she ducked behind a screen of well-trimmed boxwoods.

The heels stopped, and Zelda held her breath. Heavy footsteps marked the entrance of someone else to the gallery.

"Aurelie," a man's voice broke the silence.

"Rafe—" the headmistress said, frustration audible in her voice.

Is she talking to Lord Scarlet, the headmaster of EAMS?

"I already told you, I'm not getting involved," the man said. Zelda tried to remember what Lord Scarlet looked like. He was quite reclusive, and she'd only caught a glimpse of him on a couple of occasions throughout her time at school.

"We can't sit back and let this sort of thing happen. You can't hide out in this school of yours. What happens in our country's government affects us all," Madame LeBleu said.

"Enough with the dramatics. You and your professors are making something out of nothing."

"Professor Weymouth foresaw—"

Lord Scarlet's voice cut Madame LeBleu short. "Not that charlatan. What will be, will be. My academy has weathered many a storm. A shift in the monarchy is nothing."

Are they talking about Leo?

Madame LeBleu huffed. "For you and your financial backers, I'm sure."

"I've heard enough. I won't criticize how you run your school if you won't criticize how I run mine," Lord Scarlet said with finality and he and Madame LeBleu left the cloister in opposite directions.

At the sound of feet rustling on grass, Zelda pressed herself deeper into the hedge, desperate not to be caught eavesdropping. The light of the moon caught Lord Scarlet's face as he stalked across the lawn. He was a tall, slender man with a fair complexion. Graying blond hair and blue eyes. He was more handsome than she remembered, but also more severe. His nose was straight, and his mouth was set in a firm line.

Shivering, Zelda hurried away from the lawn and down the hall toward the dormitories.

Leo's room was easy enough to find. The doors were each labeled with the occupants' names. Zelda knocked quickly, eager to avoid another run-in with a school administrator. Leo opened the door with a grin and yanked her inside. He shut the door behind her as she took in the room.

It was long and narrow with a twin bed, desk, and wardrobe against each wall. The right side of the room looked unoccupied, but the wall above the bed to the left was covered with an assortment of maps. The best part was the smell. Zelda inhaled deeply. Most boys' rooms smelled of unwashed gym clothes and microwave mac and cheese. Leo's room smelled of old wood, expensive cologne, and freshly laundered shirts.

Leo leaned against the door and watched as she examined his room, his dimples bookending his smile.

"How is it you managed to get a single room?" she asked.

Leo laughed. "I didn't. That's Felix's half of the room. He's not much of a decorator." He pushed off from the door. "Why did you need to see me, Zelda?"

"I needed to clear my head."

"Did something happen tonight?" Leo took a seat on his bed and motioned for her to join him. With legs crossed in front of him, he propped his back against a constellation map.

Zelda hesitated. Her hands tugged awkwardly at the twirly skirt of her blue velvet skater dress. She couldn't remember the last time she'd been on a boy's bed. *Stop being ridiculous.* She slipped off her shoes and seated herself at the foot of the bed. It was easier said than done in a dress with a short skirt.

Leo had long legs, and even with them crossed he took up a large portion of the bed. Zelda tried to make herself smaller with her feet tucked underneath her, but her knee somehow still brushed against Leo's leg. She ignored the rush of feeling deep in her gut when Leo's eyes flicked to where she'd touched him.

"I ran into Dante tonight."

Leo's lips pressed into a frown.

"Actually, I think he might have found me on purpose," Zelda said.

"What did he want?"

Zelda folded her arms and kept her eyes on the map of the November sky behind Leo's head. "He was all concerned about me spending time with you. He seems to think I'll get hurt."

Leo's eyes fell to his lap. "What do you think?"

"I think he doesn't know you like I do."

Leo didn't reply, and they fell silent. They hadn't been alone like this since he'd tried to kiss her. His schoolwork, crew team practice, and royal duties on top of it all had made sure of that. Zelda had explored every corner of the library stacks with him looking for any form of literature on elves, but a curious Imogen or Felix had never been far away.

So far, Leo had respected her rules and had, for all intents and purposes, seemed to put his romantic feelings on pause. He hadn't even brought up his invitation to the Wishmaker Festival Ball. But the unspoken hung heavily in the air now that they were alone.

Leo cleared his throat. "Well, I'm glad his concerns seem to have been ignored." He tried to flash her a confident grin, but he wavered. Blotches of red colored his cheeks. "So, I've been meaning to ask about our investigation. Have you had any more luck researching on your own?"

Zelda shook her head. "No. I think we've exhausted the school collections."

"Then the time has come to take bolder action," Leo said. "I think we should revisit the idea of taking a factory tour."

"But we're not supposed to be interfering, remember?"

"We're not interfering." Leo's smile widened and a sparkle returned to his eyes. "We're simply conducting a parallel investigation."

"I don't know." Zelda tucked her hair behind her ears.

"Come on. You can't make Happily Ever Afters on the sidelines. Get off the bench, Zelda Ravensdale."

Every fiber of her being told her to say no. To do as she was told and keep the prince away from the elves.

"I'll put it this way then," Leo said. "Can we trust your professors? Implicitly?"

Zelda hesitated. She wanted to say yes, but she wasn't sure. Madame LeBleu and the other teachers seemed trustworthy to some degree, but after what she'd just overheard in the cloisters, any one of them could have an agenda of their own. "Maybe we should keep working—just in case they miss something."

Leo bit his lip to hide a smile. "I was hoping you'd agree with me. We can still keep this on the down low. A tour of the factory to shake hands and kiss-up to an influential family is exactly the sort of royal frippery that's expected of me."

"It's not a bad idea," Zelda admitted.

"It's settled then. I'll get Felix to add it to my schedule." He slid off his bed and moved to open the door for her. "If that's all we needed to talk about . . ."

Something compelled Zelda to stay where she was. "You know, I don't have to be anywhere before curfew."

Leo froze with his hand on the doorknob. The smile he threw her over his shoulder was a dazzling thing. "We could watch a movie. Or would that cause Dante too much concern?" He turned and tucked his hands into his pockets.

Zelda sat a little taller. "I would love that."

Leo pulled out a laptop. "What do you want to watch?"

"What's your absolute favorite?"

"My *absolute* favorite?" Leo grinned, a blush coloring his cheeks. "It's really old. And black-and-white."

"If it's your favorite, then I have to see it."

"Well, if you're sure." Leo angled his laptop toward the bed.

Zelda turned to rest her back against the wall. "I'm sure." After he started the movie, Leo rejoined her, only this time he sat close enough that his shoulder rested against hers. She tried to settle her mind and pay attention to the film, but she couldn't focus on anything besides the warmth Leo's arm spread into hers. *I should move.* It took every ounce of her will to shift away from him, but it didn't relax her in the way she'd hoped. She'd left a charged empty space between them that begged to be closed.

Does he feel it too? She snuck a glance at Leo from the corner of her eye and caught the whisper of a smile on his lips.

He moved a hand from his lap and let it rest on the bed just inches from where Zelda's hand gripped the hem of her skirt. Zelda's fingers tingled at the open invitation, but she wouldn't let herself take it.

He didn't move it for the duration of the film as if to say, *whenever you're ready, I'm here.*

Chapter Sixteen

It took Leo two weeks to find a gap in his schedule to get a closer look at the finer details of St. Germain's operations. He'd requested a tour of the emporium but was instead offered a tour of the factory itself. On the evening after his tour, Zelda tried to focus on her spell drills. She texted him asking how it went right after the scheduled time, but she hadn't heard from him. How had Leo's first contact with George St. Germain gone? Her phone sat beside her, maddeningly silent. She wanted to nudge him for a reply, but she didn't want to double-text him and seem desperate.

Despite the distractions and an endless stream of giggles from the common room, Zelda's drills went well until Maud Woods burst into their room. "Come quick. Susan is on the news with Prince Leo."

Was this news about his tour? Susan hadn't been part of Leo's plan. Zelda looked nervously between her phone and the list of spell drills on her desk.

Imogen sensed her hesitation. "Come on. Homework can wait. Let's just watch to see if Susan makes a fool of herself."

Imogen pulled Zelda into the common area. The common room was part of the dormitory's towering entrance hall. The long room with vaulted ceilings was divided into smaller areas by large ornate rugs. The study areas at each end of the room sandwiched a lounge area with large groupings of leather chairs and a TV mounted above a massive stone fireplace. A banner hung above, emblazoned with the Madame LeBleu's crest. GITs crowded the TV while the dorm matron sat at the front desk with her face buried in a glossy tabloid that claimed to have leaked medical records detailing the king's secretive ailments.

Zelda and Imogen squeezed together into the only remaining armchair—the one with the farthest view of the screen.

Maud perched herself on the arm of their chair. "Susan's segment will be on after this commercial break."

Susan sat toward the front of the room where a group of her friends peppered her with questions.

"What was he like?"

"Was he nice?"

"Do you think he's going to ask you out?"

Susan, looking pleased with all the attention, answered each question with carefully crafted half-answers that left girls begging for more. Leo's dimpled, smiling face appeared on the television and ended the inquiry when several girls collapsed into giggles.

As the news segment started, Zelda wondered if anything she could glimpse during the broadcast would confirm what they'd seen in the window of the store. The prince and the media entourage were somewhere outside the city of Erimount in front of an old Tudor-style building that sat amid the rolling green foothills of the Black Forest Mountains across the border. It didn't look large enough to house a massive shoe manufacturing operation, but it was rumored that most of the St. Germain's factory ran underground.

Leo gave the gathered crowd a graceful wave, and the news anchors took turns making comments on his choice of clothing and whether he had developed the bearing of a king. Beside him stood George St. Germain and Susan. Zelda could see where Susan got her looks. Her father was pale skinned with grayish blond hair and kind, crinkled eyes.

The cameras moved in tight as Leo said something to Susan that made her laugh.

"What did he say? What did he say?" a chorus of girls asked.

Susan grinned and blushed demurely. "I probably shouldn't tell you."

Zelda didn't like the way a twinge of jealousy shivered over her skin when Leo offered Susan his arm and they ascended the steps to the factory doors.

Zelda wanted to look away from the screen but couldn't. Susan already had Dante. Now she was flipping her hair and batting her eyes at Leo? Several students glanced at Zelda to see her reaction; she was practically the only GIT who ever hung out with Leo. She wrestled her features into a mask of emotional indifference. Leo wasn't hers in a romantic sense, but it stung to think of Susan taking something else from her. He was her godchild and she'd sworn to protect him, but he was also a friend.

That was it.

The news channel showed clips of Leo as he walked through the main factory floor and the ordinary, human, non-pointy-eared workers eyed the camera nervously. The anchors talked labor policy over the montage of Leo shaking hands, asking questions, and nodding his head along to their answers. To Zelda, the prince looked regal, but approachable, which seemed to put the workers at ease. He'd made her feel the same at their first meeting.

The broadcast cut to a dazzling showroom and a brief clip of an impassioned speech about labor rights that Leo gave at the end of the tour. Zelda's chest swelled with pride. She was now part of his future and it was her job to make sure he got his Happily Ever After.

The broadcast ended and Zelda returned to her room before she had to listen to more of Susan's commentary on Leo. Zelda checked her phone to find a missed call and two messages from Leo.

8:15 p.m.: **Sorry I didn't reply to your text. I went to the castle for my weekly dinner with my father right after the tour. He wanted to be debriefed and to critique my every move. He just finished. I'm staying at the castle tonight or I'd come see you. The tour of the factory was interesting. We need to talk ASAP.**

8:30 p.m.: **What are you doing? Can you call me when you get my texts?**

Zelda smiled to herself. He had totally double-texted her.

I can't call. Imogen's in the room. What's up? I can't wait to hear about the tour.

Leo's reply was instantaneous. **The tour wasn't as informative as I thought it would be.**

Zelda sighed. **So no proof? Maybe St. Germain doesn't know about the elves in his shop. I wish he would've given you a tour of the emporium.**

Zelda started her spell drills again, but she kept her phone close.

I didn't see any indication of elves, but there was something strange about that place.

What do you mean? The factory had looked perfectly normal from behind a television screen, but Zelda had to admit that she'd been distracted by how well Leo carried himself during a public appearance. It was such a difference from the boy who rolled up his sleeves to stress bake and loved watching black-and-white movies. He wasn't different in public in a bad way. She liked both sides of him.

Leo's text took a while to come through, like he was trying to put something together he didn't understand. **It was like Disneyland.**

Zelda laughed but stifled it when Imogen glanced up from her ethics book. **Disneyland?**

Like it was made to look like a shoe factory—you know, staged just a little too well.

That's interesting. Maybe it was all for your benefit.

Maybe. Leo answered.

Make sure to write down everything you saw so we—

"Who are you texting over there?" Imogen said from her bed, an arch grin on her lips. "You're smiling like you're talking to a guy."

Zelda's pulse fluttered. "No one—one of my sisters," she answered, but her voice wavered.

The smile fell off Imogen's face and was replaced by something that looked more like hurt. Zelda wanted to tell Imogen what was going on, but the privacy of Leo's wish and the true nature of their relationship was at stake. Thankfully, Imogen didn't ask any follow-up questions, and they both silently returned to their studies.

Imogen was in a strangely foul mood the rest of the week.

"Are we going to talk about why you're being weird?" Imogen said out of nowhere as they stopped to get water during fencing team practice. The evening sun threw long panels of light across the gym floor. The athletic facilities were technically part of the EAMS campus, and they had the heavy, Victorian Gothic features to match—vaulted ceilings and pointed arches.

Zelda's stomach jumped into her throat. "What are you talking about?" She pulled on her mask before Imogen could see her cheeks flush.

"I don't know," Imogen said. "I've noticed Prince Leopold has a way of finding us, finding you. 'Help me figure out how to check out books, Zelda.'" She mimicked Leo's deep voice. "And you're always slipping off somewhere or texting *nobody*."

"I think Prince Leopold just wants some friends." She made sure not to call him Leo.

Imogen let out a loud cackle. "Don't get me wrong, we're awesome. But don't you think it's crazy that out of all the students between EAMS and Madame LeBleu's, he's chumming it up with us?"

Zelda tried a nonchalant shrug. "I don't think it's crazy."

"So, where did you go after the Halloween mixer? I stopped by the room to get a bigger coat before I went out to The Swan and Raven with Fletcher. You weren't there—and don't give me that line about the library again. If you're sneaking off to be with Dante—"

"No," Zelda said. "He's with Susan now, remember?"

"I don't care who he's with. I want to know what you're keeping from me. I thought we could trust each other with anything?"

"It's complicated. You know I'd trust you with anything, right?"

Imogen didn't answer. She turned on her heel and stalked to the farthest piste, away from their teammates and the coaches.

Imogen settled into en garde. She raised her foil to signal she was ready for the bout. Zelda did the same, and they both brought their swords down with a swish to signal the start. Imogen advanced and lunged first, but Zelda was quick to retreat and parry.

Zelda turned her block into a jab at Imogen's shoulder.

Imogen dodged the tip of Zelda's foil with a dancer's leap. "If you trust me, why haven't you told me what's going on? Unless you can't tell me."

"I can't tell you all of it." Zelda moved so Imogen's thrust missed her waist. She used her blade to knock Imogen's away and took the opening for a riposte and landed a point on Imogen's chest. They stopped to reset. "But I think I can tell you some of it."

Imogen lowered her foil. "What? There's really something going on?"

Zelda closed the distance between them, and they pulled off their masks. "You can't tell anyone . . . I'm Leo's fairy godmother, and that's all I can say about that," she whispered.

Imogen nodded. "I see." It was considered bad form to talk to anyone about a particular godchild's wish. "And that's it?"

Zelda grimaced. "There's more."

"More?" Imogen's eyes widened.

"We may have discovered the existence of a race of fairy tale creatures . . . and Leo tried to kiss me."

"Prince Leopold tried to kiss you?" she whispered.

"Well, he just leaned in—"

"You know it's frowned on to be involved with a godchild, right?" Imogen asked. "Not that I'm judging. Prince Leopold leaned in to kiss you."

"No. I know. That's exactly what I told him."

Imogen's mouth pulled into a smirk. "Can't you just grant his wish and then lay a kiss on him? What's taking you so long?"

Zelda pulled Imogen off the piste to get another drink of water so they wouldn't be scolded by their coach for standing around and talking. "It's a complicated wish. That's all I can say. Did you hear what I said about discovering a race of magical creatures?"

"Oh yeah. What is that about?"

"Leo went with me to get potion supplies earlier this semester. We had to talk about wishing stuff, and we saw an elf polishing shoes in the window of St. Germain's."

A worry line formed between Imogen's brows. "An elf?"

"Yeah, she had pointed ears and couldn't have been taller than eight inches."

"Wow. I thought they were long gone—if they ever were around. My halmi used to tell me a story about elves when she told me the fairy stories her grandma used to tell her."

"I'm glad you don't think I'm losing it."

"You're yampy for not kissing the prince at least once, but if you say you discovered a race of elves sneaking around in St. Germain's, then I believe you."

"Really? Cause I think Leo and I are going to need some help."

"Help with what?" Imogen took a swig from her water bottle. "I mean, whatever you need from me, I can help."

Zelda's chest swelled. She hadn't expected Imogen to brush her off, but it was nice to be reminded how much she could lean on her. It'd been hard to keep so much to herself. "Thanks. You're really amazing."

Imogen's lips cracked into a grin. "And don't forget it."

"I won't. We have no idea what an elf was doing in St. Germain's, but it raises some questions."

Imogen snickered. "I feel like that would be common knowledge if they were using elves to run the store."

"Right? That was our thinking. As far as anyone knows, elves don't exist. It's now up to you, Leo, and me to find definitive proof that George St. Germain is harboring them."

"Do you think maybe he's keeping them safe?"

Zelda paused. "I hadn't thought of that, but this girl was smudged head to toe with shoe polish and jumped at the sight of us. It wasn't exactly the picture of great working conditions."

"Then we need to figure out what's going on," Imogen said with a definitive nod.

Chapter Seventeen

Professor Nutt gave Zelda a warning glare when she slipped into ethics class after the starting bell.

"Now that Ms. Ravensdale has joined us, we can begin," Professor Nutt said. Zelda ignored the jab. At least she hadn't gotten a demerit. The professor fiddled with the spring-loaded projector screen before it snapped upward into its case above the blackboard. A question had been hidden behind the screen.

What does it mean to be a fairy godmother?

Professor Nutt read the question aloud. "You will have to answer this question in your own words for your final evaluation with the International Council of Godmothers. It is always the final question on the test, and it should be the easiest. After years in my class, every fairy in the granter track should have a clear idea of what this job would mean to you."

Zelda wrote the question in her notebook.

"Being a fairy godmother can accomplish a lot of things. It can bring you fame and fortune, but those things will not sustain you throughout your tenure unless you have a reason for what you do. When you begin your placement, the ICG will pay you a stipend and find you housing, but from the moment you begin, the territory is yours. Your predecessor will advise you during the first year, but beyond that, it is up to each godmother to determine how she manages wish granting in her territory."

They broke into discussion groups to talk about the meaning of godmothering before they wrote their practice essays.

"Do you think godmothers really get famous in their region?" Imogen asked as they pushed their desks together with Ava and Maud.

"Definitely," Ava said. "In America, godmothers are practically celebrities."

The thought of using her position for fame made Zelda's stomach churn. "Who would want that? People demanding wishes wherever you go?"

Maud snorted. "That sounds awful. I'd much rather be at the ICG offices analyzing wishes and passing them on to the field workers. You couldn't pay me to be a granter." Maud was in the godchild management track.

Zelda underlined the question in her notebook anxiously as a clear answer eluded her.

Imogen straightened confidently in her desk. "I'm not going to be famous," she declared. "But I *am* going to be free. That's why I'm going to be a Happily Ever Specialist. You're responsible for you and your godchildren. That's it."

They looked to Zelda, but she wasn't sure how to respond. Wanting to be a fairy godmother because her mom was one suddenly didn't seem like such a great reason anymore. Maybe she really did want prestige. She'd watched all of her sisters become top granters with the ICG. Three of the five now had degrees in advanced magical arts.

Maybe it wasn't about following in their footsteps. Maybe it was a way to become a part of all the fairy stories she'd read growing up. Maybe it was okay not to have a specific answer, but Zelda still didn't like not having one.

When she didn't chime in with what being a godmother meant to her, they all started writing out their answers.

After class, Imogen hooked her arm through Zelda's as they left the academic building to head to lunch. "Is Leo going to be at dinner tonight?" she whispered. "We need to start making plans to prove your elves exist."

They followed a stream of GITs toward the dining hall, but a bitter wind nipped at their ears and carried their voices away.

"He has a state dinner tonight."

Imogen snorted. "I don't know how he gets his homework done with everything he does."

Zelda shook her head. "I don't either. His parents haven't let him slow down with his royal obligations."

Imogen leaned in closer. "I forgot to tell you. Specs told me Dante has started hanging around Leo lately."

"What?" Zelda exclaimed and several heads snapped to look in their directions. Hadn't Dante just warned her away from Leo?

Imogen nodded and lowered her voice. "It looks like he's trying to cozy up to him, but Leo's figured out that Dante will leave him alone if he's around Specs."

"Why does Dante want to be friends with Leo?" Zelda asked as they jogged up the steps to the dining hall, desperate to be out of the cold.

Imogen shrugged and pulled Zelda around a first-year who had spilled the contents of her potion kit right inside the doors. "Power. Influence. So he can brag about it to anyone bored enough to listen. Some people have no class."

They stopped to help the flustered, red-faced first-year chase the last of the vials that had rolled out of her reach. Zelda didn't know what to think. Imogen's explanation was highly plausible based on Dante's recent behavior. But after Dante had just warned her away from Leo at Halloween, it seemed like Dante was up to something.

They handed the first-year her potion ingredients and found a table to drop their bags.

"Well, Dante may not be a problem for much longer," Imogen whispered.

"What?"

"He's failing out—at least that's the rumor going around EAMS. He's been in and out of Lord Scarlet's office all semester. Word is that he may not come back after break."

"Woah," Zelda muttered.

As if on cue, Dante blew in through the other doors to the dining hall like a slow summer breeze. Easy and self-assured, he sank into the open chair next to Susan. The idea of Dante getting kicked out of school was unsettling. She didn't mind the idea of Dante leaving, but Zelda didn't like that she may never have really understood the intelligent boy she'd dated for a year.

Zelda was so engrossed in her potions homework that the tap on her dormitory window made her jump. She gasped when she found Leo smiling at her from out in the courtyard. He waved, and Zelda pushed open the window.

"Hey," Leo said.

The cool December air sent shivers over Zelda's skin. "What are you doing here?" she asked, then noticed his navy-blue tuxedo. "Did you come straight from that state dinner?"

His breath puffed out in diaphanous clouds. "Can I come in? It's freezing out here."

Zelda hesitated. "Guests aren't allowed in the dorms on school nights."

He glanced over his shoulder to check that the courtyard was empty. "Can I sneak in?" Leo's brows raised suggestively.

Zelda had to bite back a smile, but she nodded and opened the window wider. Leo clambered through the window, toppling a cup of highlighters and a lamp from her desk on his way in.

Leo straightened his tux and looked at Zelda with a smile that made her regret sneaking him into her room. "Climbing through a window is harder than it looks. Did I at least look cool doing it?"

Zelda laughed. "No. No, you didn't." She shut the window behind him and pulled the curtains closed.

Leo's eyes crinkled at the corners. "I thought the tuxedo would've helped."

Zelda shook her head. "What are you doing here?"

She sank onto her bed, but having a boy in her room made her jump at every sound in the hall.

Leo kicked off his polished shoes and joined her on the bed. "I thought you'd be interested in what happened at the state dinner tonight."

"I am," Zelda said. "But Imogen is working on calculus homework in the common room, and she'll be back soon."

"I'll make this quick if I must. I also thought since you saw my room, it was only fair I see yours." He didn't seem eager to leave as he settled in against the wall. "I met someone interesting at the dinner—the head of the Ministry of Labor."

"Was that so interesting that it warranted breaking the rules to tell me in person?" she teased. Sitting so close on her bed, Leo's smile was familiar in the most comforting of ways. Those dimples could make her forget all about charm drills and practice exams. And the tailoring of his suit did wonderful favors to his figure which made him the best kind of study break.

"We talked about workers' rights and labor reform and all the political talking points that I'm supposed to touch on at these events, but something she said intrigued me. Apparently, anyone can make an anonymous tip to the ministry's tip line if they feel workers are being treated unfairly."

Zelda's heart skipped a beat as she realized where Leo was going with this. "What happens if we tip them off about St. Germain's?"

"They would send someone out for a surprise inspection." Leo looked pleased with himself. "I told you how staged the factory tour looked."

"A surprise inspection would catch them off guard." Zelda didn't bother to hide the excitement in her voice.

A grin flashed across Leo's face. "I already called it in."

"Leo," Zelda scolded and hit him lightly on the arm.

Leo's grin fell. "What? I thought this was a good thing."

"You called the tip line tonight? Right after talking to the head of the ministry? What if someone traces it back to you?" Zelda pushed her loose hair behind her ears.

"It's anonymous remember?" Leo placed a reassuring hand on the bed just inches from hers.

His hand was there for the taking. Zelda's fingers prickled teasingly at the invitation. Everything in her wanted to take his hand, but she knew she shouldn't. "You should've let me do it."

"Well . . ." Leo withdrew his hand and pushed his fingers through his hair. "I was mad."

Zelda sat up. "At what?"

The joy left Leo's face as he remembered something. He shook his head as if to chase it away. "It's my dad. He was in one of his moods, which means he was on my case all night."

"About what?" Zelda leaned closer, eager to know everything about Leo's difficult relationship with his dad. His dad's approval was one of the reasons he wanted to give up his crown. It was for his Happily Ever After, of course, but deep in her gut, she cared about his hurts in a way that made her physically ache.

"Tonight, it was everything. My slouching, my manners, my hair, my blue tux, my socializing. It was awful. Apparently, my cousin, the Duke of Brockford has been lambasting me and my father to anyone who will listen."

Zelda froze at the mention of Brockford.

"And he's taking out his frustration on me like *I'm* the weak link. My mom tried to get him to let up, but I eventually couldn't take it anymore, so I just left and came straight here."

"You just left?"

Leo's deep-blue eyes met hers. "He can be so toxic. I had to get out."

Something fluttered in Zelda's chest. "And you came here."

Leo sensed what she meant. She hadn't phrased it as a question, but her statement still begged to be answered. "Of course I came here. Being around you—you're so hopeful. You have so much purpose. You make me feel like I have purpose too."

Warmth swelled in Zelda's chest. "I think you bring that out in me too," she whispered.

Leo opened his mouth like he had something more to say, but instead he glanced at his watch. "I should get going before I get you in trouble."

Zelda wrapped her arms around herself. "Imogen won't care." The sound of girls giggling and running down the hall made Zelda wish she'd locked their door. But nobody locked their doors. A locked door would only draw more attention to the boy hidden in her room. "The dorm matron might, but—"

I don't want you to go.

Leo waited as if he wanted to know what came after that "but."

Zelda willed her lips to move, but she'd lost her nerve. Instead, she slid off the bed and tugged her desk away from the window so Leo could climb out more easily this time.

"I guess we just have to wait and see what comes of your anonymous tip," Zelda said.

Leo seemed to understand that this was goodbye, so he clambered over the sill. Before he slid off the ledge and into the night, he stopped. Everything slowed. He touched the top of Zelda's hand where it rested against the window frame. Just the brush of his fingertips sent a ripple of shivers up her arm.

"This was the best part of my day," he said.

Zelda didn't draw away. When Leo slipped her hand into his, she found her nerve. "We need to find time for more of this."

"I agree," he said.

Despite the cold air that seeped through her clothes, Zelda didn't want Leo to go. She didn't want to go back to textbooks and essays. Schoolwork only reminded her of First Fairy and doing what was expected of her. But there was more at stake now—elves and political conspiracies that she was supposed to be keeping the prince away from. *Be a good girl. Keep your head down. Study hard.* That's what her mom and dad told her every Sunday when they called to hear about her week. But Leo was right, she had purpose now.

And she knew what to do with it.

Chapter Eighteen

The picture made it look way worse than it was.

Zelda couldn't believe her eyes when she opened social media first thing in the morning. The photo was grainy, but there, plain as day—Leo climbing out of her window. One leg in and one leg out, he balanced on the sill, his profile lit by the glow of Zelda's room. Someone had been watching all of it through a telephoto lens.

"Creep," Zelda said under her breath.

At least from the angle of the photo, Leo's arm, propped against the window frame, blocked Zelda's face from view. It could be any girl in the photo, and it was zoomed in far enough that it could be any first-floor window. That was a blessing. The headlines were not.

Playboy Prince Skips Out on State Dinner for a Secret Rendezvous.

His Grace Makes a Less-than-Graceful Exit.

Prince Leopold Caught Sneaking out of Mystery Coed's Room.

A guttural groan came from Zelda's throat—a sound loud and strange enough to wake Imogen.

"Wha?" Imogen mumbled.

"This is so bad."

Imogen threw off her quilt and slouched over to Zelda's bed. She snuggled up to Zelda's side and put her head on her shoulder. "What's so bad?"

Zelda held the phone for Imogen to see.

Imogen had to squint to see the screen without her contacts in. "Is that Prince Charming?"

"Mmhmm."

Imogen's head popped off Zelda's shoulder. "And that's our room. You sly dog."

"No. It wasn't that. We were just talking."

"Right." Imogen drew out the word to mean she was highly skeptical. "So, he snuck into our room because his phone wasn't working?"

"He had some important news about the elves." Zelda didn't have a good answer for why she let Leo sneak into their room instead of talking to him over the phone. She tucked her hair behind her ears and quickly changed the subject. "So far it looks like only we know where he was. No one's tagged me in a post about it."

Imogen scoffed. "People may still think it's you. He talks to you all the time."

Zelda crawled out of her bed and fisted her hands in her hair. "I don't care if people think it was me. Leo is going to get in so much trouble. He's already pushing his dad's limits by insisting on going to EAMS for his final year of schooling."

"It's just the gossip rags tweeting about it right now. It's not even major news. It'll blow over with the next news cycle. You'll see."

Zelda's stomach was in knots, but not for her sake. She could earn a demerit for sneaking a boy in, but she was more worried about what Leo's dad would do. The thought of Leo being pulled from EAMS was far worse than a demerit now.

"I hope you're right."

The news traveled fast, but aside from a stern reminder about dormitory visitation rules during morning announcements, Zelda had avoided detection. All morning, professors had difficulty keeping their classes in order as speculation about the mystery girl and the prince passed around in furtive whispers. Zelda couldn't shake her nerves. She'd yet to hear back from Leo whether he was okay. She was so distracted that during demonstrations in charms class, her pumpkin didn't turn into a carriage. Instead, it exploded and spewed slimy pumpkin guts on the entire class.

To Zelda's mortification, girls were still picking pumpkin seeds from their hair when they arrived to history class. Professor Weymouth entered, briefcase in hand. His gaze met Zelda's as she tried to ignore the loud complaints from her classmates about the lingering smell of pumpkin. He gave her a wry smile that seemed to convey his sympathy before he silenced the class with a cough.

"Distractions aside, we have lots to cover today." Professor Weymouth picked up a piece of chalk, flipped it skillfully between his fingers and wrote on the board. "We're covering the First International Magic Conference of 1702. This was a pivotal moment in the movement for fairy godmothers' rights, and it's almost always included in the written portion of your ICG certification exam. You'll want to take extra notes today."

By the end of the lesson, Zelda had filled three pages of her composition book with statutes of wish privacy and wishmaker limitations. Professor Weymouth stopped the class a few minutes before the ending bell. "I believe Miss Pickett has an announcement about the Wishmaker Festival Follies."

Iris bounded to the front of the room. "As you know, every spring, Madame LeBleu's and EAMS puts together the Wishmaker Festival Follies for the first night of the festival." Her mousy blond ponytail swished behind her as she spoke animatedly. "Each class must put together a ten-minute skit or feat of talent, and we need to get working on ours. Madame Olivier has put me in charge of our skit."

Of course. Iris was a first soprano and the uncontested darling of the choir director, Madame Olivier.

Iris placed a clipboard on the desk nearest to her. "Please sign up with any hidden talents you might possess and the best times you are available to rehearse on Saturdays. I already know which parts you all sing, so there's no need to put that down." She heaved a dramatic sigh and looked at Zelda. "And remember, participation is mandatory."

Zelda broke into a sweat at the idea of singing on stage. Madame Olivier had tried to coax a tune out of Zelda with religious fervor, but after two years without success, she reluctantly deemed Zelda completely tone deaf and lacking all rhythm. For the past three years, she'd been intentionally positioned in the back and commanded to mouth the words only.

"Zelda couldn't find a harmony if it arrived at her doorstep in a pumpkin carriage," Madame Olivier wrote in a note to Madame LeBleu to permanently excuse Zelda from choir class. She sometimes wondered if Madame LeBleu had the note in her permanent file.

The bell rang while the clipboard was still being passed around. Zelda received it last, but she still wasn't sure what to write down as a special talent. *Exploding pumpkins, perhaps?* Instead, she put down "costumes" in the hopes she wouldn't actually have to appear on stage.

On her way out the door, Iris stopped her. "Hey, Zelda, quick sidebar?"

Sidebar? Zelda held back an eye roll. "What's up, Iris?"

Iris gave her a brilliantly toothy grin. "So listen . . ." From the nervous look on her face, it was clear she wasn't sure how to politely say she didn't want Zelda messing up the fourth-years' act. "You're friends with Thaddeus Asher from EAMS."

"Specs."

"What? Oh yeah, that's what you guys call him. Anyway, it was the headmistress's idea to put together a combined act with the tinkers in addition to our other act for the Follies this year. Lord Scarlet put forth Thaddeus, and he said he'd be willing to work with us on it. I thought you might want to work with Specs on a special act—"

"Yes," Zelda said before Iris could even finish. She was glad for any opportunity to be in control of her theatrical fate. Plus, she knew Specs wouldn't force her to sing, dance, or balance a spinning plate on a broom.

"Wonderful." Iris looked just as relieved as Zelda. She collected the clipboard and bounced into the hall.

After classes ended for the day, Zelda met Specs at their usual booth in the corner of the Blackbird Café. A glance at the tiny table at the front window reminded her of Leo. The memory made her itch to pull her phone out and check for a reply she knew wouldn't be there.

Specs examined a notebook spread out before him, a tepid-looking cup of tea forgotten beside him.

His face lit up when she slid onto the seat beside him. "I didn't even see you come in."

Zelda gave him a slightly awkward side hug thanks to the tightness of the booth. "You were studying so intently, I couldn't resist sneaking up on you."

She stood to go order a coffee, but Specs pulled her back down. "Wait. We need to talk about why the prince was sneaking out of your room last night."

Zelda's mouth fell open. "How did you—"

"Well, I'm pretty sure you're Leo's closest friend at school."

"It wasn't how it looks." Zelda held up her hands in defense. "He needed to vent."

Specs shrugged. "If that's what you say, I believe you."

"I'm glad you don't jump to conclusions." She paused. "Was he in class today?"

Specs shook his head. "I haven't seen him at all." He blew on his tea before realizing it had gone cold and he downed a large gulp.

"Thanks." Zelda was glad Specs indulged her curiosity without forming judgments about her relationship with Leo. She pulled out her phone and typed a new text to Leo.

Please just let me know you're alive, okay?

"Should we talk about the Follies?" Zelda said. "Do you have any ideas for a combined act for a tinker and a GIT?"

Specs shifted in his seat, an anxious grin on his face. He ran a thumb over his upper lip. "After doing some research on the properties of wand-making, I think we could find a way to meld tinkering and fairy magic," he gestured between Zelda and himself, "into one."

"One what?"

Specs dragged his hand across his jaw. "That's up to us. I was thinking a stage magic show, but instead of tricks and sleight of hand, it's real magic."

Zelda laughed. "So, like, pulling a rabbit out of a hat?"

"Exactly. But we can find something more interesting than that."

Specs beamed with excitement, but something urged Zelda to be careful. "I'm not sure. Magic is dangerous enough as it is. Trying to combine it with anything to make it function outside of a fairy and her wand is risky."

Specs flipped to a blank page in his notebook and took a pen from the pocket of his scarlet blazer. "Okay, but what about a simple transportation charm?"

Zelda shook her head. "There's nothing simple about a transportation charm. Besides, I can't travel using magic until I have my wings."

"Then how do you travel by phone?"

"It's charmed."

"So, what if we created the transportation charm, but with tinkering?"

Zelda still wasn't convinced.

"What if we didn't transport a person. Would you be more comfortable if we made someone's handkerchief appear in a box?"

Zelda bit her bottom lip. It sounded less risky if it was just a square of fabric, but also much less interesting. Was she being too cautious? She didn't want to let her own magic troubles hold them back. "Perhaps a transportation box will be fine. We'll need plenty of practice," she mused. "And I could definitely enchant a handkerchief into a white dove if we wanted."

"Okay. If it makes you feel any better, I'll make sure to get Lord Scarlet's approval on anything I create. He seemed eager for one of his students to work on a project like this with the GITs."

Really? That seemed strange after Lord Scarlet's disagreement in the cloisters with Madame LeBleu. He'd been pretty clear about wanting his school left well alone. Why was he suddenly eager for cooperation between the schools? Zelda trusted Madame LeBleu, but she wasn't so sure about the reclusive Lord Scarlet.

"I'll run this by my professors too." If Lord Scarlet *did* have anything to gain from such experimental magic, he'd have to go through Madame LeBleu to get it.

A buzzing at Zelda's elbow made her jump, and she scrambled for her phone. She nearly gasped at the sight of Prince Charming on her caller ID.

"It's Leo," she said to Specs before she answered with a swipe of her finger. "Leo."

"Zelda," Leo's voice came from the other end. Her name sounded like a sigh of relief. "Where are you? I need to see you. Now."

"I'm at the Blackbird Café with Specs."

"I'm close. Stay there. I'm coming to you."

When Leo entered the coffee shop, Zelda's stomach knotted at the sight of him. He scanned the patrons until his gaze landed on them and he crossed the café in long strides.

He looked worse than the night before. Last night, he'd been upset. Now he looked angry. Zelda had barely slid out of the booth when Leo reached the table.

"Leo." It was all she could think to say.

He didn't hesitate when he pulled her into a hug. Startled at first, it took Zelda a moment to realize what was happening. One of Leo's arms held her tight around the waist while his other hand slid up her back and came to rest on her shoulder. In reply, Zelda threw her arms around Leo's neck. She had to rise onto her toes to do it.

He let out a long sigh.

With her cheek pressed into Leo's soft hair, Zelda could barely form words. "What happened to you?" she sputtered.

Leo slowly released her, but his hand lingered on her elbow. "My dad sent a car to pick me up this morning."

"Oh," Zelda said.

Leo took a seat beside Specs, and Zelda took the space opposite him.

"When I got to the castle, he said he was pulling me out of school."

No. Leo couldn't be done at EAMS. She didn't want to think about walking into the cafeteria or the library and not finding him waiting for her. "He can't take you out of school."

"I'm sorry, man," Specs said.

"It took all day, but I've finally convinced him to let me stay."

Zelda let out a sigh of relief. "Leo, you need to be more careful. Where's Felix? Does he know you're here?"

"No," Leo said. "I've been careful my whole life. I'm done with it."

Specs' eyes widened, flicking between Leo and Zelda.

"What do you mean?" Zelda asked.

Leo ducked his head before he met Zelda's gaze. "There was a surprise inspection at St. Germain's this morning. They didn't find anything."

Specs cocked a brow. "What?"

"I'm so sorry. That's not what we wanted," Zelda said.

Leo pressed his palms flat against the table. "That's why we have to do something. We know what we saw. We have to act."

Specs looked even more confused. "What are you two talking about?"

Zelda glanced between Leo and Specs. "You're right. We do need to do something."

"We need a plan," Leo said.

Zelda shook her head. "No. First, we need a team."

Chapter Nineteen

The fencing gym was dark when Zelda and Imogen slipped inside. Two figures stood in the middle of the room, the smell of sweaty fencing gear and lemon floor cleaner hanging in the air. Zelda quickly recognized Specs' towering frame and Leo whose wavy head of golden hair only reached Specs' chin.

Imogen tugged on her high pony so it was even bouncier than usual. "Hey, boys. What do you think of all this cloak and dagger? Fun isn't it?" Her voice echoed off the high, vaulted ceilings.

Both Leo and Specs shushed her.

"Sorry," she whispered. "Is someone going to call this secret meeting to order, or do I have to?"

Zelda elbowed her in the ribs. "This isn't a secret meeting. We're here so we can fill Specs in, then we're coming up with a plan."

"A plan for what?" Specs asked, his voice tight with unease.

Zelda and Leo told him what they'd seen in St. Germain's window, of the little woman in rags polishing shoes, and the staged factory tour.

Specs fidgeted with the hem of his shirt and nodded along until they finished. He contemplated everything for a long moment before he spoke. "If you really saw what you saw, there's definitely something strange going on."

"Right." Leo clasped his hands together. "We need a plan. I'd like to get a closer look at the emporium. What do you think?" He looked to Zelda.

"That's a great idea, but you can't waltz in there. You're way too noticeable. And after the inspection and your 'spontaneous' tour, it might be best if you stayed away."

Imogen settled herself cross-legged on the mat and opened her phone. The light of the screen cast the room in an eerie glow. "What if I got a job there?" Her thumb flicked across the phone screen. "They're hiring seasonal sales associates to help with the holiday rush. I wouldn't mind giving it a go—I could always use the quid."

"Are you sure?" Specs leaned down to read over Imogen's shoulder. "You'd be comfortable spying?"

Imogen looked up at him with a little smirk. "It's not spying. I'd be observing and reporting back."

"If you're up for it, I say apply," Zelda said.

"Fine then." Imogen's smirk slid into a wicked sort of grin. "I will."

"A fifty percent discount," Imogen blurted as they walked to the potions lab. "Fifty percent."

Several first-years stumbled over each other as they tried to give Imogen and her flailing a wider berth.

Zelda shushed her. "Can you keep it down? We don't need everyone knowing you're working at St. Germain's." By everyone, she meant Madame LeBleu. "This is a covert operation, remember?"

"Oh, right." Imogen put a do-it-yourself manicured finger to her lips. "Hushity hush."

Zelda batted the conspicuous hand away from Imogen's mouth as they turned into the classroom.

Professor Ballentine propped herself on her desk and crossed her stockinged legs. Her red vintage pump bounced impatiently while she waited for the shuffling sound of arriving students to die down.

"Let's get started," she said. "On page seventy-eight you'll find instructions for a cloaking potion. This is a handy one if you need to move around unseen. The potion makes you untraceable to recording devices and imperceptible to people you pass—but it won't make you invisible. If you bump into someone or strike up a conversation, they'll see you. The stronger the potion you brew, the stronger the cloaking. If made to perfection, you might as well be invisible."

Zelda scanned the procedures and list of ingredients. The directions were intricate, but something about a complicated potion sent a thrill through her veins. She knew Professor Ballentine would expect a superior potion from her.

Ballentine continued. "This will take longer than we have time for in this class. The cloaking potion should take at least a week to complete, so don't fall behind. Work smart, work steady, work fast. You must reach step five by the end of class, at which point you'll bottle and start again on Tuesday."

Zelda set to work with a determined fervor. Step one had at least four parts of its own and the other steps looked just as long. By the chime of the ending bell, she'd broken out in a sweat and removed her navy jumper. Professor Ballentine paced the room to make sure every girl had their potion components and ingredients stored properly.

Zelda's breath stopped short as the professor examined her stoppered vial. "Stay after class please, Miss Ravensdale."

Her heart sank like a coin to the bottom of a fountain. *What have I done now?* She glanced over the potion steps, but she hadn't missed a single one. As she packed her bag, she tried not to think of the worst possible things Professor Ballentine could say to her.

The class filed out the door and Zelda stopped at Professor Ballentine's desk.

"I'm sorry," Ballentine said. "I didn't mean to alarm you."

Zelda's face must have betrayed her panic. She schooled her features into her best attempt at a casual grin. "I'm fine."

Professor Ballentine didn't look convinced. "I just wanted to let you know that the potion you've made is beyond exceptional."

The grin fell from Zelda's face. "It's what?"

"Don't look so surprised. This is your best subject. Your mother was a great brewess if the stories are true. She makes wine with magical properties, right?"

Zelda's chest warmed. "She made a table wine that prevented dinner conversation from lagging or turning dull."

"Right," Ballentine said with a laugh. "And I'm sure it's outside of my budget."

"Mine too." Zelda laughed nervously. There had to be a more important reason than discussing wines for Ballentine to keep her after class.

"Zelda, I want to talk about your after-school plans."

"I want to be a granter," Zelda blurted. It was almost a reflex.

It'd been her answer to the question "Who do you want to be?" ever since she could form sentences.

"I know, and I have no doubt you will be an amazing one," Ballentine said. "With most students, we expect they'll fulfill their mandatory tenure, then enter the workforce. With others, the best of the best, we expect they'll make a career of godmothering."

Zelda leaned forward. *Which one am I?*

"I believe you're one of the latter."

Zelda's lips formed a slow smile. "You're serious?"

"Of course. All your professors agree. It seems the only person who doesn't believe in you, is you."

"But my magic. It's erratic and uncontrollable. I'm sure you've heard about the pumpkin disaster by now."

"Something is out of line. I know how hard you work, but magic flows from a clear heart and a calm mind—belief is a big part of that, Miss Ravensdale. Work on trusting your magic again."

"That seems easier said than done."

"Then think about this: in order to get approved for a second tenure, you need to finish an advanced degree. The University of Erimount has an excellent potions program, a very competitive one. I would suggest getting settled in your territory for a year, but I wouldn't hesitate to apply. If that's something that would interest you, I'd be happy to write a recommendation."

Zelda's mouth went dry. Her tongue was too thick to form words. "Thank you," she managed to say. Dread crept thick and slow into her chest and at any moment she worried a tear might form in her eyes. It was nice to be recognized for her potential, but she still had to live up to it.

Professor Ballentine offered Zelda a rare, warm smile. "Brewing a great potion takes more than talent, Miss Ravensdale. I've seen what you can do with a wand, a graduated cylinder, and a Bunsen burner, and it's nothing short of miraculous."

Doubt licked icily at Zelda's ribs. Brewing a potion was like breathing, but she didn't like to think about what she could do with a wand. With how the semester was going, magic had become something she avoided, something she feared. Before she could think of a reply, the second bell rang. She was going to be late.

"I'll write you a pass," Ballentine said. "Just remember what we talked about. Trust your magic. To do that, you'll need more than sheer force of will."

"But how do I—"

"I can't say. It's different for everyone." Ballentine held out a slip of blue paper with a looping gold script.

Zelda took the pass and made a beeline for the classroom with the hotlines. She was so tired of hearing about how much potential she had, that only her lack of belief was holding her back.

I have belief in bucketfuls. She'd wanted to be a godmother for as long as she could remember. Now she had a chance to be the godmother of Olisand, the birthplace of the first wish. The dream seemed so real and so close. Of all the girls in her year, she was the most capable, if not, surely the most driven. Except for Susan, perhaps.

"Isn't that proof enough?" Zelda asked the empty passageway. Her voice echoed of the polished marble floor. Hollow.

Proof, yes. But not belief.

She entered the classroom, her eyes hot with a feeling close to anger, but not far enough from sadness. Professor Weymouth took her pass. She dropped into her chair and hoped he'd assign her a cut-and-dry, simple wish.

"It should be a busy day with the holidays coming up," Weymouth pulled out an extra thick stack of cards. "Get ready."

Despite what she'd hoped, Professor Weymouth called her name five minutes into the hour.

"Yeah?" She swiped a finger under her wet eyes to make sure her mascara hadn't run.

Professor Weymouth raised a brow. "This card is for you, Miss Ravensdale, if you feel able."

Professor Weymouth never asked students if they were okay to grant wishes. This turned several heads, and a flame of panic fluttered in Zelda's chest.

"I'm fine," Zelda assured him. He handed her the card, and she hurriedly punched in the number.

"Hello?" a male voice answered on the first ring.

"Madame LeBleu's School for Godmothers. How may I assist you?"

"Yes, um. I-I have a wish."

Zelda paused. The speaker was young, and his voice sounded vaguely familiar. "I can help with that. Would you like to discuss it over the phone, or should I come to your location?"

"My location would be best, I think."

"I'm on my way." Zelda pushed the button on her phone, and the room went black.

She opened her eyes at the screech of a loud whistle. To her surprise, she stood in the main terminal of the Olisand train station. People hustled to board trains, but a few stopped and stared because she'd appeared from midair. The speakers overhead crackled to life as dispatch announced boarding for a train headed to France. Doors to one of the sleek bullet trains opened on the nearest platform.

"Zelda?"

She whirled around at the sound of her name. Her heart nearly skipped a beat as she found Dante standing behind her. *What is he doing here?*

He slipped his phone slowly into his pocket. "I didn't know if it would be you when I tied my wish to the gates. I'd hoped it would be." A scuffed leather suitcase sat at his feet.

Zelda's eyes fell on the suitcase. "What's going on?"

Dante tucked a casual hand into the pocket of his navy trousers. His dark hair was groomed like it always was—soft and pushed to the side like he belonged on the set of a black-and-white movie. The expression on his face was almost neutral. A hint of a smile faded as he seemed to sense her distress. "Are you okay? Did I upset you? I didn't want to ambush you, but I was out of options."

Zelda wasn't sure how to answer. "How I feel is not important now. You have a wish—"

Dante took a step toward her and put his hands on her shoulders. They were heavier than she remembered. "Your timing is impeccable. I need your help. I need to leave—no, I need to disappear."

Zelda's brows pushed together and she shrugged his hands off her shoulders so she could think clearly. "That's your wish? To disappear?"

"Yes. I need cards that can't be traced. A new name would help, too, but you can't ask me where I'm going."

Zelda's stomach turned sour. "But term is almost over. Why do you have to disappear, Dante? Why now?"

"You can't ask me that either." His expression was tender, like he was trying to console a child.

The air went out of Zelda's lungs. In the chaos of the bustling train station, the moment felt so strange and dream-like. They were largely invisible even as streams of people passed, their focus only on their next destination. Dante was clearly in trouble, and she had no idea why. She took a rapid mental inventory of everything that'd changed in him since their breakup. Nothing could be gathered from his carefully crafted presentation, so she combed through memories, testing each one for a reason why he had to disappear.

"I–I can't," she sputtered, trying to understand the consequences of what Dante was asking. *Is this because he's failing his classes?* "I can't grant your wish with so little information. I have to know more if this is best for your Happily Ever After. If this is about grades, you don't need to run away. You just need a tutor."

Dante's reached for her hands and gave them a squeeze. "This isn't about school, but I can't tell you more. If there's any chance you'll get hurt—if anyone hurt you, I would hate myself for that."

Can he really mean that? Did this have something to do with Leo? Something to do with his warning about the prince?

Zelda couldn't believe it, but it almost sounded like he still cared about her. "I can pass your wish to Madame LeBleu." She didn't pull away even though he held her hands with too much familiarity. "I'm sorry, but that's all I can do."

Dante ducked his head. When he lifted his gaze to meet hers, hope flashed in his eyes. "Do you trust her?"

"Yes," she said. Doubt flickered in her mind, but she pushed it aside. "Yes, I do."

Dante released her hands and picked up his suitcase. "Okay, then. Pass it on." The train doors to the bullet train closed with the sigh of hydraulics.

"I'm sorry I can't do more," Zelda said, the desperate ache of guilt setting heavy on her shoulders.

"You don't have to say you're sorry. The hope is a wish granted enough in itself."

"Hope?"

"Yeah. Isn't that the purpose of a fairy godmother?"

Zelda wrinkled her brow. "We're supposed to grant wishes."

Dante pursed his lips in thought. "You know, the way I always saw you guys wasn't so much about the wishes, but that you give all of us without magic the hope for something better."

The words tugged at something in Zelda's chest the way Ballentine's had. He picked up his suitcase.

"Where are you going?" Zelda asked hurriedly.

"I'll see you at school, Zelda." Dante threw a wry little smile at her over his shoulder and joined the mass of people that streamed toward the exit of the station.

Chapter Twenty

Students packed The Swan and Raven to say goodbye to friends before everyone left on Christmas holiday. From where Zelda sat, she could see across to the corner booth where Dante held court with a group of tinkers.

He now occupied Zelda's thoughts more than she cared to admit. After he'd confessed his wish to her on the train station platform, nothing happened. In the dining hall and when they passed on the sidewalks, Dante ignored her as had been the norm. If he wanted to pretend it hadn't happened, then Zelda would too. She'd done as she said and passed the wish along to Madame LeBleu.

A booth seat squeaked and broke her reverie as Leo slid into the seat next to her.

"Why are you sitting all alone?" he asked.

A shudder passed through Zelda's chest as her breath caught there. She almost hadn't recognized the prince. His damp hair peeked out from the hood of his crew team jumper. "Imogen and Specs are ordering some mulled wine," she said. "Did you come from crew practice?"

"Yeah. How'd you know?"

Zelda turned in the booth to see him better. "Your hair is wet. I've never seen it wet." Her fingers itched with the urge to reach out to brush it from his forehead, to twist a soft lock of golden hair. She swallowed the thought as her cheeks reddened.

"I'm technically not allowed to be seen in public like this." Leo lifted a casual shoulder. "But I just showered after my team workout and thought, why not? Who's gonna stop me?"

Zelda choked on a laugh. "You're such a rebel. Felix didn't give you any grief?"

"No. He was too busy fussing like a mother hen because I wanted to come to a bar to notice."

"Where is he?"

"He's brooding over by the bathroom doors." Leo waved at the man in the dark suit who watched them from across the bar. He didn't wave back, only glowered with a subtle shake of his head.

Laughter burst from Zelda and Leo, but his smile quickly faded. "How many days till your fall term ends?"

"A week. I go home next Friday."

Leo nodded and hung his head. "Me too."

An idea crossed Zelda's mind, and the words tumbled out before she could stop herself. "You could spend Christmas with me and my family."

Leo's head snapped up. Something sparked to life in his eyes that made Zelda lose her breath all over again. "Y-yes," he sputtered. "I'd love to. I mean, if that's okay with your parents."

"They practically beg me to have friends home. I'll ask, but I don't think they'll mind."

Leo smiled, and it felt like Zelda had swallowed sunlight. Would he read something into the offer? And did she want him to? She hadn't dared address the tremble that went through her whenever she saw him.

Imogen and Specs appeared with drinks and stopped Zelda's thoughts before she could question what she was feeling about Leo.

Imogen slid Zelda her mulled wine. "Sorry, Prince Charming. If I'd seen you come in, I would have gotten you something."

Leo sat a little taller. "Is that my nickname?"

"It's what Zelda has you in her phone as."

Zelda shot Imogen a dirty glare before Leo turned to her. "Is that true?"

She couldn't read him, but she hoped he wasn't upset. "I think it suits you for a nickname."

Leo smiled and ducked his head bashfully.

"Can I call you Prince Charming?" Specs asked before he blew a straw wrapper at Leo.

Leo batted the projectile away. "You can call me whatever you want. But you," he stuck a finger at Imogen, "you can call me Your Highness."

"I will." Imogen propped her elbows on the table, her fingers laced under her chin. "If you all call me Your Majesty."

Zelda laughed, but a part of her wasn't convinced Imogen was joking. "So, Imogen, you had something to share with our . . ." She wasn't sure what to call their group.

"Coterie," Specs suggested.

It seemed to fit. "Do you have an update for the coterie, Imogen?" Zelda asked.

Imogen sat taller, a little smirk on her rosy glossed lips. "You'll all be so proud of me. I think I have a career in espionage if godmothering doesn't pan out."

Beside Zelda, Leo's knee bounced violently. She wanted to reach out to still him, but she thought better of placing her hand on his leg. Instead, she pressed fingers to his forearm which rested on the sticky tabletop between them. He flinched at her touch, so she drew her hand away. A look of regret flashed over his face. He opened his mouth as if to offer an apology but seemed to think better of it with Imogen and Specs watching them. He cleared his throat. "And what is it you called this meeting for, Your Majesty?"

Imogen smiled and flicked her hair over one shoulder. "Well, this was the first week I've been scheduled to close up shop—it only takes a few of us to do it."

"Really?" Specs said. "The whole emporium?"

"Yes, that's what I'm getting to. Apparently, there's a cleaning crew that comes in each night."

When they'd passed the shop windows, St. Germain's had been closed. Had they seen a member of the "cleaning crew?"

"Friday night was the last night I closed, and since I'm still new, they scheduled me to open Saturday too—everyone hates when they do that." She took a long sip of her mulled wine and cupped it under her chin. "Anyway, Friday night when we locked up, the shelves in the repair room were filled to the ceiling with shoes in dire straits. I mean scuffed, dirty, frayed stitching, and worn soles like you wouldn't believe. It looked like weeks of tedious work getting them all repaired." She paused for dramatic effect.

"When I got in this morning, every single repair order had been completed. Every. Single. Pair. They were all on the opposite shelves, waiting to be returned to their owners. So of course, being the good spy that I am, I asked around. Apparently, the cleaning crew does those too."

The flutter of excitement in Zelda's stomach bubbled over into an audible squeal. "Imogen, you brilliant superspy. That's probably who we saw." She grabbed Leo by the arm. This time he didn't jump, and she didn't let go.

Imogen's eyes fell to where Zelda's hand rested on Leo's sleeve. Zelda thought it would be better to release the prince, but she desperately needed him to steady her as she pressed on. "We have to see this cleaning crew. If we're right about this, all we do is wait inside St. Germain's until they come. There'll be some security measures we have to avoid but—"

"I'd like to be there."

All heads at the table turned to look at Leo.

"I *need* to be there," Leo corrected.

Zelda looked to Imogen and Specs, and they both appeared equally uncomfortable with Leo taking yet another risk.

"Leo," Zelda said. "That's way too risky. If you get caught—"

"You have magic," Leo said. "Can't we use that to make sure we don't get caught?"

Zelda shook her head. "Magic has limits. Even the world's best cloaking potion can't make you totally invisible."

Specs gave a hesitant little cough. "What about a shrinking potion?"

Imogen shot him a suspicious look. "How do you know about those? You know you can't brew without magic, right?"

Specs gave a little smile and ducked his head. "No, I know. It was just out of curiosity that I stumbled across the mention of one once."

Zelda shifted nervously, but Specs had a point. Shrinking down to the size of elves would make them inconspicuous and less intimidating if they did come across one. "Maybe," she said. "Those potions are way, way, way advanced. Think university level."

Leo's face lit into one of his brighter smiles. "You can handle it—you're always bragging about your brewing skills."

"Well . . ."

"Come on." Leo turned to fix her with a brilliant grin. "Do you think you can say 'no' to my smile parentheses?"

Zelda's cheeks flushed with fire. Of all the things, why did he remember that?

"Your what?" Specs asked.

Zelda ignored him. "Fine. Specs, Leo, and I will hide out in St. Germain's and get a look at this cleaning crew."

They agreed that the best time to go undercover had to be a night when Imogen was closing. Imogen was scheduled to close before she went back to London for Christmas holiday, but that still left the shrinking potion.

Nothing. Not a single shrinking potion in the entire contents of the school library, Zelda texted Leo.

We need to find a better library, he replied.

That's it. Zelda smacked her forehead with the heel of her hand. Why hadn't she thought of it sooner? **I know of a better library**.

Imogen gave her a sideways glance as they headed for the charms classroom. "What's wrong with you?"

Zelda laughed. "Nothing. I'm just an idiot."

Imogen snorted. "What else is new?"

Zelda shoved her. "Rude much?"

"Are you gonna tell me why you're an idiot or is it because you've spent more time worrying about today's First Fairy rankings than all the rest of the fourth-years combined?"

"No," Zelda said as renewed anxiety stole her grin. "I wasn't thinking about that at all, but now I am."

"Oooo. Were you thinking about Prince Charming?"

"No."

Imogen looked doubtful. "Then come on. Let's go look at the rankings list and get it over with."

Zelda stopped in her tracks and let out a long groan. "Ugh. I don't want to."

"Yes, let's go." Imogen moved behind her and started to push.

Zelda locked her knees and planted her feet. "I can't move my legs. I forgot how to walk."

"No," Imogen shouted playfully as she pushed harder.

The smooth bottoms of Zelda's saddle shoes slid on the polished marble. "Oh my giddy gourds, you're strong."

Imogen cackled wildly before she was cut short by a sharp "Girls."

They whirled around and found Professor Nutt with hands fisted on her hips. "No rough housing in the halls."

"Yes, Professor," they said in unison.

"And if I see your phone out again, Miss Ravensdale, I'll give you a demerit."

Zelda's gaze dropped to her shoes. "Yes, Professor." She grabbed Imogen, and they hurried down the hall and up the stairs before they got a lecture on lingering in the halls too.

"She scares me," Imogen said.

They neared the crowd of GITs that surrounded the piece of paper hanging outside the classroom door and picked their way to the front.

Zelda clutched Imogen's arm for support. It didn't take long to find her name on the list. It was right below Susan St. Germain's, firmly at number two. Second. To her surprise, relief spread through her body. Second was fine. After all she had been through this semester, second would do. She still had all of spring term to get ahead of Susan.

"Second." Imogen rolled her eyes. "All that worrying and you're still second in the class?"

Zelda turned and gave a sheepish shrug of her shoulders. "Sorry?"

"I'll accept your apology as long as you start acting like a normal person when you come back from holiday."

"Define normal," Zelda said as they headed back toward the stairs.

"You know what I mean. If you stay wound this tight, you're eventually going to snap."

They exited the academic hall through arched doors and headed out into the chilly December air. Zelda pulled up the collar of her peacoat tight under her chin. The wind howled against her ears and snatched her breath away as they ran across the quad.

Once inside, Imogen fumbled for her key. "Next semester I don't want to see you skipping meals to run spell drills or camping out in the stacks."

"You don't get it." Frustration pointed her words. "I have four sisters and a mother who were First Fairy before me."

"No." Imogen whirled around. "See, I do get it. My parents weren't exactly pleased when I gave up on a career with the Royal Ballet. Every time I go home, I get to hear how disappointed they are that I refuse to dance in addition to being a fairy godmother."

"Oh," Zelda said. Imogen had almost gone pre-professional, but she hardly ever mentioned it.

"Yeah. I willingly chose a different path from what was laid out for me, but that doesn't mean it hurts any less that my parents don't get why I'm doing this, why I want the life of a granter."

"I'm sorry," Zelda said. "I didn't know this was so hard for you. You seem so freaking strong—like nothing fazes you."

"Most of the time it doesn't, but it's always harder when I know I'm heading home."

"I'm glad you told me."

Imogen unlocked the heavy wooden door to their room, and they moved inside. In the throes of packing for the winter holiday, suitcases lay open in the middle of the room with stockings, jumpers, and skirts thrown about as they tried to figure out who was taking what home for Christmas.

Imogen sank down in front of her floral-patterned duffle. "First Fairy is what it is." She chucked a pair of lace-trimmed ankle socks into the bag. "It just means the professors like you best. It doesn't even mean you'll be a good fairy. It's, like, ninety percent political. Just look at Susan. She's been the favorite to become First Fairy since she walked through the gates of Madame LeBleu's four years ago, and she is a bloody awful person to be around. Your rank doesn't matter, and it doesn't change what kind of godmother you'll be."

"I get it," Zelda said, but something still sat uneasy with her. First Fairy had seemed like a link between her mother's success and the success of her sisters. Could she trust that she would be a good fairy godmother without Madame LeBleu's top seal of approval? She wanted to believe so, but that was easier said than done.

"Good. Then we need to discuss Prince Charming."

Zelda's face flushed as she plopped into her desk chair. "What about him?"

"We need to discuss what you're going to do about your feelings for him." A smirk lifted the corner of Imogen's lips.

Zelda's mouth fell open before she mustered a convincing scoff. "I'm not—I don't—we're not—" She halted to collect her racing thoughts. "I'm his godmother, remember? In order to grant his wish, everything must appear above reproach."

"Yes, but you like him, don't you?" Imogen watched her with a knowing look.

"We're close friends."

Imogen laughed. "I don't look at my friends the way you look at him."

Zelda couldn't stop the smile that spread across her face. "Okay, fine. Maybe he makes my insides warm and fuzzy whenever he's around, but I've already rejected him, remember? That ship has sailed."

"He looks at you too," Imogen said gently.

Zelda's pulse sputtered. "He does?" She wanted to comb each memory of her interactions with Leo to see if Imogen was right. That Leo still hoped that she might return his romantic feelings.

"Yeah. And he's going home with you for holiday. So, are you going to make a move or not?"

"I don't know." Zelda picked up a pile of clothes from her bed and threw them into her suitcase. "I can't think about that now. I have to pack. Leo is picking me up in—" she glanced at her phone. "Ten minutes."

"Please," Imogen begged. "For my sanity, consider snogging him under some mistletoe, okay?"

"Imogen." Zelda made the mistake of imagining such an act and it resulted in a high-pitched giggle. "I guess I'll consider it."

Chapter Twenty-One

A sleek, black, two-door car idled in the road between Madame LeBleu's and EAMS. It was squat and so flat, Zelda wondered how they were going to fit inside along with their luggage. In her haste, she'd definitely overpacked. Felix stood over the car, his arms crossed. He glowered at Leo as the prince opened the trunk and placed Zelda's bulging suitcase inside.

"I don't like this," Felix said darkly.

Leo rounded the car and opened Zelda's door for her. "Everything is going to be fine. I'll be with the most promising and powerful godmother to walk the halls of Madame LeBleu's."

Felix growled, and Zelda could have sworn she saw muscles bulge in his shoulder where she didn't know muscles existed.

"You will drive straight to her parents' vineyard, and you will drive straight back. You will not stop. You will not take detours from the route pre-programmed into the GPS or do anything that would draw attention to yourselves."

Leo motioned for Zelda to get in the car. "That's exactly what we intend to do."

Zelda slipped into the low seat, and Leo closed her door. The car smelled like soft leather, and as she nestled deeper into her seat, she realized Leo already had the warmer on for her. Leo and Felix exchanged a few final words, but she had to strain to hear them.

Felix didn't look happy. "Are you sure you should be leaving the city with your father—"

Zelda couldn't make out the rest. Whatever Leo said, Felix pulled him into what looked like a painfully tight hug. He released him, and after a pat on the shoulder, Leo jogged to his door and slid in.

"What was that about?"

Leo laughed and put the car in drive. "Felix? He's such a worrywart."

"I meant the hug."

Leo adjusted his seatbelt. "That? He was just wishing me a happy Christmas since I won't be at the castle."

Zelda nodded. The words rang true, but she couldn't shake the feeling that Leo had left something out. They pulled out of the alley and onto the road where they were immediately forced to wait for a passing trolley. "I can't believe Felix is letting you go alone."

Leo chuckled behind closed lips. "He wouldn't if he'd had his way. Felix was overruled by my mom. Christmas is a slow week for royal duties, and she thinks I need some time away from everything." Before Zelda could ask what he meant, he changed the subject. "So, about this library you texted me about?"

"Oh yeah." Zelda jumped in her seat; she'd almost forgotten about it in the packing frenzy—and her conversation with Imogen. "There is a wing in the National Archives that's exclusively dedicated to the International Council of Godmothers' collection of resource materials for spells and potions."

"You're kidding." Leo shook his head. "I actually knew about that. I'm thick for not thinking of looking there before."

Zelda giggled. "That's what I said too."

"No, no, no," Leo said. "I'm not thinking about potions. The National Archives has extensive records from the International Magical Relations Committee. They're the non-magical counterpart to the ICG, and they might have something we can dig up on magical creatures."

"You really think we'll find a paper trail to St. Germain's elves?"

"If it has to do with magic, and it happened in Olisand, there'll be a record of it in the archives."

Leo's excitement rolled off him in waves, and it made Zelda's pulse race. "That would be amazing."

"You're not exaggerating. If we have something besides our own word, that would be a coup if we need to expose St. Germain for shady labor practices."

"Right."

Afterward, they fell into silence. Leo focused on following the overly complex instructions Felix had put into the car's GPS, so they would throw off anyone trying to follow them out of the city. Zelda tried to get comfortable in her seat, but there was a shocking lack of room between her and Leo. She gave up squeezing against the door and propped her elbow against the negligible hump of an armrest between them. It was silly. She'd never been nervous to be close to him before. It was all Imogen's fault she now had to analyze everything she did around Leo.

Leo made a sharp turn near the city limits, and Zelda couldn't stop her arm from leaning into his.

"Sorry," she muttered as the car straightened.

"No worries," Leo said.

Zelda snuck a glance at Leo and found a slight smile on his lips and the dimples that always came with it. Her cheeks heated on cue. She couldn't deny Imogen's observation. Zelda Ravensdale had a devastating crush on Prince Charming.

Before long, they were out of the city, and zipping through the rolling hills of Olisand's countryside. There still wasn't snow on the ground, but the cold and the gray skies overhead cast the world in muted colors.

"Will your family miss you if you're gone for Christmas?" Zelda hazarded to ask. She hoped it wouldn't seem prying, but these were the things they'd talked about before.

"Astara is furious. My mom will miss me, I'm sure, but she has a lot going on at the moment."

It wasn't hard to figure who was left out. The sadness on Leo's face made Zelda's gut roil with anger. The strength of the emotion surprised her. No one should feel like their parent didn't want them around, but she knew not everyone was lucky enough to have parents like hers.

"My family is excited to meet you," she said.

That cheered Leo significantly, and Zelda was glad to see his smile return.

"I'm excited to meet them," he said. "What do they think about you being friends with a prince?"

Zelda laughed nervously and clutched her knees for support. "Actually . . ."

"What?" A twinge of panic tightened his voice.

"They kinda don't know exactly who I'm bringing home."

Leo's head snapped to her so fast he turned the wheel too, and the car almost ended up in a ditch. He righted the car and returned his eyes to the road.

"Why didn't you tell your parents you were bringing me?" he asked, his voice charged with concern

"Relax." Zelda placed her hand on his arm and some of the tension eased from his shoulders. "I-I didn't want them to freak out. I know my family, and if we catch them off guard, they won't have time to prepare and get all weird and polite. I want you to meet the real Ravensdales."

Leo's smile broke through his concern. "I see," he said, but his hands tightened almost imperceptibly on the steering wheel. "I want to meet the real Ravensdales too."

Zelda shifted in her seat, conscious of the lack of space between them. *Why is he so nervous?* When she'd invited him home as a friend, she'd thought all chances of something more between them had passed. But, if Imogen was right, he looked at her like she looked at him.

She snuck a glance at Leo and found him already looking at her.

"What?" he asked.

"Nothing. You just keep your eyes on the road," she said quickly and turned to look out the window. She would have to be more careful than ever not to cross her ethical boundaries.

Leo stopped the car at the start of the long driveway that led to the Ravensdale's vineyard. Mountains rose far in the distance, and the medieval vestige of the winery stood in front of them. Rows of skeletal grapevines lined both sides of the road.

"That's where you live?" Leo gestured to the building at the top of the hill.

It wasn't even comparable in size to the royal castle in Erimount, but the stone edifice was still an impressive sight from where it loomed over the neat columns of well-tended vines.

"Part of it is. Most of what you see is wine production and an inn." She felt a twinge of pride at the business her parents had built on grapes, love, and a little bit of magic to help it along the way.

Leo sucked in a deep breath, then let it out slowly. "Okay. Here we go." He took his foot off the brakes and inched the car up the driveway where it formed a circle by the front steps.

Zelda's dad was at the front door where he fussed with a wreath he was trying to hang on the front door. He turned at the crunch of tires on the gravel drive and his warm brown eyes widened at the sight of the sports car.

"Park here," Zelda said.

Leo did as instructed and turned off the engine. Zelda leaped from the warm vehicle into the biting air. She crossed the distance between her and her dad at a sprint, then threw her arms over his shoulders. "Dad."

He kissed her on both cheeks. "Ma petite." His deep voice rumbled through her chest, his warm breath mingling with her hair. But there was hesitation in his voice. "Whose car is that?"

"Dad," Zelda waited for Leo to emerge from the car. "This is Leo."

Recognition dawned slowly on his face. When he realized who'd driven her home, he dropped the wreath at his feet.

"Hello, Mr. Ravensdale." Leo put on a polite smile and stuck out his hand. "Prince Leopold Barrois, but you can call me Leo."

"Ian Ravensdale." He shook Leo's hand slowly. "You—you're Zelda's friend from school." He looked like he almost didn't believe his eyes.

"Yes," Leo said kindly. "Zelda is my friend at school. And outside of it."

Ian laughed at the joke—a little belatedly—before he turned to Zelda. "Should I bow?"

"No," both Leo and Zelda said in unison.

"Okay," Ian said, snapping out of his daze. "It's cold. We really should get you both inside. Your sisters will be glad to see you—both of you, I think."

Zelda was glad to see her dad snap back to his normal self. It confirmed her decision to spring Leo on them rather than give them a heads-up.

Inside the entryway, the smell of cinnamon and freshly cut pine boughs hung in the air. They dropped bags at the foot of the staircase, and Ian gestured for them to move to the sitting room. "You'd better go say hello to your sisters. They're all in there."

Chattering voices swirled through the air as Zelda guided Leo through the stone halls. They rounded the corner and found Zelda's four sisters and her brother-in-law in the living room, a giggling baby in her brother-in-law's lap.

A fire roared in the fireplace, and her dad's Christmas jazz music played through the speaker system. Warm woolen blankets wrapped worn leather chairs and an emerald chesterfield sofa boasted an inviting pile of pillows, but all sat unoccupied as Zelda's sisters lounged on the floor, vying for the attention of baby Sophia.

The second youngest of the Ravensdale girls, Ramona, caught sight of Zelda first. She emerged from the cluster of doting aunts to pull Zelda into a hug and kiss her on both cheeks.

"Zelda's here, everyone," Ramona exclaimed, her black ringlets bouncing. When she spotted Leo hiding behind Zelda, her face fell, and she went white. "Oh my giddy gourds!"

"What is it?" Caterina, the second oldest sister, ceased shaking her keys in front of her laughing baby niece.

Maria, the eldest, jumped to her feet. Her husband was trapped on the floor with Sophia propped up in his lap. He, too, paled as he spotted Leo in the doorway.

"Hi," Zelda said as they all froze. "I brought a friend home—please don't be weird about it."

Helene, the dramatic middle child, jumped behind the chesterfield with a scream. This seemed to amuse Sophia who matched her aunt with a screech of laughter of her own.

"How could you do this, Zelda?" Helene cried from behind the sofa. "Give us no warning you were bringing a royal home? I'm still in my pajamas."

"Zelda, you sneaky little troll." Ramona stuck out her hand for Leo, and he shook it kindly.

"Do I need to curtsey?" she whispered to Zelda.

"I'd prefer it if you didn't," Leo said. "And we can dispense with the formality of titles, 'Leo' will do fine."

"Did anyone know Zelda was friends with a prince?" Helene called from behind the couch.

"No," Maria said, a motherly scowl of disapproval on her face. "She's been very tight-lipped."

"I know," Zelda said. "Does this make up for it?"

A smile cracked Maria's lips. "A little bit."

Leo made his way around the room to introduce himself to everyone. It was a little awkward at first, but Leo proved his skill of putting people at ease once again. He seemed to remember every little detail she'd told him about each sister, and he miraculously didn't mess up a single name when Zelda knew how easy it was to mistake one pale brunette for another.

Once Leo had made his round, Caterina pulled him onto the couch with Helene; she had been coaxed out of hiding when Leo had offered to change into his pajamas if it would make her feel better.

"So how did you and Zelda meet?" Caterina asked, her arm wrapped through Leo's.

Zelda pushed aside her panic at how Leo would answer that question and asked a question of her own. "Where's Mom?"

Ian finally spoke up. "She's in the kitchen finishing up a batch of croissants. You'd better go say hello."

"Come on, Leo," Zelda said to a chorus of groans from her sisters.

Leo jumped up from the chesterfield a little too fast and followed Zelda into the hall.

"Sorry," Zelda said. "They can be a little much."

"They're great." He bumped his shoulder against Zelda's. "No apologies necessary."

Zelda lowered her head to hide her smile.

Sabine was standing in front of the stove when Zelda and Leo entered the kitchen. The air wiggled with the heat from the open oven door, while steam rose from a tray of croissants. Zelda's stomach rumbled, and she hoped her mom had remembered to stuff some with chocolate.

To Zelda's surprise, her mom's snow-white swan's wings were out, folded against her back. "Mom," Zelda said. "Your wings."

Her mom spun round with a smile. "Zelda." Her gaze fell on Leo, and her eyes widened in shock. "Oh good heavens."

"This is my friend Leo," Zelda said before she gestured to her mom's wings. "Are you baking with magic?"

"I laced them with a little Christmas cheer. But you know how baking with magic tends to go." She waggled her eyebrows at Zelda. "I needed a little support from my wings."

Leo crossed around the old, butcher block island in the center of the kitchen and extended his hand to her. "I'm so pleased to finally meet you, Mrs. Ravensdale."

Sabine gave his hand a firm shake, even though she still had on a crocheted oven mitt. "So, you're Zelda's friend." She gave him a once over with a contemplative gaze. "She failed to mention the royalty."

Leo shook his head. "I told her she should have let you know."

Sabine tilted her head back and laughed. "And I'm sure she convinced you otherwise."

Leo smiled. "I didn't need much convincing. I've learned to trust her."

"Just don't let her near the kitchen," Sabine said.

"Ha. Ha," Zelda said dryly and rolled her eyes.

"I feel like there's a story here I haven't heard," Leo said.

"Oh, there is." Sabine filled the kitchen with a full laugh. "She got it into her head that she wanted to make a cheese soufflé after reading a cooking magazine. Long story short, she tried to use magic to inflate the fallen soufflé. By the time she thought to run it out into the garden, it was too big to fit through the door."

Leo's mouth fell open with sheer joy. "How big did it get?"

"It was larger than the old van we have sitting out in the garage."

"Wow. Did it at least taste good?"

Zelda shook her head. "No, it did not."

Leo crossed back to where Zelda stood on the other side of the kitchen. "No wonder you're so terrified of baking."

He threw an arm over Zelda's shoulders, and her thoughts fuzzed like radio static. What did her mom think of their friendship? After godmothering for a full tenure, her mom had become quite perceptive. Would she figure out that Zelda was Leo's godmother? Or worse, would she ferret out the undeniable feelings Zelda harbored for the prince deep in her heart?

Zelda stepped out from under Leo's arm. "Would you like a tour?"

Leo looked a little unnerved by her abrupt changing of the subject, but he recovered quickly. "I would love a tour."

"Before you go—" Sabine tossed them each a warm croissant. "They're better when the chocolate is still melty."

"I was hoping you'd make chocolate for me."

"Take your things to your room first," Sabine said. "Leo can stay in one of the guest rooms. The inn is closed for the holiday, so give him one of the suites."

"Okay."

"And don't be long. I'll need everyone's help preparing dinner."

"Fine." Zelda grabbed Leo by the hand and led him from the kitchen before they could be given any more orders.

Chapter Twenty-Two

Leo was an excellent sport when it came to Ravensdale family Christmas. Two days of board games and overly personal questions about life as a prince from her sisters confirmed everything Zelda admired about him. Her mom discovered his knack for cooking early on and made use of his help often. He made great company and even volunteered to help around the winery when her dad needed a hand.

With stomachs full of Christmas Eve roasted chicken and chestnut soup, her dad pulled out a bottle of the "conversation wines" the vineyard was known for. And then another. Everyone seemed in a particularly truthful mood as they lounged around the sitting room.

People wandered off to bed one by one until finally only Leo and Zelda remained. They sat on opposite ends of the emerald-green couch with their feet sharing the edges of a blanket in the center. Leo watched her with a curious sort of look that made Zelda ask, "What are you thinking about?"

"This seems like a wonderful way to grow up." The corner of his mouth turned up into a smile.

The fire in the hearth snapped and guttered gently while the floors above them creaked with the padding of feet as Zelda's sisters tiptoed between bathrooms and beds.

"Yeah. It's a wonderful place to call home," Zelda said. "The castle seems wonderful too—from what I remember. They took us on a tour in primary school once. It was my favorite field trip."

"It may seem wonderful." Leo sighed and ran a hand through his hair.

"It isn't?" Zelda finished the last sip of wine in her glass.

"It's easier to appreciate from the outside." Leo's gaze looked through her as he spoke.

She rubbed her arms, though they weren't cold. "Leo." His eyes met hers at the sound of his name. "Is something wrong? What was Felix really talking to you about before we left?"

He ran his fingers over the little brass tacks along the edge of the couch's back. "It's my father. I confess, there's more than one reason for my wanting to come home with you. Of course, I wanted to meet your family, but Erimount was getting to be too much. On top of the pressure my father already puts on me, the doctors are saying my father's heart is failing him."

Zelda pulled her knees up to her chest as she resisted the urge to tackle Leo and pull him into a massive hug. "He looks so young. He can't be more than . . ."

"Fifty. Yeah. They said something about on-the-job stress. Everyone is saying I should be preparing myself."

"For his death?"

"And to rule. I'm of age now, so I'd be crowned king within the year."

Zelda swallowed. "Are you scared?"

"Of losing my father? I don't know what to think. I know I should be sad, but with our relationship so strained, I've already mourned the loss of what we used to have since I started taking on royal duties. I don't know how I'll handle losing him when the time comes. You must think me horrible."

"No. No, I think you are still young to be carrying such heavy burdens."

"It's strange," he said with a weird sort of smile. "I thought I'd be more scared knowing I could be king sooner than I ever feared."

Zelda couldn't help but think of his wish.

"How did you know you wanted to be a fairy godmother?"

The question startled her. "My mom was a fairy, so I was born a fairy," she answered. "It's been my destiny since I performed my first feat of magic." The answer didn't feel as satisfying on her tongue as it sounded.

"You couldn't have been something else if you wanted? Or you never wanted anything else? There's a big difference."

Zelda considered her answer. "I think it's always been assumed that I would be a fairy godmother, but truly I've never wanted to be anything else." Being a fairy godmother was everything to her. She'd watched each of her sisters get their wings and dreamed of getting her own in turn. "What about you?"

"I-I do believe I want to be king. I want the honor and the challenge and the chance to do some good for those who need it most. But I know it comes with a lot more. The pressure, the balancing, the politics—knowing when to intervene—that part terrifies me."

Zelda understood all too well. "There's a lot of pressure when it comes to people's Happily Ever Afters. Sometimes I wish there was a way to be absolutely certain that I was meant for this—that everything will turn out fine."

Leo smiled. "It sounds like you're looking for your own Happily Ever After."

Zelda smiled too. "Someone once told me that the purpose of fairy godmothers was not just to grant wishes but to bring people hope for something better."

"I can see how they'd think that."

Zelda burned under the look Leo gave her. Was this the sort of look Imogen had told her about? A meaningful, I'm-not-saying-everything-I-want-to-say sort of look. The warm air from the fire made her head feel fuzzy. Or maybe that was the magic in the wine. "Do you want something to eat?" she blurted.

Leo's eyes fell to her empty glass. "Have you had too much to drink? Do you feel okay?"

Zelda shook her head. "No. No. I'm fine. But this wine is great with cheese. Do you want cheese?"

He looked a little shocked at the abrupt turn of conversation.

Do you want cheese? I could kick myself.

His smile recovered, and he threw the blanket off his feet. "I'm not really hungry, but I'll always make room for cheese."

They headed into the kitchen, where Zelda pulled out a wedge of soft camembert and Leo went through drawers until he found a cheese knife. Zelda tried to feel less awkward, but she couldn't get Imogen out of her head. Her heart sputtered into high gear every time she got within a few feet of Leo, and he didn't make it easy on her; he moved close to her any chance he got.

His arm brushed hers, sending a jolt of electricity from her shoulder to her fingertips. "Water biscuits," she shouted like a madwoman and jumped out of Leo's reach.

"Zelda? Are you sure you're all right?"

Rotting, stinking pumpkins! He was on to her. She just needed a second to get her head together. Zelda darted for the pantry and to her dismay he followed.

"Can't have cheese without water biscuits," she said.

The pantry was dark and cool and smelled of the dried lavender and basil that hung in thick bunches from the rafters. Zelda loved the smell and was reminded of how much she'd enjoyed being sent into the pantry after an ingredient when she was little.

"Zelda. You're acting strange. Have I done something wrong?" Leo asked, his silhouette framed by the light from the kitchen.

"No. Nothing's wrong," Zelda squeaked as she climbed on to an antique pie safe to reach the water biscuits on the top shelf.

"Yes, something's wrong. Get down before you hurt yourself."

She grasped the long box, but not before Leo's hands grabbed her by the waist and pulled her back to safety. "Everything's fine. See, now we have biscuits."

"Enough with the biscuits." Leo reached to wrest them from her hands.

"No." Zelda giggled nervously as she turned her back to Leo and hugged the box to her chest.

Leo wrapped his arms around her and soon all was lost. "Ha." He hoisted the box over his head. "You'll get these—these aren't biscuits. This is a box of dried spaghetti. What's going on?"

Zelda's cheeks flushed, warmer than they already were after her mad scramble for what she'd thought had been a box of biscuits. She buried her face in her hands. "I can't," she mumbled.

"Since when can't you tell me something?" A sadness in his voice made Zelda lift her head.

"No. It's not—It's . . . see here's the thing—I, well—I'm feeling certain things about you, and I don't think it's fair of me to say after everything." She gave an exasperated groan. "I have feelings of a *romantic nature* toward you."

Leo set aside the box of pasta. Even in the dim light, Zelda could make out the crease that formed between his brows.

"I have it under control," she continued. "I won't let this affect how I grant your wish, so you don't have to worry. I can remain impartial, and if the Wishmaker Festival comes and you still want to have a normal life, I'll grant you that wish—"

"Zelda." His voice was heavy, the weight of her name enough to silence her.

Leo took a step toward her. "Stop for a second. I still don't want to be king. I don't want that power or the weight of that responsibility, but something has changed." Another step and the little room left between them vanished. "You've changed the way I think about a lot of things. From the moment I met you, I felt like I'd met myself for the first time too—like I'm the person I was always meant to be when I'm around you."

Zelda tried to swallow the lump in her throat. No one had ever said anything like that to her before.

"Furthermore, you've made me realize, you and Imogen and Specs too, that it's not really about me, because I'm not alone. It's about who I surround myself with, and with the right people I can be anything, do anything." His hand reached out and brushed Zelda's cheek.

Everything stilled under his touch. It seemed even the house quieted. The rich, spicy-sweet smell of cologne filled her nose. "Does this mean you're keeping your crown?"

Leo's lips parted into a lopsided, dimpled smile. "I think I'm going to save my wish for something else. I have another Happily Ever After in mind and it doesn't involve you being my fairy godmother."

A shiver ran down Zelda's spine as Leo's eyes flicked to her mouth. Her pulse thundered in her ears as she urged her body to move, willed her frozen limbs to do something, but what?

Leo's hand slid around her waist and with a gentle tug he pulled her in. He started to lean in but stopped just a breath away. "A while ago you told me not to kiss you."

Zelda was sure she couldn't form words, so she mumbled a "Mmhmm."

"Then I need you to tell me if this is okay—if I may kiss you." His hand slid along her jaw, his thumb brushing softly against her cheek.

"You may," she said, then brushed her nose against his as if to grant him permission into her space.

He sank into her, lips first, and kissed her softly. Slowly his mouth formed to hers, a gentle brush of a kiss. Even after waiting so long, Leo held back. With a tenderness that made Zelda ache deep in her bones, he drew out every stroke of his lips against hers.

Zelda pressed a hand to his chest and felt the rapid tattoo of his heart against her palm, but she could only think of the tingle in her lips as she craved more of him. She slid a hand up to his neck and greedily pulled herself closer. Leo didn't miss a step and smiled against her lips as he surrendered to her want for more.

A creak from one of the floorboards upstairs sent them flying to opposite walls of the pantry. Zelda gasped for breath as she watched Leo bring a hand to his mouth. He had the startled look of someone who'd just been kissed for the first time.

"That was . . ." Leo's voice trailed off.

Zelda couldn't keep from smiling. "What?"

"I think we should go to bed."

A breath escaped in a gasp as Zelda's lips parted.

"In our own rooms," Leo clarified, a lopsided smile dimpling his cheek.

Zelda's face burned. "Of course."

Unanswered questions rattled around Zelda's head as she put out the fire in the living room with a muttered spell and a sweep of her wand over the flames. They turned out the lights, and Zelda grabbed Leo by the hand to lead him through the dark.

She was going to have to face her family in the morning. What would she say? What would she call Leo now? Were they *together* together? Or did he still have to ask her for that?

They paused at Zelda's bedroom door.

The hall was quiet and dark and cold, and Leo stood close enough that she could feel his warmth. Everything was different now—uncertainty and excitement hung heavily on every moment. Zelda's insides twisted and taunted her with want at the thought of kissing him again. Would he dare when anyone could wander out of their room at any moment?

"Goodnight," Zelda said.

A smile tugged at the corner of Leo's mouth. "Goodnight." He placed his hands on her arms and drew her in close to place a kiss on her forehead. Zelda touched his chest to feel the soft tapping of his heart against her fingertips again.

She let out an awkward sigh and slipped from Leo's hands to open her door. "Goodnight."

"You already said that." The prince slid his hands into his pockets with a lopsided grin.

Zelda slipped into her room and held the door open just a crack. "I know," she said. "It's just been a good night."

"So it has." Leo smiled at his feet before he brought his eyes up to meet Zelda's. "Goodnight and sweet dreams, Zelda."

Chapter Twenty-Three

Zelda lay in bed for hours, trying to find sleep, but the feeling of Leo's kiss ghosting on her lips kept her awake. As she stared at the exposed rafters of her childhood bedroom, she regretted not pulling him in for another kiss when they'd said goodnight. *There'll be more opportunities*. Especially, now that he wasn't her godchild anymore and she could close out the ICG case on his disastrous wish. Her legs were restless, but she didn't dare get up to pace her room. Instead, she drew the cream-colored quilt over her head to muffle the sound of her tired groan.

Bad idea. The blanket smelled of lavender from the sachet of dried flowers it had been stored with. The scent brought her right back to the pantry and her heart sputtered at the memory. A faint knock sounded at her door, and she pulled the covers from her head.

Her face still burned when she answered the tapping. Leo stood on the other side, his hands clasped behind his back and a smile on his lips that dimpled his cheeks.

"What are you doing here?" Zelda grabbed Leo by the neck of his chunky white sweater and pulled him into her room before her sisters spotted him and started getting the wrong idea. "It's almost three in the morning."

"Sorry, did I wake you?"

Zelda's brows pushed together. "I couldn't sleep."

"Neither could I, but that's not why I'm here."

"You wanted to be the first to wish me happy Christmas?"

Leo took a seat on an antique, spindle-legged chair with embroidered cushions. His face fell. "I have to go."

Zelda sank onto the edge of her bed. "Go where?" For an instant, she wondered if she'd scared him off, but she chased the silly thought away when she remembered that it was Leo who had asked to kiss her.

"My father was hospitalized an hour ago."

Zelda's mouth went dry as her pulse rocketed. "Is it serious?"

Leo ran a tired hand through his golden hair. "They don't know, but my mom needs me. I have to look out for Astara too. Felix will be here soon to take me to Erimount."

Zelda didn't know what to say. She couldn't promise Leo everything would be okay when they both knew it might not. Moonlight through her window hit Leo's profile, illuminating the muscles of his angular jaw which fluttered as he clenched his teeth. Zelda could easily guess what was going through his head. Despite their complicated relationship, Leo was about to lose his father. They'd both expected more time before he would take up his father's role as king. And would he come to regret giving up his first wish?

He was about to discover whether his worst fears about becoming king were unfounded or not.

"Do you need anything from me?" Zelda asked.

"Wait for Felix with me?"

Zelda nodded, and they tiptoed downstairs to the living room. Leo sat on one end of the sofa while Zelda used magic to start up the fire again. She took a seat at the opposite end of the couch, feet tucked beneath her.

Leo watched her curiously. "What are you doing?"

Zelda laughed. "I don't know. What am I doing?"

"Sitting all the way over there."

Zelda's insides went warm and fuzzy. "Oh." She tried not to smile like an idiot as she slid down the sofa to sidle under Leo's waiting arm and nestle into his side. This was certainly different. Good different. This was one of those things that changed after a kiss—how much they could touch. It was like an invisible wall had crumbled. If she wanted to reach out to him, to touch his hand, she could.

And she did.

With only the sound of the crackling fire, she ran her fingers over the shallow and deep lines of his palm. She wanted to learn every part of him and hold it in her memory for when he went away.

Leo shifted and pulled a small, rectangular box from his pocket. "Sorry, this isn't wrapped. I wasn't sure I should give this to you, but I—well—just open it."

Zelda took the felt-covered box and pried open the lid. Inside, a pair of pronged hairpins with sparkling stars sat on a satin cushion.

"Leo," she said breathlessly. The pavé crystals twinkled as they caught the warm, flickering light of the fire.

"It reminded me of your wand."

The star was similar to the five-pointed, diamond star that tipped her wand. But this star, made of a precious metal and embedded with little white stones, had eight points like a compass rose. Still, Zelda couldn't remember receiving a more precious gift. "It's gorgeous."

"I wasn't sure what to get you. I wanted to give you something nice for how wonderful you've been for me—I just didn't want to make you feel weird like I was pressuring you toward something other than friends." He took a pin from its satin cushion and squared himself to face her. Zelda bit back a contented sigh as Leo pushed his fingers through her hair. He gathered the hair at the back of her neck and stuck the pin into the mass of loose, dark waves. "I like that we're now *more*, I just want you to know our friendship isn't a consolation prize to me. It's everything."

Leo withdrew his hands and while a few pieces of hair fell around her face, the majority of it stayed. He took the second pin and slid it into Zelda's hair. The tines scratched teasingly at her skin, and she shivered.

"I couldn't leave without telling you," he whispered. "You've become very dear to me."

Zelda thought for a moment. "You make me glow," she said.

Leo smiled. "What does that mean?"

"I don't know. Whenever you're around I feel all warm and jittery. Like I have a stomach full of sugary hot cocoa."

Leo tilted his head back and laughed.

"Don't laugh."

"I'm sorry. I won't laugh." He wrapped his arms around her waist and pulled her into his lap. "That was such a wonderful thing to say."

Zelda wrapped her arms around Leo's shoulders and pressed her face into the soft hollow of his neck. She took a deep breath and smelled something sweet and heady alongside the fresh fabric-softener scent of his knit sweater.

She lifted her head off his shoulder. "I got you something too."

"Oh. You didn't have to—"

"Of course I did." Zelda dragged herself away from his side and padded over to the tree. "I wasn't sure what to get a prince for Christmas, but I think I did well."

"Zelda," Leo said with a lopsided grin when she handed him a long tube. He tore off the wrapping and pulled the rolled piece of time-aged paper from inside.

His lips pressed together as he unfurled the delicate, antique star map of the Leo constellation.

"Is that okay?" Zelda nestled back into her spot at his side. "I don't think I saw that one on your wall."

Joy glistened in his eyes.

"It's not valuable or anything. I got it in a charity shop—"

"It's perfect." Leo gently replaced it in the tube.

He pulled her close and they sat for a long while with only the sound of crackling fire to fill the room. Zelda let her eyes flutter closed as she traced the events of the past few days and committed each quiet moment to memory. She must have nodded off, because she awoke to the rhythmic beating of helicopter blades outside the house.

Her head popped off Leo's shoulder. "Is that your ride?"

"Yes." Leo grinned sheepishly. "I hope it doesn't wake your family, but I need to get back to the city as fast as possible."

"I understand, but your car's here. Is someone going to drive it back to Erimount for you?" Zelda stood up, the absence of Leo's warmth at her back startled her with a dose of cold reality. These idyllic days with Leo and her family had reached an abrupt end. And what was next for her and Leo?

"One of my security team can, unless you want to drive it back to the city? I don't want to put your parents out since they weren't planning on driving you back to school."

Zelda shook her head furiously. "I can't."

"You don't know how to drive a manual?" Leo stretched and tucked his new star map into his suitcase where it sat by the front door. "I can teach you sometime if you want to learn."

"No." Zelda laughed. "I can drive a manual. Your car's just too nice. If I wreck it, I'll never be able to pay you back."

"I see." They headed out the door and the helicopter got louder. "You needn't worry about that, but then again, the handling on sports cars can take getting used to; I don't want to worry about you making it back safely."

"I think you have enough on your mind without worrying about me ending up in a ditch on my way back to school."

Leo's face turned dark and Zelda could probably guess where his thoughts had ventured.

"We'll get through this. If there's anything you need, I'm a phone call away."

He gave her a weak smile. "I'll call you as soon as I know more."

The helicopter touched down in the empty field near the road. Dark figures jumped from the aircraft as the blades slowed. They approached, and Leo rounded on Zelda. He dropped his suitcase, grabbed her around the waist and pulled her into a hug that lifted off her feet. Zelda threw her arms around his shoulders and buried her face in his neck.

Felix was the first to reach the turnaround at the end of the drive. "Your Highness, we're ready to leave as soon as you are." His silky, dark curls were thrown into chaos by the wind from the helicopter blades.

Leo slowly released Zelda, and her feet found the solid ground.

"I'm ready," he said to Felix, his eyes still on her.

"Goodbye." Zelda didn't know if she should kiss him in front of Felix. They hadn't discussed whether they were officially in a relationship. How did one start dating a prince? Did she need the king and queen's approval? Did she need to feel a pea beneath a pile of mattresses to prove she was worthy? The sight of the helicopter with the Barrois crest at the end of the driveway was strangely unsettling. She wanted to pull Leo back into the house where they were just a boy and a girl who kissed each other in a pantry and cuddled on the sofa while the rest of the world slept.

Leo's eye's flickered with amusement as he caught what was probably a look of panic on her face. "Whatever you're thinking, we'll figure it out. Together." He took her hand and brushed a kiss to her knuckles.

The warm, gentle touch of Leo's lips made Zelda's legs tremble. She glanced at Felix to gauge his reaction to Leo's display of intimacy.

The faintest grin twitched on Felix's lips, but he averted his gaze politely.

Heat flushed to Zelda's cheeks.

"I'll see you soon," Leo said.

"See you soon."

Without Leo's arms around her, Zelda shivered against the cold. Her breath puffed out in fleeting clouds as Leo jogged down the driveway. Someone placed a heavy coat on her shoulders, and she realized her dad had joined her. It was his long, wool coat, and it smelled like cedar and French cologne. She pulled the front closed and let the familiar scent chase away her anxiety.

"Where's Leo going?" Ian asked.

"He has to see his dad. He's in the hospital." As the words left her mouth, Zelda hoped she hadn't revealed sensitive information. She looked up at her dad in panic.

He placed an arm around her shoulder. "Don't worry. I won't tell anyone."

"Thanks." Leo was going to have to coach her on this sort of stuff.

"Come inside," Ian said. "I'll put on coffee and we'll figure out what to tell the rest of the family, so they don't think we scared him away."

"Okay."

"It's a shame he couldn't stay." He guided Zelda back toward the house. "I like him."

Zelda laughed—a hum through her closed lips. "Me too."

Chapter Twenty-Four

Within an hour of his leaving, Zelda got a text from Leo saying he was back in Erimount. She tried not to think about it too much, but every time her phone buzzed, she imagined the worst had happened. Over a large breakfast of her dad's famous crêpes, everyone bemoaned Leo's sudden departure.

Ramona scowled and stabbed a strawberry with her fork. "Someone could have told me he was gone before I did my hair and makeup this morning."

"I did," Marie said as she bounced baby Sophia in her lap. "You were probably blow drying your hair when I yelled it down the hall."

Baby Sophia reached for the remaining crêpes on Marie's plate. Marie pushed them out of her reach, and Sophia expressed her disappointment with a piercing scream.

After breakfast, they went to the fireplace to see what treats Père Noël had left for them in their Christmas clogs. Leo had given her parents great gifts too, which made her heart ache for him all over again. He'd given her mom a fine wool scarf of Olisand wool, and her father a vinyl of an obscure French jazz-folk band that made him giddily run off to play it on the record player.

With only a dusting of snow on the ground, the family piled into vans and headed to downtown Montvian for the Christmas Market where the locals set up shop on the main square to sell their winter vegetables, meats, wines, and cheeses. Each year, the Ravensdales set up their own stall with the season's best wine.

Their wine was well known throughout the region both for the quality and its magical properties—a side effect of the occasional charms and spells Sabine used to help the fussier grapes along during the growing process. They'd brought cases of the 2009 Muscat to sell, a rich, buttery wine that had a knack for helping people remember the exact location of something they misplaced.

The market was crowded when they arrived at noon. It was all hands on deck as Zelda helped set up tables and stocked them with enough wine to buzz the entire region. Customers quickly flocked to the rows of dark bottles. Soon, there wasn't room for all the Ravensdales to work the market stall at once, so Sabine suggested to Zelda they take a walk. Zelda thought nothing of the excursion to peruse the offerings of the market until her mom let out a long sigh through her nose that meant she had something on her mind.

"Bébé." Sabine wound her arm through Zelda's. "I've been meaning to talk to you."

Zelda's jaw clenched with unease. "Do I want to know where this is going?"

"I don't know. I want to make sure you're okay."

The crowds jostled them about before Zelda could make her reply. Sabine pulled them over to a produce table and examined a supply of radishes.

"I'm fine, Mama."

"We got your grades from Madame LeBleu's. Your marks in charms are the lowest we've ever seen from you." She picked out a bundle of radishes and handed over a few sovereigns to the merchant.

Zelda bagged the bunch of red, bulbous vegetables. "There was a mishap with a snowstorm, some tulle, and a pumpkin—not all at once—but I've been doing extra credit to make up for it."

"I believe you, but I'm worried. You've never struggled in school."

They headed back into the stream of marketgoers. Zelda hoped the conversation would be over soon, but her mom was undeterred by being shoulder to shoulder with shoppers.

"This is your last term. I probably don't need to remind you that your class rank will affect your choice of available territories for placement."

Zelda's stomach knotted at the reminder of her slipping class rank. "No, Mama." She didn't mean to sound short, but another reminder her entire future would be decided in a few short months was the last thing she wanted to hear. "I know how tough Madame LeBleu's is. There's a real chance I might not be First Fairy."

Sabine sidestepped a woman standing in the middle of the street eating a galette. "I don't care about First Fairy. I just want you to make sure you're prepared to enter the field once you graduate. Being a godmother will be the hardest, most rewarding thing you ever do."

Zelda stopped short and a man ran into her. He mumbled something about teenagers under his breath as Sabine pulled Zelda out of the way. She led them away from the harried crowd of Christmas shoppers, and they took a seat on the wall around the dormant fountain at the center of the square.

"You were First Fairy, and you pushed all the rest of us girls to be First Fairy. I thought you'd be disappointed if I didn't get it," Zelda said.

Sabine tucked a stray curl behind her ear. "A mother always wants to see her children excel, but we always knew you'd be a different kind of fairy."

The words stung more than Zelda wanted to admit. "What does that mean?"

"Nothing." Sabine held up her hands in defense. "That sounded worse than it did in my head."

Zelda folded her arms across her chest. "I could be First Fairy if I sucked up to the professors as much as Susan St. Germain does." She didn't want to descend into a full snit, but this was the last thing she needed to hear. Not after how much she'd pushed herself to make it to the top of her class.

"I don't want that. What I mean is you are more passionate than the other girls, more creative. You take after your father more than the others, and like him, you like to question the rules—especially when they contradict what you think is right and just." Sabine wrapped an arm around Zelda's shoulders to pull her into her side. "I'll never forget when Madame LeBleu called during your first year to tell me that you'd released the school's mice claiming they were tired of being turned into horses only to be turned back into mice again."

Zelda's face burned with anger as her voice grew tight. "What does that have to do with being a different kind of fairy?" Her words sounded more hurt than she wanted to let on. Did her mom really think she wouldn't make First Fairy? She wasn't sure she liked hearing that she took after her non-godmother parent.

Sabine brushed a stubborn stray hair from her face again. "Look. Just keep up the hard work and know that I wouldn't change a thing about you."

Zelda toed a tuft of dead grass that had once sprouted to life between the cobblestones. She didn't know what to say when her mom's "reassurance" only left her more concerned about her future as a godmother.

Sabine eventually broke the prolonged silence. "We really like Leo." She stood and helped Zelda to her feet.

Zelda could do little to hide her smile at the mention of Leo. "He'll be glad to hear that. He really liked you guys too."

"It's a bit strange he wanted to be away from his family on Christmas—and they let him."

"He seems to get along with his mom and sister, but his relationship with his dad is strained." It almost didn't feel like she was talking about a crown prince. "I think his mom was giving him a break."

Sabine gave her a nod, but despite her fondness for Leo, she didn't seem at ease.

Zelda wasn't sure how to reassure her. Maybe people didn't like to know their ruling families suffered the same pains as all families did.

Her phone buzzed in her pocket. She pulled it out, and Leo's name and face smiled up at her from the screen. Panic and excitement fought to dominate her mind, but more than anything Zelda was reminded that she missed him already.

"Go on," Sabine said with an all-too-knowing grin.

Sabine returned to the stall, and Zelda turned down a quiet street where she could answer Leo's call in peace.

She held the phone to her ear. "Hi."

A warm chuckle came from the other end. "I only lasted a few hours without you." He sounded tired, verging on exhausted.

"How are you? Is everything okay? Is your dad . . ."

"My dad is being released today. I'm—I'm okay."

"Leo, if there's anything you need from me, I'm here for you."

"Funny you should say that. There's been a change of plans. It's all over the media that my father's health is failing, and some have made claims it has affected his ability to fulfill his duties as king. He and his advisors want to host a lavish New Year's Eve party at Erimount Castle to restore everyone's faith in his health." Leo didn't seem thrilled with the plan. "Will you come? My parents want to meet you. Astara threatened me with bodily harm if I don't introduce you to her soon."

Zelda smiled. He'd been talking about her. "Well, I *would* like to save you from bodily harm."

"Before you say yes, it's a whole weekend affair starting the twenty-ninth. I don't want to pull you away from your family on such short notice, but I could send a car for you tomorrow."

"Tomorrow?"

"If you're going to be coming as a guest of mine, they want you to be trained in the castle's rules and customs," Leo said.

"Oh." Three days of training was no small request; it made the reality of dating a prince all the more real—and far less simple. And what would her family think of her leaving so soon?

"I know it's a lot to ask, but I could really use you here."

Zelda swallowed the lump of anxiety constricting her throat. "I'll do it, but I need to get my parents' permission first."

"Let me know what they say, and don't worry about what to bring. I'll have the clothes you need for the weekend's events ordered for you if you'll just send me your size."

"Okay." Zelda's heart glowed at the thought of seeing Leo within a day's time. "I'll let you know as soon as possible."

Leo loosed a sigh. "I miss you."

A shiver like magic zipped from Zelda's chest to her toes. "I miss you too."

Chapter Twenty-Five

Sabine and Ian seemed hesitant at first when Zelda brought up Leo's request. They came around eventually, but Ian insisted that he drive Zelda to Erimount. When they returned from the market, Zelda packed and spent the rest of the day playing cards with her sisters. Sabine relegated the task of setting the table to her while the other girls helped cook, but Zelda was allowed to frost the Yule Log.

Ian and Zelda left early the following morning.

Her dad tapped his fingers to the wheel of the old van in time to the radio, but it was a nervous tap. He had something to say, but he didn't speak until they passed the old Norman wall that marked the outer limits of Erimount.

He ran a hand through his dark mess of salt and pepper ringlets. "My darling."

For the sake of her sanity, Zelda hoped this conversation wouldn't go in the direction of school. "Yes, Papa?"

"You'll be careful, ma petite?"

"What do you mean?"

"These people you're going to be spending more time with—princes, royalty, politicians—they aren't the same kinds of people you're used to dealing with."

Zelda folded her arms across her chest. "As a godmother, I'll have to deal with all kinds of people."

"I know, but I don't want any one of them to make you feel any less than what you are: the greatest fairy to ever walk the halls of Madame LeBleu's." A wide smile spread over his face to crinkle the corners of his deep-brown eyes—her eyes.

"Thanks." Zelda liked this conversation much better than her pep-talk from Sabine, but she wished she had as much confidence in herself as her dad did.

"People in power are always concerned with maintaining their power. Or getting more of it. I trust Leo, but for all I know, everyone you come across could have ulterior motives."

Zelda didn't reply, but he was probably right to warn her. She silently worried a hangnail until they reached the large, gilded gates of the palace. A guard in a royal-blue coat and stark white trousers came out of the guard house. He checked the license plate tag, which Zelda had given to Leo, and then checked both of their IDs. He waved them forward and the gates swung open to admit them.

Ian drove slowly up the winding drive to the castle at the top of the hill. It made an impressive entrance, and he let out a long whistle.

"Magnificent," Zelda confirmed.

"Positively palatial," Ian said with a laugh.

A guard motioned for them to turn into an area behind the castle that looked like it might have once been used for the storage of horses and carriages. They stopped, and before Zelda could even grab her door handle, a man in blue livery stepped forward and opened the door for her.

Zelda stepped out of the car as three figures descended the steps to the castle's entrance. Leo was in the center flanked by a short woman in a tidy, white wool dress and jacket, and a young girl with Leo's bright eyes and golden hair. Queen Antonia and Princess Astara. A servant helped Zelda with her bags as the trio crossed the gravel lot toward them.

Ian rounded the front of the car and froze. Queen Antonia stood before them in all her glory. Zelda was equally stunned.

The queen was short in stature, but Zelda wouldn't have known it if she hadn't been standing next to Leo for reference. Her pale blond hair was pulled into a low knot at the nape of her neck, her hands folded neatly in front of her.

"Your Majesty." Ian bowed.

She broke from the line and extended a hand to him. "Queen Antonia."

Ian shook her hand with gentle reverence as if he might break her, but she looked far too steady to be broken by a handshake. “I’m Ian Ravensdale.”

The queen turned and fixed Zelda with a luminous smile. “And you must be Zelda. We’ve heard so much about you.”

Zelda curtseyed to the queen as Astara left Leo and bounded to her mother’s side. “Leo’s told us so much.”

Zelda’s cheeks heated as her eyes met Leo’s bashful smirk. “He talks a lot about you too.”

“I can show you what room you’re staying in,” Astara said with an eager bounce.

Zelda smiled. “Sounds good. Let me say goodbye to my dad first.”

Ian wrapped her into a tight embrace. After checking twice to make sure she hadn’t forgotten anything, he turned her over to Leo with a brief handshake and a stern look.

“I know,” Leo said.

Zelda’s gaze flicked between them, and she got the sense that there had been some conversation that happened without her knowledge.

Astara wound her arm through Zelda’s. “Come. I’ll show you your room—it’s my favorite one aside from mine.”

Zelda waved goodbye to her dad as he got back in the van, then allowed the ten-year-old to pull her up the castle steps. She glanced over her shoulder and found Leo smiling up at her as he and the queen followed behind them.

“Astara will show you the ropes. I have a few things to do, but I’ll see you at lunch,” Leo said.

Zelda didn’t want Leo to go before they’d even really said hello, but as soon as they entered a small foyer with a winding staircase, Leo headed off down one of the long, first-floor hallways. The marble floors were polished to a shine and white busts of important-looking figures lined the walls. She craned her neck to see more of the castle, but she didn’t feel properly dressed to go wandering the halls of the royal residence in jeans and a lumpy, knit sweater.

Astara pulled Zelda toward the staircase. “Your room is in the Renaissance Wing.”

They climbed three flights of stairs and stopped at a landing where a honey-skinned woman with long, coal-black hair waited for their arrival. She didn’t smile at them when they crested the top of the steps. Her maroon lipstick matched the deep red of her two-piece suit, and her dark eyes focused on Zelda from behind thick-framed, black glasses.

"Zelda, this is my equerry, Group Captain Tiffani Beck," Astara said. "She'll be helping you get ready for this weekend."

Tiffani ran a discerning gaze over Zelda from head to toe, then gave a satisfied nod. "It's a pleasure to finally meet you, Zelda."

"Are you really a fairy godmother?" Astara blurted.

Tiffani gave Astara a reproaching glare. "Your Highness, that is not a polite question to ask."

"Yes, I'm a fairy godmother in training," Zelda answered.

"Well then this should be an interesting weekend." Tiffani turned on the heel of her tasseled, leather loafer and headed down the hall without a look back.

Astara grinned and motioned for Zelda to follow, and they hurried to catch up to Tiffani's long strides.

"The crown likes to control the narrative," Tiffani said, "and this weekend will set everyone's mind at ease about King Theodore's health."

Tiffani was intimidating, to say the least, but Astara seemed at perfect ease around her equerry. This settled some of Zelda's nerves.

They rounded a corner and stopped in front of a large wooden door. Tiffani lifted the latch, and it swung open with a low groan. The room was as grand as Zelda expected, but it didn't feel lived in like Leo's room when she'd visited so many months ago. The walls were papered in a teal-blue exotic bird motif with climbing gold vines that matched the hangings on the canopied bed. A tall armoire practically scraped the ceiling in one corner, and a matching desk of dark, polished wood sat in the opposite corner. A servant had somehow already reached the room and deposited her ratty duffle on the luggage rack at the foot of her bed. *Does the castle have secret passageways?*

"Your stylists will be here in a moment with some spare outfits we have on hand until your garments arrive tonight. Now, listen carefully, Miss Ravensdale. You have been invited at His Royal Highness Prince Leopold's request. Whatever you are to him, I don't care. What Prince Leopold needs, what the crown needs, is for you to blend in. This weekend must—and I mean absolutely must—be about King Theodore's stability. There have been rumors, people calling for a regency."

Was one of those people the Duke of Brockford?

"When every journalist and Olisand elite leaves the castle next week, there must be no doubt of his ability to rule. Do you understand?"

Zelda swallowed the lump of fear growing in her throat. Had she made a huge mistake in coming? Had Leo been wrong to invite her? "Of course. I understand."

"Good. Then prepare yourself."

"For what?"

"For His Royal Majesty," Tiffani answered.

"For the king?"

"Because kings don't like fairy godmothers," Astara said from where she'd climbed onto Zelda's bed and hugged an oversized sham with more birds printed on it.

Zelda's mouth fell open, and she looked to Tiffani for an explanation.

"Because godmothers are always sending peasant girls to their balls dressed as princesses."

Chapter Twenty-Six

Zelda's stylists prepped her for lunch in a mad fury. One wiped away her chipped nail polish while another rolled her hair into oversized hot curlers. Nude polish was brushed onto her fingertips, her brows were plucked into neat lines, and finally she was zipped into a stiff taffeta tea gown in a pale yellow. The buttery hue might have looked lovely on a blond, but it didn't fit Zelda's dark hair and pale skin.

When Zelda entered the parlor with Astara and Tiffani, she was surprised to find the room empty. "Leo said he was going to meet us for lunch," she said, failing to hide her disappointment.

"It's likely he's been detained by His Majesty." Tiffani pulled out Zelda's chair, so she could take a seat at the table.

Astara took the place across from her. Zelda wished Leo was there, but it was a relief to realize she wouldn't have to meet the king just yet. Tiffani tugged Zelda's shoulders so her back pressed into the uncomfortable wooden chair.

"I know Madame LeBleu gives her students etiquette lessons. While we aren't starting from scratch, we have a long way to go before we have you acting the part of a royal lady."

"But I'm not royalty." Zelda shifted to cross her legs.

A glare from Tiffani stopped her. "As Prince Leopold's guest, you're royalty by association."

Proper posture in an uncomfortable chair was the least of Zelda's worries. Tiffani had notes on poise and polite conversation. On top of that, there were rules of decorum that dictated who Zelda could speak to and how she would greet dignitaries and other members of the nobility. Zelda's head was bursting by the time they even arrived at the subject of dining etiquette.

They ate lunch slowly, so Tiffani could critique Zelda's every move. Luckily, Zelda had Astara to watch for hints on things like which fork to use for salad.

"Drink on the left, bread on the right," Zelda recited as she reached for her glass of water.

Tiffani clicked her tongue. "No. No. The other way around, Miss Ravensdale. Bread is on your left. Your drink is on your right most of the time."

Zelda bit back a groan. "When isn't it?"

She didn't get an answer.

A uniformed servant opened the door, and Leo swept into the room, shoulders back, head high. He wore a pale-blue, collared shirt tucked into a belted pair of camel trousers, and his golden hair was parted and combed to the side. Everything about him was neater—stiffer—than usual.

He locked eyes with Zelda the moment he entered the room and clasped his hands behind his back. His movements were steady and slow, and conveyed a strength that would be enough to carry the weight of Olisand's crown. Zelda's breath caught in her throat.

Tiffani stood and dropped into a curtsey. "Your Royal Highness." She rose and turned to Zelda. "Unless you're in line for the throne of another country or you've married Leopold in secret, you must curtsey to all members of the royal family, Miss Ravensdale."

Leo held up a hand. "That's not necessary."

Tiffani straightened her maroon blazer with a tug. "I'm afraid it will be. Zelda will draw excessive attention to herself if she doesn't observe these protocols. Your father has been very specific in his instructions."

Leo pursed his lips and gave a curt nod.

Zelda's stomach churned at the thought of upsetting the king. "Leo, it's fine. I don't mind. Really." She stood and dropped into a passable curtsey.

There was a slight wobble as she rose, and a smile broke across Leo's face.

"Absolute perfection." He rounded the table and extended a hand to Zelda. "I think that's enough training for this afternoon."

"Don't take her away," Astara said. "We haven't gotten the chance to talk yet."

Leo fixed his sister with an apologetic grin. "I'm sorry. I'll return her to you both once she's had a proper tour of the castle."

Zelda took Leo's hand, and he led her to the door.

"Your Highness," Tiffani called after them. Her eyes fell on their linked hands. "There is much we still have to cover, and we're already behind."

"We won't be long," Leo said. "I promise I will have her back to you to be prepped in time for dinner."

Tiffani curtsied with a stern glare in reply as she gave in to the prince's wishes.

In the hallway, Leo's stiffness slipped away, and he seemed less like a future king and more like the boy from the school across the street.

"Hi," he said with a lopsided grin.

"Hi," Zelda parroted. "Do I really get a tour of the castle now?"

Leo chuckled. "Of course. I got to see where you grew up. Now, it's your turn."

"I can't wait." Zelda glanced at the towering paintings and tapestries that hung on the light stone walls. "Are there any secret tunnels? Hidden doors?"

Leo laughed. "This isn't a mystery novel."

"Oh," Zelda said, only slightly disappointed.

"But yes, there are loads."

They started the tour in a long gallery full of uncomfortable-looking couches and paintings of important-looking people. A portrait of a bright-haired young man in the official prince's uniform made Zelda pause. "Is that you?"

She moved closer, but Leo grabbed her around the waist and pulled her away. "Nope. This is a walking tour, not a stopping tour."

"Leo. Let me see it," Zelda cried. "Wait. Are you cross-eyed?"

Leo wrapped his arms more securely around her middle and lifted her off her feet. "I hated that painting, still do," Leo muttered under his breath, but there was a smile in his voice. Zelda shook with a fit of laughter as he carried her out of the gallery.

From the tallest towers to the damp cellars, servants scurried about everywhere to ready the castle for the weekend's festivities. When Leo entered, they all stopped to give the prince a bow or curtsey before returning to their work.

"I'm fairly certain I wouldn't make it back to my rooms from here," Zelda said as Leo ushered her into a cozy study with bookcases lining the walls.

"You said you wanted to see a secret door."

Zelda looked around the study. "There's a secret door in here?"

"Yes, but before we go . . ." He crossed to a large wardrobe and pulled open the doors. Inside were a few pieces of clothing. He pulled out two blazers. "You'll want something to wear outside."

"Outside?"

Leo helped her into a heavy, navy-blue blazer. It was a little big in the shoulders, but it wasn't too bad of a fit. The other was fitted perfectly to Leo's slender, athletic frame.

"Is this your study?"

"It is." He approached one of the many bookcases and pulled a lever hidden somewhere underneath one of the shelves. The bookcase swung open to reveal a hidden staircase.

"That was even better than I expected," Zelda said, but she was torn. She wanted to stay and get a closer look at Leo's study, but he also seemed eager to show her whatever was outside.

The secret staircase led to a hidden exit that deposited them in the castle's manicured gardens. Despite Leo's blazer over her shoulders, Zelda shivered against the chill in the December air. The castle grounds were immaculately kept, even in the winter. While flowers wouldn't bloom for a few months, a charming blanket of frost sparkled on the neat evergreen hedges. They passed frozen reflecting pools and trellises wreathed in bare tangles of vines.

In a remote corner of the gardens, they reached a circular courtyard walled with mossy stones. A battered stone fountain bubbled over into a small pool at its center.

"What's this?" Zelda asked when Leo stopped in front of the fountain.

"I thought you'd like this." He gestured to the shabby little fountain in the courtyard and handed Zelda a bronze sovereign.

She pushed her brows together in confusion. "And this is?"

Leo's playful smirk was unbearably adorable. "This is the site of the first wish. Ever."

"Oh," Zelda said. Stunned, she stepped closer, and a strange tingle crackled in her fingertips and toes. "Magic. Is that why it's not frozen over?"

"There's a natural spring here that once fed a well. It's believed the founder of Olisand wished upon the well to find a place of safety where he could live happily ever after with his star-crossed love. That wish created this country."

Zelda had heard plenty of folktales about the wish that founded Olisand, but she'd never heard the part about the forbidden lovers. "So, the fountain in Founders Square is . . ."

"A common misconception," Leo said with a knowing smile. "The St. Germain family installed the fountain there to draw more visitors to their location."

"Ah ha," Zelda said. "This place—I can feel its magic."

"Really?" Leo stepped up to her side. "What does it feel like?"

"It tingles in my fingertips and toes like when they fall asleep, but in a good way."

Leo held out his hands and examined them. "Only fairies feel it?"

"Yeah, why?"

"No reason—just curious." He lowered his hands and looked down at the coin in her palm. "Are you going to make a wish?"

Zelda looked at the coin too, and warmth flickered in her chest. "I don't know if fairy godmothers get to make wishes."

Leo sidled in closer and slid an arm around her waist. "Everyone gets one wish. It's rule number one."

Zelda stepped up to the fountain and recalled her wish from the first day of term: to be First Fairy and the godmother of all Olisand. She still wanted it in a way that made her heart ache just thinking about it, but it somehow didn't seem worthy of a wish. When she thought about what Leo had given up to save his for a different happily ever after, she didn't want to waste hers on something so trivial as a title.

For his sake, she hoped her professors had been right. If not for Olisand, she hoped she'd been right to let Leo give up the chance to wish away his crown. Zelda held her hand out over the water. *I wish . . . I wish Leo won't regret holding onto his crown—that I haven't made a mistake in listening to Madame LeBleu.* She wanted so much for him, but she didn't know how to fit it all in one wish.

With a tip of her hand, the coin fell into the water with a satisfying plop. When she looked up at the prince, she saw the weight of his potential, his compassion, his kindness. He had so much ahead of him, and she didn't want him to wish it away.

Leo eyed her curiously. "What is it? Are you too cold?"

Zelda didn't reply. She grabbed a fistful of his collar and pulled his lips down to hers.

He stiffened at first, as if she'd caught him off guard, but he sank into the kiss. The arm around her waist slid up so he could settle a hand on the back of her neck. The feeling of his hand on her bare skin set a shiver down her spine. Leo deepened the kiss as he set his left hand on the side of Zelda's face. His thumb brushed the line of her jaw, and Zelda's breath hitched.

Leo drew back and sighed. "Wow. I'm not sure what that was for, but this isn't even the best part of the tour."

Zelda laughed breathlessly. "I don't think I can take any more surprises like this."

"Come on. We have one more stop before I return you to Tiffani."

He took her hand, and Zelda could have sworn she felt the tingle of the fountain's magic grow stronger.

Chapter Twenty-Seven

Leo pulled open a pair of French doors and ushered Zelda inside. Light poured in the windows from the lowering sun and filled the massive ballroom with a golden glow.

Zelda stepped gingerly toward the center of the room. The wood floors glistened with a freshly waxed shine and reflected the gilded filigree of the towering ceiling in a mirror image. Crystals dripped from unlit chandeliers and tossed the warm sunlight around the ballroom. Zelda laughed.

Leo's hands found her waist. "Shall we dance?" He spun her around and pulled her into a flawless ballroom dance frame.

A nervous laugh escaped Zelda's lips. "If you don't mind me stumbling my way through. Madame LeBleu's teaches us to make glass slippers, gowns, and Happily Ever Afters but they don't teach us to dance, but I know a little trick for that."

Zelda took her wand from her dress pocket and transformed her ballet flats into glass slippers. She charmed the crystal heels to know the steps for the fancy ballroom dances she could never remember herself. The spell tried to add several extra inches to the heels, but Zelda fought her magic to keep them short. She tucked her wand away, and Leo tugged her in close.

"Do I smell lavender?" Leo asked.

"A side effect of the spell. It must have been on my mind."

"You mean our first kiss was on your mind?"

Zelda tried unsuccessfully to bite back a smile.

"It's been on my mind too." He hummed a slow tune and began to spin her across the dance floor. After two turns around the ballroom, he snugged her in close enough to vanish what little distance there was between them. Zelda's pulse fluttered at the sensation his voice made as it vibrated through her chest. He twirled her under his arm. Though her shoes moved her through the steps, it was hard to know what to do with the top half of her body. Luckily, Leo knew just when to grab her hands and pull her back to him.

Dread set in as Zelda imagined the empty ballroom filled with guests for the weekend's festivities. The thought made her stumble.

Leo slowed to a stop. "Is everything okay?"

Zelda looked up at the prince, her head swimming. "What am I doing here?"

Leo's brows pushed together. "You're here as my guest."

"I'm just your guest?" She didn't mean to sound hurt.

Leo frowned. "No. You're not just my guest." He brought up a hand to cup Zelda's cheek in his palm. "I need you here to steady me, but I've been thinking. I have already asked so much of you, and I would like to be with you." He shook his head and flicked his gaze upward. "You have no idea how much I wanted this."

They shared a giddy laugh, but Leo quickly sobered. "As a prince, being with me comes with more obligation than most people comprehend."

"So, is this weekend a test? To see if I'm up to the task?"

"No." Leo pressed a fervent kiss to Zelda's lips. And then another. "No. It's not a test, but I don't want you to agree to a relationship without the full picture. Please, take this weekend to think about it. See what my world is like, and if by the end of all the chaos you're still interested in this mess, I'll tell the world my heart belongs to you."

Warm feelings fluttered high in Zelda's chest. "Leo, I don't need the weekend to know—"

"Please." Leo's thumb stroked her cheek. "It will make me feel better."

"Fine," Zelda said with a playful glare up at the prince. "But when I decide to be with you at the end of this weekend, no matter what unfolds, know that I already think you're worth the trouble."

Leo melted into her, something sparkling in his eyes. His thumb moved from Zelda's cheek to trace her lower lip. "And for that, I'll try to make it up to you every chance I get."

"You're off to a good start." Zelda's eyes fluttered closed as she waited for the kiss, but they flew open at the sound of feet clomping across the floor. Leo's hands fell from her face. A tall, slim man with thick waves of gray hair strode in their direction. There was so much of Leo in his features, but none of his kindness—King Theodore.

Zelda swallowed her nerves and sank into a curtsey.

"Leopold." The king's baritone voice filled the entire ballroom.

He's so much more intimidating than in pictures. King Theodore stopped in front of them and barely glanced at her before turning to his son. "Is this what you've been up to? I've been searching for you everywhere. There are pressing demands on your attention before our guests arrive."

"Father." Leo stepped in front of Zelda, his voice a mixture of shock and anger. "We have two, almost three days left to prepare—"

"And I need you focused. Nothing, and I mean *nothing*, can distract from the message this party is going to send."

Leo's shoulders tensed. "Of course. I know that—"

"Yes, but do you *understand* it?" King Theodore took a step toward his son, a menacing finger pointed at Leo's chest.

Zelda would've given anything for Leo's father to stop interrupting him. It made her feel like they were being scolded when she didn't know what she'd done wrong.

Leo held stock still, only a faint tremble in his hands. King Theodore turned on his heel and headed back the way he came. "I'll see you in my office in ten minutes," he said. "Miss Ravensdale can entertain herself however she pleases." He didn't bother to look back.

Zelda was as shocked at hearing her name come out of the king of Olisand's mouth as she was injured at being so unceremoniously dismissed.

Leo spun around and pulled Zelda with him.

"Where are we going?"

They burst from the ballroom into a long hallway lined with ornate doors and crimson carpet that stretched endlessly in both directions. Castle servants readying the halls for the festivities stopped their work and bowed as they passed. Zelda had to dodge a woman carrying a towering floral arrangement as Leo pulled her through another set of gilded doors.

"Slow down," she cried as they stumbled into a dining hall.

Leo pulled to an abrupt stop and made sure they were alone. "My father is out of line. I can't believe he spoke like that in front of you." He yanked open the top button of his collared shirt as if it were choking him and fisted his hands in his hair. "No. Actually, I can."

The sting of her brief encounter with the king was still raw, but Zelda wasn't here for his good opinion. It mattered a little bit, but his disapproval wouldn't stop her from being with Leo if it came to that. "Leo. He's probably still recovering, and I'm sure he's stressed about this weekend."

Leo folded his arms across his chest. "Everyone gets sick. Everyone gets stressed. It doesn't mean he gets to treat you like you're invisible." He looked rather handsome with his blond hair all out of place.

"Don't let him get to you."

A muscle in Leo's jaw fluttered. "He doesn't make that very easy."

Zelda brushed a stray curl from Leo's forehead back into place. "You have your own responsibilities now. I hate to say, but with his health in question, everyone will be looking to you. Show them, and your father, what kind of person you are and what kind of king you're going to be. That's what matters."

A smile twitched on the corner of Leo's lips. "You know, this weekend may be good for something."

"What's that?"

"You'll get to hang out with my sister. Astara already loves you, and I know my mom will too."

Zelda laughed. "I can tell I'm going to like Astara. She said something interesting."

Leo chuckled. "Oh no. What did she ask you?"

"She said kings don't like fairy godmothers. Does your dad know I'm a fairy?"

Leo's face fell, and he sighed. "Yeah, he knows you go to Madame LeBleu's, so I assume he's figured it out."

Zelda didn't like the sound of his sigh. "So, he really doesn't like fairies because we send 'peasant girls' to balls?"

"I don't think it's just that. Magic has always made his job more complicated. When people don't have it, they want it, and for some people one wish isn't enough. He's always dealing with the International Council of Godmothers on some new piece of legislation."

"Oh." Zelda's stomach knotted.

"You'll be fine. Just keep your head down. Maybe don't conjure up a snowstorm in front of him, and you'll be a huge success."

"Right." The knot tightened. *Keep my extremely volatile magic under control. Easy.*

Chapter Twenty-Eight

Zelda winced as a stylist twisted her hair into a Tiffani-approved knot at the back of her head. Her scalp already ached from the hidden pins holding it in place.

"Here. Add this." Zelda handed the stylist the star-shaped hair pins from Leo.

The woman slipped the star among the other pins and passed Zelda a mirror for a final inspection.

"Marvelous." Tiffani strode into Zelda's chamber wearing a midnight-blue satin pantsuit. "It's a fine piece from the crown jewels. Very fitting for you, in my opinion." She squeezed Zelda's shoulder in a comforting gesture.

Zelda's hand flew to her hair, but before she could touch the pin, Tiffani knocked her hand away. "Ow. Did you say crown jewels?"

"Yes. I believe it has a lovely tiara and earrings to match." Tiffani crossed to the pale-blue, silk gown Leo had ordered for her for the Friday night welcome dinner and fussed over a wrinkle on the hem with a hand steamer. At their first meeting, Tiffani had seemed intense and unapproachable, but after their days spent together in royalty boot camp, they'd developed their own rapport. Zelda's perseverance in light of King Theodore's distaste for her seemed to earn her some sympathy from the equerry.

"Crown jewels," Zelda whispered as she looked at the glittering pin in the mirror. Leo had neglected to mention that when he'd given it to her. "Is he allowed to just give them away?"

"He's allowed to do whatever he wants with them." Tiffani replaced the steamer on its rack. "He inherited them from his grandmother's private collection."

Zelda had been too young to remember when Leo's grandmother, the late Queen Irene, had died, and King Theodore had assumed the throne.

"You must mean a lot to him." Tiffani unhooked the gown from where it hung on the wardrobe doors and brought it to Zelda. "And he must really trust you."

Zelda shivered as she tossed her robe onto the bed. She had to clutch a bedpost for stability to step into the gown's layers. The dress glided softly over the nude silk stockings and the reinforced strapless bra that was more of a body suit than an undergarment.

"Remember, royals don't fidget or adjust their clothes in public," Tiffani said. With the skirt of the gown over Zelda's hips, Tiffani fastened the waist to little metal hooks on her satin body armor.

"This feels excessive," Zelda said. She slid her arms into the sheer silk sleeves of the bodice.

"You'll thank me when you don't have a wardrobe malfunction at your first royal event."

With a tug and a zip, Zelda was finally battened into the gown. It was heavier than expected. Intricate beading layered the plain satin bodice and sheer sleeves that extended to Zelda's wrists. The skirt of the gown was much simpler with layers of thin, gray-blue tulle that floated as it moved. Zelda ran her hands over the skirt as she thought about what was ahead.

Tiffani grabbed Zelda's hands to still them. "Everything is going to be fine. I've taught you everything I know."

Zelda smiled weakly. "I just need to remember it all."

"And if you don't, I won't be far, and neither will Astara. Now, let's go." Tiffani placed a pair of simple nude heels in front of Zelda. "Guests will be arriving soon, and we don't want to draw too much attention to you tonight."

Zelda slid her feet into the heels. "And what do I say if anyone asks who I am?"

Tiffani paused for a moment. "You're the student ambassador from Madame LeBleu's."

"That sounds plausible."

Tiffani escorted Zelda to the ballroom through the maze-like corridors and at least one secret passageway. They entered the ballroom through a door hidden in one of the wall's panels, and Tiffani deposited Zelda at a table in a far corner of the room. The ballroom was a sight to see with the chandeliers lit and the floor full of tables draped in white and crowned with floral centerpieces. Royals and their honored guests would sit around a long table on a low, raised platform.

Tiffani excused herself to finish preparing Astara for the dinner, and Zelda was left to watch as the first of the guests trickled in. A small orchestra began to play from the gallery, and an elderly woman swanned into the ballroom with so many diamonds around her neck she looked like she might tip over from the weight of them. The room slowly started to fill with more important-looking men and women, each adorned in an array of jewels, tiaras, glittering medals, and colored sashes whose meanings were lost on Zelda.

She thought she spotted the actor who was in all the action movies Leo liked to watch, and then a more familiar face caught her eye. Dante Sadler strode into the room alongside a tall, tanned man with a beard and a crown atop his dark hair. Zelda's stomach hit the floor. As the pair moved further into the room, Zelda inched her chair around so the massive centerpiece hid her from view. *Who is he with?* She'd met Dante's father on one occasion, but he wasn't the man with Dante.

Zelda tried to steady her breath, but another pair entered the ballroom that made her throat close shut: Susan and her father, George St. Germain. Dismay fluttered in Zelda's chest. *What are they doing here?* Thankfully, Susan, in her butter-yellow, silk gown, floated in the opposite direction. Zelda wouldn't be able to avoid both Susan and Dante the entire weekend, but they appeared to be seated at the other end of the ballroom.

A few well-dressed people found seats at Zelda's table before the orchestra struck up the Olisand national anthem. Everyone in the room stood, and Zelda followed suit. As the players reached the final chorus, a pair of towering double doors opened. The royal family entered the ballroom, King Theodore and Queen Antonia in the lead, with Prince Leo and Princess Astara behind them. All the air left Zelda's lungs at the sight of Leo in his ceremonial uniform and crown. The guests around her clapped politely, but Zelda was too stunned to move.

The boy she'd baked pies with and shared lavender-scented pantry kisses with, had been replaced by an actual prince. She'd known he was a prince, of course, but seeing him stride into a ballroom in a crown made everything feel different. It should have looked weird on him, but he wore it as well as he wore crew pullovers or white collared shirts. The royals made their way to the head table and the evening began with a welcome speech from King Theodore.

From her view in the back corner, Leo was the picture of grace and poise while Zelda managed to keep all the food on her plate from ending up in the laps of people who sat beside her. She even conjured up polite conversation with the Minister of Foreign Magical Relations through dessert.

After dinner, the guests were ushered across the hall into the long dining room where cocktails were served. The massive table had been removed and replaced by a smattering of small high-top tables.

Zelda successfully avoided Susan in the transition, but as she positioned herself behind one of the tables, she felt a tap on her shoulder and found Dante standing behind her. His dark hair swept elegantly to one side, and he wore a black tuxedo that was tailored perfectly to his lithe, athletic frame. His lips pulled into a smirk.

"Dante." Zelda wasn't sure what else to say. They hadn't spoken since his wish, and until now, Dante had pretended she didn't exist.

"Zelda." Dante mimicked the high, panicked tone of her voice. "I was wondering if I'd see you here. I suppose this means the prince is still hanging around you." He slung his hands into his pockets, as self-assured as ever.

"I guess so. Are you going to warn me about him again?"

Dante shrugged one shoulder, and his head tilted to meet it. "I've already said my piece. I'm just here to say hello to my school peer. There aren't many of us here."

"Who's that man you came in with?" Zelda's eyes flicked to the bearded man in the circlet who was making his rounds through the crowd.

Dante's lips pursed. "That's my uncle, Prince Lionel, Duke of Brockford."

Zelda's stomach pulled a somersault. "Your uncle is a duke?"

"Well, I guess he's not technically my uncle." Dante rubbed the back of his neck like it was sore. "He's a friend of my parents; he's my guardian for the time being."

Zelda's gaze jumped from the duke to Dante. Her brows pushed together in concern. "What's going on with your parents?" She hadn't heard even a whisper of a rumor about Dante's parents.

"They split up this summer. Uncle Lionel is watching me while they *figure out how to be single again.*" Deep sadness darkened in Dante's eyes as he focused on something Zelda couldn't see.

"I'm so sorry, Dante," Zelda said.

"I'm fine." He failed to sound reassuring.

Zelda paused to make sure none of the other guests were within earshot. "Does this have to do with your wish?"

Dante flinched as if she'd touched an open wound. "I'm fine. Really, Zelda." His eyes met hers. "You didn't want to grant my wish, and you're definitely not my girlfriend. I'm not yours to worry about."

Zelda's mouth gaped. "You're the one who wished—"

The Duke of Brockford approached with a saccharine smile, and Dante straightened like a soldier snapping to attention. Something about the toothy grin made Zelda uneasy. The pale-blue eyes shining bright beneath his too-dark hair and artificial tan looked like they could see straight under her skin and know all her secrets.

"Dante." The duke's baritone boomed above the din of voices around them. "Who is your friend?"

Dante shifted awkwardly between his feet. "This is Zelda Ravensdale. She is a student at Madame LeBleu's."

Zelda smiled politely at the duke and gave him a curtsey because he was also a prince in line for the throne. "Your Grace," she said, remembering Tiffani's lessons on reverences for nobility.

"It's actually Your Highness, since I am in line for the throne," Brockford corrected.

Zelda's cheeks heated. "I'm sorry. I didn't mean any offense—"

"None taken. Madame LeBleu's you say, Dante? I pegged you as a fairy the moment I saw you. You're all so short. Tell me, Zelda Ravensdale, are you on track to be a granter?"

"Yes, sir."

"We don't usually get many young attendees at events like this. What brings you here tonight?" Brockford asked, his voice silky and deep. He slipped his hands into the pockets of his black coattails.

"I'm the official student ambassador from Madame LeBleu's."

Lord Brockford cocked his head while a look of obvious confusion shadowed his brow. *Did he expect a different answer?*

"It's a new program," a voice replied from Zelda's side.

Leo.

Zelda's pulse flew into high gear at the sight of the uniformed prince beside her. He held a flute of champagne delicately with one hand, and he placed the other on the small of Zelda's back.

"Your Royal Highness," Brockford said, and he gave Leo a mandatory bow as Leo was ahead of him in the line of succession. "I was unaware we had programs like that. If you decide you need an ambassador from EAMS, I hope you will consider my ward, Dante Sadler." He clapped a hand on Dante's shoulder, but his eyes fell to Leo's hand on Zelda's back.

Zelda stiffened as she remembered the public wasn't allowed to touch royalty unless the royal offered them a handshake or a hug. Leo's contact was definitely a bit too familiar.

"When I'm no longer at EAMS perhaps," Leo said, "but until then, I think I have a pretty good sense of the school and its goings on."

"Right. Right," Brockford said with a mirthless chuckle.

"If you don't mind, I'm going to steal Zelda from you. There are a few members of the magical community here that I'd like to introduce her to."

There was another round of pleasantries and bows before Leo used the hand on Zelda's back to steer her toward an unoccupied table in the corner of the long room.

"Thank you." Zelda breathed out a long sigh once they were out of Dante and Brockford's view. "How did you know I needed rescuing?"

Leo's hand slid from her waist, and he moved to stand at a respectable distance. "I can't stand Brockford. If he asks you to dance at the ball on Sunday, find any excuse to refuse. I've heard he's handsy." His gaze traveled from her head to her toes. "You look stunning."

Zelda's insides warmed. "You picked it out."

"I know, but wow." Leo sunk his teeth into his lower lip.

Zelda pushed one of her loose curls behind her ear. "You're going to have to stop looking at me like that. People will get suspicious."

"Fine," Leo said with feigned annoyance. "My father is glaring at me anyway, so I probably shouldn't linger with you any longer."

"I understand." Zelda wanted to reach out and hold his hand—anything to reassure him. "You're doing wonderful tonight."

Leo's shoulders relaxed a mere fraction. "Thank you. I'll come find you as soon as I can."

"Okay." Zelda gave him a hopeful smile as he returned to his father's side.

The cocktail party carried on for hours with no hope for another visit from Leo. Feet throbbing in her heels, Zelda decided to call it a night. Without Tiffani as her guide, she was left to maneuver the castle's twisting passageways on her own. After a few wrong turns, and walking through the same gallery twice, she found her suite by almost walking right past it.

Zelda kicked her shoes across the floor and shut the door behind her. With a groan, she flopped onto the oversized bed. The cloud-like comforter swallowed her whole in its inviting softness. Before sleep could pull her under, she fumbled for the phone Tiffani had ordered her to leave on the nightstand. There were three missed calls from Imogen in her notifications. Zelda hit "call back" but the phone only beeped in reply.

No service.

"Great." She kept forgetting to get the password for the castle's wifi. Zelda tossed the phone aside and rolled off the bed onto her aching feet. Of all the nights she needed to call her best friend, tonight she needed it most. Apparently, Imogen needed her too.

Zelda tried to ignore the feeling of loneliness that clung to her chest as she got ready for bed in the large, cold chamber. She nearly popped a shoulder from its socket as she tried to extract herself from her gown. Successfully removed from her couture prison, she padded to the en suite bathroom to brush her teeth and wash her face. The cool stone floors soothed the aching pads of her feet.

With heavy eyes, she jumped back in bed as soon as her dress was stowed carefully in the armoire. Nestled deep under the covers, she begged for sleep, but every sound roused her.

She pulled her phone off the nightstand again. Even if she couldn't make calls, she hoped a message would go through. She opened a group text with Imogen and Specs.

SOS. I'm stuck at Leo's this weekend with both Susan and Dante. I'm freaking out. Dante is being weird.

With the phone on her pillow, Zelda let her eyes fall closed as she waited for a reply.

Chapter Twenty-Nine

A knock on Zelda's door pulled her from a fitful dream where she chased Dante through a train station. "Come in," she croaked, rubbing her eye with the heel of her hand.

Leo slipped through the door, carrying a tray full of food. "Good morning, sleeping beauty."

Zelda pushed herself onto one elbow, blinking sleep from her eyes. "What are you doing?"

Leo grinned as he set the polished silver tray at the foot of the bed. He walked around to the other side of the bed, kicked off his shoes, then crawled onto the covers beside her. "This is to say thank you for last night." He leaned over and pressed a kiss to Zelda's forehead before he pulled the tray to sit between them.

The kiss and the smell of coffee and cinnamon scones was enough to wake Zelda the rest of the way. She moved to a sitting position, and Leo poured coffee into the pair of cups. "You didn't have to do all this. I talked with you for maybe a minute."

"I know—and it was just what I needed." He spooned two sugar cubes and a large helping of cream into his coffee. "Having you there was more comforting than you know."

"Then I'm glad I was there."

"This is an apology too," Leo said. "I wanted to talk to you all night, but now is not the right time to be broadcasting our new relationship to the world."

"I know; this weekend is about your father. It's not about us."

Leo pushed the plate of scones closer to Zelda. "I know, but these are my best apology scones yet. You have to try them."

Zelda took a bite of scone. Crisp on the outside and fluffy on the insides, the soft, cinnamon-y crumbles melted on her tongue. Zelda groaned. "Oh wow. These are fantastic." She took another oversized bite. "What's your secret?"

Leo chuckled. "Butter. Really good butter."

"If you weren't a prince, you could make a great career as a baker."

"Don't tempt me," he said with a rueful grin.

Zelda swallowed. "I'm sorry. I shouldn't joke about that."

Leo bumped his shoulder against hers. "Darling, it's quite all right."

Zelda straightened. "Darling?"

"Oh." Leo's brows pushed together. "Is that okay to call you? Are terms of endearment off limits for you?"

"No," Zelda said emphatically. "I like it. A lot."

Leo's shoulders relaxed. "Good. I wanted to use it at least once before this weekend is over should you decide that dating me isn't worth the trouble."

Zelda frowned. "You need to give yourself—and me—more credit."

A smile flickered at the corner of Leo's mouth. "If you insist." He tilted her chin up to press a slow, lingering kiss to her lips.

As he drew away, a shadow of contemplation clouded his face.

"What is it?" Zelda asked.

Leo's lips parted, but he closed his mouth as he stopped his reply. He glanced at the clock beside the bed. "I'm afraid I've made you late."

"What?" Zelda set down her cup of coffee and jumped from the bed. "Late for what?" She flew to the wardrobe and threw open the doors as she tried to remember what Tiffani had planned for her to wear.

Leo slid off the bed. "Well—"

"What were you doing plying me with scones when I was supposed to be up and ready?"

As Zelda pawed through the hanging garments, arms came around her waist. "Because I'm selfish and wanted you all to myself for a few minutes."

"Leo." Zelda sank against him. His warmth pressed invitingly against her back. "Where am I supposed to be right now?"

Leo pressed a kiss to the top of her hair, released her, and headed for the door. He slipped into the hall and returned seconds later with a long wooden bow and a leather quiver filled with arrows. "The queen's archery tournament is starting soon. If you hurry, you won't miss the first round."

Dressed in stretchy caramel pants, high leather boots, a plain white collared shirt, and a quilted jacket, Zelda hurried through the castle gardens with her new bow and quiver slung over her shoulder.

The morning sun hung low over the trees and chased the cool mist from the air. Wispy, gray clouds streaked the sky, but the sun's rays broke through enough to make the blanket of frost sparkle like diamond dust.

Zelda tried to remember Leo's instructions for finding the archery range, but none of the garden paths seemed to follow a straight line. She passed a frozen pond, a hollow of yew trees, and more than one stone pavilion. Leo had mentioned something about a Corinthian column, so when Zelda found a giant stone arch, she realized she was somewhere in the correct vicinity.

A flash of blond hair caught Zelda's eye as she passed through the arch. Susan St. Germain, with a bow over her shoulder, hurried down the crushed gravel path and disappeared into a copse of towering Juniper trees.

Zelda followed her in the hope that Susan knew the way to the archery range. She veered off the path toward the trees where she'd lost sight of Susan, but as she approached the gathering of bushy evergreens, the sound of a man's voice gave her pause.

"No, Susan. I won't allow it."

The smooth baritone sounded vaguely familiar. Zelda pressed her back to one of the Juniper trees and peered through a gap in the branches. Susan stood at the center of the grove beside her father, George St. Germain.

Susan's voice carried clearly through the dense branches. "Why not? You know they're onto us, right? You know what they want."

"I'm the adult. I'm handling the Consortium. You need to focus on school."

"The longer you put them off, the worse it will be—"

"I'm not handing you over in place of the Heartstone."

Heartstone? Zelda wondered. She'd never heard the term before.

"Not after what happened with your mother." George St. Germain's voice trembled with pain.

"That was a fluke. I'm stronger—"

"No," he roared. "End of discussion."

Feet clomped across the frozen ground, and Zelda shoved herself further into the tree. George St. Germain stomped toward the castle, and Susan left the copse and scurried away in the other direction. Zelda waited a few seconds before she followed Susan in what she hoped was the direction of the archery range.

She didn't have to go far before the chatter of voices filled the cold air.

The archery range was set on a long rectangle of grass surrounded by low, manicured shrubs that remained green through the winter. A row of circular targets painted with concentric circles stood at one end, and a crowd of women stood at the other. The women were paired off; the tournament had already begun. Queen Antonia stood at the first lane where she released an arrow that found the yellow circle at the center of her target. A din of polite applause rose from the people around her.

Zelda approached the group of archers and tried to slip in unnoticed, but Tiffani found her before she could disappear into the crowd.

Tiffani's hand locked around Zelda's arm, and she steered her toward the end of the range. "Where have you been?" she whispered. She wore a hunter-green suit and her long, black hair was braided into a crown.

"Sorry, I got lost." Zelda thought it best to leave out Leo's apology scones and the eavesdropping.

Tiffani rolled her eyes exaggeratedly, but a smile twitched at the corner of her lips while she examined her clipboard with the tournament bracket. "You're lucky. You'll have to play into the tournament from the loser's bracket, but one other girl was late too, so you'll pair off first."

Zelda's stomach sank as they stopped in the last lane. Susan St. Germain stood at the end of the line with no partner to be seen.

"Ravensdale," Susan said icily.

"St. Germain." Zelda returned the greeting with much better cordiality.

Tiffani straightened. "Oh. You know each other?"

"We go to school together."

"Well then, since you were both *late*—" Susan flinched at this and fixed Zelda with a withering look. Zelda tried to school her features into something that resembled innocence. "You'll have plenty of time to catch up while you wait to play into the loser's bracket." Tiffani turned and went to another lane to record the tournament's proceedings.

There would be no pleasantries or small talk. Susan faced forward, her mouth in a hard line. Zelda and Susan didn't speak until it was their turn to shoot. "How many arrows per end?" Zelda asked.

"Six." Susan tested the flex in her bow and the tightness of the string. As the captain of the school archery team, the weapon looked at home in her hands. "We'll shoot three ends each at different lengths."

"Thanks." Zelda stepped up to her lane and placed her quiver of arrows on the waiting stand. Susan took the adjacent lane.

Zelda tried to ignore the feeling of discomfort as she turned her back on Susan and waited for the whistle to blow. Magic tingled in her fingertips as she grasped the bow in her wand hand. Her palms went sweaty. *That could be dangerous.* Fairies were forbidden from using magic without a wand. Zelda hoped the wood of the bow would be too poor of a conductor for any of her magic to escape. She shook out her hand, hoping the shivers down her arm would disappear.

The whistle blew, and Susan loosed a ready arrow. Her arrow hit the yellow center of the target with a satisfying thwack.

Zelda nocked an arrow, drew back the string, aimed, and released. Her arrow wobbled in the air, but it at least hit the target. All six of her arrows found the target, but they were all over the place. Susan's arrows were heavily concentrated in the center. Another whistle sounded and they went to score and collect their arrows.

With a closer look at Susan's target, a flare of competitive frustration flamed in Zelda's chest. It was clear that Susan would be advancing. If the official sport of Olisand were fencing instead of archery, Zelda would actually have a chance.

They returned to the line, but Susan did a double take and made a beeline for Zelda. Brow furrowed, Susan reached out and grabbed something from Zelda's hair before Zelda could swat her hand away. She wasn't gentle about it either.

"Ow. What's wrong with you?" Zelda rubbed her head where her scalp smarted.

Susan held up a sprig of evergreen needles with a clump of dark berries. "This was in your hair. Have you been hanging around shrubs a lot lately?"

"No," Zelda exclaimed. "I have no idea how that got there—probably something I brushed against when I was walking here."

Susan brought the sprig to her nose. "Juniper. That's used in lots of potions—quite poisonous if the wrong amounts are used."

"So?" Zelda crossed her arms, but it probably didn't help her seem any less suspicious. Did she know the grove she and her father had been in was surrounded by Juniper trees?

The whistle blew to begin another end. This time the targets had been moved even further back on the lawn.

Zelda stepped up to the line and knocked an arrow. She released, and Susan loosed hers a second later. The arrows raced for the targets, but Susan's got there first. It hit the target with a pop and a blast of air blew Zelda's arrow off course, so it sailed far to the right of her target.

Zelda whirled on Susan. "What did you just do?" *Did Susan just channel magic through her bow and arrow?* That definitely wasn't allowed at Madame LeBleu's, but this wasn't a school archery tournament.

Susan straightened herself to her full height and stepped up to Zelda so they were nose to nose. "Have you been spying on me?"

"No." Even to her own ears she sounded too defensive.

"Mind your own business, Zelda Ravensdale." Susan drew another arrow. This one hit the target dead center. "If you don't start focusing on that erratic magic of yours, someone is going to steal your precious spot as First Fairy from right under your upturned nose."

Anger bubbled in Zelda's chest. She would not be threatened and insulted by Susan St. Germain. "Thanks for the concern, but my magic is fine." When Zelda nocked an arrow and lifted her bow, a shiver of magic raced down her arm. It tapped at the pads of her fingers, asking to be freed. Zelda released her arrow, but she held the magic in check; she wouldn't give Susan the satisfaction of seeing her lose control. The arrow hit the outer rim of the target without incident.

"Whatever. Just stay out of my way if you know what's good for you." Susan shot another arrow, and it landed in the yellow center too.

Something snapped in Zelda's chest and heat raced to her cheeks. "Why? Have you and your dad been up to something you shouldn't?"

Susan's brow furrowed as surprise flickered over her face. "What are you talking about?"

Zelda couldn't stop the words that flowed from her mouth. "I know what you're doing, and I'll expose you both for your abuses to magical creatures."

Susan's face paled. Triumph roared in Zelda's chest as she realized she'd struck the right nerve.

"Stupid girl. You may think you know what's going on, but you understand nothing—"

"I know more than you think," Zelda said as she found her composure. She turned to release another arrow, but Susan beat her to it.

Susan gave an exasperated cry and released her third arrow. It hit the target and sparks exploded from her arrow. Several shouts rose from the crowd. The pyrotechnics sparked the straw backing, and in a blink, the entire target was engulfed in flames.

Zelda rounded on Susan, but before she could confront her, Susan threw down her bow, and stalked away from the range in the direction of the castle.

Tiffani's hand on Zelda's arm brought her back to the range. "What's going on?" She flung her hand toward the flaming target.

Zelda's voice trembled as the reality of Susan's words and actions sank in. "It was an accident," Zelda said, still stunned by Susan's outburst. She pulled her wand from the inner pocket of her coat. "Susan didn't mean to do it, but I can clear this up."

She lifted the wand and said the words for a rain spell "dribble drabble drangle" before she even gave a thought to her erratic magic. A dark cloud unfurled just above the flaming target where Zelda willed it to form. The whorls of mist formed a small cumulus nimbus cloud and a downpour of rain drenched the target. The flames sputtered, hissed, and died.

All eyes were on either Zelda or the charred target. Zelda smiled weakly as she tucked her wand away. Tiffani shook her head and scratched off something on her clipboard. "I guess Susan St. Germain has forfeited this round. You'll move to the next round, Zelda."

The cloud dissipated without Zelda's magic feeding the spell, and uniformed servants came to remove the burned target from the field. She didn't want to think what she might've said that would jeopardize the coterie's plans to free the elves from St. Germain's clutches. She may have tipped off Susan to their plans, but was Susan right? Had Zelda misunderstood what was going on? Zelda pushed the notion aside, but a sick feeling turned in her gut.

The archery tournament continued, but Zelda couldn't focus. She went out in the next round, and on the cold walk back to the castle, ran through her confrontation with Susan, so she could remember every word to report back to the coterie.

Chapter Thirty

Queen Antonia glided into Zelda's room in a simple white gown with an attached white cape that fell from her shoulders and trailed behind her. Zelda smiled up at the queen through a cloud of hairspray as Tiffani added the finishing touches to her hair for the New Year's Eve ball. Tiffani curtsied and Zelda tried to stand, but Queen Antonia stopped her with a wave of her hand.

"Don't get up. Leo asked me to loan you these for the night." She handed Zelda a rectangular jewelry box. Inside, a pair of teardrop pearl earrings and a single teardrop pearl on a gossamer-thin gold chain rested on a velvet pillow.

"They're beautiful."

"Allow me," Queen Antonia said, and Tiffani stepped aside.

While Zelda threaded earrings into her earlobes with trembling fingers, Queen Antonia clasped a necklace around Zelda's neck.

"You're almost there," Queen Antonia reassured. Her hands came to rest on Zelda's shoulders. "Just one more event and then it's over."

As nervous as she was about the ball, Zelda looked down at the empty inbox on her phone. Imogen and Specs hadn't replied to her detailed report on Susan's strange behavior and the mysterious conversation between Susan and her father. "Fairy godmothers don't go to balls. We make dresses and turn pumpkins into carriages. I—" She glanced at her reflection in the ornate, gilded mirror. Someone unfamiliar stared back. "I feel like I've wandered too far from my place in the story."

Queen Antonia's lips pulled into a sympathetic, closed-lip smile. She pulled a stray hair from Zelda's face and tucked it back into the neat, French twist. Her eyes sparkled with emotion as she examined Zelda in the mirror. "You know . . . everyone deserves to be the Cinderella of their own story."

Sadness welled like a lump in Zelda's throat. She tried to swallow it down, but it wouldn't budge. "You're just being nice," she said. The words *I don't belong here* were strangled along the way.

"Zelda." Tiffani stepped up to stand beside Queen Antonia with a determined scowl. "As I'm sure you've learned, I don't do nice. I'm not paid to be your friend. I'm paid to protect the reputation of the crown." She patted Zelda's shoulder with a firm hand. "You did well this weekend. If given a couple of years, I don't doubt I could make a princess out of you."

Zelda laughed. "A couple of years? Thanks a lot."

"Nobody is a natural at this. Nobody. Leo and Astara have grown up with this." Queen Antonia waved a hand around the room as if gesturing to the castle's general opulence. "So, have most everyone who will be in attendance tonight."

"I gathered that," Zelda said.

Queen Antonia helped Zelda to her feet, and Tiffani handed her the nude shoes that went with her lavender ballgown. "Don't let them make you feel less than for being who you are," Queen Antonia said. "We need more outsiders around here. They bring a needed perspective to this crowd."

Zelda wasn't sure she wanted to bring perspective to Olisand's elite. She was supposed to be here for Leo. "You don't think everyone's still talking about the incident during the archery tournament, are they?"

"Probably not, but I think Susan St. Germain is the one who should be worried about that," Tiffani said.

Zelda entered the glittering ballroom with a stream of other guests. Orchestra music and the delicate scent of fresh flowers hung in the air. People crushed against her on all sides. More guests seemed to have arrived just for the ball, doubling the crowd. Dancing had already begun at the center of the room, but Zelda hung back.

A fanfare of trumpets broke through the music and the din of voices. The royal family entered through a pair of gilded doors at the far end of the long room. Zelda's breath caught. Queen Antonia and Princess Astara sparkled with the shine of diamonds against their simple gowns. King Theodore looked the definition of regal composure at Queen Antonia's side while Leo escorted Astara on his arm.

Leo scanned the crowd from the moment he entered the room. Zelda hoped he was looking for her, but he was clearly distracted. He tugged at the blue sash that crossed the chest of his white, high-buttoned court uniform. A gold circlet on his head and the medals that decorated his uniform flashed in the light of the chandeliers.

The four of them moved to the center of the dance floor and officially began the ball with the Barrois family's traditional waltz. The king danced with the queen, and the young royals danced with each other.

Zelda watched intently until a presence at her side made her jump. The Duke of Brockford had sidled up to her in the crowd.

"Miss Zelda Ravensdale," he said, as if she was a curious thing to be analyzed.

Remembering Leo's warning, Zelda's heart raced. *Don't ask me to dance. Don't ask me to dance. Don't ask me to dance. Don't ask me to dance.* "Your Highness." She curtseyed politely but kept her eyes on the royal family.

"It's such a shame watching the king try to keep up this charade," the Duke of Brockford said.

Zelda wouldn't be baited. "I don't know what you mean."

He scoffed. "You wouldn't know then, since you're not privy to the gossip circles of my peers. The king is ill, and all the court knows it."

Zelda furrowed her brow in what she hoped looked like confusion. "I've heard quite the opposite," she lied.

A grin appeared on Brockford's thin mouth that made Zelda wish she hadn't said anything. "Interesting." He combed his fingers over the salt-and pepper-whiskers on his chin. "My ward, Dante, mentioned your special relationship with the prince. Perhaps you can give a more accurate account of the king's health?"

Zelda forced a laugh. Did Dante somehow know they were more than friends? *It has to be a bluff.* "It's like you said—I don't have access to your circles. I know what the crown tells the people of Olisand, nothing more."

Brockford didn't look convinced. His eyes pinched at the corners like he was trying to see through Zelda's lie as he absently twisted a ring on his finger. It was a thick, gold thing with a flat surface etched with a strange symbol. She would have missed it entirely if she hadn't been avoiding eye contact with the duke.

"That's a lovely ring." It wasn't, but any subject other than the king's health would do.

Prince Lionel looked at the ring and furrowed his brow. "Oh. It's an old family heirloom."

Zelda tried to catch a second glance at the symbol, but the Duke twisted the ring so the symbol no longer faced out on his finger.

"Enjoy your evening, Miss Ravensdale." He turned his back on her and sauntered off through the crowd. He slipped the ring from his finger and tuck it into the pocket of his coattails, then stopped to talk with George St. Germain. Something about the two men with their heads bent together sent a shiver of suspicion down her spine.

Zelda tried not to stare at them, but Professor Weymouth's warning from the start of their investigation came to mind. He was definitely right about the Duke of Brockford being close with St. Germain. Professor Weymouth and Professor Ballentine were supposedly handling it, but Zelda had seen little evidence of their efforts and she still had no idea how that whole situation put Leo in danger.

A hand on her elbow drew her away from George St. Germain and the Duke of Brockford. She turned and found Leo standing behind her. He held a gloved hand out to her.

"May I have this dance?"

Zelda curtsied to him. "Of course." She placed her hand in his. His face lit up with a smile that made all the corsets, tweezing, and etiquette lessons worth it.

All eyes seemed to follow them as Leo guided her to the center of the dance floor. The other dancers made room, and Leo took her right hand in his left. The orchestra transitioned into a solemn, haunting waltz that she didn't care for, but Leo's hand in hers made the rest of the world fall away. Leo slipped an arm around her back. Zelda's feet jumped into line on their own accord. She held on tight as he began to move her through the steps, her charmed shoes following along without assistance.

"You look lovely," he whispered.

"And you look very princely."

Leo chuckled, and his breath tickled Zelda's neck.

To avoid drawing too much attention, they continued the dance in silence, but each touch of Leo's hand to her waist, her arm, her hand, made Zelda's skin ripple with magic. The music slowed, and their dance came to an end too soon. As Leo escorted Zelda off the dance floor, Zelda couldn't help but notice Dante and Susan watching her from the front of the crowd. She felt a pang of regret for even hinting at her suspicions to Susan, but nothing could be done now. Susan's reaction had been equally concerning, enough to make Zelda wonder if her assumptions had been wrong.

No. She's trying to cover her tracks. It was the only explanation Zelda could think of.

Leo bid Zelda a brief goodbye with a fleeting kiss on the back of her hand. "I will find you again. I promise."

As a foreign minister pulled the prince aside to offer him a dance with his elegant daughter, Zelda expected it would be difficult for him to make good on that promise.

A ball wasn't anything like Zelda expected. She spent as much time making small talk with the other guests as she did dancing. The younger women seemed much more interested in making her acquaintance after Leo had chosen her for the second dance. In the moments she was left alone, she was forced to watch Leo smile and dance with every young female in the room. After the first hour, the novelty of glittering gowns, champagne, and tiaras under candlelight had worn off. There was no place to sit when her aching feet craved it, and not a server in sight to offer her refreshments when she wanted it most.

The giant, ornate clock mounted on the wall above the orchestra read eleven o'clock, but Zelda wasn't sure if she would make it to midnight. She'd quickly learned few members of the nobility knew the steps to ballroom dances as well as Leo. The enchantment on her heels kept time a little too well and left her stumbling and stepping ahead of her less experienced partners who merely shuffled their way through the dances.

Zelda escaped to the women's powder room to avoid the pressing attentions of an overly cologned young earl. On her way back to the ballroom, she found a door opened just a crack that hadn't been open before. Light streamed from within, so she poked her head inside.

Princess Astara sat alone, propped up in a gilded armchair in the rosy-hued sitting area. Her arms wrapped around her knees, and she scrolled mindlessly on her phone.

"Are you hiding in here?" Zelda asked.

Astara's eyes popped up to meet Zelda's face and a grin burst across her face. "Of course. What are you doing in here?"

"I need a break. Can I join you?"

Astara perked up in her seat and patted the cushion of the chair beside her. "No one ever talks to me at these things." She lowered her feet, but they didn't reach the ground.

"You have me to talk to now." Zelda sank into the open seat.

Astara studied Zelda with wide eyes. "I saw you dance with my brother."

"Yeah?"

"Do you like him?"

"I do."

"Do you love him?"

Zelda almost choked on a laugh. "Wow. I don't know about love, but I *like* like him if that helps you out."

"Oh, I see," she said with a knowing smirk. "He definitely loves you."

A strange flutter burst into Zelda's chest, but she tried to tamp it down with a steady breath. "Well, I don't know. It's a bit early for that and he hasn't said—"

"No. I know my brother, and he has never brought a girl to meet us." Astara folded her arms, confident in her logic.

"Never?" The flutter reared in Zelda's chest.

Astara shook her head. "I don't think I would've liked those other girls anyway."

"No?"

"They probably wouldn't have talked to me either."

Zelda smiled at Astara, and she felt a pang of loneliness. She'd seen the same look in Leo when they'd first met. Then he went to school and made friends. Zelda wanted the same for Astara.

Astara's face lit up as something dawned on her. "Want to take some selfies?"

Zelda laughed. "Sure, I'd love to."

After Astara left the sitting room to sneak off to bed, Zelda was forced to return to the ball alone. She instantly regretted her decision not to follow Astara's example once she saw who was lurking in the crowded corridor outside.

Chapter Thirty-One

Dante lounged against a towering marble pillar between Zelda and the ballroom. She hoped in vain he wouldn't notice her rush past.

"Zelda Ravensdale," Dante called loudly enough for anyone in the castle to hear.

From the way his tongue tripped over consonants, it sounded like he'd had one drink too many. Zelda's stomach pitched, and she put her head down. She wished for anything but to be in the same room with him in this state. His hand latched onto her arm as she tried to slip by without engaging him.

She jerked her arm from his grip and spun to face him. "What are you doing?"

"Come dance with me?" Dante pleaded.

Zelda took a step back. "No."

"What? I'm not good enough for you anymore?" Dante gave her a look of feigned injury, his voice too loud. It earned them both appalled glances from the others in the hall.

"No. I won't dance with you because you're making a scene," she whispered.

"Oh, a scene?" Dante's words rose to a shout. "Look at you putting on some fine airs. I seem to remember you begging me not to break up with you last spring."

Anger flared in Zelda's chest. The heat of humiliation rushed to her face as she willed herself anywhere else. "That never happened."

Dante shoved off the wall and would've crashed into Zelda had she not pushed him off. Putting her hands on him seemed to have the wrong effect. Dante grinned wildly at her.

"Does the prince know how things were between us?" Dante reached for Zelda's hand, but she yanked it out of reach. "How desperate you were to keep me?"

"I didn't—I never—" Zelda sputtered, unable to find the words to silence Dante for good. *Why is he being like this?* "Don't talk to me." Tears of embarrassment welled hot in the corners of her eyes. It was the last thing she wanted.

Dante noticed, and his face fell. He took a step back and downed the last dregs of champagne from the crystal flute in his hand.

"What's going on here?"

Zelda flinched at the sound of Susan's voice and quickly swiped the wetness from beneath her eyes.

Susan snatched the empty glass from Dante's hands. "What's wrong with you?"

"Nothing." Dante swayed on his feet. "What's wrong with you?" He booped Susan on the nose, and she rolled her eyes.

"Okay. You're done for the night." Susan gave Zelda a glance that looked embarrassed and almost apologetic.

"No," Dante whined. "It's not even midnight yet, *Mom*."

"That's it. Fun's over." Susan grabbed Dante by the flesh of his arm and pulled him toward the stairs. Dante tried to follow, but he stumbled over his feet and ended up in a tangled pile on the ground. "You can't even walk, can you?" Susan asked.

Zelda watched dumbfounded until Susan gave her a silent, pleading look as she tried to pull Dante off the floor by herself. She had never in the entirety of their relationship seen Dante like this. Zelda rushed to Susan's side and between them they hoisted Dante to his feet, his arms across their shoulders.

“He’s staying in the Duke of Brockford’s suite,” Susan said as they pulled Dante away from more prying eyes. She led the way, and they soon reached the door to the suite. Dante’s head lolled on his shoulder as Susan tested the handle and found it unlocked. She glanced at Zelda with a frown. “Thanks. I can take it from here.”

Zelda looked at the barely conscious boy between them. “Are you sure?”

“Yeah.” Susan shifted the bulk of Dante’s weight onto her shoulder. “I can handle it. Go enjoy the rest of the party—Prince Leopold was looking for you the last time I saw him.”

Zelda gave Susan a weak smile as she let Dante’s arm fall from her shoulders. “Thanks.”

Susan nodded, her face emotionless, and pulled Dante into the darkened room.

Zelda didn’t hang around. She hurried back to the ballroom where she found Leo waiting outside its doors.

His face lit up at the sight of her. “Where have you been?”

Zelda stopped herself just short of throwing herself into Leo’s arms. “Susan and I had to take care of something.”

Leo’s brows rose. “You and Susan? I feel like there’s a story here you aren’t telling me.”

“There’s a story, but right now I just want to be with you.”

“Me too. I’ve been trying to get away all evening.” Leo took Zelda’s hand and pulled her into the ballroom and the crush of bodies that filled it. The crowds parted for Leo as he swept her to the center of the dance floor.

Leo turned to face Zelda as they took positions for the dance. “My father kept pushing me into dance after dance, but I promise, I’m all yours now.”

They made it halfway through the first set of steps before the music slowed to a stop, and they paused along with the rest of the room. Leo let out a long sigh.

“We can’t catch a moment, can we?” Zelda said.

“No. We can’t.” He released her from the dance frame and moved to stand at a respectable distance.

The master of ceremonies directed the crowds to make their way to the terrace for the final minutes of the year.

“We’d better go,” Leo said. He didn’t take her hand, but he motioned for her to follow.

Zelda stayed close. The night air was cold, but the terrace was packed with bodies. She shivered against the cold.

Someone began a countdown from ten. Leo's lips pulled into a smile as he joined the countdown with the crowd. Zelda counted too, but the look on Leo's face made her wonder what was coming.

The countdown reached one, and a loud whistle cut through the cheers of the crowd as a rocket soared skyward. With a bang that rattled through Zelda's chest, the firework exploded against the dark sky in a shower of twinkling gold. Zelda tried to read Leo's face in the flashes of light.

Someone bumped into Zelda and sent her flying into the prince. He caught her against his chest, and his arms wrapped around her waist almost instinctively. When he didn't release her immediately, Zelda's breath caught in her throat. For a moment, she thought he was going to kiss her, but he didn't.

With what seemed like great reluctance, he finally released her. "Your dress isn't going to change into rags, is it?" he teased.

"Please." Zelda held a hand to her chest in mock outrage. "I'm no amateur."

His lips formed a thin line. The weekend had drawn to a close; it was time for Zelda to give him her decision on their relationship, but this wasn't the place for it. Instead, they remained silent while the crowd ooh'ed and aah'ed at the pyrotechnic display of light and color.

A large black sedan idled in the gravel drive, waiting to take Zelda back to Madame LeBleu's. The guests had left the castle, but Leo still rippled with nervous tension. The crushed stones beneath Zelda's feet sparkled with a layer of morning frost, and she pulled her coat closer.

"What do you think?" Leo asked, his hands tucked bashfully into the pockets of his tan pants. "Did I scare you away?"

Zelda placed her hands on both sides of Leo's face, so he looked her in the eyes when she answered. "No. I'm not going anywhere."

Leo's mouth pulled into a wide smile, and his shoulders relaxed. "Good. We'll coordinate a public release with Tiffani and Felix to go out when things with my father's health have stabilized."

"I can't believe we're doing this."

Leo answered her with a long, slow kiss that made Zelda regret all the time she'd wasted not kissing him. They broke apart, and Leo opened Zelda's door for her. "We're doing this and we're doing it right."

Zelda didn't want to leave, but she was desperate to see if Imogen had arrived at Madame LeBleu's before her. It wasn't like Imogen to go totally off the grid. The drive between the school and the castle passed quickly as Zelda tried to collect her thoughts and remember everything she'd been dying to tell her best friend.

She found the door to their dorm room unlocked and Imogen hunched over her desk. The floor around her wastebin was littered with used tissues and the wrappings of a Christmas candy massacre. Zelda dropped her bag on the floor and the sound made Imogen jump in her chair. Her brown eyes were rimmed red and puffed from crying.

"Imogen." Zelda left everything at the door. "What's going on? What happened?"

"I can't get this charm to work for more than thirty seconds," Imogen cried between shuddering gasps for air.

"What?" Zelda moved to see several compacts of pressed powder spread across the desk.

"And Fletcher and I broke up." Imogen blew her nose.

"Oh no. I'm so sorry." Zelda grabbed the bin and picked up the tissues and candy wrappers that had fallen on the floor. "What happened?"

Tears welled in Imogen's eyes. "Fletcher came to visit me in London after Christmas, and when I wanted to work on my filtering foundation he said I was being boring."

"That's why you broke up?"

"No. Well, sort of. He thinks I don't want to spend time with him. With working at St. Germain's and school, he doesn't like me working on a big side project like this." She gestured to the makeup on her desk.

"The filtering foundation?"

"Yeah." Imogen sniffled. "We got in a fight about something stupid, but it helped us both realize that we didn't have much in common except being attracted to each other."

"I'm sorry," Zelda said.

"It's for the best, but it still stings." Imogen reached for a compact. She took a brush and tapped it in the pan. "Let me see your wrist."

Zelda held out her hand and let Imogen swipe foundation across her skin. Imogen caught her staring. Zelda didn't want to know what her expression looked like. She tried to wipe any signs of pity from her face with a sincere, hopeful smile.

"Take a look before it wears off," Imogen said as she released Zelda's hand.

Zelda examined her wrist. The morning light through the window hit the swatch of foundation, and it almost glowed. There was a blurring effect too that smoothed out the coloring. "Imogen. This is amazing."

Imogen glanced at the time on her phone's lock screen. "Aaaand it's gone."

Zelda checked the spot on her arm, and it had turned back to normal—no more luminescent glow. "There has to be a way to make this work."

"Can you imagine if I get the skin-clearing charm to work too?" Imogen lowered her head to rest in her hand. "Now, it's your turn. Distract me, *please*. What's been going on with Susan? And Leo?"

"About that text." Zelda laughed. "I have so much to tell you."

Imogen's face lit up, and she sat a little taller. "How much? Do we need snacks? If there was kissing involved, I'm going to need you to be as detailed as possible."

Heat bloomed on Zelda's cheeks. "We're definitely going to need snacks."

Chapter Thirty-Two

The start of the second term began like a whirlwind. With their final godmother certification exams mere months away, the pressure was on. Between the snow and the freezing rain and the piles of homework assignments, Zelda didn't know when she'd escape to comb the archives for a shrinking potion recipe. On top of it all, they had a talent act to put together for the Follies.

At the soonest opportunity, Zelda and Imogen met Specs and Leo at the small iron gate that led to the EAMS academic buildings. Specs used his student key to unlock the gate and let them through. He had his many-lensed glasses perched on his head, and wore a crimson blazer over a rumpled white shirt.

Leo was dressed for a crew workout. Everything that had made him a regal prince over New Year's weekend disappeared when he wore black joggers and a hooded team zip-up. Even though they were now dating, an official statement hadn't been made, so they had to keep PDA to a minimum. The king's weekend-long party had been well received by the press, but it still seemed too soon to announce a royal relationship.

They hurried up the main steps to the nearest building and scrambled inside to get out of the cold. In the foyer, a lead glass dome filled the space with cold, gray winter light. Zelda had never liked the look of the interior of EAMS much. Everything was made of dark wood and covered with ornate carvings.

"This way," Specs said as he led them to a hallway off the foyer. At the end of the long hall, he turned into a towering room full of worktables and all sorts of machinery that puffed and whirred—mechanisms whose uses escaped Zelda's knowledge. The workshop's towering windows lined the far wall and gave them a commanding view of the building's courtyard, the manicured gardens, and the doleful sky.

Imogen wandered among the tables, examining the half-finished projects that lay on their surfaces.

Specs watched her as she moved through the workroom. "I heard about Fletcher. Is she okay?" he asked Zelda.

"She'll be fine. It was a mostly mutual breakup."

Specs pulled the magnifying spectacles from his head and wiped a smudge from one of the lenses. "How'd it happen?"

"She said they both realized they didn't have much in common."

"Really?"

"Ask her for yourself." Zelda nudged him in the ribs. "She'd be glad to know you're concerned."

"S'pose I will." Specs jogged off after Imogen.

Leo assumed the place at Zelda's side.

"We should let them catch up," she said. "Which of these contraptions is the one Specs has been working on?"

"You know, I've been working on it too," Leo said with feigned indignity. He grabbed Zelda by the hand, and her fingertips tingled with electricity. He laced strong fingers between hers, leading her to a large pair of wooden boxes. A shiny metal crank on the side of the box was attached to a series of gears, and a large curl of copper wire ran between the tops of the two. The invention was supposed to represent magical cooperation—something that required fairy magic and tinkering to work together.

Zelda didn't know what the components did, but she could see the pride on Leo's face. "This looks . . ." She reluctantly released Leo's hand and circled the first box to get a closer look at the mechanics of it. "Impressive. Will it really work?"

Leo shrugged. "I hope so. We haven't had a fairy try it yet."

"That's what we're here for," Imogen said as she and Specs joined them in front of the contraption.

Specs pulled his glasses down over his eyes. "Well then. Should we give it a go?"

Imogen raised her hand. "I'll try it."

Specs opened the hinged door on the front of the left box and motioned for Imogen to step inside. "For you, Miss Yang."

Imogen smiled and took Specs' hand. He helped her into the box, then closed the door behind her.

"What do I have to do?" Zelda asked.

Specs pointed to the crank that stuck out from Imogen's box. "Just turn this here. It will draw out a bit of magic from you and use it to transfer Imogen to the box on the right."

"Of course, we can make a bigger show of it during the actual performance," Leo said.

Zelda positioned herself in front of the crank. "As long as I don't have to sing." She rapped her knuckles against the wood. "You okay in there, Imogen?"

"Hurry up," a muffled voice replied. "I'm getting claustrophobic."

Specs gave Zelda a nod, and she started to turn the crank. Slowly at first, the gears turned one by one, but they soon began to whir and hum. Zelda turned faster. Something in the mechanism gave off a bright spark. Then, as if something bit the tips of her fingers, the copper crank shocked her.

"Ow." She released the handle and shook out her sore fingertips.

Leo was there immediately to examine her hands. "Are you okay?"

Zelda sucked the smarting tip of her little finger. "I'm fine."

"Imogen?" Specs exclaimed, panic in his voice.

Imogen jumped from the first box with an enthusiastic, "Ta-da!" Her grin faded when she realized she hadn't left her box. "It didn't work?"

Specs sighed in relief and rushed to one of the worktables and retrieved an ancient-looking book.

"Lug nuts," he cursed and stepped behind the transportation contraption.

"Is it bad?" Imogen asked. "Because I definitely felt something happening when I was in there."

"Here—" Specs held out the book for Zelda to hold while he adjusted something in the gears. A loud clanging came from behind the machine. "I guess we'll have to keep messing with it."

Zelda took the book, and her breath stopped. The cover had a familiar symbol embossed on its spine—the strange symbol she'd seen on the Duke of Brockford's ring. "Where did you get this, Specs?"

Specs peered around the corner. "Uh, the book? Lord Scarlet gave it to me so I could work on this."

Zelda's fingers traced the foil lettering on the cover. "Doyle's Study of Magical Conduction," she read aloud. She flipped to the first pages and found the copyright. "Published by the Consortium of Thaumaturgy. Copyright 1889." Suddenly, she saw the symbol correctly. It wasn't some fancy rune, but the letter "C" with a "T" inside. *What was the duke doing wearing a thaumaturgy ring?*

"What is it?" Imogen moved to read over her shoulder.

"Lord Scarlet gave this to you?" Zelda asked, ignoring Imogen.

Specs looked at her like she was crazy. He nodded slowly.

"Did he say anything about this Consortium?" The word sounded so familiar, but Zelda couldn't remember where she'd heard it recently.

"Thaumaturgy?" Imogen repeated. "That's a study of magic, but not fairy magic." They both looked to Specs. Thaumaturgy had been outlawed by the International Council of Godmothers long ago. Zelda knew little of what the practice entailed but based on how little it was talked of, she could guess it was nothing good.

Specs held up his hands in defense. "Don't give me that look. It's not thaumaturgy—this is tinkering stuff—numbers and equations."

Zelda held up the book, so he and Leo could see the symbol marked on the spine. "Look. I've seen this symbol on a ring the Duke of Brockford was wearing, and he got really weird about it. He . . . he's . . ." She looked to Leo to find the right words.

"He's not someone I'd trust," Leo said.

"And he's close associates with St. Germain," Zelda said. *The Consortium.* "I heard St. Germain talking with Susan, and he said something about handling a Consortium."

"What?" three voices asked in unison.

When Zelda finished relaying the short but tense conversation she'd heard between Susan and her father, Specs took the book back and scanned the pages like they might burn him if he looked too long. His dark brows pushed together and formed a deep worry line between them. "I have a theory," he said. "Unlike regular tinker equations, these formulas require a source of magic other than the naturally occurring aether in the immediate environment. These equations require an actual living source of magic. For our experiment, our machine can't work on aether alone, it needs to borrow a little bit of the force that's inside a fairy that allows her to perform magic."

"What do a duke and a shoe store owner need with magic like that?" Imogen asked.

They all looked at each other, unsure of the answer.

"Could that mean they want to use this *Heartstone* as a source?" Leo asked. "Maybe it's a lost source of magic Susan and her father are hiding?"

"I've never heard of a Heartstone," Zelda said.

"But it sounds like Susan didn't want them to give it over to the Consortium," Specs said.

Leo shook his head and ran a hand through his hair. "So, what does this mean? Would the Consortium use the elves if they can't have the Heartstone? You said it needs a living source of magic. Do elves even have magic?"

"We'll figure it out one thing at a time. First, we go to the archives. Then, we find our elves. Let Susan and her father worry about their Heartstone," Zelda said.

Specs examined the book in his hands.

Imogen took a step toward him. "Specs?"

"I didn't know," he said, his voice barely above a whisper. "I wasn't trying to cross a line into thaumaturgy, but Lord Scarlet said the book would help. It's all numbers and theories on aether conduction."

Imogen gently removed the book from his hands. "It's okay." Her voice softened. "Can you finish the transportation box without the book?"

Specs rubbed his forehead, a slight tremble in his hands. "I've already used some of Doyle's formulas, but I think I can finish it."

Imogen placed a reassuring hand on his shoulder. "Of course you can. Just be careful. Thaumaturgy is outlawed partially because its methods are cruel, but it's also dangerous. Accidentally exposing someone without the gift of magic to a large amount can have serious physical consequences like stopping the heart."

She passed the book to Leo. "Leo can hold on to this. Zelda and I will work on the shrinking potion, and you guys can figure out what a bunch of influential men would want to use thaumaturgy for."

Specs nodded and removed his glasses to scrub the bridge of his nose. "Sure. Sure."

Leo gave Zelda a weary smile like he, too, felt in over his head. Maybe Madame LeBleu had been right to tell them to stay away, but a feeling deep in Zelda's gut told her she wouldn't be able to anymore. It was part of a fairy's nature to help those who needed it most. Now, perhaps, it wasn't just the elves. They couldn't turn back. *We're not in over our heads,* she reassured herself. *Not yet.*

Chapter Thirty-Three

When Leo didn't have any ribbons to cut, public appearances to make, or a crew team workout on his schedule, Zelda agreed to accompany him to the national archives. There was never a good time to fit an afternoon of non-school-related research in, but Zelda found it anyway. Even if it was for their secret mission, moments alone with Leo were few and far between. The fourth-year GITs had more advanced spells crammed into their course load in the first month of second term than they'd learned in all of first term.

Dating Leo in secret was harder than she'd expected. There was a slight bit of chatter around the prince's love life when Princess Astara had posted her selfie with Zelda to her private snapchat. It had been screenshotted and passed around on social media as people wondered who was getting cozy with the royal family, but no legitimate publications picked up the story.

The marble-columned building of the Olisand National Archives was hidden in the crooked streets of Erimount's Castle District. Leo signed them in at the receptionist desk in the nearly empty rotunda. The young librarian did a double take as he realized who was signing in.

Leo nodded to him, and they breezed out of the rotunda and up the wide marble stairs to a towering room filled with endless rows of books.

Zelda eyed the thousands of spines that filled the shelves. "Where do we even start?"

Leo hooked a thumb in the pocket of his red EAMS blazer. "Lucky for you, when I was privately tutored, I did all my research in this library." He placed a hand on the small of Zelda's back and steered her down the nearest aisle. "I know just where to start."

They headed up a winding, iron staircase to a gallery full of shelves that overlooked the first level of the library. There was no one in sight, and Zelda's skin sang with the warmth of Leo's hand through her sweater. They hadn't been alone like this in ages, and she relaxed at Leo's side. She didn't know when they'd get another opportunity to just be themselves—together.

Leo stopped in front of the furthest section of shelves which were filled with leather folios. "Welcome to the gallery of records for the International Magical Relations Committee. If it has to do with magic, or it happened in Olisand, it will be recorded or kept in here. I'll look for the last known documentation of magical creatures in Olisand—"

"And that would be in here?" There had to be a thousand folios in that section alone. The dark wood shelves extended high out of reach, with files only accessible by ladder.

Leo nodded. "If you want to start looking for books on shrinking potions, you'll want to start on the other side of the gallery. If you work your way around clockwise, you'll eventually run into case files for misuses of magic. We can meet up there and look for more information on thaumaturgy."

"Sounds good." Zelda begrudgingly left Leo's side to start on the far side of the gallery. The first section was all volumes of spell books, but she eventually found her way to the titles on potions and brews. She recognized several books they'd used over her school years, but a vast number of them were unfamiliar. Zelda scanned the titles, unsure where to begin.

A hardback textbook *Brews for Biochemical Manipulation: Collegiate Brews Level 1* seemed to be a good place to start. A quick glance at the table of contents told her these were only mood and mind-altering potions. The back listed *Potions for Biophysical Transmutation: Collegiate Brews Level 2* as a title from the same publisher, and Zelda found it on the next shelf.

Zelda flipped open to the index in the back of the book. Shrinking Potion, Page 197.

She opened to the page, and there it was. *Shrinking Potion (For human and fairy use only. Not suitable for animals.)* The ingredients list was extensive, but there wasn't anything out of the ordinary. Zelda closed the textbook, tucked it under her arm, then headed for the sections of folios on the misuse of magic.

It was much harder to find anything related to thaumaturgy than it was to find a recipe for shrinking potions. With only case numbers and brief names handwritten and only occasionally printed on the covers of the folios, each file had to be searched. One by one, Zelda skimmed the contents of each folio. File after file contained cases brought before the ICG where humans and fairies alike attempted to use magic to make unnatural gains in the world. The most common thread seemed to be magic and tinkering use to create vast amounts of wealth that would damage world economies by deflation.

Zelda thumbed through files for what felt like hours. She snuck glances at Leo across the gallery and several times caught him watching her as well. A curious look flitted across his face that Zelda couldn't get out of her head, even with the monumental task in front of her. She was trying to focus her drifting thoughts when the first remotely relevant title caught her eye: *Lord Barnabas and his gold-spinning imp.* It was the first mention of a magical creature besides fairies. With a hunger that made her fingers tremble, she unwound the leather cording that bound the old leather folio together.

Inside was a police report from the Erimount Royal Officers in a faded typeset on time-yellowed paper. The first page was a missing person's report filed by a Lord Edmund Barnabas at the disappearance of his eldest daughter. The report indicated that his daughter of eighteen years, dark skin, and dark hair, might be found with a pointy-eared gentleman. The second page of the report detailed the results of a raid on the ancestral mansion of Lord Barnabas himself when the lady of the house tipped off inspectors that her husband had made a deal with an imp. The man with pointy ears, dark hair, and green skin had taken their daughter as a reward for the treasure he created for the lord. A room in the house was found filled to the ceiling with spools of gold thread, but any evidence that an imp had been kept on the premises couldn't be found. An inspector from the International Council of Godmothers confirmed the gold had been created by magic, and it was promptly destroyed.

The case, dated 1902, was still marked as open. The thought of being missing for over a hundred years made Zelda shiver. There were a few tintype photos of the spools of gold thread and a ring of mushrooms found in the woods outside the mansion, but the case didn't offer much help in their search for elves.

In another section, between more shelves of folios, Zelda found a shelf of ancient-looking books. The bindings were frayed and faded beyond recognition. A folio marked the start of a row. It contained an old piece of paper with a handwritten list: *The Confiscated Titles of Lord Rafe Scarlet II.*

The full title of the headmaster for the school for tinkers was Lord Rafe Scarlet IV. *Or maybe the fifth?* Zelda exchanged the folio for the first book on the shelf. *Thaumaturgy for the Novice*. If Lord Scarlet was loaning out books on thaumaturgy to students, it was quite likely he'd built his family collection back up.

She flipped through the first pages, but like the book Specs had, it was mostly equations. There were other books confiscated from other citizens of Olisand that followed after the books of Lord Scarlet. Zelda picked up a book bound in black leather that had belonged to a cobbler whose name didn't have any meaning to her. Finally, words. And pictures. Brittle paper crinkled in her hands as she turned the pages. Her fingers stopped at an illustration, and for a moment everything went numb.

In the illustration, a man with a wicked grin stood over a fairy with a pair of scissors in one hand, and the fairy's clipped wing in the other. The one-winged fairy's face contorted into a scream as she writhed at the man's feet.

A hand on her waist made Zelda jump, and the book fell to the floor with an echoing thunk.

"I'm sorry." Leo's voice came from behind her. "I didn't mean to startle you."

Zelda picked up the book and several of its pages which had gotten dislodged in the fall. "It's fine," she said despite the thrumming in her ears.

Leo examined the book. "You actually found a book on thaumaturgy?"

"Yeah. These were all confiscated from citizens of Olisand." She shoved the loose pages back into the foul book and handed it to Leo.

He flipped it open to the illustration of the wingless fairy. The muscles in his jaw clenched. "These should be under lock and key."

The image ghosted in Zelda's mind. Her breath caught in her throat, and a ripple of gooseflesh ran over her skin.

"Would this kill a fairy or take her magic forever?"

"No. It would just cripple her magic for a long time until she could replenish her stores."

Leo seemed to sense her distress and snapped the book closed. "We'll stop them from stealing magic." He wrapped Zelda in his arms, and the deep rumble of his voice soothed away the panic rising in her chest.

"But why would Susan go anywhere near this kind of magic?" Zelda said, her face buried in the soft fabric of Leo's shirt. "Fairies are supposed to help those in need. This is the furthest thing from a Happily Ever After I've ever seen." Her stomach knotted as she breathed in the heady, warm musk of his cologne.

Leo's hand ran up her back and into her hair as he clutched her head to his chest. "I don't know. Maybe, like us, she didn't know what she was getting into." He let her go to replace the book on the shelf. "Let's get out of here. I have something that will make you feel better."

On the other side of the gallery, Leo had discovered precisely what they had come to the archives to find. He pulled out a file whose location he had marked by turning the folio on its side so it stuck out from the seemingly endless row of others. Zelda took the folio from his outstretched hand. She scanned the contents, and her mouth fell open.

Leo watched her with a self-satisfied look and a dimpled grin. "Over two hundred years ago, a man with the surname of St. Germain was fined for failing to register his employment of elves in what was then a hole-in-the-wall cobbler's shop."

"It says here, when inspectors returned, the elves were gone."

Leo folded his arms, looking pleased with himself. "Perhaps. Or was that what spurred the St. Germain family to hide their workforce?"

Finally, some tangible proof that they weren't chasing a ghost. Zelda's smile bubbled over into a laugh. She scanned the contents, then in a moment of unbridled joy, she threw her arms around Leo's neck and planted a kiss square on his mouth.

"Don't celebrate yet," he said once they came up for air. "We still need to find the elves, but I found something else that can help us there."

Zelda followed Leo again. He stopped in the far corner of the gallery and climbed a ladder to a high row of books that looked like it hadn't seen a visitor or a dusting in fifty years. Leo lifted a small green book from the shelf and brought it down to Zelda.

She read aloud from the title page: "*The International Magical Relations Committee Inspector's Handbook of Magical Beings: From Sprites to Warlocks, with a special foreword from International Council of Godmothers founder Brigitte LeBleu.*"

"Turn to page twenty-eight."

Page twenty-eight had a neatly numbered list of all the steps it took to find and befriend skittish elves. She looked up at Leo with an open smile. "George St. Germain isn't going to know what hit him."

A strange smile crept over Leo's cheeks.

"What?" Zelda asked, hitting him in the shoulder with the book.

Before she could protest, Leo wrapped his arms around her and lifted her off her feet. "I didn't even know it was possible to feel this way with someone—so happy that you're actually mad with it."

"You're madly happy?" Zelda asked. She gasped as Leo pressed her up against the opposite bookshelf. "With me?"

Leo smiled and nodded. "You're going to think I'm crazy."

"I already think you're crazy."

Leo considered his words by working his lower lips.

"You can tell me anything," she said.

"When I think of us, I don't know, something about *us* feels like Forever After." On the word "forever" he moved his mouth to Zelda's jaw to whisper it against her skin.

Forever After? She'd never heard anything so wonderful. "I like that idea. Forever After." She tasted the words for herself while wrapped in Leo's arms.

Yes, she could deal with being this happy *forever after.*

Chapter Thirty-Four

Zelda read through the inspector's handbook late into the night, so they could formulate a detailed plan for finding St. Germain's elves. Apparently, elves were shy, intelligent creatures, which made them hard to find.

The book suggested an offering of berries or small, shiny trinkets to draw them out. Then all they'd have to do was follow them back to their home. With no idea when they'd be able to put their plan into action, they opted for a handful of brass buttons from one of Leo's blazers.

Brewing a usable shrinking potion, however, turned out to be harder than expected. Despite classes and homework and certification exam prep, Zelda attempted to perfect the potion in her remaining spare time. The potion's shelf life was short, and it had to be consumed within a few hours of brewing. This meant they only could attempt the complicated brew when Imogen was at work, and they were ready to put their plan into action.

On a Friday night when Imogen had a closing shift at St. Germain's, Zelda set about attempting the potion again. Leo watched nervously from the edge of Zelda's bed while she brought the delicate potion to a simmer on a hot plate in the center of her floor. The last three times she'd done this, she'd heated it to a boil, and the result was a shattered beaker.

The clear liquid bubbled slowly in the jar, turning to a shimmering lilac as it hit the exact temperature. Zelda snatched it off the hotplate before it could explode. "You can relax." She swirled the liquid in the beaker to cool it, then used a pipette to portion it into vials. The batch yielded only enough for two; it would just have to be her and Leo.

St. Germain's Shoe Emporium closed at eight, which would hopefully give them enough time to find the elves and make it back before Friday's midnight curfew.

"It's seven-thirty," Leo said as he checked his watch. "We have a half hour to get to the alley behind Founders Square. Imogen will let us in the back door."

Zelda threw on a coat and filled a pocket with the brass buttons they hoped would attract the elves.

After they signed out with the matron, they headed straight for Founders Square. Even on a Friday night, the city was quiet on cold evenings after dark. Leo pulled his hood over his head to hide his face, but the city felt like it was all theirs. "Where does Felix think you are?" Zelda asked.

Leo grinned. "He thinks I'm studying in the library with you. I gave him the night off when he said he didn't want to watch me make lovey eyes at you across the table. The library closes at midnight so as long as we make it back by curfew, he won't suspect a thing."

They hurried past glowing restaurant windows and soon arrived outside the staff entrance to St. Germain's Shoe Emporium at five till eight. Zelda and Leo clung to the shadows when a door flew open, and some girls in matching gold skirt suits sauntered down the alley. Another girl appeared but held the door ajar. Zelda quickly recognized Imogen with her slicked-down high ponytail and matching golden eyeliner.

"I'm so getting fired if we get caught," Imogen whispered.

Zelda emptied the contents of her coat pocket into Imogen's waiting hands. "You don't even need this job; you took it so we could have a spy inside St. Germain's."

"I get a fifty percent discount," Imogen moaned.

"Yes, but for all we know, these shoes are made with slave labor." Zelda unstopped the vials and handed one to Leo.

"If you find these elves aren't getting paid, I'll quit. Now drink your stupid potion," Imogen said. "I need to lock you in."

Zelda tipped back the vial and swallowed the bitter, purple liquid. She hoped she'd brewed it correctly as her legs began to tremble. She looked at Leo.

"My mouth tastes like flowers." He grimaced.

The walls of the alley pitched before Zelda's eyes to a dizzying effect. Once her brain seemed to catch up to her quaking limbs, she was looking at Imogen's shin. "Leo?"

Zelda turned and found Leo farther away. She tried to slow the pounding of her heart as she tried and failed to wrap her head around the fact that she was less than a foot tall.

"You're so tiny." Imogen's voice boomed overhead. She bent down to get a better look at them.

Leo looked up at Imogen, stunned. "This is . . ."

Zelda ran over and grabbed his hand. "Come on. We don't have time for you to freak out."

Imogen held the door open. "I'll stand guard for as long as I can, but if anyone comes by, I may have to leave, okay? You can get out the door from the inside, but you'll have to wait for the potion to wear off."

Zelda and Leo skirted around the door and into the darkened hall inside St. Germain's.

Imogen opened her fist to examine the pile of brass buttons. She looked between the gleaming pile and Leo and Zelda. "Here," she gave them each one to carry. To Zelda and Leo, the buttons were now the size of dinner plates. "And stay away from the fifth floor. St. Germain has an apartment there, and I don't know if he's home tonight."

Zelda nodded.

"Good luck," Imogen said and closed the door. The lock slid into place with an echoing thunk and then everything went silent.

Leo slid the loop of the button onto his arm, carrying it like a shield. "Where do we want to start?"

Zelda eyed the length of the hallway and had to suppress a smile. At her new size, the arched ceiling made it feel like walking through a cathedral. There would be a lot of ground to cover at only one foot tall. "Let's find somewhere close to hide, we don't want to wander too far from the back door and get lost."

The first room they found was a long, dimly lit workroom filled with stools and worktables. Floor-to-ceiling, square, wooden cubbies, each occupied by a pair of shoes, stretched across the longest wall in the room.

They dropped their buttons under a worktable and climbed into one of the low cubbies that held a relatively non-odorous pair of shoes. Zelda wasn't quite sure how long the potion would last, but she didn't want to be stuck in a cubby when they grew back to their original size. The book said three hours, but potions could be temperamental, and this was her first successful attempt.

"They have to come for the buttons," Leo whispered, his voice dripping with eagerness.

This was their best chance, and likely their last, before they were swept into the chaos of the Wishmaker Festival in May and then final examinations after.

"They'll come," Zelda said as she met Leo's gaze over the pair of red pumps with a busted t-strap.

They both returned their eyes to the buttons, too afraid to miss the elves. After fifteen minutes, Zelda started to wonder if the *Guide to Magical Beings* had any merit to its information. Elves had been declared extinct, a forgotten thing of fairy tales, so the inspectors couldn't have been too good at their jobs in the first place.

Just when Zelda was ready to give up hope, a musical tinkling of laughter filled the workroom. Zelda gasped. From the darkest corner of the room, a parade of minuscule workers emerged from a crack in the wall. Zelda almost didn't believe the sight. They marched in a single file line, each wearing dark blue smocks and crisp white aprons.

Thirty or so elves entered the workshop, and after pulling hidden levers and cranks out of the floorboards, baskets on pulleys lowered from the rafters. The elves climbed into the baskets and set to work on repairing the shoes that filled the cubbies.

Zelda kept watch on the buttons, and just as the book said they would, a pair of giggling female elves in matching smocks stole over to the suspicious set of loose buttons.

"Look," said the pale elf with a mane of fiery curls.

The other elf had copper skin and thick dark hair pulled back into a braid. She hoisted a button and propped it on her hip. "I do not recognize these. They are not from our shop."

"Fallen off a shop girl's uniform?" the redhead asked.

"They must have. What shall you do with yours? I think I will take mine to the smith and see if she can remove this loop here; t'would make a great serving bowl—"

Zelda grabbed Leo's hand, and they emerged from their hiding place in the cubby. "Excuse me," she said.

The elf with the red hair dropped her button with a shriek. She dashed behind the table leg while her companion stared dumbfounded at the new arrivals. Her eyes narrowed as her gaze flicked to Leo's rounded ears.

"Don't be alarmed," he said. "We mean you no harm."

They slowed their approach as they neared the elves.

"W-what are you doing here?" The dark-haired elf's voice shook.

Zelda held up her hands in surrender. "Please. We saw one of you in the front windows, and we wanted to make sure you were okay. The rest of the world doesn't know you exist."

The girl with the dark hair dropped her button. "And we intend to keep it that way." Before Zelda could react, the elf reached into a pocket of her apron and pulled out a blue glass vial sealed with gold wax. She threw the vial at Zelda and Leo's feet, where it smashed against the unforgiving wood floor. When the glass broke, a plume of red smoke engulfed Zelda's vision. She tried to hold her breath and reached for Leo in panic, but the heavy, dragging weight of sleep slammed into her. In seconds, everything went black as she was pulled under the spell.

Chapter Thirty-Five

"Do you know what you just did, Nahia?"

A male voice echoed in the darkness of Zelda's mind. A light flickered behind her eyelids, but they didn't respond when she willed them to open. She urged her sleepy limbs to move, but they ignored her as well.

"The fairy is fighting off the curse," a nervous female voice squeaked.

"Do you know who this is?" the male with the deep voice asked.

"The fairy?" another voice asked.

"The boy is the crown prince of Olisand."

Suddenly, as if a heavy blanket had been ripped off her, Zelda woke. She blinked against the light of the towering chamber. It looked like they'd been transported to the great hall of a castle—an old castle. The floor and walls were made of stone and the ceiling of wood. Fantastic patterns of suns, moons, and stars were painted on the beams. Circular wooden chandeliers lit with candles hung from the rafters and filled the room with a warm flicker, but a cold light glowed on the other side of the tall, paned windows.

The moon? What time is it? How long were we out? As Zelda gained her bearings, she realized why she hadn't been able to move her limbs. Her wrists and ankles were tied to a wooden armchair.

"Leo," Zelda cried when she only saw the two female elves in front of her.

Something moved at her back. "Right here," Leo's voice groaned.

A glance over her shoulder confirmed that Leo was tied to a chair behind hers. Relief flooded her until she saw the man who belonged to the deep voice she'd heard through her sleep. He was tall, pale, and had a head of dark-red hair. A single teardrop pearl hung from one of his pointed ears. He looked to be only a few years older than Leo, but Zelda wasn't sure how elves aged. The way he was dressed gave Zelda pause. He looked like some prince from a Shakespearean play. His maroon brocade doublet was embroidered in vines of gold thread, and he wore thick, black tights that were tucked into knee-high black leather boots. A wreath of gold vines crowned his head.

Zelda flinched as he bent down and unsheathed a jeweled knife from his boot. "Don't," she cried even though she could do nothing to stop him.

The elf paused and fixed Zelda with a set of arresting green eyes. His lips lifted into a playful smirk. "So, I should not cut the prince's bonds? Is he dangerous?"

"No." Zelda's muscles loosened with relief. "He won't hurt you. Neither will I."

"Good," the elf said. He cut Leo's bonds, then dragged the prince and his chair around so he and Zelda sat side by side.

"My apologies for the rude welcome," he said as he knelt in front of Zelda. His warm fingers brushed her wrist as he made room for the blade to slip between the rope and her skin. "I am King Rían. You have already had the pleasure of meeting Nahia and my sister, Edrie." The girl with the crimson curls waved. Zelda guessed she was his sister. Nahia only glared at them with arms folded across her chest.

"Hello, Your Majesty," Leo said with a bow.

King Rían brushed him off. "Before we all get to know one another, I need to know what you were doing hiding in my kingdom."

Zelda and Leo glanced at each other. "Your kingdom?" they asked at the same time.

Rían ignored them. "Does anyone else know you are here? Who have you told about us?" He had a formal way of speaking that matched the old-fashioned appearance of his clothing. Both girls spoke with a similar lilt.

Zelda wanted to stand, but she wasn't sure she trusted her legs to hold her yet. "We've told a few people we trust, but no one I wouldn't trust with my own life," Zelda said.

Leo nodded. "We just wanted to know why George St. Germain kept you a secret—and to know that George St. Germain wasn't holding you against your will."

It was the elves' turn to look confused.

Nahia moved to stand at King Rían's side. "Against our will? George St. Germain is our protector. His family has kept our existence secret for over two hundred years. We owe him our lives." She got visibly angrier with each word.

"I'm sorry," Zelda said. "We mean no offense, but if that's true, George and Susan St. Germain may need some help. There's a society of Thaumaturges trying to get their hands on a Heartstone. Does that mean anything to you?"

The three elves exchanged furtive glances.

"If Susan is in trouble, I think we should tell them," Edrie said.

Rían dragged a hand over his angular jaw.

"I do not like this," Nahia said.

"If Susan and George St. Germain can't protect you, then what?" Zelda rose slowly from her chair. "We have friends who can help. We even have someone who works in the store who could defend you if needed."

Rían's verdant gaze fell on Zelda. His lips lifted into a grin. "I appreciate the kindness of your offer, but who are you? I know the crown prince, but I have not seen your face before."

"Zelda Ravensdale. Student of Madame LeBleu's." She extended her hand for a handshake, but the elf king swept it up and placed a kiss on her knuckles.

"A fairy godmother in training and a prince? How interesting," Rían said.

"A story for another time? We're on a bit of a time crunch," Leo said. There was a measure of annoyance in his voice.

Rían dropped Zelda's hand. "What I am about to show you is Olisand's best-kept secret, and if there are indeed Thaumaturges out there looking for us, you are putting my people at great risk by being here. The Heartstone is the source of our magic, and if someone were to *steal* it, well, you shall see."

Zelda helped Leo from his chair. When his legs wobbled, Rían offered him an extra hand, but Leo ignored it.

"Right this way," Edrie chirped as she led them to the end of the great hall and massive set of wooden doors. She and Nahia each grasped one of the large metal loops and pulled. The pair of arched doors opened to reveal a sprawling, medieval-looking town.

Zelda's mouth gaped. Thousands of yellow windows glowed in the night. *Where are we?* She looked up, expecting to see the moon and stars above her head, but instead, she could make out the crisscrossing wooden rafters. The lunar glow wasn't the moon, but a large, uncut gemstone. Mounted in a bell tower of sorts, the stone emitted a steady stream of blue light.

Rían appeared at her side. "Beautiful, is she not? Welcome to Fifth Floor. We have eight thousand residents here, with more throughout the emporium and beneath it." He moved down the stone steps to a cobblestone street that wended its way through the patchwork of buildings.

"Is this? Are we still in St. Germain's Shoe Emporium?" Leo asked.

"Of course," Edrie said. "This is the attic."

Questions raced through Zelda's mind. Most importantly, *how did an entire race of elves build a thriving society within the walls of St. Germain's?*

The Heartstone. Magic was the only explanation for something like this.

"I am certain you have many questions," Rían said. "I can take you to my house where we can talk more."

Zelda looked to Leo. "What time is it?"

He glanced at his watch. "Ten. We have time, and the potion doesn't feel like it's wearing off. Do you feel okay?" He took Zelda's hands in his.

A feeling like electricity surged in Zelda's fingertips. "I'm fine. We can stay a little longer."

"Excellent," Rían said as he set off down the street. "Follow me."

Leo didn't release Zelda's hand as they followed the elf king through the city streets. The road they followed curved and banked through the city—past storefronts for a bakery, a tailor, and a host of other services. Zelda almost forgot they were small until she spotted a metal bottle cap that had been painted over with the name of a public house and hung outside. Eyes followed them everywhere, but Zelda wasn't sure if it was them or Rían they watched.

The street rounded upward and ended at a row of newer looking townhouses with a commanding view of the city. Their style was simple and Elizabethan like the rest of the city, but they had a little more grandeur.

"Here we are," Rían said. He opened the front gate and plodded up the front steps.

Zelda was surprised to find neat hedges and flowers growing in his front garden. The white petals of the tiny flowers glowed almost blue in the light of the Heartstone. Zelda reached out and brushed a petal with her fingertip. "All this can grow indoors?"

Rían smiled. "Fifth Floor has dormer windows so we get a little light during the day, but we can grow whatever we need here, thanks to the Heartstone."

He ushered them inside, and Zelda was struck by the simplicity of his accommodations. For a king, he certainly didn't live like one. The manor was warm with dark wood walls and long curtains of pale-green velvet. The ceiling was white with ornate plasterwork. The front door deposited them in the candlelit main hall which was dominated by a long table with simple benches and a massive stone fireplace that could fit all five of them inside.

"If you would follow me," Rían said. "We shall go into the study. It really is the best part of the house." He turned to his sister. "Edrie, would you mind preparing tea? My staff has likely gone to bed."

She gave Rían a look of annoyance, but she obliged him anyway and disappeared through a darkened doorway.

There was more to the manor than Zelda had originally thought. As Rían led them through cramped hallways and up winding staircases, she wondered how much of St. Germain's Shoe Emporium was like that.

Rían wasn't wrong about the study.

They entered through a door they all had to duck their heads under and were met with a stunning view of the city. A large, paned-glass window stretched two stories high with a massive latch on the side which meant it could open. King Rían's study was built against one of the dormer windows of St. Germain's and offered them a commanding view of the city's night skyline. In the distance, Zelda could even make out the outline of the castle.

"This is fantastic," Leo said as he crossed to stand at the window.

Zelda joined him.

Figures scurried through Founders Square, but there were few people left in the streets. Rían settled himself on one of the pair of large, green velvet sofas that faced each other in front of the window.

Zelda hadn't seen it at first, but a wall of books sat opposite the window. Nahia helped herself to one of the books and took a seat at Rían's desk. She kicked her feet up onto the desk, opened the book to one of its center pages, and proceeded to look disinterested despite her unease with them there. Her relationship to Rían was unclear, but she certainly looked at home in his study.

"I am certain this is all quite confusing," Rían said. His eyes twinkled as he watched them.

Leo and Zelda moved to sit opposite him.

"It's hard to wrap my mind around," Leo said. "So, you're . . . king?"

Rían chewed his bottom lip. "Yes. It is an old title without the job security. It has not always been so, but now it is an elected position."

Zelda's brows pushed together. "You're not a monarch?"

"No." Rían fingered the pearl hooked into his ear. "Think of me as a magistrate with a lifetime appointment. My people, however, can call for a popular election at any time. It keeps me honest."

"And your arrangement with George St. Germain is what exactly?" Zelda asked.

"He offers us protection and lets us keep to ourselves. We in turn help him make shoes. Not all elves enjoy making shoes—many have found other professions as you may have seen on your way here—but we of Fifth Floor have been passing down the skill for generations. We have become quite adept at it," Rían said with a look of pride.

"Interesting," Leo said. "So, you're entirely self-governed within the physical boundaries of the emporium?"

"Yes, but as we have always existed within the bounds of Olisand, we fully submit to the authority of its crown." Rían dipped his brow to the prince.

Leo sat a little taller. He seemed to falter for words. "I'm sure my father would thank you, but he has no idea you're even here."

"Tell me," Rían said when Edrie appeared with the tray for tea. "Does King Theodore need to know of our existence? Would he be content to let a kingdom of elves govern themselves within his?"

Zelda looked to Leo nervously. She didn't know what his answer would be, and she didn't know what hers would be either.

"King Theodore has enough on his plate," Leo said. "If you think it's best to keep hidden, I can respect that request. My father doesn't need to know what we've seen here tonight."

"I trust your discretion, Your Royal Highness," Rían said with a twinkling smile. "Now, let us have some tea, and you can ask me anything you like, after you tell me what you know about this business with a Consortium of Thaumaturges."

Edrie scampered up to the table and placed a steaming copper kettle and several cups in front of them. "I did not know what blend you would prefer so I selected Rían's favorite evening tea."

Nahia glanced up from her book and fixed them with a look like she wanted to kick them out the oversized window. Zelda ignored the cold reception and helped herself to the tea.

Edrie took the seat beside Rían and tucked her bare feet underneath her. "The tea is made from flowers and plants grown here on Fifth Floor."

Zelda wasn't sure about drinking a strange concoction of elven tea, but Edrie looked proud and truly eager for Zelda to take a sip. She took a tiny sip first, but it wasn't too hot. With a real drink of the tea, she tasted the fullness of its herbal and fruity flavors. Not a hint of sharp bitterness to the brew. "Amazing," Zelda said. "Do I taste apples?"

Zelda glanced over to see if Leo liked it, but he'd already finished half of his cup.

"I'll have to come back for more of this," Leo said.

Rían grinned, and it creased the corners of his green eyes. "Your Royal Highness is welcome to visit us anytime—discretely, if you please."

"Of course," Leo said, and he drained his cup.

"Thaumaturges?" Nahia prompted from her place at the desk.

"Yes," Zelda said. "We believe Susan and George St. Germain seem to be having some trouble with Thaumaturges looking to use your Heartstone as a source of magic."

"That is grave indeed," Rían said. "After what you have seen tonight, I hope you understand why it is so important for Fifth Floor to remain secret. If someone were to take the Heartstone, life on Fifth Floor would be decimated. The stone is not only the source of our magic, it is the life that flows through our entire ecosystem. Without it, we would wither away and have to leave to find a new one, but the St. Germain family has protected us for centuries against just that kind of threat. I will bring up your concerns with Susan the next time I see her, but if she has not brought this to our attention, then I believe we have nothing to worry about."

They talked for what felt like hours, but Zelda kept one eye on the minute-hand on Leo's watch. As midnight inched closer, Zelda's eyes felt heavier and heavier in the warm study. She was usually in bed by eleven, but Leo didn't seem ready to leave, and Rían was kind enough to answer his questions. They still had an hour to get back to school when Zelda let her head rest on Leo's shoulder.

"Don't fall asleep," Leo whispered against her hair.

"I'm not," Zelda murmured.

Well maybe just for a second.

When Zelda opened her eyes, light streamed through the dormer window. She felt the steady rise and fall of Leo's chest on her cheek. As she stirred, his strong arm around her pulled her in close. The scent of his cologne was intoxicating until she realized they were still in Rían's study. Zelda bolted upright. Someone had put a thick fur blanket over her while she slept. Leo had settled into a corner of the cushy sofa, his head on the back cushion.

Zelda's pulse kicked into overdrive. "Leo." She pressed a hand to his chest. "Wake up."

Leo's head popped off the sofa and his eyes blinked open. "What?" he groaned. He sat up slowly, his limbs still groggy with sleep.

"We fell asleep." Zelda grabbed his wrist to look at his watch. "It's nine-fifteen. We were out all night."

"We're still small. Aren't we supposed to be bigger now?" Leo said, his voice still deep and rumbly from sleep.

"I don't know."

Leo groaned and rubbed a hand over his face. "Felix is going to kill me—my dad is going to kill me."

Zelda stood and pulled Leo off the sofa. "Yeah. And I'm going to be expelled." She didn't release Leo's hand as she dragged the groggy prince to the door. *Where is Rían?* More surprising, Nahia had left them alone.

Her sharp memories of the night before led her back to the dining hall where they found Rían, Nahia, Edrie, and a host of twenty elves enjoying a breakfast feast fit for royalty.

At the sight of them, Rían stood from his place in the middle of one of the long tables. "Your Royal Highness." He bowed to Leo. "We were wondering when you would awaken. I am afraid I forgot how our teas can affect young elves. We give it to the little ones to help them sleep, but I did not think the brew would be too strong for humans. I hope you will not mind that we started the feast without you." He gestured to the long table filled with overflowing dishes of food.

"We have to go," Zelda said, panic tightening her voice. "We were supposed to be back at school last night."

"Oh." Rían seemed to sense her distress. "I am terribly sorry. I would have woken you if I had known."

"It's okay," Leo said. "Can you have someone show us the way out of here?"

Rían ushered them to the door. "Of course. I will show you out myself."

"I can't believe the potion has lasted this long," Zelda said as they hurried through the city's streets.

"What potion?" Rían asked over his shoulder.

"A shrinking potion," Zelda said.

Rían whirled around. He sized up Zelda with an admiring gaze as he walked backward. "A shrinking potion surely cannot last this long. I thought for certain you had used a spell that would need to be broken to be reversed. That is extraordinary."

Zelda let a smile creep onto her lips.

"You're going to run into someone," Leo said to Rían, less amused.

Rían turned back to face the direction they were going. "Do not fret. I will set you both right once we are outside of the building."

They reached the attic wall and a gaping doorway that led to the narrow space between the interior and exterior walls. Zelda glanced once more at the miniature city in St. Germain's attic before they disappeared into the dark. A tiny wooden staircase went down and down and down into the dark of the wall with only a few lanterns to light the way. Their blue flames mimicked the cold light of the

Heartstone. *Magic fire?* Zelda didn't have the breath to ask Rían as they flew down the steps. By the time they reached the ground floor, Zelda was slick with sweat.

"This way," Rían said as he led them through the dark passageway. He threw open a door, and they burst into the light of the alleyway behind St. Germain's.

The sight and smell of towering waste bins was overwhelming. Zelda turned to Rían who casually rolled up the sleeves of his emerald doublet. "Can you change us back?" she pleaded.

With a smirk on his lips, Rían raised his hands, his palms turned toward them. Zelda took a step backward. Did he really intend to do magic bare handed? Could elves control magic spells without a wand? She didn't have time to react before a flash of white light exploded from Rían's palms.

Her eyes closed on instinct. When she opened them, the bins were a normal size and a full-sized Leo stood beside her. The rapid change had left her a little lightheaded and she stumbled into Leo to catch her balance.

"Woah there," a small voice called from somewhere at her feet.

Zelda looked down to see Rían take a few steps back to get a better view of them. "Sorry," she said.

Rían waved her away.

"I'm sorry we can't stay longer," Leo said diplomatically. "I'll do my best to visit again soon, and we'll set up a line of communication."

"I look forward to it," Rían said.

Chapter Thirty-Six

As they dashed down the alley, a pit grew in Zelda's stomach. They emerged into the morning bustle of Founders Square and Leo grabbed Zelda's hand as they snaked through the crowd. Voices rose from the crowd.

"Is that the prince?"

"Did you see him?"

"Prince Leopold."

Thankfully, no one reached out to stop them, and once they were through, they were just blocks from the schools. Zelda didn't want to think about what was waiting for them. In all her years of school, she'd never heard of GITs staying out all night.

Zelda and Leo, hand in hand, rounded the corner onto the street that ran between the schools. The road was filled with royal guardsmen, uniformed police officers, and teachers from both Madame LeBleu's and EAMS. The search dogs seemed a little much, but then she had gone AWOL with the crown prince.

At the sight of them, Felix broke off from a group of men all in similar dark suits. He jogged over to them before anyone else dared to move. Dark circles rimmed his deep-brown eyes. It took every last ounce of courage to meet his gaze when he stopped in front of them. He looked tired, but he surprisingly didn't look angry.

"I'm sorry," Leo said, his words strangled with emotion.

Felix heaved a sigh. "Whatever it was, I hope it was worth it."

Leo didn't reply.

What else could he say? Zelda didn't know what they'd tell everyone now that they had to keep the elves secret. They hadn't had time to catch their breath, let alone come up with a believable alibi. As Felix walked them the rest of the way, Zelda tried to think of any excuse. A broken-down trolley. An illness. Anything besides what everyone would think she'd been doing with Leo all night. Even then, better that than the real reason they'd been gone so long.

When they reached the crowd gathered in the street, the concerned horde overtook them.

"Is anyone hurt?" a paramedic asked.

"Your Royal Highness, did someone hold you against your will?" a royal guardswoman asked.

"Your father wants to see you," Felix said.

Madame LeBleu stood at the center of it all. She fixed Zelda with a stern glare that made Zelda's insides churn with guilt. Zelda stopped in front of the headmistress, head bowed. "I'm sorry. I didn't mean to—"

Madame LeBleu placed a gentle hand on Zelda's shoulder. "Come. We'll discuss this in my office."

Zelda followed the headmistress until a voice rose up from the din of chaos around the prince. "Wait."

Leo pushed past through the crowd and closed the distance between them with long strides.

"Zelda," Madame LeBleu warned.

Zelda ignored her when she saw the look on Leo's face and the panic there as he grabbed her around the waist. His hand cupped her chin as he placed a kiss on her lips. It was a different sort of kiss—needy and deep. *Let everyone think what they're already thinking.* Zelda sank into Leo despite the many eyes watching them. A new emotion she wanted to name filled the kiss.

When Leo pulled away, he looked almost sad.

"Leo?"

He reached up and brushed a strand of hair from her face. "Zelda, I—I—" He struggled to find words for the emotions warring on his face.

"Leo, what is it?" Panic rose in Zelda's voice.

"I have to go." Glistening eyes locked with Zelda's. "This is not goodbye."

Zelda's trembling legs threatened to give out underneath her. What did he mean? "Leo?"

"I have to go," he repeated before he slipped away to duck into a waiting black sedan.

With the prince safe and sound, the crowd of police and other security personnel quickly dispersed. Zelda had nowhere to go but to follow Madame LeBleu through the school gates. Faces of students peered down at them from what seemed like every window as they headed directly for the headmistress's cottage.

Inside the cottage, Professor Ballentine waited in Madame LeBleu's private office. She looked about as pleased as Madame LeBleu.

"Take a seat, Miss Ravensdale," the headmistress said, her voice reedy and tired.

Zelda took the seat farthest from where Professor Ballentine lounged against the window bench, arms folded across her chest. She lowered her eyes to her hands as she waited for her telling-off. Tears burned in her eyes. She was going to cry. It was just a matter of when.

"Never in all my years . . ." Madame LeBleu began with thinly veiled disappointment. The wood of her desk chair creaked as she sat. "The police. The royal guard. I think this goes without saying, but this behavior does not represent the school and its students in any way, shape, or form. I think I was quite clear when we allowed you to be Prince Leopold's godmother that you were to keep him out of trouble."

"I'm so sorry," Zelda blurted. "I didn't mean to—"

"Miss Ravensdale." The restrained anger on Madame LeBleu's elegant features chilled her to the core. "I don't want to hear about your good intentions. I never would have expected such reckless behavior from you, nor would I have thought you foolish enough to develop a romantic relationship with your godchild. Surely Professor Nutt has taught you about the lack of ethics in granting a wish for someone who has a personal relationship with you."

Zelda sat up to her full height. "Leo doesn't want to wish away his crown. He hasn't wanted to for months now."

Ballentine shook her head. "I knew it. I told you all we shouldn't have gotten a student involved with Prince Leopold's wish—"

"Helga," Madame LeBleu said. "You know very well why we couldn't get involved. In fact, I think Professor Weymouth should be here."

"I'll get him," Ballentine said, but she didn't move to pull out her phone or leave to go get him.

Madame LeBleu turned back to Zelda. "Now. I'd like to hear from you. Where have you been all night?"

Zelda swallowed the lump in her throat. She'd already been told to keep Leo away from St. Germain's elves. Furthermore, she didn't have any idea whether telling Ballentine and LeBleu would help or hurt the elves. Could they really be trusted? Would they keep their secret, or would they risk exposing them to the Thaumaturges? Her silence was deafening.

Say something. Anything. Zelda willed her lips to move, but words wouldn't come.

"Well?" Ballentine said. "You don't have anything to say for yourself?"

Zelda was rescued by the sound of a door opening and closing. Professor Weymouth appeared in the doorway to Madame LeBleu's study. His mouth pressed into a severe frown. "Ellie—Professor Ballentine," he corrected at the sight of Zelda. "How many times do I have to tell you? Do not *summon me* by planning my murder in graphic detail. It's a very unpleasant vision to get in the middle of breakfast."

Ellie? Zelda had heard professors address Ballentine as "Helga," but never "Ellie."

"Weymouth, please," Madame LeBleu said. "We are hoping you can give us some insight into whatever Zelda and Prince Leopold have been up to."

Weymouth looked to Zelda, concern etched into the lines on his face. "My gift doesn't work that way—"

Ballentine scoffed. "Did you foresee her romantic attachment to the prince? You should have told us if you had any inkling. There are serious ethical boundaries that may have been crossed."

"No," Weymouth asserted. "I saw inklings of a spark, but I knew Miss Ravensdale wouldn't dare cross a line. In fact, I'm fairly certain she convinced Leo not to give up his crown *months* ago. That's what we wanted, right?"

Zelda's shoulders loosened with relief when he confirmed her story unprompted. A look passed between Madame LeBleu and Ballentine as if to confirm they'd both heard him right.

"Very well then," Madame LeBleu said. "But you should have updated us, and we still don't know what she was up to all last night. Miss Ravensdale has not been forthcoming."

Weymouth took the seat beside Zelda and examined her face. Zelda's cheeks went hot as she wondered what he would see there. She begged him with her eyes not to tell them anything. Even though he never saw concrete specifics, she hoped he would see why she had to keep the elves secret.

"It's okay, Zelda," he said. "You can tell us. I-I can't help you unless you tell me what you've been up to because Prince Leopold is still in danger."

Zelda's face fell. *What have I done?* She didn't want to betray Rían's confidence, but it also had been her duty to protect Leo. She hadn't stopped him from getting embroiled in this mess. Something about the look on Weymouth's face felt trustworthy, so she gave in. "Please, you mustn't tell anyone what I'm about to tell you."

"Go on," Ballentine said, her features softening. "What you tell us will not leave this room."

"We were with the elves in St. Germain's Shoe Emporium," Zelda said.

"Thank you for trusting us," Weymouth said. "But there's more to this, isn't there?"

Zelda recounted everything she'd learned leading up to the discovery that George St. Germain was hiding the elves, so the thaumaturges couldn't use the Heartstone.

When Zelda finished, Ballentine was the first to speak. "What I want to know is why Lord Scarlet was handing out books on thaumaturgy to his students."

Zelda shifted nervously in her chair. She was still apprehensive for bringing Specs and Imogen into this. "What does this have to do with Leo?"

Weymouth ran a tired hand over his jaw. "Yes, about that. The fact that a thaumaturge was involved was why we decided to keep you in the dark in the first place. There are stirrings in the non-magical world. Some people, the Duke of Brockford for one, believe that magic is too strictly controlled by the ICG; they believe that others should be free to explore the magical arts. The duke has proposed some very concerning legislature that makes concessions to certain thaumaturgical practices. Even worse, it was backed by Lord Scarlet."

Zelda's mind drifted back to the heated conversation she had overheard between Madame LeBleu and Lord Scarlet on Halloween.

Professor Weymouth continued, "King Theodore has always pushed for heavy regulation of fairies and their magic, but it's magic he doesn't like—not fairies. He isn't pro-fairy per se, but he was *not* receptive to his cousin's legislation. In all the public hearings on the issue, Leopold has stood behind his father's position in keeping magic under the control of fairies and the ICG alone."

"You placed me near Leo so I could protect him?" Zelda asked. "What about his father? Do you really think the duke would try to take both Leo and the king out of the picture?" Panic fluttered in her chest as she wondered what thaumaturges would do to Leo if they didn't get their way.

Professor Weymouth nodded. "The King's health is tenuous, as you know. If the worst should happen, if he and Leo were disposed of, Astara wouldn't be old enough to take the throne. The next in line would be made regent."

Zelda's gut sank. "Which would be Brockford." It all made sense. If the Consortium of thaumaturgy wanted to practice magic without fear of repercussion from the ICG, they would need someone to change laws. After seeing what thaumaturgy entailed—forcibly taking it from magical beings—Zelda fully understood why Madame LeBleu, or anyone for that matter, would want to see the ban upheld.

"Don't worry, Miss Ravensdale. We won't let them win," Weymouth said.

Zelda nodded as guilt thickened her throat. "Are the royals in danger now . . . because of me?"

"No." Professor Weymouth placed a reassuring hand on her shoulder. "They have plenty of protection, but this is no longer your concern. We'll make sure they're caught. Professor Ballentine has been tracking them across Erimount, and she's getting close—"

"Yes, and what I'm doing is a top-secret investigation for the ICG, not something for a GIT to be meddling in," Ballentine said, annoyed.

"I'm not meddling. Just . . ." Zelda fumbled for the right word. She opted for Weymouth's. "We were investigating. I brewed a shrinking potion since Imogen was closing the store, and she let Leo and I slip inside. We weren't looking for any thaumaturges."

Professor Ballentine's brows shot up at this. "A shrinking potion? Those are extremely difficult. Do you have some left over?"

"Now is not the time," Madame LeBleu said. "Miss Ravensdale, I specifically told you not to get involved. We were aware of George St. Germain's affiliation with the Consortium of Thaumaturgy."

Zelda straightened. "But now you know how he is trying, and on the verge of failing, to keep the Heartstone away from them. The elves need that stone for their entire civilization to survive."

"She's right," Ballentine said. "I had been chasing whispers, but now I have at least some idea of what the Consortium is up to."

Madame LeBleu folded her hands on her desk and fixed Zelda with a stern glare. ""Regardless, you have disobeyed a direct order to keep the prince away from this mess. These matters at hand are so far out of your depth—we can't have a student in the mix. We expressed that to you, and you deliberately ignored it. Your actions have given me no choice but to issue you three demerits."

Zelda's stomach fell like a brick.

Madame LeBleu got up from her chair and retrieved a thin file from her cabinet. "That puts you at four demerits for the year which means you are officially on probation. One more demerit and you will be put before the disciplinary board for expulsion. Understand?"

Zelda nodded and swallowed the lump in her throat.

Madame LeBleu set the file on her desk. "Furthermore, your off-campus privileges are officially revoked with the exception of school-sanctioned activities and when you're working the hotlines."

"Yes, Madame LeBleu," Zelda choked out.

"Professor Ballentine, please escort Zelda back to her dorm."

Zelda bolted out of her seat, eager to put as much distance between herself and their conversation.

Chapter Thirty-Seven

Felix didn't speak the entire way back to the castle. Maybe he didn't know what to say. Maybe it was a kindness. Leo knew what waited for him at the castle looming at the top of the gravel drive. His father was a miserable bully even when Leo was on his best behavior. He was going to get the verbal thrashing of a lifetime—and pulled out of EAMS— that much was certain. Yet he wasn't filled with the usual terror of facing his father's wrath.

He was more scared of the giddy feeling that bubbled in his chest. He pressed his palms against his legs to steady his breath when he knew he should be worried. Zelda was in as much trouble as him, and the guilt over his part in that warred with what he'd almost said.

"Are you okay?" Felix asked from the driver's seat. "I don't want to clean your sick out of my car mats."

"I'm fine," Leo said. He wasn't.

The car eased into the mews, and Leo got out before they came to a full stop. Tiffani waited at the door, her ever-present clipboard in hand.

"Your father wants to speak to you straight away," she said as he brushed past.

"Where is he?" Leo asked, fisting his twitching fingers.

"Dining room—and you'd better hurry."

Leo knew he should've been getting his excuses in order, but all he could think about was Zelda and that kiss. He didn't know what was going to happen after what they'd done, so in a panic, he had almost said some precious words.

"What's wrong with you?" Astara appeared and jogged to match his quick stride. "Tiffani said you're in so much trouble."

Leo turned up the grand staircase. "Go away."

"Don't be rude." Astara's voice came from behind him. "What did you do?"

Leo didn't want her following him right into a confrontation with his father, so he turned and fixed her with a glare. "I was careless and foolish, and I may have hurt Zelda and . . ."

Astara's eyes went wide. "And what?"

He shouldn't have said more. "You wouldn't understand. You're too young."

"And you're stupid," Astara retorted.

Leo rolled his eyes and continued up the stairs. "You just proved my point, and don't use the s-word."

Astara followed him. "That's not the s-word. I know what the s-word is. I'm not a baby."

Leo stopped on the top step, so Astara had to stop below him. "It's something you wouldn't get. You've never been in love."

The scowl on Astara's face was replaced by excitement. "Please tell me," she said, changing her tune. "Please. I'm telling you I can handle it. Don't decide what I can't understand—that's what Dad would do."

Leo groaned. She knew just what card to pull to bend him to her will. "Fine. I almost told Zelda I loved her."

"What? Why didn't you?" Astara poked him hard in the muscle of his arm.

"Ow." He rubbed his bicep. "I didn't tell her because it was the wrong time. We were surrounded by people, and it was too soon—there's no way she already loves me back."

Astara threw her hands in the air, a gesture that looked much too old for a ten-year-old. "Leo. You're such a buttmunch."

"I'm a what?"

"Of course she loves you. She came out for New Year's Eve and wore all those really uncomfortable dresses you picked out and sat through all Tiffani's lectures. She even entertained Mom and Dad's snobby friends, and she never once complained about it. No one would do that for a guy they just liked. Even if she didn't know it, that was love-level stuff she did for you."

Stunned, Leo's heart pounded in his ears as a heady warmth filled him from head to toe. *Is my ten-year-old sister right about this?* "It was the wrong moment," he said.

Astara shook her head. "There is never a wrong time to tell a girl you love her. She probably saw it coming and is now freaking out because you didn't say it."

Panic crept up in Leo's chest. "Well, then what do I do now?"

"My professional advice—"

"Your professional advice?" Leo teased.

"As a girl," Astara continued, "is now you really have to tell her you love her, and soon."

"Soon?"

"And it would be better if you made a big show of it. You chickened out in front of a crowd, so you need to prove to her that you're not ashamed of her."

"I have to do what now?"

"Leo." His mother's voice carried from down the long hall.

The smile fell from Leo's face. "I have to go. We'll finish this later."

"Fine," Astara said with a smirk on her lips. A loud crash sounded down the hall, and her grin faded. "Good luck," she said before flying down the stairs in the opposite direction.

Leo tried to swallow his nerves, but the anxious flutter refused to leave his stomach. He headed toward the sound of the crash. It wasn't out of the realm of possibility for his father to smash something in anger.

"Father?" Leo called as he neared the dining room.

It was his mother that replied. "Leo?" Her voice carried from the closed doors to the dining room, high and tremulous with alarm.

Leo entered the formal dining room, looking for the sound of the crash, and for a moment, nothing seemed amiss aside from the untouched platters of food that lined the center of the table. Then, he saw his mom's face, blanched with shock. His eyes followed her gaze to what was truly wrong with the scene. A pair of legs in black trousers and gleaming wingtips stuck out from behind the table, twisted and tangled at an unnatural angle. Unmoving.

"Get help," Queen Antonia said between shuddering breaths. "Your father has collapsed."

Chapter Thirty-Eight

Leo never came back to school. At lunch the following Monday, Specs brought them the news that Leo's room had been packed up. On Tuesday, the real news broke. The king had suffered a medical event and had been hospitalized. Details weren't clear, but it was serious enough that Leo was made regent while the king was incapacitated.

It was weird to see Leo step into the role of regent, but he was every bit the part: eloquent, serious, dependable—almost like he was born for it. Zelda wanted to understand his silence. For all intents and purposes, he was ruling the country now. He'd been about to say something before they were separated. She didn't want to assume, but his final words told her not to lose hope even if every day of silence brought her closer and closer to losing it.

This is not goodbye.

The week of the annual Wishmaker Festival arrived with all its pomp and circumstance and the first break in icy temperatures for spring—perfect weather for the outdoor concerts, street fairs, and parades to come. The royal family decided that despite the king's health, the festivities would continue as usual.

"Have you tried calling him?" Imogen asked.

Zelda grabbed Imogen's hand and saved her from making the grave mistake of adding stardust to the vision-enhancing brew, instead of powdered moonstone. A mistake Susan had failed to avoid minutes earlier. The potions lab had filled with thick, acrid smoke, and Susan was forced to clear away all her progress with a swish of her wand. A mistake from Susan was a rarity, but it didn't give Zelda the satisfaction it would have before. Susan was starting to look tired, but Zelda didn't enjoy seeing her like that—like she'd given up on school. It made her feel less guilty for telling Madame LeBleu and her professors about the elves. If Susan and her father failed, she had no doubt now that Professor Ballentine would stand up to the thaumaturges.

"Of course," Zelda said. "But my phone isn't connecting to his number anymore. He might have a new number, or his phone got messed up when we took the shrinking potion. Mine is a mess. It keeps deleting apps at random—we should have given you our phones before we took the potion."

Imogen flicked her long ponytail over her shoulder. "He should have at least tried to call you."

"I think he did. I had a missed call from a restricted number at fencing club practice."

"It was definitely him."

"He invited me to the Wishmaker Festival Ball months ago. Do you think I should still try to go?"

In the days leading up to the festival, the only subject discussed in the halls of Madame LeBleu's, other than the Follies, was who had managed to get a date to the Wishmaker Festival Ball. In the chaos of last-minute preparations for the Wishmaker Festival Follies, Zelda had barely a moment to think about the ball. She spent her nights magicking costumes together and working out the final touches on their act with Specs and Imogen. Though the transfer machine hadn't worked in any of their rehearsals, Specs had assured them it would be in working order for the show.

"Of course, you should go," Imogen said as she pulled their potion off the heat.

"Are you going?" Zelda knew Specs had asked her, but Imogen hadn't said anything about it.

Imogen groaned. "I don't know. Specs asked me, but he also told me he liked me."

Zelda's stomach flipped. "And that's bad?"

"Yes. He told he's liked me for a long time, but he hasn't had the chance to tell me till now. *Now*."

"He's shy."

"But we have like two months of school left and then who knows where I'll be on my placement. I just . . . I wish he wouldn't have waited so long. So yeah, I'm kinda mad at him."

"But do you like him?"

"I don't know. I never thought of him that way." Imogen blushed to her ears. "He's going to be all weird if I reject him, and I don't want to lose my friend."

"Maybe you can tell him you want us all to go together, as friends, so I'm not left out," Zelda suggested.

Imogen sighed. "I guess that could be okay."

"Unless you really do want to go with him?"

"I need more time to think," Imogen said.

Professor Ballentine instructed them to wrap up at a good stopping point and dismissed them early, so they could get to the Olisand National Theater to prepare for the Follies. Zelda and Imogen arrived at the theater with the rest of the GITs. It was the first time Zelda had left campus since Madame LeBleu had put her on probation. Thus far, she hadn't set a single toe out of line, and that wasn't going to change.

They entered through a towering lobby with a ceiling that boasted a mural of cherubs and angels playing on wisps of clouds in a blue sky. The theater was smaller than the one Zelda had visited in Paris, but no less decadent. The walls were draped in maroon velvet and lined with a subtly shimmering gold wallpaper. Zelda's neck began to ache as she tried to catch a glimpse of each trompe l'oeil they passed. A nervousness slicked her palms as they passed rows upon rows of seats that would be filled with bodies in a matter of hours.

They found Specs and the rest of the tinkers backstage. For tonight, Specs would play the "bumbling" magician, and Imogen and Zelda would play his more competent and magically inclined assistants. Imogen had worked out the comedic bits, while Zelda had perfected the charms on their props. She only had to do a few simple spells made to look like classic magician's tricks and turn the crank on the box for the final part of the act. It seemed simple enough, but that hadn't stopped her from rehearsing the act with Imogen each night that week.

Specs gave Imogen an awkward wave and hopeful half-smile that made Zelda cringe with secondhand embarrassment. She left them to talk and squeezed herself into a spot at the crowded greenroom mirrors. Zelda wasn't sure how normal theater productions ran, but the chaos backstage bordered on overwhelming. Layers of makeup were applied with heavy hands, and half-dressed students scurried about looking for missing elements of their costumes.

Imogen eventually found Zelda to help her apply makeup. "Come." She pulled Zelda out of the greenroom and into a brightly lit hallway. "We can do our makeup here. I'm not going to get a flawless winged eye with Iris Pickett elbowing me in the ribs." She produced a shiny gold compact with a wicked grin. "And I don't want to debut it yet, but I've stabilized the filtering foundation, and you're going to be my first tester."

"Really? It's not going to make me look blurry is it?" She didn't like using the really intense photo filters.

"It's subtle. You'll like it," Imogen said as she tapped the powder puff to Zelda's cheeks.

Once they were in makeup and costume, they joined Specs backstage for sound checks. Even from the wings, Zelda could feel the heat rolling off the stage lights. She shook out her hands which, of all things, had started to sweat. Imogen guided her onto the stage when their act was called.

It took a moment for Zelda's eyes to adjust to the bright light. When they did, she found she couldn't see past the first row, and it calmed her immensely. She might as well have been performing for a very bright lamp.

Back in the greenroom, sandwiches were delivered for dinner, which meant the show was starting soon. The excited chatter fell to a nervous hush after Iris announced that the curtains to the stage were closed for the start of the show. Zelda picked absently at a chicken sandwich while they waited for places to be called. She rehearsed the order of the lines for their act silently, and in her concentration, almost didn't notice the total silence that fell over the dressing room.

"What's going on?" she asked.

Imogen shrugged.

A group of people in imposing dark suits came through the stage door and began a scan of the room.

"What's happening?" a bolder tinker asked.

"Security sweep," a woman with a no-nonsense ponytail said. "A VIP will be attending the performance."

"Who?" several eager students cried at once.

The security officers didn't answer, but Zelda jumped to her feet when she spotted a familiar face among them. Felix. Air left her lungs in a rush. Felix met her excited gaze, but his expression was unreadable. Was Leo really coming to the Follies? How was she supposed to keep her focus when she knew he would be watching? The twisting in her gut felt like the days when she'd first met the troubled prince. Everything had been easier around him, and perhaps, she was glad to know he would be there.

After the security officers finished the backstage sweep, a haggard Iris Pickett came around to call everyone to their places for the opening act. Their skit was after the intermission, but Zelda left Imogen and Specs in the greenroom to try to catch a glimpse of the VIP from backstage.

The wings were dark, lit only by a blacklight, and the curtain did little to hide the chatter of the crowd. She could see part of the audience and an empty set of box seats through the sliver of a gap between the wall and the curtain.

Then she saw him. Prince Leo and Princess Astara entered the box closest to the stage. The audience rose to their feet and applauded the prince regent. Leo gave a friendly wave, and he and Astara took their seats.

The audience sat as Madame LeBleu and Lord Scarlet took to the stage to welcome everyone and give special thanks to the royal guests. Applause thundered, the curtain opened, and the fourth-year tinkers began the show with a campy musical mash-up of songs with tinkered stage effects. Applause thundered at the end of their number. Dante ignored Zelda when he left the stage, but she brushed it off.

The rest of the first act flew by and before she knew it, the second-year GITs had finished their performance. Zelda tried to catch a glimpse of Leo before the curtains closed for intermission, but he and Astara had disappeared from the box.

Imogen and Specs were gone too.

Chapter Thirty-Nine

"Where are they?" Zelda muttered under her breath. Iris was calling for places, and Imogen and Specs were nowhere to be found. After checking backstage and the greenroom, Zelda set up their act herself. She rolled the transfer machine and Specs' steamer trunk of props into place and waited.

"One minute to curtain," Iris called.

"Come on," Zelda groaned under her breath.

Just as the curtains were about to open, Imogen and Specs rushed onto the stage.

"Are you kidding me?" Zelda said at the sight of their beaming smiles. "We're going on now. What were you doing?"

Specs and Imogen shot each other a furtive glance. "Uuhhh—"

"Ew," Zelda cried. "You chose right now for your first makeout session?"

Specs made a strangled sound. "No that's not—"

"This wouldn't be our first makeout," Imogen said over Specs.

Zelda's eyes went wide. "What?" She didn't have time to ask when their first kiss had been before the curtains opened.

The music came on, and they plastered on smiles while Specs introduced himself as "The Great Disillusioned: the eighth best magician in Erimount" to a hesitant laugh from the crowd. He began by juggling three red balls while he carried on a soliloquy about all the bad reviews he'd received.

Then, mid-juggle, he used both hands to fish out another ball from his jacket and the balls juggled themselves in midair. The audience laughed as they realized Zelda was using her wand to juggle for the bumbling magician. The laugh was Zelda's cue to hide her wand behind her back and let the balls tumble to the floor. This got another laugh.

Zelda glanced to the box where she'd hoped to spot Leo, but she couldn't see past the stage lights.

Specs produced an obviously fake bouquet of flowers from his sleeve, and Imogen tapped her wand to change them into a lush spray of lilies when Specs had his back turned. He did a double take at the sight of the flowers and tossed them to Imogen. Specs pulled the top hat from his head. "This wouldn't be a magic act if I didn't pull a rabbit from a hat."

Zelda's breath caught. *What is he doing?* They hadn't rehearsed this part of the sketch. She watched, helpless, as Specs waved his fake wand over the hat. "And now I'll get a little help from my assistant." He handed the hat to Zelda who took it apprehensively.

It was surprisingly heavy for a hat.

"Show us what's inside, Zelda," Specs said with suspiciously large grin.

Zelda half expected to feel a soft rabbit kicking around inside the hat, but her hand closed around something hard. She pulled out a glass slipper that sparkled brilliantly under the bright stage lights.

"Oh," Specs said as if he hadn't expected a glass slipper to be in the hat. "That's . . . Is anyone missing a glass slipper?" he asked the audience. Only scattered chuckles answered him.

"Is it yours?" he asked Zelda.

"I-I don't think so," Zelda sputtered. *This wasn't in the script.*

"Why don't you try it on?"

Zelda's hands went sweaty as she shot Specs a glare. She was going to let him have it once they got off stage, but she didn't have any option other than to go along with the skit. Zelda slipped off her black, patent-leather shoes with a wobble and tried the glass slipper.

It slipped onto her foot like it had been made just for her.

"Where's the other one?" Imogen asked.

"Right here," a familiar voice said.

Zelda whirled around to see Leo stride onto the stage. Her pulse thundered half in panic and half in shock. He held up a glass slipper to match hers.

"Leo?" she managed to say.

His lips parted into a grin. "Zelda Ravensdale." A microphone clipped to the front of his blue button-up shirt magnified his gentle, even voice. There were a few cheers and scattered applause from the audience. The royals had never made a cameo appearance in the Follies.

Zelda forgot how to breathe as the prince regent knelt in front of her and held out the shoe. Excited murmuring briefly drew her attention to a crowd of tinkers and GITs watching from the wings.

"Zelda," Leo said, drawing Zelda's attention back. "May I?"

She nudged her other shoe from her foot. Leo took her ankle, his touch through the silk of her stockings sending a shiver up her leg. He slid the matching glass slipper onto her foot. It went right on, but Leo didn't stand.

"Zelda Ravensdale, I've come here with one purpose. To tell you I love you and to ask you to accompany me to the Wishmaker Festival Ball."

Several gasps rose from the audience.

Zelda's heart was full to bursting at the earnest and dimpled half-smile on Leo's lips. She couldn't contain her smile as she burst into a laugh. "Of course."

Leo jumped to his feet and swept her into his arms. Zelda grabbed his face and pulled his lips to hers. He didn't hold back as he kissed her in front of all the world. It might have been unbecoming for a prince regent, but Zelda didn't care. When they finally broke apart, she whispered, "I love you too."

Leo's face looked like how she felt—like this was the happiest moment of his life. He gave her another short kiss before he left the stage. Dazed, Zelda almost missed Specs' cue to start their final trick.

"I have still one more act of disillusion to perform," he said, "and it is the trickiest of all." He gestured to the two boxes which had been ignored until this point and opened the door to the first box.

"If my lovely assistant will step into the box of befuddlement." He placed a kiss on Imogen's hand as he helped her in. Imogen fluttered her lashes, playing it up on the stage.

It took all of Zelda's will not to look off stage for Leo. Every inch of her ached to run back into his arms and kiss him again and again for every second they'd been apart.

"Now," Specs lowered his voice, "my second assistant will turn the crank and transfer my first assistant from one box to the next. This is a dangerous feat, never performed before, so I will need complete silence."

The lights lowered to cast eerie shadows over the stage. Zelda hoped the box would work, but all she had was Specs' word that his math had been corrected. If not, she didn't think the audience would care much after Leo's cameo.

Zelda turned the crank, and the copper gears which climbed the side of the box began to whirr. Then the metal coil stretched between the boxes glowed like the filament of a lightbulb.

Specs had actually gotten it to work.

She turned faster and faster until the machine made a loud pop. A pain unlike anything she'd ever felt before shot up her arm and through her chest. She fell to her knees as a strangled cry escaped her lips. She tried in vain to release her hand from the crank, but her fingers grasped it, white knuckled, as if some unseen force held them there.

Zelda's eyes darted to Specs who stood frozen in panic. *What had he changed on the machine?*

Another jolt of pain surged through her and spread with white hot agony. The force that kept her hand in place relinquished its hold, and she collapsed to the ground. Her ears felt like they were stuffed with cotton. Faraway sobs muffled around her, but she realized they were her own. Her head swam and then all the lights in the theater went out.

Chapter Forty

When Zelda woke, she found herself looking up at a paned-glass ceiling. It took a moment for her brain to catch up and remember the glass ceiling from the nurse's ward at Madame LeBleu's. Her mind lagged as she took in the rows of beds around the empty room. Stringing thoughts together felt like sifting pudding through a sieve—her limbs felt even slower. Her legs felt heavy and her muscles trembled at just the thought of moving.

The strange heaviness on her legs turned out to be Leo. With his head nestled into his folded arms, he'd pulled a metal chair up to the foot of the bed and fallen asleep. Zelda watched the slow rise and fall of his shoulders until she finally figured out how to make her voice work again.

"Leo," she croaked. The words sounded distant, strangled. She tried to sit up.

The movement tugged at the blanket beneath Leo's arms and roused him.

"Zelda." He looked up at her with bleary, red-rimmed eyes. Large wrinkles creased the front of a familiar blue shirt. He'd rolled the sleeves up to his elbows.

"What happened?" Her body ached like she'd gotten hit by a trolley, and she couldn't shake the feeling she'd forgotten something.

Leo got up to stand at her side. "The nurse said you shouldn't move too much. Your body was put through a great ordeal." He brushed away the hair that was matted to her forehead.

Through the inky blackness of her memory, the last bit of their act for the Follies came to mind—and the pain. She'd passed out almost instantly. "What happened to me?"

"I'm not as familiar with magical injuries as your nurse, but she says the contraption you used to transfer Imogen . . . it took all of your magic."

"What?" Zelda sat up quickly. The movement made her head feel like it was about to split down the middle.

"Not permanently, from what I understand," Leo said.

Zelda flopped back onto her pillow, her energy spent. *How did this happen?* Specs was so sure . . . "And Imogen? Is she okay?"

Leo nodded. "She made it fine. Specs feels terrible about what happened. He looked pretty shaken up when he was here. The nurse gave him a calming tonic to help him stop trembling."

Zelda looked up at the blue sky behind the glass ceiling. She had a heavy, lethargic feeling in her gut like she'd been asleep for a long time. "How long was I out?"

"Three days. The nurse says you're rebuilding your supply of magic, and it takes a lot of energy since no fairy can naturally dwindle her entire store of magic on her own," Leo said, his hand on hers. His thumb traced hypnotic circles over the soft skin. "Don't worry. I called your parents and told them what happened."

Zelda smiled weakly. "Leo, how long have you been here?"

His blue eyes cut to gaze at the frayed edges of the blanket. "Since they brought you here after the Follies. I've come and gone a few times, but I wanted to be here when you woke up to make sure you were okay," he said. "I can go if you need some space."

"No." Zelda wrapped Leo's hand tightly into hers. "Please stay."

Leo's smile finally reached his eyes and he lowered his head to rest against hers. "I was hoping you would say that."

Zelda's heart was in her throat. Despite her weakened state—and what was possibly the worst case of morning breath ever—her skin tingled all over at Leo's proximity. For a moment, it looked like he might kiss her, but the nurse entered the ward, a clipboard in her hands. Leo took a step back to stand at a respectable distance.

"I see you're awake, Miss Ravensdale. How are you feeling?" the nurse asked. She looked her over with a kind smile.

"Tired," Zelda admitted.

"Yes, having your entire store of magic drawn out will do that to a fairy." She dug a hand into the pocket of her white smock dress. "This belongs to you." She held out a glass orb filled with what looked like shimmering purple smoke. "It's all the magic that contraption took from you. It stored it in here for use. Madame LeBleu and the other professors have already had a look at it, but they can't find a way to get it out."

The school nurse set the orb on Zelda's bedside table. "I suggest you get more rest. You should have drawn in a little bit of magic by now, but you still have a long way to go. I believe His Royal Highness has a ball to get to?" she said, implying heavily that it was time for him to leave.

"Oh no," Zelda exclaimed. "That's tonight?"

"I'm afraid you'll have to stand up your date. You're in no state to attend a ball."

Leo gave her a sullen glance. "It's okay, Zelda."

"No. I can go."

Leo gave her a reassuring smile. "Don't rush yourself." He looked at his watch. "I'm expected to make at least a short appearance at the ball, but I promise to be back here by midnight."

Zelda didn't want to let Leo go, but her eyelids were already starting to feel heavy. As consolation for his leaving, he placed a kiss on her forehead.

"I'll make it up to you," he said. "I'll make up for every day we've been apart as soon as you're feeling better."

He left with the nurse, and Zelda was alone in the ward again. She didn't even bother to resist as she drifted back into a dreamless sleep.

She couldn't tell how many hours had passed when a sound roused her from sleep. The sky above was the inky lavender of dusk. Upon turning onto her side, she found her phone buzzing on the table beside her bed. She fumbled to grab it in her weakened state.

The number was unregistered. "Hello?" she answered groggily.

"Zelda," Professor Ballentine exclaimed from the other end. She was gasping for breath, and her voice sounded alarmed

"Professor? What's going on?" Zelda propped herself up on her elbow.

"We're stuck in St. Germain's Shoe Emporium. Greyson had a *hunch* that the Consortium was going to come for the elves tonight, so we went to head them off. We had to fight off about twelve curses to just get past the third floor, and now we're stuck—some sort of intruder entrapment charm. I called for backup, but Madame LeBleu is already at the ball. Zelda, I don't think a thaumaturge could create curses like this. Only a fairy could. Who—"

Before Zelda could hear the end of Professor Ballentine's warning, the phone was snatched from her hand. Zelda turned to glare at what she expected was the nurse, but she found Susan St. Germain standing over her bed.

"Susan? What are you—"

"I'm sorry, Zelda," she said. Susan looked about as bad as Zelda felt. Her hair hung limp and stringy around her face and sad, dark circles hung under her eyes. She tossed the phone across the room where it made loud clatter as it hit the wooden floor.

Susan then reached out and took the glowing orb filled with Zelda's magic from the nightstand.

"What are you doing with that?" Zelda made a desperate lunge for the orb, but Susan jumped out of her reach.

"You shouldn't have gotten involved with this—the Consortium. They aren't patient, but you should know—I don't have a choice." Susan looked almost apologetic as she slipped the glass sphere into her bag.

"Of course you have a choice," Zelda exclaimed. "You don't have to do what they say. Thaumaturgy is dangerous, Susan. There's a reason it's outlawed."

"You really are ignorant if you think I can just say no to them," Susan spat. "The Consortium is everywhere. I'm always watched." She turned on her heel and headed toward the door.

"Don't. Susan, please."

Susan paused with a hand on the door. She looked back at Zelda. "I really am sorry. They'll hurt my friends if I don't. I hope you've gotten to see Leo one last time. He may not last the night."

Zelda screamed after the desperate blond, but she was gone. Across the room, her phone was buzzing. She couldn't believe the school nurse hadn't appeared in all the commotion, but that was probably Susan's doing.

In the deadly silence after Susan's departure, the room seemed to spin. Zelda slid her aching legs out of the bed. Her feet hit the cold floor, and she stumbled in the direction of her phone. Her mind reeled somewhere between unbridled fear and shock as she tried to reach her phone. The only thing she could think was that Leo was in danger. Professor Weymouth had told her as much over and over again.

She found the phone beneath a cot along the far wall. A jagged crack ran the length of the screen, but it seemed to be working. A call from Leo showed on the screen. Zelda fell to her knees in exhaustion before she answered.

"Leo?"

"Zelda?" The sound of his voice was enough to spring tears to her eyes.

"Leo, are you okay? Susan St. Germain just stole the magic the transfer machine took from me. She said you were in danger. The Consortium of Thaumaturgy is coming for you." The words flew out fast and high. Hopefully, she'd reached him in time to keep him from danger.

"Zelda? I can't hear you. I'm heading into the ball now, so I have to leave my phone with Felix. Zelda?"

"Leo, no."

"Hopefully you can hear me," he continued. "I love you. I'll see you later tonight if you're awake."

Her phone beeped. *Call lost.*

The panic in Zelda's stomach made her want to vomit. She pulled herself up from the floor, using the metal frame of the cot for support. "I'm coming, Leo," she said to the empty room. She didn't know how, but she had to move fast. Without strength. Without magic. She would have to find a way.

Fear, dark and sick, tightened in her chest until it hurt. She couldn't lose him. Not after how long it had taken them to find what they had. An adrenaline rush gave her the strength to gather her personal items from her nightstand and rush to the doors, but they were locked. She pounded her fists against the solid wood and screamed until her throat was raw. Zelda sank to the floor as the realization set in that no one would hear her cry.

Susan was too smart. She hadn't left anything to chance. There would be no getting out of the ward without magic. Zelda let herself ugly cry as she lay on the cold floor. Through blurry, tear-filled eyes, she saw the first stars of twilight, and she wished on the brightest of all that Leo wasn't meeting his untimely end at that very moment.

"You are useless," she cursed at the star. As she swiped away tears, the distinct scent of rain and ozone on a hot summer's day filled the nurse's ward.

"Now what kind of attitude is that for a fairy godmother?"

Zelda startled at the foreign voice. She was no longer alone.

Chapter Forty-One

For a moment, Zelda couldn't understand the scene before her. Queen Antonia stood over her, wearing a great layered ballgown of Barrios Blue and a cream sash across her chest. She extended a hand to Zelda and helped her to her feet. Wings. Queen Antonia had a set of black hummingbird's wings folded against her back. She turned and paced down the center aisle of the nurse's ward. The feathers of her wings shimmered emerald when they caught the light of the moon.

"What?" Zelda choked out. "You're a . . ." She couldn't bring herself to say it.

Queen Antonia turned to face Zelda, her dress swishing across the floor. "The fairy godmother of Olisand? Of course, I am." She gave Zelda a curious glance. "I thought you would have sensed my magic when you stayed with us over the winter, but I suppose you are still quite young. That ability gets stronger with maturity."

Zelda didn't believe it. "But King Theodore—he doesn't like fairies. At least that's what Astara said." She silently cursed herself the moment the words left her lips. It was probably rude to bring up bad feelings while the king was still so sick. She blamed the lack of a filter on her exhaustion.

Queen Antonia formed a thin smile. She seemed amused with Zelda's lack of tact more than anything. "He isn't too fond of magic in general lately, but he is fond of me. But that's a long story for another time. I've heard all your wishes, Zelda. Most importantly your wish to save my son's life—which is strange because I just left him at the ball. Is there something I should know?"

Zelda clutched her shattered phone to her chest, her last connection to Leo. "He called a few minutes ago. Susan St. Germain said he was in danger—she just left, and she took my magic with her. My professors and St. Germain's elves are in trouble too. I don't know what's going on, but something went wrong at the emporium. Please. I promised the elves I would do everything I could to protect them."

Queen Antonia nodded and placed her small, warm hands on Zelda's shoulders. Nose to nose, they were the same height, and the queen had the twinkling eyes and rosy-cheeked glow of a fairy. Now Leo's hesitation to involve the godmother of Olisand made sense. *Why didn't I see it before?*

The queen pulled a slender, pink quartz wand from a pocket hidden up her sleeve. "I can see about your professors and these elves, if you will act to protect Leo." Her lips thinned with concern. "I would like to grant your wish. It's Leo's best chance, but it would be your one and only wish. I know how much you have wanted to be First Fairy. I can certainly advise, but the choice is yours. Just know, if you choose to wish for First Fairy I will understand and will do everything in my power to save Leo and the elves."

Zelda's heart pounded in her chest as she sensed something the queen held back. "But . . ."

Queen Antonia pressed the heel of her palm to her temple. "I believe a fairy's magic is at its strongest when someone's Happily Ever After is on the line. If I'm granting your wish to save him, magic is going to be on our side."

This was all too much. Zelda's head was still foggy from her recent injury, but even with all her mental faculties intact, Queen Antonia's words would have still sounded impossible. She'd never heard of magic spoken of this way, as if it had a will of its own—as if it worked as a force for happiness in the world. She wished she believed that were true, but she knew that granted wishes didn't always guarantee Happily Ever Afters. Magic couldn't fix all of life's tragedies, and it certainly couldn't conquer death. She wanted to help Leo more than anything, but the more she thought about it, the more helpless she felt.

Tears sprang to her eyes. "There's no guarantee. Magic doesn't work like that."

Queen Antonia pulled her into an embrace. Again, the smell of rain and ozone filled Zelda's nose. "I know it seems that way to a young fairy. Magic is the thing that fills your textbooks and is measured and calculated out in potions recipes. Someday, when you know magic as well as I do, you'll see that it's not such a cold and distant thing. Have a little hope, dear."

Hope. It was what Dante told her wishes gave the rest of the world. *Hope for something better.* She had to have hope. For Leo. And the thought of losing First Fairy was nothing compared to the thought of losing him.

Zelda straightened, swiping away the wetness from her cheeks. "I wish to save Leo."

Queen Antonia brightened. "Wonderful. Let's get you your Happily Ever After."

"What do I have to do?"

"The easiest way to proceed would be to restore your magic, but as that's against the law—"

"But is it?" Zelda interjected. "I already have the gift of magic."

Queen Antonia shook her head. "The ICG has had to take magic from fairies before. The rule applies to all."

Panic surged again. "Even when a life is at stake? It's the life of your son."

"I know, but magic always finds a way. If he is your Happily Ever After, you can protect him from harm without breaking the rules of the ICG." Queen Antonia squared herself to face Zelda. She eyed the white hospital gown that hung limp over Zelda's shoulders. "We need to get you to the ball, so you need a dress. And shoes. You'd be surprised at the number of Happily Ever Afters I can make by providing someone with the correct footwear."

With a swish of her wand, pale pink silk and gossamer-thin thread enveloped Zelda and replaced the hospital gown with a blush, V-necked satin gown and a skirt of layered tulle. Another wave and she found herself no longer barefoot, but in a pair of glass slippers. Zelda went to sweep her hair into a ponytail but found it already pulled into a sharp French twist.

"Are you ready to travel by magic?" Queen Antonia asked, offering Zelda her arm. "I'll get us to the ball, and we can search for Leo."

Zelda gathered her wand and slipped her arm through the queen's. The room faded to black. Like traveling through the magical phones for their field experiences, she felt a familiar tug as she was pulled into the aether. Zelda expected to hear the sounds of the ball, but when the tension in her chest released, they hadn't left the nurse's ward. She looked to Queen Antonia for explanation.

The queen furrowed her brow. "Someone sealed off the state building and the surrounding area from external transfer for the security of the ball."

"If we can get out of here, the school greenhouse always keeps a ready supply of pumpkins," Zelda suggested.

The queen gave her an appraising smile before turning her wand on the door. "I like your thinking, Zelda."

She raised both hands toward the towering planes of wood and squared her shoulders as if she were about to wrestle a bear rather than take down a door. A ribbon of red light shot from the crystal in her hand and worked its way through the wood until every grain glowed with magic. A sound like breaking glass filled the chamber, and the magic dissipated into nothing.

"That should have done it," Queen Antonia said. She hurried to the door and, to Zelda's relief, pried it open with a hefty pull of the handle.

In the greenhouse behind Madame LeBleu's cottage, they picked out a large, white pumpkin from one of the raised beds. Careful not to get dirt on her pristine blush gown, Zelda lumbered toward the gates of Madame LeBleu's with the pumpkin in hand and Queen Antonia close behind. They reached the empty cobblestone street, and Zelda set the pumpkin in the center of the road. That was the trick with turning a pumpkin into a carriage—doing it someplace with enough room.

Queen Antonia waved her wand over the pumpkin and its curling tendrils of vine. The magic that coursed through the city tingled in Zelda's feet as her body tried to draw it in and replenish what she'd lost to Specs' machine. She gripped her wand and tested the flow of magic. From the shallow ripple of gooseflesh over her skin, she estimated she had gained back just enough magic for one spell. She'd have to use it wisely.

Queen Antonia worked the magic from her wand, and with a flurry of radiant gold sparks, the pumpkin swelled and grew to the size of a large sedan. The result was quite impressive. With all the filigree and finery of a French court, the glimmering carriage was a sight to behold in the dull city street.

But what's going to pull it? "We need horses," Zelda exclaimed.

"Not when we have horsepower." The queen gestured to the front of the carriage where a rumbling engine was entangled in what had been the vines of the pumpkin. "You can drive, can't you?"

Zelda smiled at Queen Antonia's ingenuity, but they didn't have time to admire the intricacy of her skill with magic. "I can drive."

The queen helped her into the idling carriage and closed the door. Zelda placed her hands on the wheel of the pumpkin, and the engine roared to life at her touch.

"Good luck," Queen Antonia said. "I'll meet up with you as soon as I can." She gave Zelda a solemn nod before disappearing with a stretch of her wings and a puff of air.

Zelda pressed her foot to the gas pedal, and the carriage took off in the direction of the state building. Her heart pounded in her ears, a dull thud even over the engine's roar. She couldn't lose Leo. She tried not to dwell on Susan's warning, but the threat of Leo's imminent demise made her all the more ready to fight. Perhaps her magic would be ready too.

Chapter Forty-Two

Zelda parked the hulking pumpkinmobile in front of the steps to the state building. "It doesn't require keys," she said as she passed a gaping valet.

She ran up the steps and reached the open door to a long, columned hallway. A pair of guards stopped her at the door.

"Name?" the woman asked. She didn't look up from the tablet in her hands.

"Zelda Ravensdale."

"Did you purchase a ticket?" she asked as she swiped her finger across the tablet.

"She's on my list," her male counterpart said. "She's a personal guest of His Royal Highness."

The woman looked up, eyes wide, and ushered her through the metal detector. "My apologies, Miss Ravensdale."

Zelda followed the trickle of other late guests toward the sounds of the ball. The state building was a large square, and the ball was held each year in the open central courtyard. Zelda never imagined she'd be going to a ball in search of a prince. As she got closer, the cacophony of a huge crowd and a full orchestra mid-waltz echoed through the hall. She reached the door to the courtyard and froze. The crowd was twice the size of the New Year's Eve ball.

How am I going to find Leo in this mess? She scanned the crowd, but not a single familiar face stuck out.

Zelda descended the stairs, but as she tried to weave through the sea of gowns and tuxedos, a pocket formed around her. People moved out of her way.

"It's her," a woman shouted to her friend.

"That's the girl from the Follies," another said.

Zelda smiled nervously and waved. *Is this how Cinderella felt when she came back on the third night of the ball?*

Deeper in the crowd, ripples of whispers followed her and people moved away to watch her like she was going to start break dancing or something. A hand on her elbow sent her heart flying. She turned, expecting to find Leo standing safe and sound behind her. Instead, she found the last person she wanted to see.

"Don't look so disappointed," Dante said. He wore a black tuxedo with a crisp white bowtie.

"I'm not—"

Dante stepped in close and pulled her into a waltz. When she resisted, he whispered, "He's not here."

Zelda's chest clenched as his breath brushed her ear. "What?"

"Prince Leo isn't here."

The throngs of ball-goers around them seemed less interested in her now that a reunion with the prince was no longer imminent.

"Do you know where he is?" Zelda's voice trembled.

"I tried to warn you, Zelda," Dante said.

"Where is he?" Zelda cried, firmer this time.

Dante stepped in close to Zelda. "The Consortium took him to St. Germain's factory outside of Erimount," he whispered, his head ducked close to Zelda.

"What? You know about the Consortium?" she rasped.

He pursed his lips. "As a tinker, my uncle roped me into it, but when I saw what they were doing, I tried to leave. To disappear. But it seems the fairies didn't want to grant that wish."

Guilt made Zelda's mouth go dry. "You should have told me more. I maybe could have helped."

Dante's face softened. "You know what the Consortium does now, don't you? I know what you're like and I knew you'd want to stop them. I wanted to keep you as far away from them as possible."

"That wasn't your decision to make. Where's the factory?"

Dante rolled his eyes. "Come on, Zelda. If you think you're going to pull some crazy rescue—"

"That's exactly what I'm going to do," she snapped.

"These people have dangerous weapons. You'll get yourself killed."

Zelda threw her hands in the air. "Fine. I'll just look up the address." She felt the pockets of her dress and realized she'd left her cracked and magic-damaged phone in the nurse's ward or the greenhouse. All she had was a wand and one spell left in her veins.

"No," Dante said as he took her hand and pulled her toward the exit. "I'm coming with you. It's not searchable online anyway."

"Zelda," a female voice called behind them.

Imogen and Specs elbowed their way through the crowd. Imogen's glittering gold, form-hugging gown matched her headband of floating stars. "No one told us you were awake—" She stopped at the sight of Dante. "Ew. What are you doing here?"

"The Consortium took Leo. Dante knows where," Zelda supplied.

"Rust rot your gears," Imogen spat at Dante.

Dante shrugged. "I think that's fair."

"Where is Leo?" Specs roared as he grabbed Dante by the lapels of his tux.

Ball-goers turned at the commotion.

"Relax. He's at St. Germain's factory." Zelda pried Specs' fist from Dante's jacket and shuffled everyone away from the dance floor. She turned to Dante. "If you're so keen to protect me, then help us. You can take us there."

Imogen folded her arms across her chest. "I don't trust him." With a flick of her wrist, her wand slid out the sleeve of her gown.

"That's fine," Dante said. "But we don't have time to stand here arguing about it. Any of you have a car?"

Specs and Imogen glanced between them. "We took a trolley."

"I have a ride," Zelda said.

Outside, the valet hadn't moved the pumpkinmobile from the curb.

"Are you kidding me?" Dante said. "That won't be conspicuous at all."

"It's all I had access too," Zelda said as she gathered her skirts and hopped into the driver's seat. "It'll be cramped, but we can all fit."

Dante got in on the other side and sat in the middle. Specs sat against the window with Imogen balanced on his lap. She still had her wand pointed at Dante.

He swatted her hand away. "Get that out of my face. I need to see where we're going."

"When you prove you don't need a wand in your face, I'll put it away."

Zelda hit the gas pedal, and the pumpkin lurched away from the curb. As they trundled out of the city, Zelda had to threaten to kick Imogen and Dante out to stop their bickering.

"We have to be close," Zelda moaned.

"A few more miles," Dante confirmed.

Soon, a stately Tudor mansion rose from behind a hill.

"Is that it?" Specs asked through gritted teeth. "My legs are falling asleep."

"That's it. Pull over." Dante pointed to a copse of trees at the foot of the hill. "We won't want to leave the pumpkin where anyone will spot it."

Zelda slowed, easing the vehicle off the road. It bounced and jostled over roots, but she was able to park it away from view.

When she took her hands off the wheel, the engine went quiet. They all tumbled out of the pumpkin and headed toward the factory on foot. They stopped at a tall iron fence surrounding the property.

"I only have enough magic for one spell, and I should probably save it," Zelda said. "This is up to you, Imogen."

"I'm really sorry about that," Specs said.

"It's okay," Zelda said. "I know you didn't do that intentionally. With you guys, I shouldn't need my magic to save Leo."

Specs breathed a sigh of relief. "I was worried you were going to hate me."

"I could never—" Zelda said.

"Shush. I need to concentrate." Imogen turned her wand on the towering metal bars. With a silent swish of her wand, a section of the fence turned translucent. The spell spread until the entire fence panel was glass.

Dante searched the ground and returned with a weighty stone. "Stand back." He took a running start and hefted the stone at the fence panel. It crashed into the bars, shattering the glass.

Only a steep grassy hill remained between them and the factory. They started up the slope, stumbling along. Specs helped Imogen as her strappy heels kept sinking into the ground. She eventually got annoyed and transformed her and Zelda's heels into trainers. Dante offered to help Zelda, but she needed both hands to hike up her voluminous skirts.

They reached the factory, sweaty and out of breath.

"Where do we go in?" Zelda asked Dante. "The front door probably isn't the best idea."

"The Duke of Brockford has brought me here for meetings with the Consortium. They enter through the orangery in the back."

Dante led the way to a large glass-walled conservatory. He rattled the handle on the door. "I wasn't given a key."

"I can pick the lock," Specs said. "If one of you has two hair pins I can borrow, I can use it to move the tumblers."

Zelda pulled two of the pins from her hair. "Thanks, Specs."

After several tense minutes of silence, Specs turned the pins in the lock, and the door opened with a subtle click.

Inside the orangery, the wilted array of plants looked in need of some care. "Where would they hold Leo?" Zelda asked.

"The attic. They meet in the attic," Dante said.

"Let's go." Zelda headed for the darkened doorway that led into the factory, but Dante didn't follow. "Are you coming?"

"I can't," Dante said. The look on his face pleaded, *Don't make me.*

"Why not?" Imogen barked.

"My guardian—the Duke of Brockford would make my life miserable if he found out I helped you."

"Well, we can't let you go," Imogen said, arms waving. "Not so you can sneak away and alert the Consortium."

"I won't, but can you make it look like I put up a fight? Knock me out if you must."

"The Duke of Brockford isn't going to get away with this," Zelda said to reassure him.

"Maybe," Dante said. "But just in case, can you make it look like I tried to stop you, but you got the best of me?"

"Gladly." Imogen's jet of pink sparks hit Dante in the chest and burst like a silent firework. When the light faded, nothing but a small lump wiggled under the pile of black-and-white formal wear.

Chapter Forty-Three

"What did you do?" Zelda ran to the jumble of clothes and hesitantly lifted off the tuxedo pants. A faint snuffing and a whine came from the lump inside the white shirt.

"Relax," Imogen said. "It's a perfectly legal spell."

Zelda found Dante inside the sweater, except he didn't look much like himself anymore. She pulled the wriggling puppy from the depths of the clothes. "He's so cute," she said before she could help herself.

Imogen had reduced the boy to a tiny spaniel puppy with wavy black hair that matched the color of Dante's. The deep brown of its eyes matched too.

"I don't think this is legal," Zelda warned.

Imogen folded her arms. "He deserved it. After everything he's done, some time with a bladder the size of peanut should make him reconsider hanging around with thaumaturges."

Specs took Dante and tucked him into the crook of his arm. "We can't leave him to go wandering off."

"Fine," Zelda said, "but we're wasting time."

She led the way into the darkened doorway. Hallways stretched in three directions. Before Zelda could decide which way to head, Dante wriggled out of Specs' arms and took off down the hall straight ahead of them.

"No." Imogen snapped her fingers. "Bad dog."

Dante skidded to a halt and looked over his shoulder at them.

"I think he wants us to follow," Zelda said.

Imogen didn't look convinced, but she followed after Dante. He led them down the hall, through the long, empty factory floor and into the grand showroom. Moonlight through the tall windows glinted off glass cases full of shoes. He stopped at a door that read:

"No Admittance. Executive Staff Only."

Zelda hesitantly tested the door handle. It was unlocked.

Specs picked up Dante again, and they ducked inside. Zelda half expected to find George St. Germain and Lord Brockford waiting for them on the other side, but they were only met with another long hall. Several doors lined the walls, but the hall intersected with another at its end.

An office wing?

They moved onward, hoping to find a further set of stairs around the corner that might lead them to the attic. At the intersection of the two halls, a dull thud from somewhere above their heads brought them to a halt.

Zelda pressed herself to the wall, and the others followed suit. She peered around the corner, but the hall was empty save for a door at one end. The frosted glass door was marked with the name "George St. Germain" and the word "Private" in gold, block lettering.

They were so close, but it felt like ages had passed since Susan had slipped in and stolen the glass orb of her magic. Zelda tried not to think what a thaumaturge would do with access to such a vast amount of magic. Dante gave a high-pitched whimper.

"We have to go in there?" Zelda asked.

Dante whimpered again.

Imogen headed for the door. "Come on then."

Zelda followed a few steps behind. A strange smell filled her nose, faintly at first, it grew stronger as they neared the door. *Black licorice and cough syrup*—Zelda recognized the possible smell of a curse just as Imogen reached out to touch the handle.

"Don't," Zelda cried, but she was too late.

When Imogen's hand made contact with the brass knob, she collapsed to the ground with a thud. Specs set Dante at Zelda's feet before he rushed to Imogen's side and lifted her head to cradle it in his hands. He lowered a cheek to her mouth.

"She's breathing," he said, his eyes fluttering closed.

Dread trickled like ice through Zelda's veins as she stared at Imogen's prostrate body. "What are we doing?" she whispered. "We should have called Madame LeBleu or the police—anyone who could help."

"Zelda," Specs blurted, his voice a firm whisper. "We have to act. We can't sit and wait for the authorities to show up. We got here much faster than they would've—if they even believed us."

Floorboards creaked overhead, and they froze.

"Stay with her," Zelda told Specs. "Get her out of sight, but as soon as you can, call the school, call the police. I don't know—tell them the prince is here and to send Queen Antonia."

"Why the queen?" Specs asked as he picked up Imogen.

"Because she'll want to see her son." She turned to Dante. "You stay with Specs. Don't wander off until we get you changed back, or some lady will adopt you and you'll spend the rest of your life getting carried around in a purse."

Dante gave a floppy-eared nod in reply, before trotting over to sit by Specs' side.

Zelda examined the office door. The smell of licorice had disappeared. Rather than use her magic to reveal any remaining curses, she used her skirts to cover her hand as she turned the handle. The door was unlocked—she hoped by accident.

Her hand trembled on the knob as she eased into the dim office. A massive desk filled the room and the spines of old books packed the bookshelves on the walls. The desk didn't look like it got much use. There were no papers or writing tools, only several strange brass instruments. She scanned the titles of the books, but they were all either old leather account ledgers or books about shoemaking. Even with paws and floppy ears, Dante had seemed confident that they were in the right place. Something stirred in her chest that felt a lot like the tingle of magic.

Just when she was about to fetch Dante, she heard the creaking of feet on old wooden stairs. Zelda gripped her wand tight. One of the bookcases swung open soundlessly, and Susan St. Germain appeared from behind the hidden door.

"What are you doing here?" Susan sputtered, her eyes wide.

"Is he up there?" Zelda said, anger surging through her veins like fire. She raised her wand higher.

Susan's eyes flicked between the stairs and Zelda's face. "I told you to stay away. It was for your own good. These are dangerous people."

"I'm here for Leo." She took a step toward Susan. "I used my one wish to get here, and I'm not leaving without him, so move aside."

Susan shook her head. "You got a wish?" Her eyes were red and glassy with unshed tears. She looked utterly broken as she held her own wand limp at her side.

"Yeah," Zelda said, bewildered. It was not what she'd expected Susan to say. "We get Happy Ever Afters too, and mine is in there, so if you have any sense at all, you'll let me pass." She hoped Susan would back down, but she just stood there. Zelda tried a different tack. "Let me through, and I'll make sure you get a wish of your own."

Susan looked at Zelda for an agonizingly long moment. Then, she took out a key from the breast pocket of her fuzzy yellow sweater. "I don't know what you'll be able to do for Prince Leo. They'll be back soon." Her hands shook as she handed Zelda the key.

Zelda took it from Susan's pale, cold fingers. "The Consortium has been stealing your magic, haven't they?"

Susan's eyes fell closed, and she gave a shallow nod. "I'm sorry for being horrid to you. They wanted me to take over the Olisand territory, so they could keep me close. Not that I minded too much—it was me or my friends."

"The elves?"

Susan nodded. "Glad you finally figured it out," she said with a familiar bitterness.

Zelda was relieved to hear Susan sound at least a little like her old self. "What's your wish?"

Susan lifted her eyes to meet Zelda's. "To destroy every last member of the Consortium." The anger in her eyes made Zelda's blood run cold. "You'd better hurry—I don't think he's faring well."

"Thanks," Zelda said. It didn't feel like enough, but she dashed through the secret door and up the staircase. At the top of the stairs, she found the door that belonged to the key. She shoved it into the lock and turned.

Zelda burst into a musty attic. Bare bulbs dangled on wires from the exposed rafters. Her sudden movement into the space made the hazy dust motes swirl violently through the beams of light.

Leo kneeled on the hard floor, sitting back on his heels. He leaned forward, spine curved, head lowered, and hands tied behind his back. Zelda was lifting up his face to look into his eyes before she even realized she'd crossed the room. His eyes were marred with dark circles, and it took a few seconds before recognition dawned in them.

"Leo," Zelda breathed.

"Zelda," he said weakly. A smile pulled up his lips on one side. He wore a black tuxedo tailored to suit him incredibly well, but he'd clearly put up a struggle. His white shirt was open to reveal the bare skin of his chest, the buttons missing as if it had been torn open.

He had a tattoo over his heart, crisp and unfaded but well-healed. Maybe six months old. It snagged Zelda's gaze. In the valley between the contours of his chest, a skilled hand had inked a compass rose like she'd seen on Leo's maps. The eight-pointed star reminded Zelda of the jeweled hairpin he'd given to her.

"What's going on? What are they doing to you?" She reached around him and began to work the knots loose that bound his hands together.

"Magic." Leo's head lolled to the side to rest against her shoulder.

Zelda grunted as her fingers tore at the rope. "I love you, but you'll have to be more specific." She got Leo's hands free, and he gave a low groan as he rolled his shoulders. From the red marks on his wrists, it looked like he'd been bound for a while.

"This," he said, touching the compass tattoo on his chest.

Zelda leaned in closer to look at the tattoo inked over his heart. There were faint red marks on the skin where something had pierced him.

Her fingers traced the marking. "Leo." She wanted to rewind time, to undo all the hurt they'd done to him. "I'm sorry."

Leo, weak as he was, pulled Zelda in. With hands framing her face, he placed a desperate kiss to her lips. His hands slid back into her hair, tightening his hold on their kiss. Zelda didn't realize the span of her relief until Leo kissed away the tears running down her cheeks.

On their knees, arms wrapped around each other for support, Zelda buried her face into Leo's neck. "We have to go. Susan let me in, and she said they would be back soon."

Zelda helped Leo to his feet and gave him her shoulder for support. They hobbled, Leo with an arm around Zelda's back, toward the door. The sound of feet on the stairs hastened her steps. *Why did we waste so much time?*

They made it to the door before Leo had to stop for a breath and brace himself against the jamb.

At that moment, the Duke of Brockford, hair askew and eyes wild with something that looked terrifyingly close to joy, came dashing up the stairs. He wore a dark gray suit, complete with the medals and sash of royal regalia and a wicked grin. George St. Germain was steps behind, but he blanched at the sight of them.

The Duke of Brockford lunged forward.

Zelda raised her wand and thought of the strongest blizzard she could imagine.

She only mustered up a flurry of flakes that did little to stop the duke from crashing into her. All the magic in her heart couldn't produce a blizzard. She tried to keep hold of Leo, but the duke was not a slight man. He wrestled her to the ground facedown and pinned her hands behind her back. Even worse, he had her wand.

Leo fought off St. Germain with a little better success. "Don't touch her," he yelled, but a well-aimed elbow from St. Germain sent the weakened prince to the ground.

A smooth voice came from the door. "What do we have here?"

Chapter Forty-Four

Zelda twisted around to find the source of the voice. Lord Scarlet stood in the door frame. He was the picture of elegance in a suit of deep maroon velvet with one hand tucked casually into a pocket. In the other, he carried something large and brass that looked awfully like a spider with a glass orb for its bulbous end. The thing with its jagged, needle-like legs made Zelda's insides squirm. Then, she recognized the orb. The purple smoke swirling inside was her own magic.

Lord Scarlet's presence made Leo stop. His eyes, wide with terror, were fixed on the spider in the headmaster's hands.

"Don't," Zelda exclaimed. "You can't—you can't use my magic. It's against the law."

The words poured out, useless against her captors. They only seemed to amuse Lord Scarlet as he advanced on the prince. He addressed Leo. "Don't listen to that fairy propaganda, Your Royal Highness. You are about to be a part of history."

Leo tried to put distance between himself and Lord Scarlet, but St. Germain held him steady. "Not willingly."

"And that's most unfortunate." Lord Scarlet patted Leo on the cheek.

Leo flinched at the man's touch.

Lord Scarlet then rounded on Zelda. "You see, Miss Ravensdale, the Consortium of Thaumaturgy is willing to take the step you fairies will not and grant the gift of magic to anyone . . . for the right price, of course." He lowered the contraption in his hands, so it was inches from Zelda's nose. "And we have you to thank. Susan St. Germain wasn't strong enough, but now we have a fairy's entire reserve of magic. I suppose I really should be thanking Mr. Asher for doing what others could not."

Zelda glared up at Lord Scarlet. "You're insane. That will never work. Magic resides in the heart. If you just stick it in someone who hasn't been born with the capability of controlling it, it will overpower the heart and stop it."

Lord Scarlet shook his head. "So naive."

He pulled a short key from his blazer pocket and stuck it into the belly of the contraption. With a turn of the key, the device made a sound similar to a clock or a music box being wound. "What your professors never told you is that anyone is capable of using magic. It's all a question of how to control it. Leo here is the key. He's already taken in quite a lot, but now we'll see how he reacts to the rest of it."

"Why him? Are you too afraid to try it yourself?" Zelda said, her voice like acid.

"I have, but my body doesn't naturally replenish a store of magic. We believe that as the descendant of both the first fairy godmother and the founders of Olisand, he'll have the best chance of the magic taking hold since it's already in his DNA. We're really killing two birds with one stone. Quite simply, he is historically in favor of supporting continued regulation of magic by the ICG," Lord Scarlet sneered.

"I wonder why," Leo retorted, still strong enough to throw a bit of sarcasm at their adversaries.

Lord Scarlet ignored him. "We also need to know how much magic a non-fairy can take before their heart stops. Leo will be the first to test this. Plus, with the princess so young, the Duke of Brockford here will be made regent when the prince has been removed."

The internal workings of the spider whirred when Lord Scarlet removed the key, and a whimper escaped Zelda's lips. The magic swirled in its glass container. Zelda thrashed harder against the Duke of Brockford's grasp, but a knee in the small of her back kept her pinned.

Lord Scarlet strolled over to Leo, tugged his shirt aside, and stuck the spider to his chest, right over his heart. The effect was immediate. Leo writhed against St. Germain's hold on him as deep purple veins of magic snaked across his skin, emanating from the legs of the spider. The muscles in Leo's jaw and neck tensed with the pain, but he didn't make a sound as her magic poured into his chest.

"Leo." Zelda's vision blurred with tears. She struggled against the Duke of Brockford as she was forced to watch Leo double over in pain. A pop in her right shoulder and flash of plain made her cry out again.

"Let her go," Lord Scarlet said without taking his eyes off Leo. He had a pocket watch in hand to time the length of Leo's ordeal.

The Duke of Brockford tightened his grip. "What's that, Rafe?"

"Let her go to him. She can't stop it unless she wants to stop his heart."

Zelda felt her hands released, and the duke removed his knee from her back. She scrambled to her feet, wincing as she moved her right arm, and tingling pain shot from her neck to her fingertips. She was at Leo's side in seconds. St. Germain leaped away from Leo when Zelda reached him.

The touch of her hands to his face drew him back to her, and for a moment, their eyes met. A low rumble and a crash sounded somewhere in the floors below them. Light swelled in the feeble bulbs that hung in the attic.

Zelda brushed the hair away from Leo's face and pressed her forehead to his. "I don't know how to help you," she said, her voice weak.

Leo took in a labored breath through gritted teeth. "I think . . . I can . . . control it," he whispered, low enough for only her to hear.

"Can you feel it in your chest?"

Leo gave her a barely perceptible nod. At this, the low rumble came again. "Give me a spell." His blue eyes burned on her, pleading for the pain to end.

Zelda knew the dangers of trying to use magic without a wand. She knew how using her magic, unfettered with the magic in the aether, could mean disaster. But if Leo could channel the magic and release it from himself, it might not overwhelm his heart.

She whispered the only spell that came to mind with lips to his ear.

Leo gripped her for support and uttered the spell. The syllables fell from his lips as a clap of thunder shook the entire building. Without warning, Leo lifted her to her feet and a dark smoke-like cloud filled the space. His arms wrapped around her, and she could feel the hum of the spider against her chest.

Then, with the clouds came snow and howling winds. Leo held her tighter against the cold. Snow and ice stung her skin as it whipped through the air. She felt him mutter something, his mouth pressed close to her ear. From the splay of his fingers on her back she could tell he was in great pain.

In the chaos of the storm, Lord Scarlet pressed himself to the wall. He covered his face with his hands. The duke dropped Zelda's wand and bolted for the door as ice gathered on every surface of the attic. The blizzard thundered as lighting and magic crackled through the clouds. Then, the shout of more voices rent the air.

Zelda realized Leo was repeating something to her. "I love you—" he yelled over the howl of the storm.

"Leo, I love you. Just let the magic out." Zelda whispered the words against his lips.

Her right arm hung limp at her side, but with her left hand, she ran her fingers down Leo's arm to intertwine with his. At their touch, a strange and familiar sensation traveled up her arm—the tingling, heartwarming sensation of magic. Perhaps it was her instinct reacting to her magic, but she could feel it, almost an extension of herself, pulsing through Leo. She reached out to it, called it with her heart.

It responded. Like using a wand, she pushed all the magic out of Leo, out of the spider and straight into the storm that swarmed them. Then, as if something slipped from her grasp, the last of her magic was drawn into the spell. Leo leaned into her and whispered, "I wish I had more time with you." His blue eyes rolled back, and he collapsed into her as they both fell to the floor.

The snow charm raged on without Zelda's control, shaking the rafters so violently that she feared the entire building would come down. "Leo," she cried, trying to shake him awake.

There were more voices now than just her own. Zelda looked over her shoulder to see Queen Antonia with a wand trained on George St. Germain. From the looks of it, Ballentine and Weymouth had escaped the emporium with her help. Ballentine fought to call back the snow charm while Weymouth grappled with Lord Scarlet. Zelda lowered her cheek to Leo's mouth. A shallow breath tickled across her skin. *Alive.*

Her entire supply of magic had traveled through his heart, and he was still alive. By all accounts, he shouldn't have survived, shouldn't have even been able to control it, but Zelda had a suspicion Lord Scarlet's theory was right.

Relief crashed over her in waves, and her body began to shake. They were safe for now, but the exhaustion of the ordeal had caught up to her tired limbs. She brushed away the snow from Leo's hair. "I'll get you more time. I promise."

The world around her felt like it moved in slow motion, and Zelda could only watch as her professor finally brought the storm down to a light flurry—watch and try not to think about how the magic had affected Leo. The pain in her shoulder was blinding with the absence of adrenaline coursing through her veins. In her weakened state, it was enough to make her vision fade at the edges. Then, as if her body was saying it had taken enough, she felt herself fall fully into the darkness around her vision.

Chapter Fourty-Five

Zelda woke from a dreamless sleep to find herself in the nurse's ward again. Only this time, she wasn't alone. Groggily, she found the bed beside her occupied by Imogen. Looking fully recovered from the curse, Imogen sat in bed, talking animatedly with Specs. On Zelda's other side, Leo slumbered peacefully, his mother and sister at his bedside. Across the room, Professor Ballentine and the school nurse fussed over the black eye and broken nose Professor Weymouth refused treatment for.

He caught Zelda's eye first.

"Miss Ravensdale." His outburst was enough to stop the nurse from trying to rub something on his swollen eye. It was not, however, enough to stop Professor Ballentine from sending a healing spell straight into his face. Weymouth didn't look pleased, but the swelling already started to go down.

The nurse hurried over as several others called out Zelda's name in surprise. Queen Antonia was instantly at her side, pressing a kiss to her forehead along with her thanks.

"Are they safe?" Zelda asked the queen.

Queen Antonia winked knowingly at her. "They're safe. Miss St. Germain and Professor Ballentine have seen to that."

The school nurse brushed the others out of the way and tenderly prodded Zelda's right shoulder.

Zelda sucked in a breath through her teeth. Her arm twitched, though not much since it was wrapped tightly to her chest.

"You're healing nicely," the nurse said. "You've certainly been through a lot."

"You bet she has," Imogen said from her bed. She extended a fist across the space between them for a fist bump. Zelda, amused, obliged albeit wearily.

The nurse wasn't so amused. "All of you need rest—plenty of it."

Zelda cast a glance at Leo sleeping peacefully. "Will he be okay?"

The nurse's brow softened as she turned to the prince. "His vitals are strong. There seems to be some magic still in him that's keeping his heart pumping after the beating it took. But it's my job to worry about him. You need to get more rest. Certification exams are coming up soon."

Zelda sank back into her pillow. She gave Imogen a weak smile. "What about Dante?"Imogen grinned. "Turned back to a prat at the stroke of midnight."

Zelda and Specs both stifled a laugh.

"Not bad for our last adventure at Madame LeBleu's together," Imogen said.

"Not bad indeed," Specs said.

They all broke out into giggles.

Zelda, Imogen, and the rest of the graduating godmothers waited impatiently on the winding marble staircase outside the school auditorium. With handmade wreaths of white flowers in their hair, they wore matching gowns of pale-blue silk that fluttered with the tiniest movement.

The thin straps dug into Zelda's shoulders, but the low-backed design of the dress would leave ample room for whatever wings she was presented with. The dresses belonged to the school, so no one's fit perfectly. It was a tradition from the days when magic was just taught in the homes of fairies—between mothers and daughters. A fairy could only get her wings once her tutor deemed her ready to grant wishes. Now, the duty fell to the headmistress.

Nervous whispers echoed off the marble. Zelda shot a pained smile at Imogen who stood at the back of the line. Susan St. Germain waited right behind Zelda, looking down at her amber wand and pretending Zelda didn't exist. No one except those who had been at the factory that night knew about Susan's involvement. A rumor still went around that she was going to postpone her placement for a year.

Would Susan hold her accountable to the promise she had made to help her dismantle the Consortium? Zelda wouldn't mind if she did, but Susan would have to eventually make eye contact with her if she wanted to work together.

Imogen wandered out of her place at the end of the line and found Zelda. She groaned and propped her elbows against the stone balustrade. "I'm so nervous. If I get insect wings, I'll freak. I hate bugs."

The type of wings depended a lot on both heritage and personality of the individual fairy, but there was no guarantee that Zelda would get her mom's swan wings. "You'll be fine. If you do, it will be totally different."

Professor Hildebrandt shooed Imogen to the back of the line, then opened the double wood doors. "It's time, ladies. Now, just like we did in practice, walk slowly up the center aisle, up the left steps, and onto the stage."

"I forgot to anti-trip charm my shoes," someone whispered in panic as the line moved toward the doors.

Zelda took a deep breath as she neared the doors. The rustle of bodies packed into a small space carried into the stairwell. Professor Hildebrandt ushered her through, and she started toward the stage. The crowd of excited families was far less overwhelming than the audience at the Follies. She heard her name shouted from her left and spotted her parents and all four sisters in the chaos. Her sisters had even made a banner with "Congrats, Zelda" on it in sparkly letters. A smile burst onto Zelda's face.

She scanned the crowd and found the only other face she wanted to see at the end of the first row with Felix right at his side. Leo had woken from his prolonged slumber just in time for the Wing Presentation Ceremony. Zelda knew she probably looked ridiculous with a goofy smile on her face, but she couldn't stop grinning.

Leo didn't take his eyes off her. Her favorite blue eyes in the world followed her all the way to her seat on the stage. To see him finally smiling at her with parentheses was enough to make her blush.

Madame LeBleu took to the stage in a high-necked navy dress that hugged her figure, and she began the ceremony with opening remarks.

Zelda knew what came next. She'd watched all her sisters awarded First Fairy before her. All her hard work came to this moment, but she wasn't as nervous as she thought she'd be. After everything she'd done, she wondered if it really even mattered anymore.

"It is always my greatest pleasure as headmistress of this school, not only to present a graduating class with their wings, but to award one outstanding student with the highest honor of her class: First Fairy."

There was no giddy feeling, no racing of her pulse.

It's going to be okay.

"We had several names in mind for First Fairy, but our ultimate choice was undeniable. Not only did she save a reigning monarch and show exemplary dedication to the field of godmothering, but she'll be the first student to be awarded First Fairy with four active demerits on her record."

Zelda laughed out loud and so did several other students.

"This year's award for First Fairy goes to Miss Zelda Ravensdale."

Cheers erupted in the vicinity of where Zelda's family was sitting. Zelda got up from her seat and walked to the podium to accept a leather-bound folio from Madame LeBleu.

"Well done," Madame LeBleu said. Her smile reached the corners of her eyes.

"Thank you." Zelda could've said more but didn't know where to start. Instead, she hurried to her seat so Madame LeBleu could begin the presentation of wings.

Freya Alvarez was called up first. Madame LeBleu put her wand between Freya's shoulder blades and muttered a spell Zelda couldn't hear. When she pulled her wand away, a pair of diaphanous dragonfly wings sprouted from Freya's back.

With a gasp, Freya examined the shimmering wings over her shoulder before Madame LeBleu directed her back to her seat.

Zelda could barely contain her excitement as it got closer and closer to her turn. She watched several other girls get wings like feathery birds or the sheer black wings of honeybees.

When her name was called, Zelda all but raced to the podium. She tried to breathe away her nerves as she felt the tip of Madame LeBleu's wand press against her spine. Zelda felt a shiver of magic drawn straight from her back. When she looked over her shoulder, the large pearl white wing of a moth fluttered behind her. She'd never met a fairy with moth wings, but for some reason they felt perfect.

Susan St. Germain went next and got a pair of dark leathery wings so wide they nearly knocked over the podium. Zelda's mouth fell open in amazement. They were too large to be bat wings. That meant—

"Dragon wings," several students muttered in shock.

Even Madame LeBleu looked surprised. She helped Susan guide her new wings closed so she wouldn't block the entire class from view. Madame LeBleu leaned in to whisper something in Susan's ear to which Susan replied with a fervent shake of her head. Susan took her seat and examined the taloned wings high above her shoulders with awe.

Zelda cheered loudest when Imogen received a pair of jet-black raven's wings and brought the ceremony to a close. They proceeded off stage and out of the auditorium in reverse order. Instead of sending them back up the stairs, the professors applauded them out into the courtyard.

Girls spun around to examine each other's wings. Imogen brushed Zelda's wing, and a flurry of shimmery dust lifted off them.

"They're so soft," Imogen said.

"Your wings are too," Zelda said as she traced the feathers of Imogen's wing.

Families trickled out into the courtyard and found their graduates. Specs wandered out and Imogen nearly tackled him to the ground with a kiss. To Zelda's surprise, Dante was waiting for Susan in the courtyard. His breakup with Susan had been all over the school along with the news of her father's accusations of thaumaturgy, but they were still inseparable. Only those who had been at the factory saw them for what they were: two survivors holding each other together.

Dante gave Zelda a nod and small, genuine smile that reminded her of the Dante she'd once been in love with. She nodded back.

Zelda's large family was one of the last out of the door. They swarmed her with a bunch of hugs and excited chatter. While Ramona and Helene argued about whether moth wings were a sign of clairvoyant aptitude, Zelda's dad pulled her into an extra tight hug.

He pressed a kiss to the top of her head. "See. I knew you had it in you."

"I did too," Zelda said with a grin. And she really meant it.

Epilogue

Music from the midsummer ball trickled out to the terrace. It was the first public event since the king had recovered his health. High in the mountains at the summer palace, nights were pleasantly cool. The evening wasn't even close to being over, but Leo had insisted on a moment alone. Even more, his hands insisted on tracing delicate lines down Zelda's spine. She'd crafted her own gown for the evening—something pale pink, flowy, and with a daringly low back.

"Please. One more time," Leo begged, trailing kisses down her neck.

"No, *Your Royal Highness,*" Zelda cooed.

Leo straightened at the sound of his formal title. He wrinkled his nose a little before diving back into Zelda's neck, his lips on the tender place just below her ear. "Please?"

Their absence from the party was likely growing more suspicious by the minute. She rolled her shoulders and finally gave in. With a shiver, Zelda pulled her magic through her shoulder blades and felt the wings sprout from her back. The sensation was a pleasant one—as if someone had loosened a belt from around her chest.

With wild eyes, Leo ran a hand down the length of the ivory wings that sat flat against Zelda's back. The sensation of his hands on her made her take in a deep breath as she settled in closer to him. The wings felt like the perfect extension of her, but Leo's fascination with them was an added bonus. Still, they left a pearlescent white dust on anything they touched—a fact they'd learned quickly after Leo backed her up against a dark, damask papered wall in a hallway after the Wing Presentation Ceremony.

She'd never be able to wear dark colors again if she intended to use her wings regularly. But getting fairy dust on Leo's tuxedo was the least of her worries. She was now the official godmother of all of Olisand and official Elf Liaison for the ICG after George St. Germain was indicted for his involvement with the Consortium and their crimes against magic. The Duke of Brockford and Lord Scarlet had disappeared in the chaos of the blizzard the night of the Wishmaker Festival Ball, but Ballentine was taking a leave of absence from teaching for a year to help track them down.

Leo seemed to sense Zelda's mind was occupied with something other than the wonderfully skilled attention he was paying to her neck. "Is everything okay?" he asked hesitantly.

Zelda shook her head to clear it. "I just can't get the Consortium out of my mind."

Leo wrapped his arms around Zelda's waist. "You don't have to worry about that—not tonight, at least. Susan St. Germain gave a full testimony to the ICG before she disappeared. We'll take down their organization together."

Zelda sighed. He was right, but she was a godmother and could never turn off the part of her that needed to help people. "Together," she said with a nod.

Now, Leo looked nervous.

Zelda straightened his white bowtie which had been knocked askew during their interlude. "What is it?"

Leo picked up a champagne flute from where he'd set it on the terrace's stone balustrade. "Remember how the fairy healers said I may need to watch for symptoms after having all that magic forced into me?"

Zelda's stomach dropped. "How do you feel?"

"Well . . ." He lifted the glass for her to see. The liquid had turned completely solid, the bubbles frozen in the ice. Crystals of frost snaked up the outside of the flute from where Leo's fingers met the glass.

Zelda's mouth fell open. "Leo." To use magic with such control without even a wand was unheard of—at least it was until she'd met Rían. "This is . . ." She didn't have words to put to her amazement.

"I don't know what it means," Leo said. "But it might have something to do with the fact that I'm a descendant of history's first fairy godmother."

Leo was developing powers of his own—powers he shouldn't have. Zelda shook her head. "We'll figure it out."

Leo set the frozen champagne aside. "Together?"

Zelda wrapped her arm through his as they headed back to the ball.

"Together."

Bonus Scenes
from Imogen's Perspective

{Page 257}

Imogen meandered through the worktables and examined the half-finished tinker tech strewn across their surfaces. She tried to guess the purpose of each machine, but her knowledge of tinkering was limited to the basics. If she wanted to get her filtering foundation to work, she might need more than magic.

As if on cue, footsteps sounded behind her.

Imogen smiled. "Specs," she said without turning around.

A soft laugh. "How do you always know it's me?"

Specs never walked anywhere. He rode his bike around town, sure, but on foot he bounded, bounced, skipped, hopped, loped and jogged. He never walked — at least not like anyone else. It was like he was always excited about where he was going, and it made Imogen want to go there too. "I have my ways," she replied and turned to face her best friend.

Specs was much taller than her, but he seemed less so with his shoulders slumped forward and a look of deep concern on his face.

Panic with hummingbird wings fluttered in Imogen's chest. "What's wrong?" Instinctively, her hand reached out and grasped his arm. Lean muscles tensed underneath his scarlet EAMS sweater.

"N-nothing," Specs stammered. "I, uh, I mean not with me. I came over here to check on you."

"Me?" Imogen laughed, and it slowed her racing heart. "You had me worried, looking at me like that. Why are you checking on me?"

"Well, I heard about your breakup." His eyes flicked to her hand on his arm.

Oops. She'd accidentally left it there too long. The physical closeness of their friendship had never bothered him before, but maybe the look hadn't meant anything.

"I'm fine," she answered. "I've cried my tears and I'm going to be sorted."

"Are you sure? You know you can talk to me about anything."

"Seriously. It was mostly mutual."

Specs laughed dryly. "Mutual? Fletcher has been moping around the halls of EAMS like a sad Victorian ghost. What happened?"

"He was mad that I don't want to spend more time with him, but I'm busy, you know?"

Specs' face melted with sympathy, and he took a half-step closer, his head tilted slightly as he listened and waited for her to go on.

"I've been working on this filtering foundation, and I can't get the charms to last more than thirty seconds or so." Imogen wanted something in her hands to fiddle with as the painful memories surfaced. She picked up an oscillating aether gauge. "He was cross I was working on it instead of coming to the gym with him, and it turned into this big thing."

It was Specs' turn to place a hand on her arm. "Gen." He was the only one who called her that. "You'll come across many guys like Fletcher who want you to follow them around to witness their *greatness*." Specs rolled his eyes, but then he squared Imogen by the shoulders so she had to look right into his warm brown eyes. "They only care about how *you* make *them* feel about themselves. They don't see you for what you are."

"What am I?" Imogen's heart thudded in her ears.

"You're full of ideas and schemes and dreams — more creative than any Tinker I've met here. You're an inventor, an artist, an innovator. You're a speeding train. A rocket to the moon."

"I'm a what?" They both laughed.

"You're going someplace fast," Specs clarified. "You just need to wait for a co-pilot who wants to chase your dreams too."

Imogen's lips parted as she sucked in a breath to steady her racing pulse. "That was the nicest thing —"

"Have you considered gold?" Specs' eyes darted away from her abruptly.

Imogen cleared her throat. "Erm, what?" When had she moved to stand so close to Specs? She took a step back to get her head right.

"For your filtering foundation? You're trying to stabilize a charm meant for a person on something inanimate, correct?"

“Yeah,” Imogen answered, but her thoughts weren’t on charms and enchantments of a magical sort at the moment.

“As student tinkers, we mostly use brass in our inventions because it’s a relatively effective aether stabilizer, but reasonably cheap. A finer, softer metal like gold could, theoretically, hold a charm. Glass could work even better.”

“Oh! I’ll have to try that. Thanks, Specs.” She threw her arms around his shoulders and squeezed him tightly. “Thank you, Thaddeus.”

His arms wound around her waist. “Of course.” His deep voice rumbled through her chest.

Imogen glanced over at Leo and Zelda. “Come on. We should join them.”

{Page 237}

Imogen found a table along the railing on the library’s third floor that looked over the rows of study tables in the center. The library was mostly deserted, but a few studious tinkers and GITs bent their faces towards their books in the waning light.

She hadn’t even bothered to change out of her work clothes before she went to find Specs at their predetermined meeting spot where they would wait for Zelda and Leo. Specs wasn’t there yet, probably wouldn’t be until his Tinkerbot team finished work for the night. There was a small Tinker Tussle league at EAMS that built aether-enhanced robots to fight each other. The winner of the Wishmaker Tinker Tussle got an invitation to the European Semi-pro league, and Specs’ team actually had a shot.

Thinking about Specs made Imogen’s stomach twist in a way she didn’t understand. Since they came back from holiday, Zelda had been absorbed in schoolwork and her new relationship with Prince Charming. And with Fletcher out of the picture, Imogen was spending more and more time with Specs — and it was becoming the best part of her days.

A strange sound made her pause, a clatter of metal clunking on the wooden floors growing louder. Something flashed out of the corner of her eye, then she jumped when something bumped into her foot. Imogen looked under the table to find a brass sphere next to her gold shoe.

Specs.

She picked up the contraption and searched for him nearby but didn't find him. The sphere had seams running concentrically around its surface, but with a little twist, nothing happened. "Aha," Imogen said with a laugh. It was another one of Specs' puzzle machines. He was always testing out a new design on her.

Her heart raced at the prospect of testing the limits of her puzzle skills. The surface was smooth, with only the seams on its surface. She applied a light pressure to twist the sphere along each seam until she finally found the right one and was rewarded with a satisfying click. She repeated this process until each sequential twist opened the final lock.

Imogen squeaked in surprise when the sphere popped itself open and landed on the table with a thunk. It had required a delicate touch, but Imogen had expected a few more steps. She examined the open contraption and realized it was meant to look like a ladybird with its wings open — more art than puzzle, though Specs' puzzles were usually both. She turned over the beautiful sculpture and found a small roll of paper clutched in the ladybird's legs.

Imogen unrolled the paper and read the note. It took her a few seconds to decipher Specs' messy handwriting.

Will you go to the ball with me?

Imogen froze. Couldn't move. Couldn't breathe. Her feelings were too much to take in at once.

A quiet cough broke the spell and Imogen turned to see Specs propped against a bookcase, watching her nervously with one hand on the back of his neck, the other shoved deep into a pocket.

"You figured that one out quick," he said, ignoring the fact that he'd just asked her to the ball.

"What's this?" She held up the note.

"I-uhm ... I want to take you to the Wishmaker Festival Ball." He tried to keep his eyes on her, but his gaze fell to his feet.

Imogen stood and joined him between the shelves. "What do you mean, Thaddeus? I didn't think you would be interested in a ball, so are you asking to go as my friend, or is this a date?"

"I know how much you love gowns and getting dressed up. I didn't want you to miss the ball your last year at Madame LeBleu's." Specs scrubbed the back of his neck nervously.

"And so you asked me as a friend?"

Specs' eyes snapped to Imogen. "Of course, as a friend, always a friend, but ... not just a friend."

"Specs!" she cried. "What are you doing?" Her pulse fluttered, but her mind reeled. *More than friends.* The thought had never once crossed her mind. Of course, she had often wondered, cute as he was, why Specs never dated anyone. She'd just assumed he wasn't interested in it, but she'd assumed wrong.

"I'm asking you on a date," Specs replied. "I thought that was obvious."

"I know, but our *friendship*. It's one of my favorite relationships in the whole world and I ... I don't want to mess it up."

Specs shifted nervously between his feet. His smile fell and his face grew deeply serious. "Imogen. I've kept my feelings to myself for as long as I can, but it's eating me up. You're finally not dating anyone and—"

"Wait." Imogen pressed her fingertips to his chest. "How long have you been waiting to tell me this? Are you saying you've liked me since *before* my breakup with Fletcher?"

Specs ducked his head and smiled sheepishly.

"Longer?"

"Fall term. When I saw you again after summer holiday, it scared me how much I'd missed you. I don't know how or when, but it was then I realized I wanted to be something more. I guess I was falling so slowly I didn't notice until I was in too deep and then I was scared," he pressed his hand on top of hers so her palm flattened against his heart. "I didn't want to lose what we had, but every time you looked at me I wanted. I wondered. I ... burned for more."

Imogen's cheeks heated. Where had Specs, her sweet, kind friend, hidden this version of himself from her? Furthermore, why? She wanted to yell at him or kiss him or both, but she was struggling to wrap her head around either. "Thaddeus Asher, I had no idea you had that kind of talk in you."

Specs chuckled. "So I'm not making a total mess of this?"

"Oh." Imogen laughed dryly. "This is a mess. A complete mess."

Specs turned and started to walk away.

"Where are you going?"

Specs stopped. "First, I'm going to take a bracingly cold walk around the outside of the library. You're going to sit and wait for me at that table, and when I get back, I'm going to say 'Hi Gen! Heard from Leo and Zelda, yet?' You'll say 'Nope,' and we're going to pretend that none of this conversation ever happened."

Imogen shook her head and pulled Specs deep into the shadows between the bookshelves. "No, you're not taking this back because–" She wrestled with the thoughts and feelings racing through her head and which to deal with first. "I'm a little mad at you."

"I'm so sorry–"

Imogen held off his sorry with a finger to his lips. The feeling of soft lips on the pad of her finger made her snatch it away before she completely lost her train of thought. "Before you start apologizing, you numpty, let me explain. I'm not mad at you for your feelings. I'm mad at you for waiting so long."

There was the truth of it. This was Specs! Imogen was choosy in who she chose to date, and even choosier in her friends. If he had given her any indication, flirted with her even in the slightest, she knew the care she had for him as her friend would have blossomed into more.

Imogen's pulse raced as she realized what was bothering her most. "I wouldn't have wasted four months on that loser, Fletcher, and we wouldn't be trying to figure this out three months before school ends."

Specs rocked back and forth onto his toes, lips pursed, like he was holding in something he wanted to say.

The air felt charged like a lightning strike. Imogen shook her head with a laugh, her high ponytail swishing back and forth. "You were going to apologize, weren't you?"

Specs chuckled, but their shared amusement did little to diffuse the tension singing in the air. "I was. Then I realized that would be disingenuous, Because I'm not sorry. I'm kicking myself, sure, but I'm not going to disappear from your life after school ends." He took a step closer and fixed his brown eyes directly on hers. "Every moment we have ahead of us, the chance for something deeper and more meaningful is worth risking our friendship for."

Imogen couldn't think straight. With all the noise in her head, the only thing she could think of to answer Specs' question was ... heat rushed to Imogen's cheeks. It had to be done. She pulled Specs' face to hers and kissed him boldly.

Specs held his hands stiffly at his sides and they broke apart seconds later when they both had to laugh nervously. Imogen touched her lips, a faint quiver in her stomach. "That was..."

"You caught me off guard," Specs said at the same time as Imogen said, "I was still in my head."

Specs shuffled closer. "Should we try again?"

Imogen shook her head to clear it. "Yes. Again."

This time, Specs took the lead and placed a hand on the back of Imogen's neck and tilted her chin up to meet his lips. His kiss was soft, tender, and Imogen tried to ignore the fact that this was Specs kissing her, but that was the whole point of this chemistry experiment. It was Specs' lips and nose brushing hers. His dark curls coiling through her fingertips. His hand on the small of her back. There was something fundamentally incongruous about kissing your best friend.

They broke apart and Imogen gave a frustrated sigh. Specs scratched his head.

"That was—"

Specs fisted a hand into his curls. "Don't say it."

"This was awkward."

Specs let his head fall back and let out an exasperated groan. "Fine. It's a little awkward. But not ... unpleasant, right?"

Imogen touched her lips. "No. Not unpleasant. As with all things, you're technically proficient, Specs. It's just, there was a spark but no flame. Those kisses weren't worth risking our friendship over."

"We're in our heads."

"In our heads," Imogen agreed.

Specs' shoulders slumped forward. He almost placed a hand on her arm, but seemed to change his mind and shoved it in his pocket instead. "Maybe just take some time and think about us, and we'll take a step back on the kissing."

"Ugh. Fine," Imogen said. "That's probably for the best."

Specs lifted a shoulder. "Unless there's a moment where a kiss would feel natural."

"Right. It's not off the table."

"Right." Specs bobbed his head towards the study table. "Come on. Let's go wait for Leo and Zelda to get back."

How was it possible to simultaneously want to kiss someone again and wish you'd never kissed them in the first place?

{265}

Specs had left Imogen completely tangled in uncertainty. She was wedged firmly between friends and romantically interested, too scared to take a step forward and too afraid she'd always wonder *what if?* if she didn't. The week of the Wishmaker Festival arrived, and she still hadn't given Specs an answer to his invitation to the ball.

The bustling greenroom started to clear out after Iris Pickett called for places and the start of the Wishmaker Festival Follies. Imogen and Specs stood beside Zelda in a cramped corner.

"I'm going to go watch from the wings," Zelda said brightly. Imogen could easily guess who she was eager to see. She'd spotted Prince Charming's bodyguard in the security sweep of the theatre.

"We'll meet you there," Specs said. "I need Imogen to help me run my lines."

Imogen's stomach flipped. *Really? Or is he going to demand an answer to know if they were actually going to the ball together?*

Zelda nodded and seemed to think nothing of leaving them alone together. She hurried off with the rest of the students toward the stage.

Even though the room was less crowded, Specs didn't move away, his shoulder just inches from hers. Imogen snuck a glance up at him. She had always been distracted by his long, dark lashes and warm, round eyes, but everything about his features was charming. His perfectly sloped nose, full cheekbones, and angular jaw were pleasant in every way.

Then her eyes fell on his full lips.

As if he knew all along what she was doing, his lips turned up in the corner. Imogen felt his hand find hers and intertwine their fingers.

"Subtle," she said.

"You're staring at me." His eyes crinkled.

"I'm trying to figure out if I'm crazy for not taking you up on your offer."

Specs' gaze danced around the room. "And your conclusion?"

"Undecided."

Specs shoved away from the wall and pulled her with him. Hand-holding was a new and strangely comfortable thing as Specs led her through the cramped halls of the theater and ducked into a large, dimly lit room filled with disparate set pieces and large props.

"Are we allowed in here?" Imogen asked.

"Probably not." Specs climbed the steps to a columned folly covered with fake ivy that looked like it belonged in *A Midsummer Night's Dream*.

"What are your intentions, Thaddeus?" Imogen tugged Specs closer. *Was she actually flirting with him? And enjoying it?*

"I want to know what's still running through your head." He released her hand and brushed a stray hair from her cheek.

Imogen's stomach sank. "I don't want to say."

"Oh. Bad news?"

"I just keep thinking of all the reasons you're going to break up with me or how I'm going to hurt you."

Specs chuckled. "That's a terrible place to start."

"My last four relationships ended on someone else's terms, not mine."

"I thought Fletcher was a mutual breakup?"

"It was, but he initiated the process. Not every relationship broke my heart, but each one stung more than the last."

Specs brows pushed together. "All right, then. Why do you think I would break up with you?"

Imogen knew the reasons. They ran through her head like a catchy song whenever she couldn't fall asleep. "I can be flaky."

"Spontaneous," Specs corrected.

"Flighty."

"Whimsical," he offered.

"I'm always absorbed in a project."

"So am I."

Imogen smiled when she realized what he was doing. "I don't even know what corner of the world I'll end up granting wishes in!"

"And I can be a tinker anywhere."

Imogen folded her arms. "You would do a long-distance thing?"

"Not really. I'll go where you go."

"What?" Imogen sputtered, and her arms fell to her sides.

"I've applied to the top tinkering programs at universities on every continent."

"What?" Imogen was so shocked she actually laughed.

"Maybe you should stop trying to figure out our relationship by its end date and consider, perhaps, that it doesn't have one."

Imogen just stared at Specs.

"Here's my proposition: we treat each other with the respect and admiration we've always shown each other, only now we think of ourselves as copilots ... who kiss a little." Specs held out his hand for her to take.

"I haven't forgotten that day you called me a speeding train and a rocket to the moon. Were you talking about yourself when you told me I needed a copilot?"

Specs grinned bashfully.

Imogen's stomach fluttered. She took his hand and gave it a firm shake. Before she could release it, Specs tugged her in and kissed her. Her worries disappeared as her heart soared and softened, letting herself fall into him. This was everything a kiss should be: tender, earnest, and electric.

They broke apart to catch their breath, and when their eyes found each other, they laughed.

"I think that proves this equation," Specs said.

Imogen blew out a puff of air and tried to collect her thundering pulse. "Thoroughly."

Specs lifted a shoulder. "Should we double-check our work?"

"Thoroughly," Imogen answered.

They fit back together with seamless ease, each kiss sending Imogen's heart further into the security of Specs' care. Imogen could have spent hours kissing him, but a cough behind them sent them flying five feet apart. Imogen turned to find Leo standing at the bottom of the steps to the folly wearing a dark suit with a blue button-down underneath.

He grinned wildly. "Sorry to interrupt."

Imogen flew down the stairs and threw her arms over Prince Charming's shoulders. "Leo! What's going on? We've missed you!"

Specs clapped him on the shoulder. "Yeah, man. Why'd you disappear on us?"

"I'll explain everything soon, but I need your help with something."

Imogen and Specs glanced at each other. "Whatever you need," she answered.

"How do you think Zelda would feel about a big romantic gesture?"

Imogen squealed. "She'd love it!"

Acknowledgements

First, I would like to thank my heavenly father for being my source of steadfast hope and peace. Thank you for putting the hope of heaven in my heart. It's only through His sustaining power and His gift of creativity that this book was possible. All honor and glory belong to Him alone.

To Sam, my critique partner, my alpha reader, my beta reader, my encourager, my true love. There would be no "I Wish I May" without you. Thank you for pushing me, challenging me, and finally, making me put down the editing pen and put myself out there.

To my stellar editors Ellen and Elle, thank you for helping me give this book a professional polish so it could truly shine in the way I always dreamed it could.

To my many beta readers, Cassie, Leah, Kim, Britain, and Laura, thank you for your honesty and enthusiasm. Each of your unique perspectives and feedback made this story so much better and you are forever part of this book's DNA.

To all my Wattpad and Figment readers, thank you for encouraging me and pushing me to keep going. Without the thousands of you leaving hearts, comments, and sending "please update!!!" messages, I might have given up on finishing this story altogether.

To Kate Y, thank you for being my lifeline while querying and trying to find a publishing home for I Wish I May. You encouraged me to keep believing in my story when I sorely wanted to put it back on the shelf.

To Benita, thank you for your expert eye on my cover design. And Tracy, for being an amazing friend, listening ear, a bounty of encouragement, and for lending your graphic expertise to the cover design.

To Mom and Dad, thanks for raising me to dream, for endless (possibly) magic woods to roam, and for feeding my imagination with shelves of fantasy books, Disney VHSs, and Enya CDs.

Finally, to the named characters I cut from the first draft, I'm truly sorry. It's not personal, I just couldn't remember all your names.

Adelyn Belsterling is a writer of all things hopeful and stories full of magic. She grew up on a steady diet of Disney VHSs, fantasy books, and musical theater. Adelyn lives in Ohio with her husband, daughters, and cavalier, Theo. She is a graduate of Grove City College with a degree in Marketing Management and spends her days chasing a toddler, baby-wearing and neglecting her garden while writing novels in her free time.

Learn more at AdelynBelsterling.com

or through her newsletter at adelynbelsterling.substack.com/

Or follow her on Instagram: @authoradelynbelsterling

www.ingramcontent.com/pod-product-compliance
Lightning Source LLC
Chambersburg PA
CBHW020458310726
48979CB00016B/2699/J